MW01131318

SHADOW
DRAGON

Lance Horton

SHADOW DRAGON

iUniverse, Inc.
Bloomington

Shadow Dragon

iUniverse books may be ordered through booksellers or by contacting:

iUniverse
1663 Liberty Drive
Bloomington, IN 47403
www.iuniverse.com
1-800-Authors (1-800-288-4677)

Because of the dynamic nature of the Internet, any web addresses or links contained in this book may have changed since publication and may no longer be valid. The views expressed in this work are solely those of the author and do not necessarily reflect the views of the publisher, and the publisher hereby disclaims any responsibility for them.

Any people depicted in stock imagery provided by Thinkstock are models, and such images are being used for illustrative purposes only.

Certain stock imagery © Thinkstock.

ISBN: 978-1-4620-0765-3 (sc)
ISBN: 978-1-4620-0767-7 (e)
ISBN: 978-1-4620-0766-0 (dj)

Library of Congress Control Number: 2012902217

Printed in the United States of America

iUniverse rev. date: 4/23/2012

To my mom

CHAPTER 1

Montana

Jake Holcomb rocked and lurched in his seat as the snowcat churned its way through the dark line of trees. Even with the lights on, it was hard to tell if he had lost the trail again. On the radio, barely audible over the roar of the cat, the morning DJ droned on, "And finally, the cleanup efforts continue as emergency crews work around the clock to restore power and clear the highways after five straight days of record snowfall in northwestern Montana, adding to the stress of local residents who are suffering through one of the harshest winters on record. State officials have announced that Highway 2 between Columbia Falls and Glacier National Park, which has been shut down due to the heavy accumulations, should be reopened in twenty-four to forty-eight hours, provided there is no further snow. Now, back to the hits on Classic 93—"

Jake grabbed the thermos wedged between the seat and the center console. He spun the lid off and took a big swig of the Kahlua and coffee.

"Ahhh." He wiped his beard on the sleeve of his snowsuit. He didn't usually drink on the job—at least not this early in the morning—but he had been putting in sixteen to eighteen hours a day for the last three days, repairing downed power lines in the freezing snow and ice. He deserved a little reward. Besides, it wasn't like he had to worry about running over anyone in the middle of the damn forest.

1

He was almost on it before he spotted the top of the sign for Graves Bay sticking out of the snow. Ahead of him, the ground disappeared. He turned sharply to his right, following the ridge for a short way before making a hard left. The cat tilted perilously as the trail doubled back on itself and then slanted downward into a small clearing. Jake hit the brakes and knocked the cat out of gear. Somewhere out there in front of him was the lake. He sure as hell didn't want to end up in there. He wiped a circle into the fog-shrouded window and peered out at the cabin to his left. There were no lights on inside.

Grumbling to himself, he grabbed his tool belt from the passenger seat and then hopped from the cab into the waist-deep snow. He pulled out his Maglite, flicked it on, and began trudging around the south side of the cabin.

When he found the utility meter, he brushed the snow from the glass lens, but he still couldn't see if the dials were turning. "Fuckin' ice," he muttered, scraping at it with the butt of the flashlight.

A *crack* sounded in the forest behind him. Jake spun around, sweeping the light back and forth among the trees. Ice crystals sparkled in the dark, but nothing moved.

He turned back to the meter, and this time he could see that the dials weren't turning. He decided to check around front.

To his surprise, an SUV sat out front. It was buried up to the door handles, its windshield and roof blanketed with more than two feet of snow. Behind it was what looked like a trailer. Whatever it hauled was completely buried. He approached and raked his arm back and forth, clearing away the powder to reveal the handlebars and cowling of a snowmobile.

Jake tromped up to the front porch. He wondered if people had been stranded here or if they had just left the vehicle behind when the storm hit. He tried looking in the large picture window facing the lake, but the curtains had been pulled closed.

"Hello?" he called out as he knocked on the front door. "Is anyone here?"

He pulled back the hood on his snowsuit and listened for sounds of activity within, but the cabin remained silent. Around back, the idling cat was the only sound to be heard.

Gong.

He jerked back, looking over his shoulder. *What the hell was that?* He shone his light on the Jeep, thinking an icicle might have fallen on the hood, but the snow there was undisturbed.

Gong.

There it was again. Only this time, he realized it had come from the other side of the cabin. He stepped back off the porch and trudged around the corner to the north.

There was another door on the side at the back corner. As he approached, he noticed the door was ajar, slowly swinging back and forth. The trees whispered as a breeze passed through their upper reaches. The door blew inward to the left.

Gong.

It came from the other side. Cautiously, Jake stepped inside, shining the light into the room. The circular beam revealed a table with three chairs around it. A fourth lay on its side on the green linoleum floor. A bowl of pretzels and four Budweisers sat on the table, surrounded by a pile of scattered playing cards and poker chips.

He pushed the door shut behind him and found an old washer and dryer in the corner. The dryer's metal hull had a circular dent in it where the doorknob had struck it repeatedly.

Jake crept on through the kitchen. The brittle linoleum crackled with each step, which sounded unnaturally loud in the silence.

In the front room, a sofa faced the large window across from him. In front of the sofa, a small coffee table had been knocked over. A foamy puddle of spilled beer had frozen into golden crystals. Next to it was another frozen pool of something dark and thick like motor oil. As he continued to pan across the floor, the light spilled over something that glimmered faintly. He stopped, trying to make out what it was.

Oh, shit.

The flashlight trembled in his hand.

Shit … shit … shit!

A part of his mind yelled at him to run, but it was drowned out by the part that was screaming in terror. He stood transfixed, staring at the man's head in the pool of frozen blood, the vacant, milky-white eyes gazing into nothingness. No body. Just a head.

A low, moaning cry escaped him. Legs trembling, he turned and ran. His breath came in short, ragged gasps.

Outside, he turned the corner and raced for the cat, but he stumbled, falling face-first into the snow. The flashlight flew from his hand and vanished into the deep powder with a soft *whump*.

Looking up, he saw a hand in front of his face, its fingers frozen in the semblance of a claw.

Jake pissed in his pants.

Screaming, he scrambled backward, struggling to get out of the thing's reach. His breathing came faster, racing in time with his heart. Spots swam before his eyes. His legs went numb; the corners of his vision went dark. Unable to stand, he clawed his way across the snow, desperate to reach the cat.

He grabbed the metal treads and managed to pull himself up enough to clamber into the cab of the big rig. He slammed the door behind him and grabbed the microphone of the two-way radio.

"Gladys, Gladys!" he screamed. "They're dead. They're dead. Oh God, they're dead!"

CHAPTER 2

Seattle

The FBI offices in Seattle resided in a plain, concrete and glass high-rise on 3rd Avenue overlooking the southern end of downtown and, a little farther to the west, Fisherman's Wharf and Puget Sound. Except for the height, the building looked similar to the bureau's headquarters in Quantico—which meant drab. To Kyle Andrews, it looked like something an architecture student might have designed overnight when faced with a project deadline. It appeared as if it was constructed of large, concrete rectangles with the windows recessed in order to provide a perfect roosting spot for the countless pigeons and seagulls. Its stark facade, however, seemed appropriate for the agency it housed.

When he stepped off the elevator into the third-floor lobby, Kyle switched the manila envelope he carried from one hand to the other as he took off his overcoat and hung it on the rack. He ran his fingers through his dark hair in an effort to help dry it out. He hated that it would get all wavy when it was wet, which was most of the time in Seattle.

Katherine, the receptionist, sat behind the large console desk, a dozen red roses taking up one corner of the counter. On the marble wall behind her loomed the seal of the FBI, flanked by pictures of the president and the director of the FBI. She looked up and greeted him with an understanding frown.

"How'd it go last night?"

"Same as always," Kyle said. How else was a mother supposed to take it when she was told her five-year-old daughter was never coming back?

Abby had been taken by her father three weeks ago. They had made their way down the West Coast to California, where he had taken her to Disneyland and Knott's Berry Farm before they headed east. The FBI had tracked them down, locating them in a cheap motel on the outskirts of Las Vegas. They had waited until the middle of the night before they had made their move. But as the agents closed in, they heard two gunshots from inside the room.

When they broke down the door, they found the father dead at the foot of the bed on which Abby was laying. He had killed her before he had turned the gun on himself.

It was the part of his job Kyle hated the most—the death notification.

"I just don't understand how some people can get so messed up," Katherine said.

"I know." It was a question Kyle had been asked too many times before, and while he knew something of the reasons and motivations, he had grown tired of trying to explain them. They never understood anyway.

Katherine shook her head. "I can't imagine—" She stopped as her extension rang. She held up her finger and answered the call.

Kyle started down the hall toward his cubicle.

"Kyle," Katherine called after him. "It's SAC Geddes. She wants to see you in her office right away."

Kyle's hand tightened on the envelope. He wasn't ready to face the Dragon Lady yet. Did she know already?

Outside her office, Kyle adjusted his tie while he made a conscious effort to stand straight. He tended to slump when he was down, which caused his suit to hang on him as if it were two sizes too big. That didn't conform to the strong, confident image the FBI wanted its employees to project. Taking a deep breath, he rapped on the door.

"Come in," Geddes said, her voice raspy from a lifetime of chain-smoking.

Special Agent in Charge JoAnne Geddes stood behind her chair, rain streaming down the floor-to-ceiling windows behind her. The wan light of the day caused her hair to look darker than usual, turning it blood red. Shadows seemed to gather in the creases of her face.

Special Agent Lewis Edwards, an older black man with graying hair around his temples and a broad, flat nose, sat in one of the chairs across from Geddes's desk.

"How'd Merideth Aames take it?" Lewis asked.

"Same as they all do," Kyle said.

Lewis nodded.

The silence lingered for a moment. Kyle cleared his throat as he thought about what he should say when SAC Geddes suddenly spoke, "Edwards here tells me you're interested in applying to become a special agent."

Kyle's eyebrows raised in surprise. He looked at Lewis, who nodded in encouragement.

He looked back at Geddes. "I've been thinking about it," he admitted as he clutched the envelope in his hands.

Geddes's green eyes narrowed. "I'll be honest with you, Andrews. I don't think you'd make it as an SA. I don't think you've got the stones for it. You're too … *compassionate*," she snorted, as if the word left a bad taste in her mouth.

No wonder everyone calls her the Dragon Lady behind her back, Kyle thought. An image came suddenly to mind: narrow-slitted, reptilian eyes and red hair flaring out from her head, cigarette smoke flaring from her nostrils. Had he not been so fearful of her response, he might have laughed out loud.

"But Edwards here seems to think differently," she continued. "So here's what I'm going to do. I'm sending you to Montana with him. We've been assigned a multiple homicide on federal land in Flathead National Park. You'll officially be serving as a victim specialist on the case but will also assist Edwards with the investigation. He thinks it'll be a good chance for you to see what being a special agent is really like."

"Isn't Montana in Salt Lake City's jurisdiction?" Kyle asked.

"Normally, it would be, but the vics all appear to be from Seattle. We'll be handling the case in conjunction with the Kalispell office, the county sheriff, and the Forest Service. Your flight leaves in two hours."

Kyle started to thank Geddes for the opportunity and assure her that he wouldn't let her down, but he knew that would be pointless. Results were all that she cared about. Besides, it wasn't as if he was getting off easy. There were still death notifications to be made, families to console.

As they were leaving, Kyle stopped Lewis outside of Geddes's office. "Hey, thanks for that."

"No sweat, cowboy." Lewis clapped him on the shoulder. "Just don't make me look like an ass."

"Thanks for the vote of confidence," Kyle said with a wry grin.

"Anytime," Lewis said as he started down the hall. "Oh, and pack warm," he added over his shoulder. "I hear there's a shitload of snow where we're going."

* * *

On his way home, inching along in the crawling traffic and frigid rain, Kyle pulled out his cell phone and hit the speed dial.

"Hola, Andrews' residence."

"Miss Vera, it's Kyle." Valeria Sanchez had served as Kyle's nanny when he was a child and had been his family's maid for as long as he could remember.

"Oh, Mr. Kyle, how are you?"

"I'm fine, thanks. How's Janet?"

"Your mother, she is not so good today," Valeria whispered. "She asked about you earlier, but she is sleeping now. The treatments make her very tired."

"I know," Kyle said. "When she wakes up, just tell her I called back, will you?"

"Yes, I tell her."

"Thanks," Kyle said. He was about to hang up when Miss Vera spoke again.

"Mr. Kyle?"

"Yes?"

"Your mother, she says you will be coming back to Dallas soon. Is this true?"

Kyle frowned. He had hoped to avoid the subject. "I don't know, Miss Vera. I ... something's come up at work. I'm going to be out of town for a while."

"Oh, I see."

"Don't tell Janet, all right? I promised her I'd let her know as soon as I decided."

"Okay, Mr. Kyle."

Kyle sighed as he hung up and looked at the envelope in the passenger seat. He could already imagine Janet's response when he told her he hadn't turned in his notice.

In an effort to improve his mood, he pulled out a Jimmy Buffett CD and stuck it in the stereo.

His love of the music had begun innocently enough when Angela, whom he had just started dating at the time, had invited him to a Buffett concert. She had just begun her residency in the emergency room at Parkland, and a bunch of the staff members there were big fans. They had invited her and Kyle to go along with them. Kyle hadn't really cared for his music and wasn't interested in going, but Angela had talked him into it.

It wound up being one of the best times he could ever remember. It wasn't just a concert they attended; it was a miniature Mardi Gras. People had dressed in Hawaiian shirts and grass skirts, sailor uniforms, bikinis, and countless other wild costumes. For three hours, they sang and danced and drank and acted like children, laughing and tickling one another. And after the concert was over, the people kept it going out in the parking lot. He and Angela had joined in, buying a bottle of homemade sangria from some hippie-looking kid with a cooler full of the stuff. They drank straight from the bottle as they danced the night away. Later, when they finally made it back to Angela's apartment, they made love for the first time. From that moment on, Kyle had been hooked. He had become a bona-fide Parrot-head overnight.

He thought about calling Angela to see if she had gotten the flowers yet, but he knew she was in the middle of her shift and he didn't want to bother her while she was working.

"Son of a Son of a Sailor Man" began playing. Normally, it conjured up thoughts of better times to come: the warmth of the sun on his face, the salty tang of the ocean air, and him at the helm of a thirty-foot sailboat making his way down the Baja Peninsula.

But this morning, his disposition remained as gloomy as the weather.

CHAPTER 3

Montana

Kalispell was a pleasant-seeming town of about twenty thousand. Situated in the middle of the Flathead Valley, it was surrounded by the jagged peaks of the Rocky Mountains to the north, east, and west and by Flathead Lake to the south. In spite of the overcast day, the entire valley seemed aglow, buried beneath a blanket of dazzling white snow.

Deputy Clayton Johnson, who had picked them up at the airport, prattled on about the valley, filling them in on all its finer points, including the fact that Flathead Lake was the largest natural freshwater lake west of the Mississippi. The deputy was a lean fellow, with a high-pitched voice and thinning hair beneath his western-style hat. He seemed as friendly as could be, like a real-life Barney Fife.

They turned onto Main Street. The street had been recently plowed, with four-foot banks of dirty snow lining each side. Clayton pointed out the shopping mall and the First National Bank building, which housed the FBI's Resident Agency office on the second floor. For the most part, Main Street retained the quintessential look of small-town America. Two- and three-story brick buildings lined each side of the street, housing drug stores, law offices, bookstores, gift shops, and even a few small casinos.

The center of town was marked by a circular rotunda, which Main Street split around like an island in the midst of a stream. In the middle of the isle was the Flathead County Courthouse, a chateau-like four-story, yellow-brick building. On its northern face, a large, square tower with pointed spires rose above the snow-covered spruces ringing the rotunda. The scene looked like something from the front of a Hallmark Christmas card.

Across the street to the west was the Flathead County Justice Center, a modern, three-story, brown-brick, and mirrored-glass building that housed the county sheriff's offices and detention facilities. Several news vans were already parked out front, antennas and satellite dishes sprouting from their roofs. A handful of reporters and camera crews huddling in their coats were camped out on the salted steps, filming introductory pieces and waiting for any signs of activity from inside.

"Look at 'em," Lewis muttered. "Like a bunch of vultures."

When they saw a county vehicle passing by, they all turned, cameras zooming in. Several followed them around to the back of the building, where they pulled into the sally port. As the large doors slowly rolled down, reporters and cameramen scampered up, filming as they shouted out questions.

"I tell you ... this town's never seen anything like this before," the deputy said, shaking his head.

They entered through the booking area past the holding cells and continued to the administration area up front.

They turned down another hall, and the deputy led them into one of the offices. "Sheriff ... the FBI men are here."

Looking out the window across the room from them was a tall, broad-shouldered man. He stood motionless like a statue. Long black hair trailed across the back of his collar.

The man turned around slowly. Kyle was surprised to find he was a Native American.

"Gentlemen," he said, his deep voice like the grinding of stone on stone. "I am George Greyhawk."

Kyle had often thought that Lewis was an imposing man. Lewis was big and strong and had a deep voice, but Sheriff George Greyhawk *defined* imposing from the way he stood perfectly erect to the penetrating steel-gray eyes above his sharp, aquiline nose, not to mention the powerful timbre of his voice. It was as if he had been chiseled from the bedrock of the nearby mountains.

Lewis stepped forward to greet the sheriff, who was several inches taller than him. "Agent Lewis Edwards," he said. "And this is Kyle Andrews, victim specialist."

"Aay, you must be the boys from Seattle," said a man with a thick, northeastern accent as he rose from a chair across from the sheriff's desk. "How you doing?" He wore black jeans and a dark blue ball cap and a shirt with FBI stenciled on the front. Kyle guessed him to be about five foot six or seven at the most, but with a stocky build. He had thick, dark brown hair and a bushy mustache that helped to hide his badly stained teeth.

"Tony Marasco, Kalispell office," he said as he offered his hand. "I'm told you boys are taking the lead on this."

"That's right," Lewis said. "So what have we got?"

"Just got here a little while ago myself," said Marasco. "We were waiting on you."

Kyle stood back, taking a moment to scan the room while Lewis sat in the remaining chair in front of the desk. It was something he often did in victim's homes to get a sense of the people he was dealing with. On a bookshelf behind the sheriff's desk was a black-and-white picture of a striking, young, Native American woman with long black hair. She reminded Kyle of Cher when she was younger. She stood behind a tall boy of nine or ten, her arms wrapped around him. Even at such a young age, the boy's strong jawline and broad shoulders left no doubt that it was George Greyhawk.

The wall to the left was adorned with plaques and certificates of commendation from the department, while behind him was a large map of the Flathead Valley. Curiously, Kyle noted there weren't any items indicative of his Indian heritage on display.

Marasco picked up two manila folders from the desk and handed one to Lewis. Kyle looked on over Lewis's shoulder as he opened it. Inside were copies of the crime-scene photographs, evidence log, and other information on the men.

"We've got at least three dead so far," said the sheriff. "The remains were discovered around 6:15 this morning by an electrician repairing downed power lines. The site is about halfway down Hungry Horse Reservoir, just off Graves Bay." He pointed at the map on the wall behind them. Hungry Horse Reservoir was a long, thin lake between two mountain ranges to the northeast of Kalispell. About halfway down the reservoir, Kyle found the quarter-moon-shaped bay.

"How long is the reservoir?" Lewis asked.

"It's about fifty-five miles from the dam to the Spotted Bear Ranger Station at the other end," said the sheriff. "We arrived on site about 8:45. The snow was so deep we had to use the Forest Service snowcats to get there."

"Any idea what happened?" Lewis asked.

"Not yet," said the sheriff. "Four men were staying at the cabin. Two nights ago, there was a big storm. Power to the cabin was knocked out. It appears at least two of them went out back to start the generator. From there, we aren't sure what happened. But one of the men's severed head was found in the living room, and another's arm was found in the snow out back. After we called in the search-and-rescue dogs, we dug out in front of the generator. We found a flashlight and another hand. The decapitated man was Steve Haskins. From the fingerprints, we were able to identify the two other men as James Darrell and Jasper Earl."

"How did you know the men were from Seattle?"

"From the luggage in the bedrooms. Their wallets were left along with the cash and credit cards."

"Was a report taken from the repairman?" Lewis asked.

"Yes, the deputy that took his statement said he had no reason to suspect him."

"I heard he pissed his pants when he found them," Marasco added with a smirk.

"We'll want a copy of the statement," Lewis said.

The sheriff nodded.

"What about the fourth man?" Lewis asked.

The sheriff flipped through a few of the pages in front of him. "Larry Henderson," he said. "We don't know what happened to him. We're still searching for him and any other remains. The truck and the snowmobiles they rented were left out front. He couldn't have gotten far on foot."

"Sounds to me like a poker game gone bad," said Marasco. "I used to see this kind of shit back in Jersey. You get a bunch of drunk wise guys bustin' each other's balls. Then suddenly someone snaps, and *boom*—you got fuckin' dead people everywhere."

"Unless he had help," Lewis said to the sheriff, ignoring Marasco's comment. "What sort of condition was the road in before the storm?"

"It had been plowed recently," said the sheriff. "A four-wheel-drive vehicle could have made it, but they would have had to have left before the storm hit. It doesn't fit with the estimated time of death."

"What about the evidence?" Lewis asked.

"It's all going to the lab in DC," said Marasco. "Including the body parts. I've already talked to the coroner."

"Good," said Lewis. "Make sure we get copied on everything."

"You got it."

Kyle knew that when he returned to Seattle, he would have to explain to the families what had happened to their loved ones and why they couldn't claim their remains yet. It was not something he looked forward to.

"Any evidence of weapons fire?" Lewis asked.

"Just one from a shotgun," said the sheriff. "We removed pellets from the fireplace."

"Any other weapons found?"

"Not yet. And nothing that would explain the dismemberment."

"Is it possible they were mauled?" Lewis asked.

"Not as the cause of death," said the sheriff. "Haskin's head was severed clean. Same for Earl's arm. According to the coroner, the bones didn't show any signs of fracturing or splintering, or any abrasions that one would expect to find if the arm had been hacked or sawed off. He says the arm was severed by something like an ax or a sword or a machete. Darrell's hand did appear to have been bitten off, but we think that occurred postmortem."

"What about these?" Lewis asked, pointing at a photograph of scratches on the hardwood floor.

"We think those were caused by whatever they used to decapitate the vic." The sheriff reached across the desk and flipped to the next picture. "The ceiling is open-joist construction, with logs about eight inches in diameter. There are also scratches around that beam there.

We think they might have looped something over, like a chain, and used that to hold them up."

"Torture?" Lewis asked.

"Maybe," said the sheriff. "Or just to bleed them out before they packed out the bodies."

"Jesus," Marasco muttered. "I ain't never seen nothing like that, not even in Jersey."

"So the bodies were taken and moved somewhere," Lewis said. "Either by someone strong enough to carry it by himself, or there were several people involved."

It didn't make sense to Kyle, and he ventured to ask about it. "What would anyone want with the bodies? If you're trying to make it hard to ID someone, wouldn't you get rid of the head and the hands instead of the body?"

"Unless they were interrupted and scared off before they were finished," Lewis said. "Or else someone was trying to make a statement."

"Could have been drug dealers," said Marasco. "Salt Lake's also running a list of all the known cults and white supremacist groups in the area. Homeland Security wants to make sure these guys weren't whacked as part of some terrorist plot. And it's a pretty fucking long list. I think there's more wackos in the woods out there than in all of Jersey."

Kyle nodded. He hadn't thought of that.

"Did it look as if the head had been moved? You know, placed in any particular position or arranged to send a message?" Lewis asked.

"No," said the sheriff

Deputy Johnson stuck his head back in the doorway. "Excuse me, sheriff, but the Joneses are here. I put them in the interview room up front and got them both a cup of coffee.

"Thank you, Clayton. Tell them we'll be right there. The Joneses own the cabin and two others along the bay that they rent out," explained the sheriff.

"I'd like to handle the interview with you," Lewis said to the sheriff. "Is the room they're in set up to allow for observation?"

"Audio and video," said the sheriff. "Agents Marasco and Andrews can watch from the room next door."

CHAPTER 4

Everyone stopped to get coffee except for Kyle, who poured himself a cup of water from the cooler. The sheriff led them down the hall to the observation room where a thirty-two-inch, flat-screen monitor sat on a desk in front of two chairs.

"All we need's a little popcorn for the show, aay?" Marasco said as he plopped into one of the chairs.

Kyle didn't respond.

Marasco looked at Kyle. "What? You got nothin' to say?"

"I just don't think it's appropriate," Kyle said.

"Appropriate? It's a fucking joke. Look, you VS guys might have to tiptoe around with the families of the vics and all, and that's fine—I understand. But don't be all high and mighty with me. You deal with it your way. I'll deal with it mine."

Kyle nodded. "Yeah, sure."

"Aay, forget about it," Marasco shrugged.

Kyle cracked a smile in spite of himself. The guy sounded like someone straight out of a mob movie. "So what brought you here?" he asked. "You don't exactly strike me as the Montana type."

"You think?" Marasco stopped when he saw Lewis and the sheriff enter the room on the monitor. "I'll tell you later."

They watched as Lewis and the sheriff greeted the Joneses. Bill Jones was a heavyset man, with broad shoulders, a barrel chest, and white hair. He had chubby cheeks and bright blue eyes. Even in winter, his weathered face was well tanned. He wore Timberland boots with jeans and a green and black flannel shirt over a thermal undershirt and held a faded denim baseball cap in his hands. There was a stricken look on his face.

Audrey Jones was a pleasant-looking lady with light brown hair laced with streaks of gray. She also wore jeans and a thick red sweater with a snowman embroidered on the front. Unlike her husband, she appeared to be more relaxed.

Lewis pulled out his notepad, made a few notes, and then said, "Mr. and Mrs. Jones, first, I want to thank you for coming in today. I know this must have been a shock to you, and we appreciate your cooperation."

"That's quite all right," Mrs. Jones replied.

"Now, according to our information, you own the cabin in which the murdered men were found."

"Yes," Mrs. Jones answered. "We own three cabins along the lake. We rent out two of them to tourists. During the summer, Bill takes them on fly-fishing trips. During the winter, we rent them out to skiers and snowmobilers."

"Did they reserve the cabin in advance, or was it rented out recently?" Lewis asked.

"It was reserved in advance," Mrs. Jones replied. "I handle all the bookkeeping for the business, and I made the reservations. I want to say that James reserved it sometime in early January. I have all the records on the computer. I'll be happy to get you the exact date if you need it."

"Yes, any specific information you can provide us with will be helpful," Lewis said. "Now, you mentioned that James made the reservation. Were you familiar with Mr. Darrell?"

"Oh, yes, James has rented that cabin from us the last three or four years. He brings some of the guys from the body shop with him each year."

"Body shop?"

"Yes, he owns an auto-body repair shop in Seattle."

Lewis nodded. "Were you familiar with any of the other men staying with him?"

"All of them except one had stayed there before. He was a younger man. I believe his name was Steve. Steve—"

"Haskins," Mr. Jones finished for her.

"Yes, that was his name."

"Did you see the men when they arrived at the cabin?" Lewis asked

Mrs. Jones shook her head, and her husband spoke again. "I—" He paused to clear his throat. "I showed them to the cabin and helped them to get settled in."

"Did you notice anything unusual about any of their behavior? Did any of them seem nervous or anything?" Lewis asked.

"No," Mr. Jones replied. "Nothing I noticed."

"Did they bring anything with them that seemed unusual?"

"Not that I noticed. Mostly just fishing gear, but I did notice they had a shotgun with them. I don't know exactly whose it was, but I know they had one."

Lewis nodded. "Can you remember for sure if you saw any other guns or weapons?"

"No, not that I can remember."

"What about an ax?" Lewis asked.

"Well, each of the cabins has an ax for chopping firewood," Mr. Jones replied.

"They never found one at the site," Marasco said to Kyle.

In the other room, Lewis paused to write down the information. Kyle was sure he was thinking the same thing. Then Lewis said, "We found the vehicle and the snowmobiles they rented at the cabin. Did they bring more than one vehicle?"

"No, just the one," Mr. Jones replied.

"What about skis?" the sheriff asked.

"No, not that I saw. At least I didn't notice any on the truck's ski rack."

"Did you know if anyone came to visit them at the cabin before the storm?" Lewis asked.

"No," Mrs. Jones replied. Mr. Jones just shook his head.

"Do you know of any reason why someone would want to kill those men?"

"No, none at all," said Mrs. Jones.

"No, me either," Mr. Jones said quietly. He acted as if he were about to say more but then stopped. He looked down at the hat he was nervously working back and forth between his hands.

Kyle could tell that something was bothering Mr. Jones.

Lewis had picked up on it too. He waited a moment before he spoke. "Mr. Jones, is there something you want to tell us?"

Mr. Jones shook his head. "I just … I went to the cabin and told them about the storm before it hit, but they said they were just going to ride it out. I didn't think … I didn't know … I just wish … I should have made them come into town with us," he sighed. "None of this would have happened if I'd made them come into town."

Mrs. Jones reached out and gently placed her hand on top of his. Her husband seemed to respond to her touch. Straightening his shoulders, he sat back up and took a deep breath. "I'm sorry," he said.

"That's all right," Lewis said. "I think we have everything for now. But before you go, there's someone else I'd like you to meet." He stood and left the room.

The door to the viewing room opened, and Lewis stuck his head in. "What do you think?" he asked.

"Not much, but I believed them," said Marasco. He sounded almost disappointed to admit it.

"Yeah, me too," said Kyle.

"Yeah," Lewis said, sounding distracted. "I was hoping they might give us something more to work with. Kyle, come with me. I want you to be the point of contact."

Kyle followed Lewis next door.

"Mr. and Mrs. Jones," Lewis said. "This is Kyle Andrews. He's the victim specialist who will be handling this case."

"Victim specialist?" asked Mrs. Jones.

"Yes," Kyle said as he shook their hands. He had never cared for the title of victim specialist. To him, it sounded like someone who specialized in *creating* victims, not helping them.

He held out one of his cards, and Mrs. Jones took it. "I'll be in touch with you to help keep you informed on the progress of the investigation and to let you know when your property will be released to you. You may not think of yourself as a victim in the typical sense of the word, but you probably do feel a certain sense of apprehension and violation over what has happened. If at *any* point you feel like you would like to talk to someone about it, please call me."

"And if you think of anything else that might help us with the investigation, don't hesitate to call," added Lewis.

Mr. Jones nodded as he and his wife stood. Clearing his throat, Mr. Jones pulled his cap back on and then reached out and took his wife's hand. Together, they walked from the room, holding on to each other for support. Watching them, Kyle thought of Angela. He wondered if they would ever be like that.

Lewis looked at his watch. "Tell the press we'll have a briefing for them in half an hour," he said to the sheriff. "I'm going to go have a smoke first."

"I'll go with you," said Marasco as the two headed outside.

CHAPTER 5

Denver

By the time Carrie Daniels arrived home, it was already well after dark. She had worked late, not because she had to but because she was trying to keep her mind off the fact that it was Valentine's Day and she was alone again. She pulled into the driveway of her townhouse and hit the garage door opener. A few scattered snowflakes had begun to fall, sparkling like tiny diamonds as they angled across the headlight beams. That didn't bother her. In fact, she liked it. Her plans for the evening consisted of dinner alone with her cat and a nice, hot bath before she relaxed in front of the fire.

When she stepped into the laundry room off the garage, she was greeted by the chirping of the alarm system she had recently had installed. She punched in the code to disarm the system and watched as the garage door rolled shut. Once satisfied, she closed the back door, locked it, and punched in the code to re-arm the system.

When she had purchased the system, she had told herself she was doing it to protect herself from the nameless, faceless criminals of the world, that in this day and age, it was foolish to ignore society's inherent propensity for violence. But she knew better. She had learned that the hard way. The harsh reality was it wasn't the nameless, faceless criminals of the world, but those closest to you who posed the greatest danger.

She stepped into the kitchen and was immediately greeted by

Chelsea, who hopped up onto the bar between the kitchen and the living room. After she satisfied the cat's desire for attention, she emptied a can of cat food into the plastic food dish on the floor. While the cat devoured its food, Carrie poured herself a glass of wine from a box sitting in the fridge. She could afford the more expensive vintages, but she didn't see the point. She wasn't a wine connoisseur. She drank for the effect, not for the taste.

Glass of box-blush in hand, she proceeded upstairs to change.

When she returned downstairs, she was wearing a pair of red plaid flannel pajamas and thick gray athletic socks on her feet. The wine glass was empty.

She poured herself another drink and then went into the living room, where she started a fire in the gas fireplace. She opened the door on her entertainment center and picked out several CDs, including The Verve, Tori Amos, Sarah McLaughlin, and Fiona Apple, which she placed into the CD changer. Then, on impulse, she added the first CD from Elton John's *Goodbye Yellow Brick Road* and *Glass Houses* by Billy Joel, both of which had been among her father's favorites. Even now, years later, she still remembered riding in the car with him, singing along and giggling at the silly face he made when he sang "Ahh-ooh, B … B … B … Benny and the Jets."

She took her time preparing dinner. While she didn't normally cook and wasn't good at it by any stretch of the imagination, tonight was about keeping herself busy, so she planned to make homemade spaghetti.

"You don't mind if my breath's bad, do you, baby?" she cooed to Chelsea as she chopped up an onion and minced two cloves of garlic for the sauce. The cat looked at her, cocking its head momentarily, and then began industriously licking its paw.

The sauce was simmering, and Carrie was buttering the thick slices of French bread for the garlic toast when the phone rang. Without looking, she knew who it was. He knew her so well. He knew she would be feeling lonely tonight and was trying to take advantage of it.

She let it ring, reaching for her glass of wine instead. The answering machine picked up.

"Carrie, it's Bret." It sounded like he had already been drinking, just enough to be charming. Reflexively, Carrie's hand lifted to the cheekbone below her right eye. Most of the bruising was gone, but it was still tender to the touch.

"I was just calling to wish you a happy Valentine's Day. Hope you liked the flowers. I know how much you like lilies and all, and roses just seem so cliché." There was a long pause and the sound of a deep sigh. "Look, I've told you like a hundred times I'm sorry about what happened. I don't know what more you want from me. Can't we just put this behind us? I love you. Don't you know that?"

A part of her desperately wanted to pick up. She wanted to believe him, to believe that everything was going to be all right, but she just couldn't do it. Not anymore.

"I'm not going to give up," he continued, the tone of his voice becoming suddenly harsh. "You know we were meant to be together ... *forever.*"

Carrie winced as the phone was slammed down.

She stood there, listening to the shrill sound of the dial tone until the machine finally cut it off. She quickly reached over and hit the button to delete the message. She knew if she didn't, she would spend the rest of the evening listening to it over and over, trying to discern the true meaning of his statement. If only she could get him out of her life that easily. She didn't know what to do. Since she had left him, his behavior had become more and more erratic to the point that she was genuinely scared of what he might do next. She had even considered taking out a temporary restraining order against him, but she was afraid that might be the thing that would send him over the edge completely.

Her hand shook as she turned off the burner beneath the sauce, her appetite suddenly gone. Instead, she went to the refrigerator and poured herself another blush. Without closing the door, she slammed it down in three large gulps and then filled it again.

CHAPTER 6

Maryland

At the corner of West Jefferson and 18th, in a quiet subdivision on the south side of Columbia, Maryland, a darkened moving truck sat next to the curb at the end of the block. In the converted cargo area sat Nathaniel Brockemeyer smacking on a mouthful of cinnamon-flavored gum. As a child, he wouldn't have dared to smack his gum for fear of a beating. But his father wasn't around anymore, so he was free to enjoy the gum as he pleased.

He wore all black, including the baseball cap turned around backward on his head. Over the top of the cap, he wore a pair of expensive Bose headphones that were typically only used in music-industry recording studios or by the most demanding—and wealthy—audiophiles. But he wasn't listening to music or even the mindless chatter of conservative talk radio. Instead, he was listening to the sounds picked up by a dozen electronic bugs that had been installed in a house halfway down the street.

The only light came from a bank of flat-screen monitors mounted along one wall. One monitor displayed the view on all four sides of the van, while another displayed the dark backyard of the house down the block. Chuckling to himself, Nathan turned a knob on the console in front of him and adjusted the gain on one of the little microphones until he could hear Letterman's monologue better.

Just as Letterman was about to deliver the punch line to a joke, there was a short *pop*, and the house fell silent. Someone had turned off the TV.

Damn it. He slapped his hand against the console. He hated it when they did that.

There was a groan of leather as someone got up out of the La-Z-Boy (or off the couch), followed by shuffling footsteps and the creaking of the stairs as the occupant made their way upstairs. Nathan pushed a small button on the console, switching the feed to the microphones on the second floor. A door squeaked open; a light switch was flipped. There was an odd clattering, followed by the sound of someone brushing their teeth. After spitting and rinsing, there was more clattering.

Nathan had done this enough that he had become good at figuring out what people were doing. As he listened to the tiny *clink*, he could picture the person dropping the toothbrush back into the ceramic holder. There was more clattering and the sound of a plastic lid being unscrewed. Inside the truck, Nathan mimicked the person, holding an imaginary bottle of mouthwash and pouring it into an imaginary glass. He leaned his head back in anticipation and laughed when he heard the person beginning to gargle. "Damn, I'm good," he said, amused by his own cleverness.

Looking at one of the monitors, Nathan waited until the light in the upstairs bedroom went out. He made a note of the time on his watch, and then leaned back in his chair to wait.

An hour later, he unwrapped a fresh stick of gum and stuffed it into his mouth. Standing, he buckled a leather tool belt—loaded with the special devices of his trade—on over his tight-fitting black fatigues. He took off the baseball cap, rubbed his hand across his stubbly red hair, and inserted a radio receiver into his left ear. He then pulled on a pair of black latex gloves and a black ski mask. He unfastened a pair of night-vision goggles from his belt and pulled them on, leaving the oculars flipped up on top of his forehead. He clapped his hands together and pumped his legs up and down as he ran in place like a sprinter preparing for a race. He took several deep breaths, mentally preparing himself for the task at hand.

Game time.

He slipped from the back of the truck and scanned the block to make sure he wasn't being observed. Overhead, the moon was blotted out behind a bank of thick clouds. The night was inky black. The only lights in the area were those still on in a few of the houses and the circular glow of the sodium-vapor streetlamp on the opposite corner. He had broken out the one nearest the truck. From behind the mask, his icy blue eyes glimmered like quicksilver.

He slipped down the alley. Years of advanced training had taught him how to be stealthy in urban environments. It had saved his life during the war with Iraq.

When he reached the back fence of the house, he hefted himself up and over. He landed in a crouch, grimacing at the momentary burst of pain in his right knee. It was an old injury that still bothered him, especially in the cold. It was a constant reminder of what he had been before.

Nathan crept across the backyard onto the patio and removed one of the tools from his belt. It bristled with a handful of thin, wire blades and metal picks. He pressed the device against the back door's keyhole and inserted several of the thin, metal wires, working and twisting until there was a satisfying *click*. He replaced the tool and carefully opened the door, making sure it didn't creak, and then slipped inside.

He flipped down the night-vision goggles. The house sprang to life in an eerie blaze of luminous green light.

He was in the living room. To his left were the breakfast nook and the kitchen. He made his way to the right, around the sofa and the La-Z-Boy recliner. He tiptoed up the stairs, stepping on the outer edges of each step in order to remain silent.

At the top of the stairs, he paused and pressed his left hand against his ear. In the truck, he had set the transmitter to broadcast the audio from the bug in the bedroom to the receiver in his ear, which he now listened to. The room remained silent.

He slipped down the hall and peered into the first doorway. A night-light next to the bed provided enough illumination for him to see without the goggles, which he flipped up. A small form lay curled up in bed—a boy, he surmised from the racing-car bedspread and the posters of sports figures and rock stars hanging on all the walls. One of them in particular caught Nathaniel's attention, which caused him to pause. It was a large photograph of Carlos Aurilio, the National's shortstop, in the process of ducking a tag as he slid into home. Dirt was flying up around him, and the umpire's arms were spread wide. The caption across the top read: "The Washington Nationals—Staying Safe at Home."

Seeing the poster caused Nathan to hesitate. He looked down at the small boy. He remembered when he had been young, the joy and admiration he had felt watching Cal Ripken Jr., play, and he felt an immediate kinship with the boy. He wished there was another way, but there wasn't. He was the one truly keeping the nation safe.

He pulled a small silver canister from a pouch on his belt. He held it near the boy's face and depressed the nozzle, dispelling a fine mist. He then turned to step from the boy's room, but paused when he saw a baseball glove lying on the dresser by the door. He picked up the glove and slipped it beneath the boy's arm before he moved down the hall.

In the master bedroom, Nathan crept to the side of the bed, his anger growing as he looked down at Jacobson. How could the bastard have been so thoughtless? Because of this man's stupidity, his entire family had been condemned. Nathan's fists clenched as he struggled to contain his rage. He wanted to pummel the traitorous bastard, to beat him to death with his bare hands. But it would raise suspicion, and that would not be tolerated.

He lifted the canister and sprayed the mist again, causing the man's nose to twitch momentarily as he inhaled the vapor. He snorted once, and then settled back down.

Nathan moved around the bed. He paused as he looked down at the woman. She was beautiful, her lustrous blonde hair aglow in the moonlight that spilled in through the blinds. Her skin was soft and smooth, her lips full. Leaning over, he breathed in the heady scent of her. He started to reach out and touch her but caught himself. Instead, he quickly sprayed two shots of the mist beneath her nose. He wasn't sure exactly what the vapor consisted of, or how it worked, but he knew it was a complex chemical agent because he had received an inoculation prior to the mission. What he did know was that within minutes all three would be dead from suffocation. The autopsies, which were certain to be performed, would reveal that they had all died from carbon monoxide poisoning. On his way out, he would simply rig the pilot light on the gas range to cover his tracks.

He waited until he was sure she would not wake, then pulled off the glove on his right hand and placed it against her cheek. He burned for her, but it was forbidden. There could be no evidence of his visit. He was already taking a big chance by just touching her.

He felt a faint exhalation leave her body—then no more. He closed his eyes, absorbing the warmth of her flesh until it began to fade.

Finally, when she had grown cold, he removed his hand, pulled the glove back on, and strolled from the room.

CHAPTER 7

Nathan drove the moving van south on Highway 29 headed toward Washington, DC. About five miles outside of Columbia, he exited the highway and turned right onto one of the rural county roads. He followed the road for two miles before he turned off onto a private drive. Fifty yards down the drive, he came to a guard station nestled among the trees. Hidden from the state road, the concrete and steel building looked more like a military bunker than a security checkpoint. A large steel gate extended across the drive, presenting an impassable barrier to virtually any vehicle other than a tank. A twelve-foot-tall, electrified, chain-link fence lined with razor wire extended into the woods on each side. Red and white signs stating "*Danger—High Voltage*" and "*Trespassers Will Be Prosecuted*" were spaced at fifty-foot intervals along its expanse.

He pulled up beside a black stanchion and stopped. He rolled down the window so that the camera could get an unobstructed view in order to run its facial-geometry and thermal-sensing scans. In years past, the gate security system had consisted of palm print and retinal scanners, but even those had been somewhat vulnerable to subterfuge, whereas the new system, based on the recognition of the thermal heat pattern of a person's face, was virtually impossible to circumvent. Additional cameras on the passenger side and thermal scanners embedded in the asphalt beneath the vehicles assured that no other occupants or stowaways were entering without being cleared first.

There was a soft *beep*, and a pleasant female voice said, "Welcome, Mr. Brockemeyer. You are authorized to proceed."

The steel gate rolled back. He drove down the asphalt roadway that wound through the trees for a half mile before it opened onto a wide, grassy plain of gently rolling hills. A stark, silver-mirrored building that was four stories tall and almost a quarter-mile long stretched across the clearing, its exterior bathed by a multitude of floodlights ringing the perimeter.

He passed the turnoff to the large circular drive in front and followed the road around back, where a second, identical building, offset by some thirty yards, paralleled the first. Driving alongside the second building, he turned down the ramp into the parking garage. At the bottom, he repeated the security check and then waited for the gate to rise.

He drove across the empty parking garage to a concrete wall at the end. Looking toward the roof of the van, he waited while the thermal scanners verified his signature. A deep *boom* echoed within the garage as the steel bolts retracted. A section of the wall slowly rolled aside, revealing a hidden bay of the garage. There were two moving vans similar to the one Nathan was driving and a red Corvette parked inside. He parked the van, leaving the tool belt draped across the chair in the back, the keys in the ignition. He walked to a panel in the concrete wall before him. After he opened the panel, he removed a foam-filled canister from its cradle and inserted the silver vial. He replaced the canister and pressed a small red button. There was a whistling, humming sound, and the canister vanished as it was sucked into the vacuum-tube system. After he closed the door on the canister panel, he turned and got in the Corvette.

With a squeal of rubber, he raced from the garage.

Nathan took Highway 29 south toward Washington. The growl of the engine and the tires humming across the pavement provided a hypnotic effect, threatening to lead his mind down roads best left untraveled. Struggling against the memories that tugged at his mind, he rolled down the window and sucked in great gulps of the cold night air as beads of perspiration trickled down the back of his neck. He changed the radio station, turning up the volume until his ears rang, but the image of the boy continued to haunt him.

A lone vehicle approached on the opposite side of the highway, its headlights momentarily blinding him like the burst of a camera flash.

He is eight years old. He huddles in the corner of his closet on a hot summer night, clutching a half-sized, autographed baseball bat and rocking back and forth as the voice of the Oriole's play-by-play announcer echoes within the darkness. The volume is turned all the way up in an effort to drown out the shouting and screaming emanating from the living room.

He imagines stepping up to home plate, a sea of fans wildly cheering him. The green grass of the outfield is bathed in the glow of the silver-haloed floodlights. There's the smell of pine tar and chalk as he scoops up a handful of dirt from the batter's box. He rubs his gloves together as he stares down the pitcher. He is not afraid. He is in control. He'll show them who is boss. And they will scream in adoration as he rounds the bases.

A razor's edge of light springs to life beneath the bottom of the door. There is a bellowing roar like the grunt of a charging bull. The door bursts open. The nauseating stink of cigarette smoke, sweat, and whisky fill the tiny space. Nathan cowers in the corner, wishing he could disappear, wishing he was somewhere else, anywhere else.

"Turn that goddamned thing off!" screams his father as he grabs him by the ankle and drags him from the closet. "I'll show you what that fucking bat is good for!" he roars as he jerks it from Nathan's grasp—

Nathan's hands clutched the steering wheel so tightly that his knuckles had turned white. His jaw muscles stood out like steel cables beneath his skin. If not for the wad of gum in his mouth, he might have cracked a tooth. The car was flying, the white lines blurring as the Corvette shot past. He was making his way around a curve, the front end of the car dipping to the inside, the tires squealing as they began to lose purchase, the rear end slipping nearer to the concrete divider. He was on the verge of losing control. He lifted his foot off the accelerator and glanced at the speedometer. He was doing over a hundred.

Perhaps it was best that the boy and his mother had been put out of their misery, he thought as he feathered the brakes to bring the car back under control.

He needed to blow off a little steam. His pent-up anger had him so wired that he knew he wouldn't be able to sleep. He would just toss and turn and stare at the ceiling, waging war with his inner demons until dawn came creeping through the blinds. Instead, he decided to head for Suzie Cue's. It had been almost a year now. It was doubtful anyone would remember him.

As its name suggested, Suzie's was a pool hall. But unlike the stereotypical version full of bikers and roughnecks, Suzie's was a modern, hip version with a full menu and hundreds of brands of beer, both domestic and imported on tap. The decor consisted of stainless steel and brick, with lots of bright neon. On Tuesday through Sunday, live bands played on a small stage in the corner. The clientele consisted primarily of young kids attending the nearby junior college, but there were always a few older barflies watching the rowdy kids and reminiscing about their lost youth.

It was a little after one o'clock when he pulled into the parking lot. He got out and made his way to the door, pausing to spit his gum into a small planter as he passed. Dressed in a tight black shirt and cargo pants, wearing combat boots and his Orioles cap backward on his head, Nathan looked enough like the other college kids that he didn't attract any undue attention as he walked in. As he passed by the hostess station, he grabbed a couple of cinnamon-flavored toothpicks from the dispenser and began chewing on one as he made his way to the bar. He sat on the stool at the end, back in the corner next to the TV. ESPN was showing highlights of the evening's NBA games. Four long-haired kids who looked like they should still be in high school were on stage, playing a poor rendition of Nirvana's "Smells Like Teen Spirit." A chubby young girl with long black hair and glasses was working the bar. He ordered a Budweiser, which she poured from the tap and placed on a cardboard coaster in front of him.

He slammed down half the beer in one gulp and ordered another. In an attempt to be friendly, the girl made a comment about him being really thirsty, but Nathan wasn't listening to her. His mind was elsewhere.

He spun about on his stool and began watching the crowd, his blue eyes narrowing as his tongue flicked the toothpick back and forth between his teeth.

He slammed down three more beers—a small fire break against the inferno raging within—while he watched for the right opportunity to present itself.

It happened just before closing time. During his surveillance,

Nathan had spotted two couples playing pool at a nearby table. Obviously college kids, they drank pitcher after pitcher of beer and became louder and more annoying with each round. The boys were both dark-haired and handsome, one of average height and well-built, the other tall and thin. Typical frat boys, they both wore Polo rugby shirts and Rolexes and had an air of spoiled sophistication about them. No doubt their parents were well-to-do DC socialites who had sent their sons to a small college in the suburbs in order to avoid the social decay of the inner-city. Nathan disliked them instantly.

The two girls with them fit the sorority-bitch mold equally well. They both had big, blonde hair—probably bleached—and wore slutty, low-cut blouses to show off their surgically enhanced tits.

As Nathan watched, one of the blondes stepped up to the pool table for her turn. Nearly missing the cue ball completely, she broke into a hysterical fit of snorting laughter before she staggered back to her stool. Head drooping, she sat down, but because she had misjudged her actual location, she slipped off the edge of the stool and fell to the floor with a loud crash. Her friends howled and pointed, stumbling about and slapping each other on the back, as if it were the funniest thing they had ever seen. The girl who had fallen, however, didn't share in their amusement. When her date grabbed her by the arm to help pull her up, she jerked away and snapped, "Don't touch me!"

Nathan seized the moment. Standing, he strode over to the table. The boy was still trying to help the girl up while she huddled on the floor, pouting and slapping at him.

"Hey, pal, leave the girl alone," Nathan said, his arms folded across his chest.

The boy spun around, the shit-eating grin slipping from his face as he looked up at Nathan.

"You work here or something?" the boy slurred.

"No, I just heard the girl tell you to leave her alone."

"She's my fucking girlfriend, jerk-off."

Nathan grinned. "Fucking girlfriend, huh? You mind if I fuck the little whore?"

"What's your fucking problem?" the boy glared at Nathan.

"You," Nathan snapped. He jammed the boy in the chest with both hands and knocked him back several feet.

Nathan crouched as the boy charged him, swinging wildly. With a quick, fluid motion, Nathan swept his left arm up, blocking the punch. He stepped forward and punched the boy square in the mouth, splitting his gums and knocking out teeth.

As the boy collapsed, Nathan whirled to face the attack he knew would come from behind. The tall, thin boy was already in motion, swinging the fat end of a cue stick at his head. Nathan ducked, and the stick whistled past, just grazing the top of his head. As he pivoted on his left foot, Nathan kicked out with his right, catching the boy square in the stomach. The boy crumpled to his knees, gasping for breath.

The gathering crowd parted. A muscle-bound bouncer came thundering across the room like a charging bull.

Nathan grinned and stepped into the attack, the roar of the crowd ringing in his ears.

As the bouncer bore down on him, Nathan grabbed him by the arm and, turning, flipped him. The beer-emblazoned pool table light shattered as the bouncer's feet crashed into it. Shards of glass and plastic rained down upon him as he landed in the middle of the pool table. Before the bouncer could rise, Nathan was over him, hammering him with a barrage of blows to his face and midsection.

"Fuck you, you worthless son of a bitch!" Nathan howled as the punches rained down.

When the fire had finally burned itself out, Nathan stopped. Without another word, he turned and made his way to the door. The crowd parted before him.

Stepping into the cool embrace of the night, he knew that he would sleep like a baby tonight.

CHAPTER 8

Montana

His breath plumed in front of him in a silvery cloud with each exhalation. His arms and legs pumped with metronomic rhythm, the thin skis carving parallel trails as they *shooshed* across the snow. He was getting tired, his arms and legs burning from the effort, but he couldn't stop. He had to keep moving.

He imagined he was a famous cross-country skier, someone named Hans or Sven, striving for the finish line while the crowd cheered, chanting his name and waving their flags as he passed.

His name was actually Adam Peterson, insurance salesman and part-time ski instructor at The Big Mountain ski resort at Whitefish. He had skied virtually his entire life, and he loved it, especially cross-country skiing. There was nothing better than being outdoors in the crisp, clean air with the sparkling glint of sunlight off the snow crystals. But more than that, it was the feeling he got when he pushed himself like he was pushing himself now. When all the troubles and issues of the outside world faded away until it was only him, his mind focused to pinpoint clarity. Push. Push. Push. Drive. Drive. Drive. Yard by yard. Mile by mile. In touch with himself. At one with the world.

The crunching of the snow and the whisking of his nylon suit were the only sounds to be heard along the valley, but even those sounds went unheard by Adam, who was mentally humming along to the sounds of Kenny G playing in the earphones of the iPod tucked into his fanny pack.

The sun had dipped behind the mountains to the west, the deep blue shadows fading to violet as he stroked along the last few miles of the trail leading back to the road, where he had left his car. He realized he was not going to make it back before it was pitch-black. Even now, it was getting difficult to make out the contours of the terrain in front of him, and he became concerned about falling and breaking a leg—or worse. His rhythm was momentarily interrupted as he slowed enough to pull his goggles onto his forehead in order to see better.

He continued on, more cautiously than before. The shadows deepened among the trees, reaching out across the trail until it was impossible to distinguish them from the dark of night. He was upset with himself for not paying better attention to the time before he had started back, but he had been in such a groove that he had lost all track of—

He was struck hard and fast on the right side like a quarterback blindsided by a blitzing linebacker. The world jerked sideways as he was knocked from the trail, tumbling down the slope to his left. His right ski smacked something, which snapped it in half and wrenched his knee. He cried out in pain as the ligaments ripped and tore.

He rolled over once more and landed on his back. His goggles were left askew on his head, and his earphones had been jerked from his ears, the cord twisted tight around his neck and tangled in his poles.

When he regained enough clarity to try to sit up, he felt a sharp pain in his right side. He looked down and was terrified to see a large gash ripped in his ski jacket. White Thinsulate lining spilled out of the rip, but as he looked, it began to darken before his eyes.

"Oh, shit," he stammered, his voice trembling with the onset of shock.

He tossed aside the broken ski pole that he had managed to hang on to and tried to pull the jacket open enough to see how bad the wound was. It was dark, and the temperature was dropping quickly. If he was unable to make it back to his car, he might freeze to death overnight.

With his earphones pulled from his ears, he was able to hear a rustling sound above him, one like the whistling of wind through the trees but different. He struggled to turn his head to look behind him for the source of the sound.

At first, he was unable to make out anything in the blue-black depths beneath the trees. But then he saw it—a rapidly moving blur amid the darkness. It was like looking through a window filled with wavy imperfections. He watched in confusion as it moved across the landscape, a shadow among the darkness, shifting and changing as it went. At first, he thought it might be another skier, but as he watched, he noticed the shape was moving through the trees at a speed no skier could match. It made a wide sweeping arc, its motion fluid and graceful. As the shadow swept down the hillside, Adam realized it was coming toward him, its speed increasing as it drew nearer. He grabbed at the other ski pole lying a few feet away.

He was too slow.

The shadow slammed into him, knocking the breath from him and driving him deeper into the powdery snow. He flailed wildly, trying to knock it loose, but it bore down on him like an avalanche and drove him down into darkness.

* * *

He wasn't sure how long he was out, but he awoke to the pressure of something on his midsection. He screamed hysterically as, one by one, his ribs began to snap. Blood geysered from his torso, spattering his face and goggles and steaming as it splashed onto the snow.

The lonely scream echoed down the valley before it was suddenly silenced as darkness settled upon the mountain.

CHAPTER 9

Seattle

Kyle made his way up the walk to the house. As he stepped onto the porch, a drop of cold rain fell on the back of his neck and trickled down his spine. Shuddering, he pulled up the collar of his overcoat. He reached for the brass knocker, but the door opened before him.

Bobbi Darrell stood in the doorway, wearing a pair of jeans and a faded Seahawks sweatshirt. It was an old one, with the old blue and silver logo. She was an attractive woman in her midfifties, but today, she looked older than her years. The dark circles beneath her eyes made it appear as if she hadn't slept in days.

"I heard your car," she said, a hint of hope in her voice.

Kyle nodded. Before he could say anything, she read the look on his face, and her expression fell immediately.

"Come in," she said as she turned and went back inside.

After they had returned from Montana, Kyle and Lewis had spent days questioning the family, friends, and coworkers of the victims in an effort to dig up leads on people who might have had a reason to kill the men. They had reviewed the backgrounds of the men and interviewed dozens of employees at the three body shops that James Darrell owned, but they had yet to find anything that suggested the murders had been committed by anyone working there.

Darrell had been the sole proprietor of the business, and therefore, no one outside of his wife, Bobbi, stood to gain anything from his murder. According to everyone they had interviewed, Darrell and his wife had been happily married for thirty-one years.

Kyle knew she didn't have anything to do with it simply from the look of utter devastation on her face the first time they had met with her. It was a look he had grown accustomed to seeing over the past few years.

Kyle followed her into the living room. It was tastefully decorated in warm earth tones, with a watercolor of the Pacific Northwest coastline hanging above the fireplace. Several photo albums lay on the coffee table along with a box of Kleenex. Videotapes with handwritten labels that read "Wedding Video" and "Paris" and "Christmas '03" were scattered across the floor in front of the TV.

Bobbi picked up the rumpled afghan lying on the sofa and folded it. She laid it across one of the arms before she sat down. Her movements were slow, mechanical.

Without sitting, Kyle took the small envelope from his pocket. Bobbi looked at it for a moment as if afraid to touch it and then slowly held out a trembling hand. Kyle gently handed her the envelope. She opened it, and then tilted it upward so that the contents slid out into the palm of her other hand.

The only thing they had recovered of James Darrell had been his severed left hand. In spite of evidence to the contrary, a part of Bobbi had clung to the hope that her husband might still be found alive. But now, looking at the gold wedding band in her hand, it was as if the finality of his death suddenly hit home.

"No," she whimpered, clutching the ring against her chest as she burst into tears.

Kyle sat next to her, and she slumped against him, sobbing. He held her gently, waiting until she cried herself out.

Finally, with tears streaking her face and her eyes red-rimmed and puffy, she leaned back and looked at him. "What am I to do now?"

Not knowing what else to say to her, Kyle said, "We'll find out who did this. I promise you." It was the best he could do.

They had yet to locate Larry Henderson, and determining his whereabouts, whether dead or alive, was currently their top priority. It had been almost two weeks since the murders, and more and more, it was beginning to appear that either Henderson had killed the other men and then disappeared, or else he was also dead. The border patrol had been provided with photographs and descriptions of Henderson. With the cooperation of the media outlets, his photo had been printed in the newspapers and broadcast on the evening news in virtually every city in the Pacific Northwest. He had also been featured on the FBI's "missing persons" website.

The report from the behavioral profiling team in Quantico—while not ruling out that the murders could have been committed by an individual staying with the men—had suggested that the crime had most likely been committed by a small group of people. The serial killer theory didn't fit the pattern, because almost all serial killers acted alone and their victims were predominately female. Also, it seemed unlikely that a single individual could have overpowered four grown men—at least one of which had been armed.

All indications were that the attack had come swiftly, in a militaristic strike, perhaps by a paramilitary group like the Montana Freemen or other domestic terrorists. Marasco, with the assistance of the sheriff's office, was in the process of investigating those organizations that fit the profile, but so far, he had not managed to come up with anything substantial.

After he promised to keep her informed of the status of the case, Kyle returned to the car as more of the cold rain fell on him.

Looking in the rearview mirror, he used his hand to brush the water from his hair. He then took out his cell phone and hit the speed dial number for Angela. He got her voice mail. "Hey, Angela, just called to see how things are going. Give me a call when you get a chance. I could use the sound of a friendly voice."

Kyle sighed as he hung up. It had been at least a week since they had talked, and then only briefly. With both of them having such hectic schedules, they kept missing each other. Fortunately, Angela was in the last year of her residency. Once she finished, the plan was for her to move to Seattle, but Kyle had sensed something different about her lately. She had seemed more distant and aloof when they had talked, as if she was having second thoughts.

He flipped down the visor and looked at the picture of Angela he kept there. He had taken it on a catamaran trip from Cancun to Cozumel. Her head was tilted back as she laughed, her golden hair shimmering in the sunlight. Even though he wasn't an experienced sailor—he had never owned anything over twelve feet long—it was still a dream of his to buy a sailboat someday and to move to the southern coast of California or maybe Florida. At times like this, he would look at that picture and imagine himself and Angela on the deck of his boat, basking in the warmth of the midday sun while Jimmy Buffett played in the background.

After he started up the car, he turned on the heater and sat there while the drizzle trickled down the windshield.

CHAPTER 10

Denver

"To Brandi!" someone called out, and everyone at the table lifted their glasses for at least the third time in the last hour. Carrie joined them in the toast, careful not to spill any of her green apple martini. There were eight or ten people from the office around the table, all gathered to give Brandi Utley a fond farewell—but mostly to take advantage of the boss's open tab. They were in a trendy, new bar in Lodo called Lime Bar, which was a few blocks from their office and just down the street from Coors Field.

True to its name, virtually everything in the bar, including the walls, was painted a brilliant lime green. The exception was the furniture, which consisted of white plastic tables and chairs that looked like something straight out of the sixties. Large flat screens were mounted around the bar, showing an endless loop of computer-animated images.

Brandi was one of the graphic artists on the staff. She had just gotten a job with a big advertising firm in LA, and tomorrow was her last day. Brandi was one of the more colorful characters in the office, quite literally. She wore dark eyeliner, had a nose ring and a pierced tongue, and wore her short, spiky hair in virtually every color of the rainbow, depending on her mood.

Across the table from her, Charlie ordered another vodka and Red Bull. It was his fourth or fifth one, and it was beginning to show. He seemed to be vacillating between morose and loud and obnoxious. Although he had never said anything, Carrie could tell Charlie had a crush on Brandi—in spite of the fact that she was a lesbian—and although he was trying to hide it, he was clearly distraught.

Then Carrie caught a glimpse of someone across the bar that caused her heart to freeze. The place was so dark that she wasn't sure, but she thought she had seen Bret. The guy picked up his beer from the bar, turned around, and leaned against the counter, his face lighting up briefly in the ever-shifting light. It wasn't him. Carrie quietly sighed in relief. She knew she was being ridiculous, but she had spent the entire evening watching for him, afraid of running into him, even though she knew he would never come to a place like this.

She checked her watch. It was a little after 9:30. She decided she had had enough fun for the evening. She leaned over and thanked Allan for the drinks and told him she was going home.

"Are you sure?" He practically yelled to be heard over the loud music. "You know I told everyone they don't have to come in until ten tomorrow."

"I know," Carrie yelled back, issuing a fake yawn. "But I'm getting tired, and I need to go check on my cat."

"All right, you be careful now," he said with a pat on her arm.

Carrie stood and waved at Brandi across the table, wishing her luck in LA. Brandi blew her a kiss and winked mischievously.

Carrie was still smiling as she walked outside. She loved working with the quirky but talented staff that Allan had put together. There was a youthful energy and a sense of family about the place that she knew would be missing at any of the big papers. That was why she had turned down the offer from the *Post*.

Her car was parked along the curb on the same side of the street about a half a block down. As she neared, she pushed the button on her remote. The horn *bleeped* twice, and the yellow turn signal lights blinked as the door unlocked. She was about to open the door when someone behind her said, "Carrie."

It was Bret. She didn't know where he had come from; he had just appeared from the darkened shadows beside the building. *He's been there waiting for me all this time.*

"Bret, what are you doing?" she asked, trying not to sound terrified.

"Me?" he said. "What the fuck are *you* doing? You going out, getting drunk, looking to get laid? Is that it? If that's what you want, I can give you that." He spoke quickly, excitedly, as if he was jacked up on something.

He was upon her before she could even think to do anything. He grabbed her and squeezed her arms painfully as he tried to kiss her. His wild eyes shone with an unnatural light. His breath stank of booze and cigarettes.

Carrie tied to pull away, but his grip was too tight. She could feel his fingers grinding against the bones in her arms. She gasped in pain, but this only seemed to excite him. He tried to turn her, to pin her against the car. They were illuminated in the headlights of an approaching car.

Please ... stop. Please stop, Carrie's mind begged, but the car continued on, tooting its horn as it passed as if in encouragement.

Carrie continued to struggle against Bret, trying to push him away. "No," she stammered, more of a plea than a command.

Finally, the frustration became too much for him. Bret shoved her explosively, the palms of his hands slamming into her chest. She stumbled backward and fell, scuffing her hands on the pavement as she tried to catch herself.

Before she could gather herself, he was coming at her again, his hands clenched in rage. She knew what was coming, and she turned her head in anticipation of the blows.

Someone coming out of the bar called out, "Hey, what's going on?"

Bret looked their way and then turned and took off, disappearing down the darkened alley.

Carrie picked herself up off the street as two guys came running around the car.

"Are you okay?" one of them asked.

"Yeah ... I think so," Carrie said dazedly.

One of the guys put his hand on her arm to help her. She flinched in pain and jerked away and then quickly climbed into her car. She didn't want anyone touching her.

Inside the car, she locked the doors and sat there as she struggled to catch her breath. She felt like she was going to puke.

CHAPTER 11

Montana

Five miles south of Poulson on Highway 93, the Flathead County sheriff's Yukon slowed as it neared the Salish-Kootenai People's Center. It was easy to miss if one wasn't looking for it among the string of billboards for lakeside campgrounds, antique stores, business parks, and car dealerships, or one of the numerous new casinos that had sprung up along the road since he had last been here. Sheriff Greyhawk looked out the window, his cold gray eyes expressionless as he passed the large tepee set up alongside the highway for the benefit of the tourists. It had been many years since he had been here, and he might never have returned had it not been for the call from someone claiming to have information about the Hungry Horse murders.

The past week and a half had been spent chasing down leads in relation to the killings only to be frustrated time and time again as they all proved fruitless. To make matters worse, a local man had disappeared while he had been skiing last week. Search teams had been organized, and his car had been found at a lookout point near Swan Lake; however, they had yet to find any trace of him. While it wasn't uncommon for someone to become lost or wounded in the wilderness, the man had been an experienced skier, and there had not been any sudden storms that might have caught him unprepared. His disappearance had only served to fuel the growing paranoia among the area residents. Leads had been pouring in from all over the valley, people reporting everything from a headless skier to Bigfoot himself.

George felt certain this one, like all the others, would turn out to be nothing as well, but when he had seen the name of the person claiming to have information, he had decided to check it out personally.

The reservation wasn't in Flathead County, and therefore, it wasn't under his jurisdiction; however, because he knew the caller, he hadn't bothered to request permission from the Lake County authorities. There was no law prohibiting a county sheriff from visiting his grandmother.

Just past the visitor center, he turned off the highway onto a gravel road. A collection of run-down trailer houses wedged between the visitor center and a lumber company formed a small neighborhood of a sort. A group of mangy dogs ran loose, barking and snapping at each other while several kids played in the dirty snow. As George made his way down the road, he fought to keep the memories of his childhood here at bay. Things had been a lot different back them.

At the end of the block, he pulled up in front of one of the houses, a faded, yellow-gold one with aluminum foil covering the windows. Up close, it was evident that the place, like most of the others in the area, was in serious disrepair.

The view beyond the trailer was that of a large, sheet-metal barn and a junkyard full of discarded refrigerators, freezers, washing machines, and dryers, all of which were slowly rusting away, their doors hanging open or missing entirely.

As he got out of the truck, George noticed a thin young boy he guessed to be about fifteen or sixteen standing in the doorway and watching him. George was certain the boy was his cousin, Joseph, but he had just been a baby when George had left the reservation. He didn't see him as a cousin. To George, he was just his aunt's son. The boy opened the door as he approached. His hands trembled slightly, and his eyes darted about nervously as George walked up. In spite of the cold, a fine sheen of greasy sweat covered the boy's face. The muscles in his jaw twitched, and he licked his dry, cracked lips incessantly.

George was sure the boy was on crystal meth. On the reservation, addiction among the younger generation had been a big problem for years, and it didn't appear to be getting any better in spite of the anti-drug programs and frequent busts.

With a dejected sigh, George pushed past the boy. Inside, incense burned in a holder on top of the TV and filled the room with its cloying scent.

"She ... she's in the back room," the boy stammered.

George stepped through the living room and down the narrow hall to the small bedroom at the back. A curtain of colored beads hung across the doorway. George paused for a moment and then parted the beads and stepped inside. The room was musty and smelled of urine.

His grandmother lay on her back, her eyes closed. Her breathing was faint and shallow. Her brown, wizened skin gave her face the appearance of an apple that had been left in the sun to dry and shrivel. Thin wisps of silvery-white hair spread across the yellowed pillowcase.

"It has been a long time, Little Hawk." Even after so many years, the voice was still the same. He looked down and found her half-open, rheumy eyes looking up at him.

"It has."

"Sit." She lifted her frail arm to point at the wooden chair beside the bed.

George sat down and waited for her to speak.

"I did not know if you would come," she said.

"I almost didn't. Why did you call?"

"I know what killed those men at Hungry Horse."

George remained silent. He knew that when the call had come in, she had professed to have information about the murders, but he had suspected it was just her way of asking him back. He knew that her health was failing and that she refused to be treated by any doctors. She was steadfastly loyal to the old ways of the tribe, clinging to the last remnants of her heritage to the very end. The same headstrong refusal to accept the modern world had kept his mother from going through with the cancer treatments that could have saved her life. After his mother had died, George left the reservation. Today was the first time he had returned in over fifteen years.

"Coyote came to me in a dream," she said. "He came to tell me the monsters have returned to the mountains."

George remembered the stories from his youth. Coyote was the wisest of all of the Great Spirit's creatures, left to watch over all the other animals when the Great Spirit returned to his home in the sky. He could remember sitting on the floor of his grandmother's house in the middle of winter, listening raptly while she taught the children the legends of their tribe. That was long ago. He had been so young that he didn't remember the stories, just the sense of warm feelings and happiness.

Perhaps because she knew he had forgotten the old stories or perhaps because she wanted to tell them to him one more time, his grandmother began speaking.

"Many ages ago," she said, "two monsters lived in the mountains. On windy nights, the sound of their howling could be heard all the way down in the valley. During the long winters, when food became scarce, the monsters would come down the mountain in search of food. They would kill some of the tribe's people, carrying their bodies high into the mountains where they would eat them. One day, the members of the tribe came to Coyote and asked him to protect them from the monsters. Coyote agreed, asking the hawk to go with him, for he had a plan. Together, they went high into the mountains where they came upon the two monsters. The monsters chased Coyote to the top of the mountain, and just as they were about to fall upon Coyote and devour him, the hawk swooped down and lifted Coyote to safety. The monsters fell from the top of the mountain. They struck the ground so hard they were swallowed by the stone, turning into two tall rocks. 'And you shall stay there forever,' Coyote said."

As he listened to the end of the tale, George remembered the feelings of pride he had felt as a boy when he had heard the stories of his namesake, the hawk, saving Coyote.

His grandmother continued, "But they did not stay forever. The rocks are gone. The monsters are free again, and Coyote has gone to live with the Great Spirit in the sky." She opened her eyes and looked at George. They were suddenly sharp and clear, and they bored deep within him. With a withered hand, she reached out and grasped his wrist.

"You must become like Coyote. You must destroy the monsters before they kill our people." The room seemed to close in around him. It was hot, and the incense was too thick, which made it hard to breathe. He rose to his feet unsteadily and made his way toward the door. He was dizzy.

He pulled the bead curtain apart and was about to step into the hallway when his grandmother's voice came to him once more.

"You must become like Coyote, Little Hawk," she repeated. "But beware, for unlike the hawk, the coyote cannot fly."

George stood in the doorway a moment longer, trying to understand what had just happened. But as it had so many years before, understanding the old ways still eluded him.

CHAPTER 12

Maryland

Dr. Myles Bennett walked briskly down the marble-tiled corridor, the bottom of his white lab coat flapping about his knees. He stopped before the large oak doors and pushed his glasses back up from the end of his nose.

His palms were sweaty as he grasped the door handle. He stepped into the office, and surreptitiously checked under his right arm to make sure he hadn't sweated through his lab coat.

"Hello, Dr. Bennett."

"Uh, hello—" He glanced at the nameplate on the desk. "Oh, yes, Linda. Hello."

Linda was tall and thin, a lady of exquisite beauty and composure with ruby red lips and long dark hair. She wore a shapely wool skirt and a silk blouse. She made Myles even more nervous than before.

"I'll tell the general you're here," she said. "Make yourself comfortable."

The waiting room looked like the inside of a law office. There was plush, dark green carpet on the floor and a mahogany sofa table with the latest issues of *TIME* and *Newsweek* in front of him. On the mahogany-paneled walls to his right and left were large, gilded-framed pictures of colonial Williamsburg that had been painted in the early 1800s.

Just as Myles was about to sit down, Linda hung up the phone. "The general will see you now."

Myles stood back up and stepped into General Colquitt's office.

"Good-afternoon, Dr. Bennett." The general stood and motioned toward the chair across from his desk.

Myles stepped up to shake his hand, but the general had already taken a seat. Even so, Myles noticed that the general was considerably shorter than he had thought. He had guessed the general to be at least five ten or five eleven like himself, but he couldn't have been more than five seven.

Myles took a seat, sinking into the low-slung leather chair, and found himself eye-to-eye with the general.

The general cleared his throat. "Dr. Bennett, I am sure by now you are aware of the tragic death of Dr. Jacobson and his family."

"Yes, sir, I am. It was a shock to us all."

"Indeed. A terrible accident ... that," the general said, picking a piece of lint from the sleeve of his suit. "I am sure you are also aware that we will have to find a replacement as team leader on the Mandarin Project."

"Yes, sir, I am," Myles said. In spite of his best efforts to appear calm, his left leg was twitching up and down uncontrollably. His heart pounded in his chest so forcefully that he was certain the general could see it.

"You don't have a family, do you, Dr. Bennett?"

Myles was caught off guard by that question. "Uh, no, sir, I don't, but—"

"I don't have to tell you how important this project is, do I, Dr. Bennett? You see, we want to be certain the person we select as Dr. Jacobson's replacement is totally dedicated to the success of this project. Committed to do whatever it takes. Someone who will not be encumbered by—shall we say ... family responsibilities?"

"Oh, yes, sir, I understand. And let me just say that I have been involved with this project since the beginning. I was the one who—"

"Yes, yes, but are you committed to seeing it through, no matter what it takes?" The general leaned forward and looked directly into Myles's eyes.

Tiny circles of fog had formed on the bottom half of each lens of

Myles's glasses. He quickly pulled them off and began wiping them clean with the corner of his lab coat. "Uh, yes, sir, I'm committed. I am." He squinted to try to see, but all he could make out was a blurry figure rising behind the desk.

"That's good, my boy. That's what I wanted to hear." The general pushed a button on his phone. "Linda, send a memo to all department heads, informing them of Dr. Bennett's promotion, effective immediately."

CHAPTER 13

Seattle

Joe's Barbeque was a small storefront restaurant a couple of blocks down Third Avenue on the ground floor of the Washington Mutual Tower. A cold wind swirled into the place, rifling the stack of yellow to-go menus beside the front register as Kyle walked in. Lewis had already grabbed them a spot at one of the tables, which was a good thing, because it was already getting crowded. It wasn't one of Kyle's favorites, but Lewis loved the place. Their claim to fame was coffee-based barbeque sauce with plenty of kick to more than just the taste buds.

It wasn't much to look at inside, even though they had tried to give the place some atmosphere. The walls were covered with weathered wood and rustic hardware like the inside of an old barn, while wooden picnic benches covered with red-and-white-checkered tablecloths filled the room.

Kyle squeezed between the people and benches and took a seat across from Lewis.

Lewis nodded at Kathy, the only waitress in the place, who in spite of her enormous bulk, slipped effortlessly down the narrow aisle.

As always, Lewis ordered the pulled pork sandwich with the espresso sauce, home-style fries, and a Coke, while Kyle ordered the sliced turkey with decaf sauce, coleslaw, and water.

"You go to Haskin's funeral?" Lewis asked.

"Yeah," said Kyle. "It was strange. His parents didn't want his remains cremated. They just had a closed casket. The whole time, all I could think about was the fact that there was nothing in there but his head."

"Shit."

"I know. The forensic report come in?"

"Yeah, I've already gone over it, and in a long-winded, scientific manner, it basically says we don't have shit."

"What do you mean?" Kyle asked.

"What I mean is that all the blood samples collected were matched to the three dead men, so whoever killed them wasn't wounded. And all the fingerprints taken belonged to either the dead men or Henderson."

"That's it?"

"Basically."

"So what do we do now?"

"We keep working the leads until something comes up."

They fell into silence. It was so loud in the place that it was hard to hear anyway. Kyle would have pressed Lewis for more information, but today, his mind was elsewhere. He stared out the window, watching as bits of loose garbage picked up by the growing wind went tumbling and bouncing across the street and into the gutter.

"You doing anything this weekend?" Lewis asked.

"Not really." Kyle knew Lewis was just trying to jump-start the conversation, but he wasn't in the mood for small talk. Thankfully, it didn't take long to get their food. The place was so small that it had to "turn 'em and burn 'em" in order to make any money.

"Ah, here we go," Lewis said and smiled as Kathy returned. She set the red-and-white paper-lined, plastic baskets down in front of them along with a bottle of the espresso sauce. Lewis smothered his sandwich with the stuff. It was thick and black and looked like used coffee grounds in molasses to Kyle. Lewis then picked up the squeeze bottle of ketchup from the table and covered his fries. Kyle just shook his head.

"Man, what's wrong with you today?" Lewis asked. "You're acting like a puppy that got whipped for pissing on the rug."

"Sorry, I just ... never mind."

"Come on, man. Spill it."

Kyle sighed. He knew Lewis wouldn't let it go until he told him. "It's Angela."

"Your girlfriend, right?"

"Ex-girlfriend."

"Oh—" Lewis grimaced.

"Yeah," Kyle said and nodded. "She finally called me back last night. Told me she had been seeing someone else for about a month now. Some doctor she works with at the hospital."

"Damn. That sucks."

"Yeah," Kyle said. "You know what really pisses me off is I should have seen it coming. I thought everything was fine, but I should've known when she stopped calling as often as she used to." It was something he had been afraid of for weeks, but even suspecting that it was coming had not prepared him for the devastation he had felt when Angela had told him it was over. He hadn't slept at all last night. He had just laid there, staring at the ceiling and trying to figure out what he had done wrong.

He had felt like a kid again, bounding downstairs with one of his finger paintings to show Janet while she gossiped endlessly over the phone about an affair one of the ladies at the club was having with the tennis pro. A cigarette in one hand and a vodka soda in the other, she had casually dismissed him with a wave and a: "That's nice, honey. Why don't you stick it on the fridge?"

"I know it may not seem like it now," Lewis said. "But things'll work out for the best in the end. You wait and see."

At least Lewis seemed to care enough to try to cheer him up. Kyle had never felt close enough to either of his parents to have a real conversation about things that were going on in his life. His father had always been gone somewhere, building his dams and superhighways, while his mother had always been more concerned with the country club's social scene and what time happy hour started.

"You know," Lewis said around a mouthful of food. "I got dumped once by this girl I just *knew* I was going to marry, and I was determined to win her back, so you know what I did?"

"What?"

"I took flowers to her place every day for a week. I didn't have them delivered by the florist. I took them myself. Every day for a week straight. And every day, she refused to come to the door. She kept sending her roommate to tell me she didn't want to see me anymore. But I was young and dumb and full of cum, so I just kept on going back for more, and you know what happened?"

Kyle wasn't really in the mood, but Lewis was just trying to help, so he humored him. "She agreed to go out with you again?"

"Hell no, she still didn't want to have anything to do with my ass, but her roommate did. On the seventh day, she handed me a note that said, 'Just because my roommate is too stupid to appreciate a good man doesn't mean I am.'"

"So did you go out with her?"

"Hell yeah."

"How'd it go?"

"Why don't you ask Rochelle the next time you talk to her," Lewis said, grinning like the Cheshire Cat.

Kyle rolled his eyes, but he couldn't keep from smiling. "Thanks."

"No problem. That's what partners are for."

Lewis's cell phone rang. He answered and mouthed to Kyle that it was SAC Geddes. "At Joe's, just finishing up lunch. Yeah, he's right here. Why? What's up?" Lewis's eyes grew larger as Geddes spoke. "No shit? All right, we're on our way," he said and then hung up.

"What is it?" Kyle asked.

"They've found Henderson's body."

They were both up and moving for the door when a booming thunderclap rattled the windows and cold, silvery rain began to spatter the pavement.

CHAPTER 14

Montana

It was late afternoon by the time they arrived in Kalispell. Agent Marasco picked them up and informed them they were going to the county morgue, where Henderson's body had been transported for the autopsy. In Kalispell, there were relatively few suspicious deaths that required an autopsy at any given time, so instead of having to wait several days, the autopsy was scheduled to take place that afternoon.

"Where was he found?" Lewis asked as they drove into town.

"He was off the Forest Service road about three miles up one of the trails leading to Margaret Lake. Poor bastard either didn't know where he was going or got lost, but he sure as hell wasn't going that way on purpose. The trail's uphill all the way and dead-ends at the lake."

"Any idea what killed him?"

"Not yet. There were no visible injuries. The corpse was in good condition, though. It had been buried under the snow, and with the warmer weather this last week, it was just becoming exposed when one of the search-and-rescue patrols found him this morning. They found the missing ax from the cabin too. It was about ten yards from where the body was found. We already packed it up and shipped it off to the lab for analysis."

"Let's hope they come up with something more than they did last time," Lewis said.

"I wouldn't count on it," said Marasco. "It looked pretty clean.

There wasn't any blood on it that any of us could see. A lot of the snow around it had melted away, but not enough to wash a bloody ax clean, and there were no traces of blood in the snow around it either. If you ask me, it wasn't the murder weapon. When whatever went down at the cabin, I think this guy just grabbed it and ran."

When they arrived at the morgue, Marasco got out and lit up a cigarette before he went inside. Lewis joined him. Marasco offered his pack to Kyle, but Kyle shook his head.

"You sure?"

"I don't smoke."

"No shit," Marasco chuckled. "Stick around. That'll change."

Kyle waited outside with Lewis and Marasco. As they stood in the small entryway, Kyle noticed Marasco seemed taller than he had thought when they had first met. As inconspicuously as possible, Kyle looked down at Marasco's feet. Along with the black jeans he always seemed to wear, Marasco wore a pair of black, square-toed harness boots, with circular metal rings on each side and thick leather bands running under, behind, and across the top of the foot. The boots didn't look to be particularly old, but they appeared to have been resoled or perhaps custom-ordered. Instead of the typical flat soles, these had thick, rubberized ones like the soles of hiking boots. The heels seemed especially tall for a man's boot. Then Kyle began to understand.

"Who's the coroner," Lewis asked.

"Technically, the sheriff is," Marasco said as he exhaled. "But since he ain't a licensed physician, the autopsies are all handled by the assistant coroner, Al Crowe."

"He any good?"

"Good enough, I suppose."

They finished their smokes quickly and stubbed them out in the sand-filled ash can in the corner beside the door. Apparently, it was a common ritual. The dirty sand was littered with at least a dozen butts.

The sheriff was waiting for them inside. When he stood up from the chair he had been sitting in, Kyle was again surprised by the size of the man. Without further discussion, he led them past the receptionist and down the stark, industrial tiled hallway toward the autopsy room.

Kyle noticed that Marasco walked on the far side of the hall from the sheriff.

As they walked down the corridor, the reason for the smoking ritual became clear to Kyle. The air was thick with the nasal-burning tang of chemicals and more noxious scents that grew stronger as they approached the autopsy room. Anything that would have dulled or numbed his sense of smell would have been preferable.

Larry Henderson's naked body lay on a cold steel table. Kyle wasn't sure if it was the body itself or the harsh glare of the fluorescent lights, but the man's skin seemed to glow with a ghostly, bluish-white tint. His mouth was agape, as if frozen in the rictus of a scream.

Standing next to the body with a clipboard in his hand was Alvin Crowe. Crowe was a lean, stoop-shouldered old man with thinning gray hair atop his head, round, gold-framed glasses, and a neatly waxed, handlebar moustache. He was already wearing latex surgical gloves, and even though he had yet to start the autopsy, Kyle was glad when he didn't offer to shake their hands.

"You've done a preliminary review of the body?" Lewis asked.

"Sure have. I'm about to start cutting if you'd care to watch. There's gloves and masks over there."

"I don't think that will be necessary," Lewis said.

"Suit yourself," the old man said with a mischievous grin. "But you're missing all the fun."

"That's all right," Lewis said. "What's your initial impression?"

"Well, considering the amount of time he's been missing, the body's in excellent condition because of the snow, but that will also make it difficult to pin down the exact time of death. The report said the body was found lying face down, which is in agreement with the fixed lividity, so it doesn't look like it had been moved. There's very little decomposition and no signs of it being mauled or damaged by any animals."

"Any signs of injury at all?" Lewis asked.

"Not externally. I'll know more after the cut."

"So what? Did he just freeze to death?" Marasco asked.

"Well, this isn't official or anything, but he was found lying face down with his right arm across his chest as if he might have been clutching or grabbing it when he fell, and I noticed a small amount of frothy blood around the lips, which leads me to think he might have died from sudden myocardial infarction. It could have been caused by several contributing factors, including alcohol and sudden exertion in the cold. We see it all the time. A big snow hits, and you can expect a least one or two to kick it just from shoveling their drive. But you mix that with intense fear or panic, and you've got a heart attack just waiting to happen. Of course, we won't know anything for certain until after the cut and the tox screen."

"So he wasn't murdered?" Lewis asked in confirmation.

"Well, it depends on the autopsy and how the rest of your investigation goes, but his death could still be ruled a homicide."

Kyle was confused. "How is that?"

"Deaths resulting from fear or fright induced by threats of physical harm can be ruled as a homicide if there is a close relationship between the inciting incident and the death, which appears to be the case with this one."

"So you're saying—"

"I'm saying it appears that he was scared to death."

CHAPTER 15

Denver

Carrie was suddenly awake. She didn't know what had caused it, but something had startled her from sleep. Without knowing exactly how, she sensed it had been something external—something out of the ordinary—that had interrupted her slumber.

She lay perfectly still, straining to hear the sound of the patio door being rattled or the creaking of the stairs as someone approached. The house remained silent except for the sound of her throbbing pulse in her ears.

There was a faint *click* as the thermostat in the hallway activated, and the familiar *shush* of air through the vents as the heater came on. She reached over to the nightstand and slid open the top drawer. After she groped about blindly for a moment, she placed her hand on the Smith & Wesson .38-caliber Lady Smith revolver she had purchased last week. It felt as heavy as an anvil when she lifted it from the drawer.

With the gun held tenuously before her, she slowly made her way across the bedroom to the door. Cautiously, she peered down the upstairs hallway leading past the stairs to the other bedrooms and the guest bath at the far end. She stepped across the threshold and cringed as the floor creaked beneath her. She quickly padded into the guest bedroom to her left. Moonlight angled in from the window, spilling across the bed, bathing the room in muted shades of silvery-blue.

She moved in front of the closet, her heart fluttering. She kept telling herself it was just her imagination, but she kept envisioning Bret crouching within, waiting to pounce on her the moment she opened the door.

She jerked the door open.

The closet was empty except for the bed linens, pillows, and the shoeboxes sitting on the shelves above the hanging rod. A few slinky evening dresses, which she no longer wore, hung limply above a shoe rack that contained a half dozen pairs of high-heeled dress shoes.

After she waited for her heart to slow a bit, she continued her search. Finding the upstairs unoccupied, she knew it would be impossible for her to sleep without being certain that he wasn't lurking downstairs. She stood at the top of the stairs and peered down into the darkness. Her legs dimpled with gooseflesh as she crept into the cooler air downstairs.

At the bottom of the stairs, she paused to wipe her sweaty palm on her T-shirt. She turned to her right and moved down the short hall toward the front door and the study on the right. The LED-indicator lamps on the security keypad by the front door glowed green, indicating that all zones were secure. She stepped into the study, checking under the desk and in the closet.

Nothing.

In the living room, the dark shadows of the sofa, love seat, and overstuffed chair could be made out. She crept around the sofa, careful not to stub her toe on the wooden corner. She made her way around the squat chair toward the back door.

The drapes hung slack and motionless before the window. She just knew that the moment she pulled back the curtains, she would find herself face-to-face with Bret, separated by nothing more than a thin plate of glass. It was a nightmare she had suffered since childhood, when she would wake in the middle of the night, terrified to look out the window above her bed, where she just *knew* the boogeyman was standing, peering down at her through the folds in the curtains.

With a trembling hand, she reached out and jerked back the curtains.

A figure stood before her in the dark.

She yelped and nearly fired off a shot before she realized it was her own reflection in the dark glass.

Carrie took a moment to catch her breath and to allow her racing heart to slow. She checked to make sure the broomstick was still in the track of the sliding glass door and then, with a weary sigh, pulled the curtains closed.

Once safely back in bed, Carrie lay there, wide awake. In spite of her relief, she hated the fact that she had become so terrified. She felt foolish for letting her imagination get the best of her, but the emotional wounds she had suffered were still too fresh and too easily reopened to be forgotten. At times, she felt as if she had been skinned alive, left to walk around with her raw nerves exposed to the world.

The little green numerals on the clock beside her read 3:13. She knew she wouldn't be able to get back to sleep—at least not without a little help. Enough moonlight slanted in through the blinds that she was able to make out her half-empty wine glass sitting on the nightstand. Without turning on the lamp, she reached into the top drawer and took out the bottle of sleeping pills her doctor had given her. She had taken one before she had gone to bed, and it obviously hadn't done the trick, so she took another, washing it down with the remainder of the warm wine.

CHAPTER 16

Montana

Kyle sat in the darkened conference room of the FBI offices in Kalispell, looking at the photo of a ramshackle, two-story building and outlying sheds projected onto the large dry-erase board. The place looked like an old, run-down army barracks.

"The man in the foreground with the red hair and beard is John White," said Marasco. "He's the leader of the Sons of Montana. His organization is an offshoot of the Militia of Montana, which his father was a member of. He's described as a fiery, charismatic man who, like all the other militant groups, promotes the white power agenda. They're antigovernment, anti-Semitic, and anti-black. Like the Freemen, they claim they were born as free citizens of Montana and the government has no power over them. Their compound is about twenty-five miles southeast of here, just past Swan Lake. It's on this side of the mountains but not too much farther south than the Hungry Horse cabins."

Lewis crumpled the empty Styrofoam cup in his right hand, dribbling coffee on the table. "Goddammit," he growled. "Hang on a minute." He strode from the room to get something to clean up the mess. Until then, Kyle had been so distracted with his own problems that he hadn't thought about how uncomfortable this must have been for Lewis. He had probably had enough of the white supremacist talk.

Marasco pushed his chair back and switched on the lights. Kyle groaned, squinting against the brightness.

"It's fucked up, isn't it?" said Marasco.

"What do you mean?"

He nodded at the photo on the wall. "Cocksuckers like John White. The only reason they're able to get away with that shit is because their rights are protected by the people they want to get rid of."

Kyle nodded. It was a sad but true commentary on the state of the nation. "So why do *you* do it?" he asked.

"Me? I don't do it for those motherfuckers—that's for sure." Marasco paused for a moment as if remembering. "My old man was a cop in Jersey back in the day," he said. "I don't know what it was exactly that made me want be like him, but I did. It wasn't like he made a lot of money or anything. I think maybe it was the way everyone else in the neighborhood respected him, you know. I liked that. It made me proud to be his kid. My brother, he's a cop too. I guess it's just something in the blood."

"So how did you end up here?" Kyle asked. "You don't exactly fit in with the locals."

"Aay, your pretty fuckin' sharp, aren't you?" Marasco grinned. "No, I was working undercover in the mob back in Jersey, and things started to get a little hairy. They were afraid my cover had been blown, so they pulled me out. Shipped me out here in the middle of fuckin' nowhere. Just until things cooled down, they said. That was a fuckin' year and a half ago.

"But you know what?" he continued. "It ain't that bad here. I've kind of gotten used to it. I mean sure, it ain't Jersey, but it's relaxing, and the people are all right. 'Course I miss the food, and it'd be hell if I didn't have satellite. I do miss going to Yankee games, though. There's nothing like—"

Lewis came marching back into the room, cell phone in hand. "You know where the Jewel Basin area is?" he asked Marasco.

"Yeah, sure."

"All right, let's go."

"What's up?" Marasco asked.

"I'll explain it on the way."

With that, they hurried out, the spilled coffee left to stain the table.

* * *

Marasco drove. Like almost everyone in town, he had an all-wheel-drive vehicle, but instead of a Yukon, his was a Ford Expedition.

In the truck, Lewis said, "The sheriff says a couple of his deputies were following up on one of the leads this morning. There were some receipts from a sporting goods store among the dead men's belongings. Apparently, the guys stopped there and bought some gear when they got into town. Anyway, the deputies went to the store and were questioning people when the manager steps up and says he remembers the guys. Says there was a bit of a disturbance when the black guy tried to buy a fishing knife. The guy at the counter—get this—a 'Jeffrey Wayne Tucker,' wouldn't help him because he was black. The manager had to step in and check the guys out."

"So what happened?" Kyle asked.

"Afterwards, the manager fired him, and as he was leaving, Tucker made some threatening comments about 'that nigger that cost him his job.'" Just hearing Lewis say it made Kyle uncomfortable.

"Have they questioned him?" Marasco asked.

"Not exactly," Lewis said. "Turns out he lives in some cabin in the backwoods, a real Ted Kazinski-like place. Apparently, Mr. Tucker wasn't feeling very sociable when the deputies showed up this morning. He met them out front with a shotgun. They tried to talk to him, but he was uncooperative. After Tucker fired off a warning shot, the deputies backed off and called it in. They've got him surrounded now. I told them to hold off until we get there."

"You think he's our man?" Marasco asked.

"Hell if I know, but I'll tell you this," Lewis said. "We've got to get him to come out and talk to us, *especially* if he didn't do it. If this thing goes south and he ends up dead, it won't matter if he did it or not. It'll be a goddamned Ruby Ridge all over again. The press will be up our ass, and DC'll try to pin it on Tucker just to take the heat off. And I don't have to tell you what that would mean to our careers. We've got to be damn careful with this one."

The cabin was located about fifteen miles southeast of Kalispell in the heart of the Jewel Basin. While much of the snow in town had melted away, it remained in abundance among the woods in the shadow of the mountains. The only access to the place was from a rough, unpaved road that wended its way toward the base of the mountains from Highway 83. At mile marker four, a narrow, winding path turned away over a small rise and disappeared into the trees. A wooden sign nailed to a tree read:

PRIVATE PROPERTY. NO NIGGERS! NO JEWS! AND NO ONE ELSE ALLOWED. TRESS PASSERS WILL BE SHOT!

They made their way up the trail another half mile before they came to a stop at the end of a line of county vehicles.

The sheriff met them as they walked up. "What have we got?" Lewis asked.

"He's holed up in a cabin just over the hill. We have eight men surrounding the perimeter." The sheriff pointed to a map spread across the hood of one of the trucks. "There are no good escape routes other than the road leading up here. He could try it on foot, but between the snow and our men, he would not get very far."

"Good. Has anyone tried talking to him recently?"

"Not in the last hour. We have spotters in the trees here and here," he said, pointing at the map. "They can see him through the window every now and then. He can't see us, but he knows we are still here."

"That's good. We want him to know he can't get away, but he can't shoot what he doesn't see."

"I also requested a search warrant from the judge," said the sheriff.

"All right," said Lewis. "He may have helped us out with that little shotgun trick. I don't think we could have gotten one otherwise. All we had were secondhand reports of him making threatening remarks. Now it looks like he's got something to hide."

"So what do you have in mind?" Marasco asked.

"Somehow we've got to get him to talk to us. Try to get him to come out voluntarily," said Lewis.

"Well, don't take this personally, but I don't think he's going to be too receptive to either you or the sheriff here."

"I know," said Lewis. "I don't think he's likely to talk to someone in uniform either. That's why we're going to send you and Kyle."

Marasco looked appalled. "Are you fucking crazy? You can't send a civilian up there. He doesn't know the first thing about dealing with a situation like this." Marasco spoke as if Kyle wasn't standing right next to him.

"You don't know what he's capable of," Lewis said. "Besides, you're not in charge here. I am. And that's how it's going to go down. You have a problem with that?"

"Yeah, I do. I may go along with it, but I want it noted that I think it's a bad idea. I'm not going to be the one going down for this if he fucks it up." Marasco turned and looked at Kyle. Then without saying anything more, he just shook his head and marched off toward the back of the line of trucks.

Lewis looked at Kyle. "You think you're up to it?"

"Yeah, sure, of course I am. I'm good at getting people to talk. It's what I do," Kyle said, trying to sound confident.

Lewis looked at him for a moment longer without speaking. Kyle struggled to keep from looking away. It wasn't that he was afraid to talk to Tucker. He dealt with people all the time, many of whom were mentally and emotionally imbalanced. But this time was different. There was more at stake now.

"Just go up there and talk to him," Lewis said. "Take your time. Just get him talking. Try to convince him we just want to talk, that we aren't here to arrest him. But don't let him know we have a search warrant, or we might never get him out. If we're lucky, he'll come out peacefully. Otherwise, we'll have to try to wait him out."

Kyle nodded and said, "Right." It was all he could manage to get out. His mouth had gone suddenly dry.

"It could take some time if we have to wait him out," said the sheriff. "To live out here, he must have enough supplies to survive for weeks at a time."

They followed the sheriff to the back of one of the trucks. Deputy Johnson had popped the rear hatch. Marasco was already shrugging into one of the black Kevlar vests.

Kyle took off his coat and slipped on the vest, fastening it with the thick Velcro straps. They had him put his jacket back on inside out so that the yellow FBI logo was hidden. The idea was to make him look like a regular guy and as nonthreatening as possible. Lewis handed his Colt Delta Elite semi-automatic to Kyle. It was American-made, of course—Lewis wouldn't carry anything that wasn't. It felt heavy in his hand. Kyle checked to make sure the safety was on and then tucked it in the back of his jeans. It was a cold, hard lump in the small of his back.

"Now listen," said Lewis. "If he starts getting hinky, just back out of there. We don't want to piss him off. And you," he said to Marasco. "Keep a close eye on Tucker. If you think he's about to draw down on you, you take Kyle down, and we'll hit him with the flash bangs. You got it?"

"Yeah, I got it," Marasco said in a surly tone. Kyle nodded as Deputy Johnson handed him a bullhorn. It seemed as if there were a million things going through his head all at once, which made it impossible for him to focus on any one thing.

"All right, let's go." Lewis said with a clap on his back.

The snow crunched loudly beneath Kyle's feet as he made his way up the trail. His senses were heightened to the point where he heard and saw things he would normally never have noticed: the sound of his breathing and the throbbing rush of blood in his ears, the chirping of a bird in the distance, sunlight slipping through the ominous-looking clouds to the west, purplish-blue shadows stretching across the ground before him. In spite of the cold, tiny rivulets of sweat trickled down his ribs from under his arms.

Just over the rise, he could see the tiny cabin tucked away among the trees. It was a ramshackle collection of logs and boards with a corrugated tin and tar-paper roof. A dented and rusting Ford pickup was parked to the right of the shack, its rear bumper hanging precariously low on the left side, where it was held to the frame with several loops of bailing wire.

"That's far enough," called a rough voice from within the shack.

Kyle stopped and raised the bullhorn.

"Mr. Tucker, I'm Kyle Andrews with the FBI. I just want to ask you a few questions," he said, letting his native-Texan accent come out. He wanted Tucker to think he was just a good old boy like himself, and therefore more likely to sympathize with his attitudes.

"I ain't got nuthin' to say to you or no one else, specially no gov'ment men."

Damn. He shouldn't have told him he was with the FBI. Tucker obviously had a problem with Big Brother. A part of him wanted to turn around and just walk away like Tucker had told him, but he was determined not to let Lewis down. He paused a moment and tried to think of the right way to approach this. He knew the first step to reaching someone was getting them talking.

"Mr. Tucker, I'm not an agent. I'm a victim's rights advocate. I make sure that people's rights are protected." It was not an entirely accurate description of his job, but he was trying to make it sound appropriate for the situation. "I just want to talk with you, so we can try and resolve this little misunderstanding peacefully."

"Ain't no misunderstanding. You're trespassin' on my property, and I got a right to defend myself. Now get outta here."

Kyle didn't want to come across as argumentative, so he waited a beat as if considering Tucker's demands. The second step was to build a sense of camaraderie, an us-against-them attitude. "You're right, Mr. Tucker. It *is* your God-given right to defend yourself, and I'm here to make sure that no one takes that away from you. But I can also assure you that there is nothing to defend yourself against right now. I just need to ask you a few questions—that's all."

There was no reply.

For a moment, nothing happened. Then Tucker finally shouted, "What kind of questions?"

"Wouldn't it be better if we could talk face-to-face like civilized adults?" Kyle tried to phrase it so that Tucker would agree with him.

There was no answer.

Kyle took a tentative step forward. "Wouldn't it be better if you came out here so we don't have to shout at each other?"

"You just want me to come out so you can shoot me in the back. I ain't no idiot. I know what happened at Ruby Ridge."

Damn. He kept underestimating the man's level of distrust. "I just want to talk with you—that's all."

"You wanna talk, you come in here," Tucker called out.

Kyle knew going in there was not a good idea, but he was making progress. He took another step forward.

"What are you doing?" Marasco whispered, but Kyle's attention was focused solely on Tucker.

"We're just going to talk, right?"

"That's what you say."

"How do I know you will let me leave when we are done?"

It was quiet for a moment as Tucker mulled it over.

"I give you my word."

"Yeah, right," muttered Marasco.

It may have seemed foolish to Marasco, but Kyle took it as a sign of progress. Men like Tucker tended to have an inflated sense of pride and honor. A man like that did not give his word lightly in a situation like this. He also knew that trust was a two-way street, and if he wanted Tucker—who already had an overt distrust of the government—to trust him, he would have to show Tucker an equal level of trust.

Kyle took another step forward. "All right, Mr. Tucker. I'm taking you at your word." He reached behind his back and took out Lewis's gun. He held it out where Tucker could clearly see it. "I'm unarmed," he announced, dropping the gun for effect. "I'm coming in. Just to talk—that's all." Kyle eased forward a few more feet.

"What the fuck are you doing?" Marasco whispered. "You can't go in there. Get the fuck back here."

"We're just going to talk—that's all," Kyle repeated as if it was some sort of mantra. He knew he sounded like a broken record, but it was all he could do to keep from being completely overwhelmed with fear. He just hoped it had the same reassuring effect on Tucker.

He took another step forward. The cabin door creaked as it was pulled ajar. Inside, he could see nothing but darkness.

"Kyle, get the fuck back here," Marasco hissed from behind, but it was as if he were a million miles away.

Kyle took a deep breath to try to calm his nerves. "I'm coming in," he said, hoping his voice didn't sound as shaky to them as it did to himself.

He stepped inside.

CHAPTER 17

"Shut the door behind ya."

His eyes hadn't adjusted to the dark yet, but Kyle could tell from the sound of the voice that Tucker was in the corner behind him. He could practically feel the barrel of the shotgun in his back.

The cabin was musty. The smell of damp wood and wet dogs and something more disconcerting—it reminded Kyle of spoiled hamburger meat—filled the air. An image of rotting corpses stacked in the next room sprang into his mind, and he suddenly realized how vulnerable he was. He wanted to turn and run, to get the hell out while he still could, but he knew that would end in certain disaster. Instead, he slowly shut the door as directed, careful not to make any sudden movements. A dog growled and scratched at the door across the room to his left. He tried to take some solace from the fact that Tucker had put the dog away, but it didn't help much.

"Sit down."

There was a rickety wooden table before him in the center of the room. On each side was a tubular metal chair that looked like something from a fifties' diner, except that the sparkly padded seats had long since disappeared, leaving just the wooden bottom. The metal legs and backs were splotched with patches of rust.

Kyle sat down and placed his hands on the tabletop where Tucker could see them.

"How come you people trespassin' on my property?"

"The deputies were just coming to ask you some questions—that's all." Kyle said, trying to sound calm. "But when you threatened them with a gun, they called us in."

"What kind of questions?"

"Have you heard about the four men who were killed in a cabin on Hungry Horse reservoir?"

"I heard 'bout it," he nodded.

"Well," Kyle continued. "We have learned that those four men came into the store you worked at. The manager says you had a dispute with one of them."

"You're talkin' 'bout that nigger I wouldn't wait on."

"Yes," Kyle said. "He was one of them."

"Ain't no law says I got to wait on no nigger," Tucker growled. "That cowardly store manager done fired me for it, but there ain't no law against it. I know my rights. Ain't no law says I got to serve no nigger."

"You're right," Kyle said, trying to calm Tucker back down. He took a breath, considering what he was about to say. "There's no law that says you have to wait on a nigger. To be honest, I can't say I blame you." Kyle hated the sound of the words coming from his mouth, but it was the only way he knew to try to gain the man's confidence. "The problem is that nigger turned up dead along with three of his white friends a couple of days later. There were several witnesses at the sporting goods store who overhead you threatening that nigger. Some of them think you might have gone to that cabin and killed him and the other men."

"I didn't kill no one," Tucker growled.

"No one is saying you did, Mr. Tucker. But you see, I need your help to prove you didn't. I need you to let me bring in some men to search your place. We have a warrant that says we're looking for any weapons that might have been used to kill those men. That's all. Nothing more. If you're innocent like you say you are, allowing us to perform this search will help prove your innocence." Kyle knew it was risky to tell Tucker about the search. If Tucker *had* killed the men and the weapon was still in his possession, he might panic. But it was also likely that he would have dumped the weapon somewhere before he had returned to his cabin. All Kyle wanted was for Tucker to allow them to perform a search of his cabin. Most people didn't realize how much forensic evidence could be gathered against a suspect without the murder weapon ever being found.

Tucker stepped over to the table and sat down across from him. Kyle's blood ran cold as he noticed Tucker wasn't holding a shotgun, but a black M16 fully automatic with a large bayonet attached. It appeared as if Tucker was ready to go to war.

"I didn't kill no one," Tucker repeated. He looked Kyle straight in the eye when he said it, drawing Kyle's attention away from the M16. They remained silent, staring at each other for several long moments, each trying to gauge the other's sincerity.

"But I seen somethin' out there one night not long ago," Tucker finally continued, nodding out the window. His vision seemed to shift focus, as if he were looking at something far away. "Never got a good look at it in the dark, but it's out there all right, blacker than the night itself. And from time to time, I heard a screeching off in the distance. Sound that'll make your blood run cold. Like the Grim Reaper hisself a wailin' in the night."

At first, Kyle began to worry that he was witnessing the ramblings of a madman. Tucker's appearance, with his long, greasy hair and wiry beard, certainly fit the part. But his eyes, which were blue and clear, didn't look like the eyes of a madman.

"Are you saying you know who killed those men?"

Tucker chuckled. "Ain't sayin' that at all. Ain't got no idea what it was. All I'm sayin' is, it wasn't me."

"Then let me bring in our men. Let them look through your things. When they don't find anything, we'll leave, and we won't bother you anymore."

"And if I don't?" Tucker raised the bayonet in front of him and pointed it at Kyle. As he stared at the finely honed edge of the bayonet, Kyle remembered the murdered men's arm and head had been cleanly severed by something like a sword or a machete … or perhaps a bayonet?

Kyle didn't like where the conversation was heading. Again, he found himself wondering how he could have made such a big mistake. "Then those deputies will stay out there until you run out of supplies," he said. "And don't think you can get away. They have the place surrounded."

Tucker stared at him as if trying to judge his response by the look in his eyes. Kyle stared back, trying to appear confident and unflinching, but inside, his guts were churning.

"How do I know you're tellin' the truth?" Tucker asked.

"Trust," Kyle said.

"I ain't had good experience trusting the government," Tucker said and then spat on the floor. "Dropped me in the middle of Nam when I was just a kid. Left me there to rot as a POW." He looked away from Kyle and ran his finger along the edge of his bayonet as if testing its sharpness.

If Tucker was trying to frighten Kyle, his actions were having the desired effect. He didn't know what to expect from the man. He swallowed hard, trying to maintain his composure. "Then trust me— same way I trusted you when I came in here unarmed," he said, trying to appeal to Tucker's sense of honor among men of similar character, not as an agent of the government. He wasn't sure what else to do.

Tucker sat silently for a moment, still staring at the bayonet, but his eyes seemed vacant. Instead of focusing on the sharp steel, it was as if they were seeing something else far away.

After several long moments, Tucker blinked and turned his eyes back toward Kyle. "I spent nearly three years in a cage in Nam. No one's gonna put me in no cell again."

"If you don't come out, this cabin will become your cell," Kyle pointed out.

"I ain't going back into no cell," Tucker repeated adamantly.

"As long as you didn't kill those men, you don't have anything to worry about."

"So *you* say. What about the warden?"

"The warden?" Then Kyle realized Tucker was probably trapping or poaching illegally. "Is that what you're worried about? The game warden's not out there."

"How do I know they won't arrest me anyway?"

"That's not what we're here for. If I get them to commit to you that you won't be arrested for poaching, will you come out?"

Tucker's eyes narrowed. "You get them to promise me that, and then we'll talk," he said with a nod.

"All right," Kyle said. "I'll be right back." He stepped to the door and yelled, "I'm coming out," so the men outside wouldn't shoot him as he emerged.

Thirty yards outside the cabin, Kyle was joined by Marasco, now holding Lewis's gun and the bullhorn. He didn't say anything as the two made their way back up over the hill.

As soon as they came into view, Lewis came forward quickly and grabbed Kyle by the front of his coat. "What the fuck were you doing back there?"

"What?" Kyle asked, confused. "I got him to talk. He wants to come out."

"What you *did* was give him a hostage," Lewis barked.

"I told him not to go in there," Marasco said.

Lewis wheeled on Marasco. "Then why didn't you stop him?"

"What the fuck did you want me to do? Tackle him and have the guys blast Tucker with the flash bangs? I'd like to see you explain that one away."

Lewis was silent, but Kyle knew he was furious. He could see the bulging veins in his temple.

"Look," Kyle said. "He says he didn't kill the men. He wants to come out. All he wants is a commitment that he won't be arrested for poaching."

Lewis didn't say anything for a moment.

He looked at Marasco and took his gun back. Then to Kyle he said, "Go tell him." He took a pair of handcuffs from behind his back and handed them to Kyle. "Don't go back in there. You get him to come out to you. And cuff him before you walk him back."

After Marasco used the bullhorn to commit to Tucker that he would not be arrested for any other crimes, Kyle walked back up to the cabin. The door opened a crack, but he did not go inside. "Are you satisfied?" Kyle asked.

"No," Tucker called out. "But I ain't got much of a choice, do I?"

"Not really," Kyle admitted.

"I have to chain ol' Blue to the tree. He don't take kindly to strangers."

"Okay," Kyle said. "But once you get the dog chained up, I have to handcuff you, for your own protection as well as mine. We want to make sure there aren't any accidents."

There were sounds of rustling and banging and a chain rattling around. "Get down," Tucker snapped. The door was slowly pulled open, and he emerged with a large, mangy beast in tow. The dog didn't look anything at all like its name implied. Its head came to Tucker's waist, and its muscles rippled beneath matted, gray fur. It snarled at Kyle, its black lips curling back to reveal long, yellow fangs. It looked more like a wolf than a dog. Kyle immediately thought of the hand found out back of the cabin. Certainly, a beast like that was capable of taking a man's hand off at the wrist.

Kyle stepped back, careful to keep his distance from the thing. He waited while Tucker tied it to a thick pine at the corner of the cabin, the trunk of which was scraped and scarred where the chain had been tied previously.

Once done, Tucker walked over to Kyle and turned his back. Kyle placed the handcuffs on him, careful not to get them too tight. Seeing this, the dog went crazy, barking and straining against the chain. As Kyle led Tucker away, he found himself hoping the chain was a strong one.

Marasco and Deputy Johnson came forward to meet them. Together, they escorted Tucker back where he was seated in one of the sheriff's vehicles. With Tucker safely situated, Kyle made his way farther down the line of trucks to where Lewis and the sheriff waited.

"Tell the forensics team they can go in," Lewis said to the sheriff. "We'll be there in a minute."

The sheriff nodded and walked over to where Davidson and his assistant waited with their cases. Lewis waited until everyone was out of earshot and then turned back to Kyle.

"Look, it was my fault," he sighed, the anger slowly leaching out of him. "I shouldn't have sent you up there. The good thing is you got him out of there without anyone getting hurt or killed, especially yourself. But next time you ask me before you go and pull some stupid shit like that."

Kyle just nodded. He had fucked up. There was nothing else to say.

"And as far as SAC Geddes is concerned, it never happened. You walked up there, and you talked him out without ever going inside, got it?"

"Got it."

"All right." Lewis turned and walked off. He had gone about twenty yards when he stopped and turned back around. "Well, come on, cowboy. Let's go see if this crazy bastard is our killer."

Kyle went with him. He still felt foolish, like an imposter trying to play the part of an agent but one who didn't know all his lines. As they stepped inside the cabin, Kyle was again assailed by the stench of the place.

"God almighty," Lewis swore as he pulled a handkerchief from the pocket of his coat and covered his mouth with it.

"It's worse in here," said a muffled voice from the room to their left.

They followed the voice into the next room. Kyle almost became sick as they stepped inside. The remains of a butchered carcass hung from a chain wrapped around one of the wooden beams. It took him a second to realize it wasn't human but that of a deer or an elk. Thin strips of filleted venison dangled from wooden hangers all around the ceiling. There was no floor, only hard, packed dirt in the center of which was a small fire pit lined with stones. A pile of smoldering embers sent tendrils of smoke curling up through a small pipe in the roof.

Davidson, the portly forensics tech, wore a surgical mask as he set up a klieg light in the corner. "Hell of a playroom, ain't it?" he said, hooking up the leads to the battery. There was a small spark, and the light sprang to life. The smoke-filled room lit up with a silvery glow, the carcass casting dark shadows across the wall. In the corner was a blood-stained workbench littered with tools and traps and knives. To Kyle, the whole thing looked like some demented stage set for a Nine Inch Nails or Marilyn Manson video, only this was real flesh and blood. It didn't matter that it wasn't human. The sight of it still made him feel sick.

Lewis stepped over to the bench and surveyed the array of traps and cutting and rending tools. Marasco stuck his head in and whistled. "This guy should be the poster child for PETA." Marasco seemed back to his old self again, the earlier conflict seemingly forgotten. Kyle supposed he should have expected that from him, being a New Jersey Italian. He called things the way he saw them and then moved on, whereas Kyle had always tended to take disputes more personally, keeping them all bottled up inside where they festered for long periods of time afterward.

Everyone jumped as someone yelled outside. The dog went crazy again, barking and jerking against the chain.

"Hey, guys, come out here. I think I found something," the voice said. It came from behind the cabin.

They hurried outside, Davidson trailing behind, careful not to step within reach of the dog. Past the back corner, they found one of the deputies who had been searching the perimeter.

He nodded at what looked to be a snow-filled pit. Part of the snow had been brushed away, revealing black ashes and garbage beneath. Twisted and crumpled aluminum cans, the labels burned away, lay amid melted plastic and the unburned corner of an Old Milwaukee twelve-pack carton. Looking closer, Kyle noticed what looked like several charred sticks and twigs among the garbage.

The deputy reached out, pointing. "Look right—"

"Don't touch anything," Lewis snapped.

"I'll get the camera," Davidson said, turning to leave.

It was then that Kyle realized that what he thought were sticks were, in fact, charred and blackened bones.

CHAPTER 18

Montana

Because it appeared that they were going to be in town for a while, Lewis arranged a rental car for them the next morning. After they picked it up, they stopped for breakfast at a place called Sarah's Kitchen on their way back in. Sarah's was a small diner that Deputy Johnson had recommended for its home-style cooking and friendly atmosphere. It should have been a pleasant way to start the day. It turned out to be anything but.

Because they had been unable to determine if the bone fragments in the fire pit were of human or animal origin, the bones had been FedExed to the head of forensic anthropology at the Smithsonian in Washington. In the meantime, Tucker had been transported to the Flathead County Justice Center, where he was being held pending the results of the analysis.

They had spent the remainder of the evening and long into the night interrogating Tucker, Kyle and Agent Marasco each using their own methods in an attempt to catch him in a lie, but it was essentially a game of good-cop-bad-cop, Kyle playing the good and Marasco the bad. But no matter what they tried, Tucker remained steadfast in his denial that he had anything to do with the murders. Even though he had no way of proving it, he swore he had weathered the storm alone in his cabin. He claimed to be a simple tracker and a loner who knew nothing about the Sons of Montana or any other militant organizations in the area. Even Marasco had to admit that they didn't have anything on file linking him to any such groups.

Kyle was skeptical of the restaurant as they pulled into the parking lot. The place looked like nothing more than a portable building with light blue siding and a wooden ramp leading to the glass door. "I hope Deputy Johnson knows what he's talking about."

"Don't worry," Lewis said. "Cops know all the best places."

Walking in, they were greeted by the rabble of conversation and the sizzling pop of bacon and frying eggs, while warm air redolent of sausage and fresh coffee washed over them. On top of the counter was a glass display case full of home-baked apple and cherry pies and a chocolate cake. It was Lewis's kind of place.

The lady behind the register smiled in greeting. "Morning! Just the two of ya?"

"Yeah," nodded Lewis.

"Okay, right this way," she said as she grabbed a couple of large menus and led them to a booth along the front windows. The smoky dining room was full of customers, the majority of whom looked like construction workers or loggers in their thick sweaters and flannel shirts and jackets. Kyle noticed that many of them fell silent, watching while he and Lewis passed before returning to their conversations.

As soon as they were seated, another lady appeared with two coffee cups and an aluminum coffeepot. She filled Lewis's cup and started to fill the one in front of Kyle before he stopped her. "I'm just having water."

The waitress just shrugged and moved to the next table to refill those customer's cups.

After she had given them a few minutes, she returned to take their order. Kyle asked if they could make an egg-white omelet, and after she checked with the kitchen to make sure, he ordered one with ham and cheddar cheese. Lewis made it easier on her, ordering the Mountaineer Special with scrambled eggs, hash browns, sausage, and pancakes.

While they waited for their food, Lewis went to get a paper from the machine in the entry foyer.

While he was gone, Kyle checked his cell phone for any new messages. He hadn't had any time alone to do it earlier, and he didn't want Lewis to see him constantly checking his messages. He felt foolish enough about it. There was one message, and what small hopes he had that it might be Angela were dashed when he heard Janet's voice.

"Kyle, it's your mother." He shook his head slowly as he listened. She had always made him call her Janet instead of Mother, constantly correcting him when he slipped, as if she had been ashamed for people to know she was his mother. She had tried to minimize it by saying she wanted to be his best friend, not just his mother, but as he had gotten older, Kyle had figured out the real reason.

Kyle's father had been a partner in a large civil engineering firm and was constantly out of town, visiting the various construction projects their company oversaw around the world. He had been significantly older than his young wife, who spent most of her days at the Dallas Country Club, flirting with the other rich old men, looking to climb even higher up the social ladder, and if any of her prospects knew she was a mother, it might detract from her desirability. On more than one occasion, unbeknownst to her, because she had been drunk, Kyle had caught her telling the lecherous old men that he was not her son but merely her nephew.

Kyle felt certain that she would have left his father for another man had he not died of a heart attack in Bolivia when Kyle was ten. Once she inherited everything, including his father's portion of the company—which she immediately sold—she no longer had any need for the older men and their money.

But now that she wanted something from him, she was suddenly "Mother" again.

"I don't know why you haven't called me back yet," came her gravelly voice over the phone. "I need you to get back with me and let me know what color you want the walls painted in your room. The decorator can't start with her design until you decide on the color scheme. If you don't hurry up, I'm just going to give her carte blanche to do what she wants, and you'll just have to live with it." She coughed then, phlegm rattling in her lungs, which then triggered a massive attack of hacking and wheezing. When the fit subsided, she sighed dramatically. "Oh, I am so tired all of the time. I just can't do this alone. You need to hurry up and get back here and help me."

Kyle deleted the message. He hadn't even told her if he was going to move back yet, and already she was trying to run his life. He didn't want to go back, at least not yet. Janet had undergone a lumpectomy recently and had just finished going through radiation treatments. Kyle had been there for the surgery, and from everything the doctors had told him, she should be fine. Kyle felt certain that she was more upset with her appearance than anything and that she just wanted him there to pay attention to her and to tell her that everything was going to be all right.

Even so, he had still been considering moving back. Just because she was a shallow, self-absorbed person didn't mean that he was. But his situation with Angela had changed things. He didn't know what he was going to do now.

Lewis stepped back into the dining room, and as soon as he did, Kyle knew something was wrong. He was looking at something above the fold on the front page, the paper clutched so tightly in his hands that they shook. His forehead was furrowed with deep creases, the veins on each side of his head bulging outward from his teeth being clenched in anger.

"What's wrong?" Kyle asked as he slid back into the booth.

Lewis plopped the copy of the *Kalispell Mountain Herald* down on the table. Printed across the top in big, bold letters the headline read, "Suspect Arrested in Hungry Horse Murders."

"But how?" Kyle asked.

"Someone leaked it," Lewis growled.

"But that's not even right," said Kyle.

"I know."

"Why would they do that?"

"I don't know, but I intend to find out."

Kyle knew Lewis loved to eat in places like Sarah's, where the coffee was only fifty cents and the buttermilk pancakes were drowning in *real* maple syrup, but this morning, Lewis was silent as he devoured his meal, his jaws clenching and unclenching with each bite. He didn't chew his food so much as he ground it into oblivion. Kyle knew better than to say anything further, and he choked down his meal as fast as he could. He had barely finished putting the last bite of food in his mouth before Lewis threw down his money and started marching toward the door.

CHAPTER 19

"What the fuck is this?" Lewis asked as he slapped the paper down. The sheriff and Marasco sat across from each other in the conference room, which had been turned into a war room, where they now held the morning briefings. Lewis stood over them at the head of the table, waiting for a response.

The sheriff didn't bother to look up from the file in front of him. "I saw it," he acknowledged.

"Yeah, what's up with that?" said Marasco.

"I don't know. I thought maybe one of you could tell me," said Lewis.

"What? You don't think either one of us had anything to do with this, do you?"

"Who else could it have been?"

"Hell if I know. It wasn't fucking me," said Marasco.

Lewis leaned over the table. "Who did you talk to about the case yesterday?"

"Aay, just because they put you in charge of this case doesn't mean I have to take this shit." Marasco jumped up and shoved his chair back from the table with an angry screech. He glared at Lewis and then pushed past him and headed toward the door.

"So how much did they pay you, Marasco?" Lewis said to his back.

Marasco spun around, his face turning bright red. "What the fuck did you say?" He started back toward Lewis. Kyle stepped in front of Marasco and grabbed him by the shoulders and held him back while

Marasco pushed against him and raised his arm to point at Lewis. "I'm no narc. You hear me? So fuck you. Fuck you!"

Marasco turned and stormed from the room. Kyle followed him into the hall. A couple of the deputies who had stopped in the corridor suddenly turned and walked off. Deputy Johnson stuck his head out into the hall. Kyle motioned to him that things were under control. The deputy nodded and ducked back into his office.

Marasco stopped. "What the fuck do you want?"

"Nothing," Kyle said. "I ... he doesn't mean anything personal by it. He just hates being blindsided."

"No shit," said Marasco. "None of us like it. That's still no excuse for what he did. That's bullshit."

"So you didn't talk to the paper?"

"Look, just so you can hear it from my lips, no, I didn't talk to the paper, okay? You satisfied?"

"Yeah, sure," Kyle said.

"Good. Now go back in there and tell that to your boss. And tell him that even if I had, I'm too fucking smart to fall for some bullshit scheme like the one you two just tried to pull. Next time he wants an answer from me," he said, poking Kyle in the chest, "you tell him to come ask me face-to-face like a man—you got that?"

Kyle thought about denying that they had tried to play him. It had been Lewis's idea, and Kyle had reluctantly gone along with it. It had probably been a mistake. He now realized that in some ways, Marasco was a lot like Tucker—someone who placed a high value on a person's honor and loyalty. But unlike Tucker, Marasco's probably came from the fact that his father had been a cop. His predisposition toward such traits would have served him well during his time undercover in the mob—and were, in fact, probably part of the reason he had been chosen for the job—where such traits were the cornerstone of the family. Kyle sensed that if he lied to him now, he would never be able to regain Marasco's confidence. Instead, he simply nodded and said, "Right."

Marasco seemed surprised by the answer. Then a hint of a smile crossed his face. "Huh, maybe there's hope for you yet. Now leave me the fuck alone. I'm going to have a smoke. I'll be back in a minute."

Kyle walked back in the room. Lewis and the sheriff were both silent, staring at each other as if it were a contest to see who would blink first. Apparently, Lewis had confronted the sheriff about the leak as well.

Lewis blinked first. Looking toward Kyle, he said, "What'd he say?"

"Said he didn't have anything to do with it."

"You believe him?"

"Yeah, I do. He seemed genuinely offended." Kyle thought he was beginning to get a pretty good read on Marasco. His loud, brash nature, the bravado, and the black harness boots were all just attempts at compensating for his height.

Lewis huffed and said, "Most perps are offended when they're accused, too, but that doesn't mean they didn't do it."

Kyle just shrugged.

"So where did he go?"

"Said he was going to take a smoke break and then he'd be back." Marasco was easily antagonized, but it didn't seem to last. "He'll calm down quick enough."

Lewis nodded. "I was explaining to the sheriff that we can't afford to have anyone compromising our investigation by leaking information to the press."

"No one in my department would do that," the sheriff said. "I have a good group of men here. They know to watch what they say around reporters, especially Wallace Hipple." He picked up the phone and hit the intercom button. "Clayton, would you come to the conference room."

When the deputy arrived, the sheriff asked him, "Do you know of anyone who might have spoken to Wallace Hipple at the newspaper about Tucker?"

"No, sir," Clayton replied. "I can't imagine any of our fellows doing anything like that."

"That's what I told Agent Edwards here," the sheriff said. "But I want you to follow up with all the men just to make sure."

"Sure thing, sheriff," Clayton replied.

The sheriff looked at Lewis.

"That's fine," Lewis said. "But I still want to see if we can get a copy of the phone records for the *Herald* and this Wallace Hipple's home and cell phone numbers. I thought it might be easier if one of your men requested them instead of us."

"Can you take care of that?" the sheriff asked the deputy.

"Uh, yes, sir," Clayton replied. "I'll handle it myself."

CHAPTER 20

Kyle opened the door to the interview room and stepped inside, followed by Marasco. The mountain man was asleep, his head on the small table. Phlegm-rattling snores reverberated off the hard surfaces within the room, which stank of rotten meat and sour body odor.

"Mr. Tucker," Kyle said.

"Hey!" Marasco yelled as he kicked the table. Tucker woke with a start.

Marasco chuckled. Kyle glared at him as he moved to face Tucker. "Mr. Tucker—"

"I told you I didn't kill no one," Tucker snapped. "You ain't gonna get me to confess to nothin'. Charlie couldn't break me, and neither can you."

"Mr. Tucker," Kyle said sternly. The man's eyes shifted from Marasco back to him. "We are not here to question you anymore. We're here to tell you that we got the results back from the forensic anthropologist and you're free to go."

"The what?"

"The bone expert, you moron," said Marasco.

"The bones in your fire pit were not human ... just like you said," Kyle said.

"I told you they was from a mountain goat."

"Yes, we know. You were right. I apologize for any inconvenience we may have caused you. You're free to go." Kyle motioned toward the open door.

"Unless you'd like for us to transfer you to one of the nice little cells in back," Marasco quipped.

Tucker wrinkled his nose in a sneer as he brushed past Marasco. "I told you I didn't do it," he repeated. "And I'm gonna go catch the thing what did too. Just you watch."

"Yeah, right," Marasco smirked as he leaned away from Tucker's foul breath. "You and O.J. Now get the fuck outta here."

CHAPTER 21

By the end of March, things were pretty much back to normal for Bill and Audrey Jones. The concern and anxiety they had felt as a result of the men being murdered in one of their cabins still lurked in the back of their minds, but since there had been no other occurrences of a similar nature in the following weeks, the event had been put behind them for the most part, written off as an unexplained act of vengeance against one or all of the men by someone with reason enough to kill.

While the winter had been one of the harshest ones in recent memory, the weather seemed to be returning to normal and other, more pressing matters filled their days now. Along with the repairs to the cabin that Bill had been working on, both he and Audrey were beginning to make preparations for the upcoming tourist season. Audrey had already booked the first fly-fishing expedition of the season for the last week in May.

After dinner that evening, Bill sat at the kitchen table, which was littered with spools of fishing line, rolls of brightly colored thread, and a craft box with little plastic drawers full of hooks, silks, furs, feathers, tinsels, wools, and hairs. Whistling, he bent over his fly-tying vise, a pair of hackle pliers in his hand, as he peered through the magnifying light at the tiny damsel fly he was working on. A fly-fishing enthusiast in the truest sense of the word, he refused to purchase store-bought flies.

Bill's blissful reverie was interrupted by a heavy *thump* from somewhere else in the house. He looked up over the top of his reading glasses, his forehead wrinkled in consternation. Fearful that Audrey might have fallen, he called out to her. "Audrey, you all right?"

"Yes, dear, why?"

"I thought I heard something. Did you drop something?"

"No, dear, I didn't."

Bill took off his glasses and laid them on the table as he stood up. He cocked his head to one side, listening for anything out of the norm. Overhead, there was the faint hiss of the heater blowing warm air through the vents and the hum of the refrigerator behind him. A wall clock over the oven ticked off the seconds.

Then he heard it again, a heavy scrabbling sound on the roof above him. He listened, trying to make sure it wasn't a tree limb, but it seemed to have too much of a pattern to it, as if someone were walking across the roof and dragging something behind.

Thump, scrape, thump, scrape.

It seemed to be making its way toward the back of the house. Audrey had come into the kitchen and was looking at him with a puzzled expression, but Bill remained motionless, listening until it stopped. He supposed it could have been a raccoon or a squirrel, but something about the way the roof creaked with its passage made him think it was much heavier. He stood up quietly and slipped over toward the window above the sink, the one that looked out into the forest behind them. A light snow had begun to fall. The light spilling through the window illuminated a rectangular patch of ground behind the cabin. The snow within that area was undisturbed. There were no tracks or other telltale signs of disturbance. Beyond, the forbidding darkness of the forest offered no clues.

A strange feeling trickled down his spine. His palms began to sweat, and he found himself backing away from the window toward the living room, his arm held out protectively in front of Audrey.

A sharp, crackling *pop* and a high-pitched, wailing scream rang out above them.

The cabin fell into darkness.

"Bill?" Audrey said anxiously.

Bill groped his way across the kitchen. He found the edge of the cabinet and used it to feel his way along to the drawer next to the refrigerator. He pulled it open and fumbled about until he placed his hand on the flashlight they kept there.

Flicking it on, he said, "Follow me." The floor creaked beneath them as they crept around the table toward the living room. Another scraping *thump* came from overhead.

"Get upstairs," he whispered as he backed into the living room, afraid of taking his eyes off the kitchen window for more than a few seconds. Once in the living room, Audrey safely behind him, he hurried across the room and jerked the curtains closed across the large picture window facing the lake.

"Bill, what is it? What's going on?"

"I don't know," he said as he hurried to the front closet. "See if you can find the cordless phone. Then get upstairs—in the bathroom without the window—and call the sheriff." He tucked the flashlight under his left arm and grabbed the shotgun, a Browning 12-gauge autoloader from the closet. He grabbed a handful of shells from the box on the shelf above the coat rod and stuffed them into the pocket of his jeans.

"The phone's on the end table by the sofa," Audrey said.

Bill kicked the closet door shut and turned around, pointing the light at the end table for Audrey to see. She quickly grabbed the phone and then headed for the stairs.

The front window exploded into the living room.

Glittering slivers of glass shot across the room, showering everything within. The curtains were ripped from the wall, engulfing something that tumbled to the floor behind the sofa.

Audrey cried out as she stumbled over the bottom step. As she tried to catch herself, she dropped the cordless phone, which bounced off the stairs and went spinning across the floor into darkness.

Bill raised his arm to shield his face. The flashlight dropped to the floor, its beam sweeping wildly about the room as it rolled.

Two loud *booms* and flashes of yellow flame leapt from the barrel of the shotgun as Bill fired at the object tangled within the curtains.

The room fell silent. The air was thick with a haze of smoke and the acrid smell of gunpowder. The thing beneath the curtains remained motionless.

Bill dug in his pocket. His hands shook as he pulled out three more shotgun shells. He dropped one but managed to shove the other two into the shotgun's magazine as he crept up to the tangled mass of drapery.

Holding the shotgun ready, he prodded the thing with his right foot and then jerked it back in case whatever lay inside was still alive. He knew there was nothing more dangerous than a wounded animal, although by the actions he had witnessed, he found it highly doubtful that it was simply a wild animal that was tangled in the curtain.

"What is it?" Audrey picked up the flashlight and began to move closer, the beam of light trembling as she held it.

"Stay back," he snapped. He was immediately sorry for the tone of his voice, but he didn't want Audrey anywhere near the thing. He reached over and took the flashlight from her. "Get the phone. Then go upstairs and call the sheriff."

Audrey gingerly stepped across the glass-covered floor, picked up the phone, and dialed 911 even as she started toward the stairs.

Bill prodded the thing again. It was surprisingly solid. And still, it remained motionless.

Sweat trickled down his forehead. He reached down with the flashlight to flip back the curtains. He still held the shotgun with his right hand, ready to fire if the thing should move.

On the other side of the room, Audrey stopped at the base of the stairs and watched.

He tossed the curtains back, sending more of the glass skittering across the floor. A dark lump lay motionless atop the cloth. He pointed the light at it. When he saw what it was, he felt as if he had fallen through the ice into one of the frigid lakes around the cabin. His breath caught in his throat. His limbs went numb.

It was one of the large fire logs they kept stacked against the back of the house.

Audrey screamed.

Bill whirled back around.

And saw the shadow coming through the missing window.

CHAPTER 22

In the middle of the night, the phone began to ring. Lewis picked it up on the third ring. Bleary-eyed, Kyle rolled over and looked at the clock on the nightstand. It read 3:27. Immediately, he knew something was wrong.

"All right, we'll be ready." Lewis hung up the phone.

"What is it?" Kyle asked.

"There's been another murder." Lewis turned on the lamp mounted to the wall above the nightstand and rubbed his face with his hand.

Kyle squinted in the bright light. "Where?"

"Hungry Horse. The Joneses' cabin."

* * *

Deputy Johnson picked them up. Agent Marasco was already riding shotgun. Without saying anything, Lewis got in the back with Kyle. They rode in an uncomfortable silence as they made their way out of town, the glow of civilization slowly fading behind them as they followed Highway 2 out of the valley and through the notch cut between the mountains by the Flathead River. What was there to say? They all felt the same. They had failed to catch the killer in time, and more innocent lives had been lost as a result.

In the backseat, Kyle stared into the darkness out the window. He wanted to become an agent to save lives. He wanted to make a difference, but now that he was involved in his first case, he was beginning to wonder if that were true. It seemed that instead of preventing the crimes, all they were doing was documenting the aftermath in an attempt to understand why, but they hadn't really prevented anything.

Maybe Janet had been right. She had always wanted him to become a lawyer or a doctor. She had wanted him to become one simply for the prestige and the money, but as Kyle thought about it now, he wondered if it might have been a better choice. Maybe he and Angela would still be together. Maybe the Joneses would still be alive.

* * *

It was a strange scene at the site. All around, the forest was pitch-black, but the cabin and its surroundings were bathed in the harsh, blue-white light of several portable floodlights. The whole thing had an otherworldly feel to it, like something out of *Close Encounters of the Third Kind*.

There were four vehicles parked in front. There were two of the county's Yukons and the coroner's white Suburban with its silver, mirrored windows on the sides and in back. The fourth was a black cargo van that had been converted to four-wheel drive complete with big snow tires. Its rear doors were open. Inside, a gas-powered generator was running, a faint plume of blue exhaust drifting away into the night.

As they walked up, Kyle noticed that the cabin's picture window was missing. In three of the corners, large pieces of broken glass still clung to the sill. Sheriff Greyhawk stood on the porch, awaiting their arrival. His eyes scanned the far side of the lake as if he was searching for something amid the darkness. It was uncanny how well his name fit him.

There were no pleasant greetings, merely solemn nods of acknowledgment as they stepped up on the porch. The sheriff filled them in as they donned the booties and gloves from boxes beside the door. "The 911 call came in around 9:30," he said. "There was no communication with the caller, so the operator did not dispatch immediately. She tried to call back but got a busy signal. It was several hours before the deputies on duty finally followed up on it. They found Mr. Jones's head in the living room and Mrs. Jones's left arm at the bottom of the stairs. Both bodies are missing. We performed a preliminary search of the cabin and the surrounding area but haven't come up with anything. We're bringing out the search-and-rescue dogs again just in case. Everything inside is exactly as it was found. We were waiting for you to get a look at it before we sent in the forensics team.

"There's a trail of blood from inside, across the windowsill and porch, and into the snow out there," he said, pointing to a small area that had been roped off with yellow tape around three wooden stakes. "But no tracks or footprints. There were a couple of inches of snow last night, so that might have covered them up."

"Was the front door open when they arrived?" Lewis asked.

"No, it was still locked from the inside," said the sheriff.

"So you think they gained entry by smashing in the front window and then left by the same route," Lewis said.

"Come with me." The sheriff led them just inside the doorway.

Shattered glass littered the floor. Beyond lay a crumpled pile of material, which Kyle realized were the curtains that had hung in the front window. Amid the tattered cloth and broken hanging rod was a fire log of considerable size.

"They took one of the logs from the stack and threw it through the window," Lewis said.

"Yes," said the sheriff. "And the electricity is out."

"You think someone killed the power and then threw the log through the window and proceeded to kill the Joneses," Lewis said.

"Yes."

While Lewis and the sheriff were talking, Kyle's attention was drawn to the television across the room. Arranged on top of a white doily were numerous picture frames.

Careful of the glass, Kyle moved across the room and leaned down to get a closer look. The photographs had been taken at various places and times over the years. One of the photographs was an old one of Bill and Audrey that appeared to have been taken at their wedding. Bill wore a tuxedo—which he looked uncomfortable in—with a yellow rose pinned to the lapel. His hair was reddish brown, and his blue eyes appeared to sparkle in spite of the age of the photo. Beside him, Audrey looked regal in her sequined gown. Both appeared blissfully happy as they held each other.

Another photo was of a family: a young man and his wife with their young daughter. The resemblance of the wife to Bill and Audrey was unmistakable.

The rest of the photographs were of Bill and Audrey and the young girl, whom Kyle assumed was their granddaughter. The pictures ranged from when the girl was around six or seven showing off her presents amid a pile of Christmas wrapping paper to a time when she was grown. In one, she wore a light blue graduation cap and gown. She appeared thin and gangly. There was a strange look about her, as if she was unhappy about graduating. Another was obviously her college graduation. Aside from the fact that Bill and Audrey looked older, the difference between the two was significant. In the latter, the girl had blossomed into a woman. The resemblance between her and her grandmother was unmistakable. She had long brown hair that trailed across her shoulders in big, loose curls and brown eyes that seemed to sparkle with an inner fire like those of her grandfather.

There were several other photos of the girl as well, some by herself and others with Bill and Audrey. Kyle found it odd that there would be so many of the girl with Bill and Audrey over the years but no others of the parents.

"Jesus," Marasco gasped. He had moved farther into the room, past the end of the sofa. "It looks like a fucking scene from *Kill Bill* in here."

Kyle looked over at him disapprovingly.

"You know, that scene in the Japanese club where Uma hacks like a hundred ninjas into little pieces," he said, motioning toward the stairs.

Kyle looked where he was pointing. The steps and wall were slathered in blood. A broken baluster laid next to the bottom step—and Audrey's severed arm.

Kyle looked away. Past the arm, in the middle of the room, he saw the broken cordless phone on the floor, its battery pack and connecting wires spilling out like the innards of a gutted animal.

And beyond, in a dark pool of blood, laid Bill Jones's severed head.

Kyle was suddenly struck by a rush of emotions he hadn't felt since he was a young boy. He had talked with these people, and in a strange way, after he had looked at all the photographs, he felt as if he knew them. He was no longer a casual observer documenting the scene from a distance but an acquaintance of the family. Imagining the horror of their last moments struck him like a punch in the gut.

He was going to be sick.

The room seemed to swim around him. Dark spots floated across his vision, and his breathing became laborious, as if he were trying to breathe through a pillow. He staggered toward the front door and lurched outside. When he caught himself on the porch railing, he leaned over and took in several deep, gasping breaths. The frigid air burned in his lungs, but it seemed to help.

Inside, he thought he heard Marasco laughing.

"You all right?" Lewis asked as he stepped up beside him.

Kyle nodded and took several slow, deep breaths. Gradually, the dizziness faded, and his vision cleared. He straightened up and looked at Lewis sheepishly. "Guess I stood up too fast," he said, feeling foolish as he looked over at the throng of men watching him.

"Ah, don't worry about it," Lewis said, taking a pack of cigarettes from his pocket. "It happens." He lit one and took a long drag.

"Does it ever get any easier?" Kyle asked.

Lewis exhaled slowly and looked at the cigarette. "You know, I never smoked before I took this job. The first murder scene I went to, the guy had been decomposing in his bedroom for several days. I got sick from the smell, puked all over my partner's shoes. So the next time, I tried smoking a Salem Menthol to numb my sense of smell before I went in. It worked, but now I'm addicted to the damn things." He offered the cigarette to Kyle.

"No, thanks," Kyle said.

Lewis shrugged his shoulders. "Some are worse than others," he said. "But it never gets easier. And if it does, you should go find yourself another line of work."

Lewis finished his cigarette in silence and then flicked the butt away into the snow.

Kyle looked out across the dark reservoir, beyond the congregation of vehicles and spotlights. The sky was beginning to lighten above the mountains, the darkness slowly turning to a rosy glow. It was a beautiful, ugly morning.

CHAPTER 23

Denver

An errant strand of hair fell across Carrie's face, which she blew out of her eyes with a quick puff, but the damage had already been done. Her concentration broken, she leaned back from the pile of documents before her and stretched. She looked at her watch and was amazed to find that it was already 12:45. She couldn't believe she had been at it all morning and most of the way through lunch without taking a break. On the other hand, it was good to be busy. It helped to keep her mind off Bret. After the latest round of threats from him, she had finally gone to the police only to be told there wasn't much they could do unless he actually assaulted her.

She was currently working on a story Allan had assigned to her. Four years ago, the State of Colorado had ordered an investigation into the underutilization of minority contractors on government projects. After the commission's findings were released, the state had instigated several new procedures in order to correct the situation. In a follow-up report issued last month, the commission indicated that the new procedures had been a great success and the state had actually exceeded its goals for minority participation. This immediately sent up a red flag with Allan. As he put it, "Anytime the government says things are bad, they're twice as bad. And if they say things are good, then they're either lying or hiding something."

So, for the past week, Carrie had been digging through the last three years' worth of public bid records for the State of Colorado. And while she hadn't found anything earth-shattering yet, she had noticed that a large percentage of the minority contracts awarded had all gone to the same contractor. She was beginning to see a pattern developing and thought she might be on to something, but she needed some more detailed information to confirm her suspicions. And when it came to detailed information, there was only one person to go to—Charlie Weisman.

Charlie was the resident computer geek/genius who worked at the *Inquirer.* Charlie could ferret out more information from the Web and other more dubious information services than anyone else could *ever* dig up. Allan had strictly forbidden Charlie to use the *Inquirer's* computers to do any illegal hacking, but strangely enough, even with his relatively moderate salary, Charlie somehow managed to have a computer setup at his home that would rival the home systems of Bill Gates and Steve Jobs.

With the information she had gathered this morning, Carrie thought she had enough to turn Charlie loose.

She grabbed the notes she had scribbled down in the raggedy notebook she always carried with her and stuffed it into her satchel. These days, most reporters carried laptop computers at which they pecked away, filing information away in categorized databases for easy retrieval at a later date, but Carrie preferred to take her own notes by hand. It was slower, but it gave her time to think about the information while she was writing it down, time to ponder what deeper issues might lie beneath the surface of an ocean of facts. She felt it made her a better reporter.

Back in her car, she pulled the notebook and her cell phone from her satchel, punched the speed dial number for the office, and hit the *send* button.

Charlie, who wore a wireless headset linked to his computer like a PBX operator, was suddenly on the line without the usual rattling that accompanied the lifting of a handset. "Hey, Carrie, what's up?"

"Wise Man," Carrie said and smiled. Charlie was in his midtwenties, but he still looked like a teenager, complete with curly brown hair, acne, and thick glasses that were constantly sliding down to the end of his nose. Most of the people at the paper called Charlie "the Mole" because of his looks and his special expertise at digging up information, but Carrie preferred to call him "Wise Man." To her, the Mole was too condescending a nickname, even though Charlie didn't seem to mind it too much. Wise Man was a more complimentary, respectful nickname. And Carrie was respectful of what Charlie was able to accomplish. In her mind, he was a modern-day technological prodigy, a virtuoso of the Internet who deserved more recognition than he got.

"I need some info," she said.

"You came to the right place."

"Of course I did," she said. It never hurt to stroke someone's ego a little, especially when you wanted something from him.

"Whatcha need?"

"I've got a list of companies I need you to look into. Pull up all you can on them, especially things like who the shareholders are, board members, annual revenue, preferred subcontractors, uh … pending litigation, and who they typically use to represent them in legal matters, things like that."

"Got it. What are the companies?"

"Ramirez Excavation Services, Inc., Johnson-Dealy Construction, and Bell Electric, Inc. And I also need you to pull up the same information for the top ten general contractors in the state. You should be able to find that out from the *Denver Business Journal's* list."

"Got it. You coming in anytime soon?"

"Yeah, I was just going to stop and grab lunch, and then I'll be in. You eaten anything yet?"

"No, you mind picking up something for me?"

"It's the least I could do. What do you want?"

"Bring me a double cheeseburger, large onion rings, and a strawberry milkshake—if they have strawberry. If not, just get me vanilla."

Carrie smiled as she jotted down the order in her spiral. *No wonder he still seems like a teenager,* she thought. *He still eats like one.* "No problem, I'll be there in a few."

* * *

Stepping within the confines of Charlie's cubicle was like stepping into the silicon equivalent of *The Twilight Zone*. Posters of hideous monsters and exotic spacecraft amid explosive battles for the fate of the galaxy shared wall space with unnaturally buxom, computer-animated, adventurous females. The only non-computer-related item hanging on the gray, cloth-covered partitions was his diploma from Cal Tech. His major, of course, had been computer science.

His glasses dangling perilously on the end of his nose, Charlie peered at one of the three twenty-seven-inch flat screen monitors in front of him. A rubber figurine of a three-eyed ogre holding a spiked club perched atop the center monitor.

"Any luck?" Carrie asked.

"Yeah, I think so," he nodded, still focused on the monitors. Then, with a snap, he turned toward the food as he took a big whiff. "Onion rings!" he smiled as he grabbed for the greasy cardboard container.

"They didn't have strawberry, so I got you vanilla," Carrie said as she handed him his shake.

"They never do," he grumbled. "But thanks."

While they ate, Charlie informed Carrie what he had been able to find out so far.

"Here's the list of the top ten general contractors in the state along with their annual gross revenue and name of their president," he said around a mouthful of cheeseburger as he pointed to the monitor on the left.

"Great," Carrie said as she leaned over his shoulder. "Can you print that out for me?"

"Sure," he replied. "Curly," he said into the microphone of his headset. "Print display to network printer five." Charlie had three processors dedicated solely to his use integrated into the office network system, and being the typical computer geek, he had named them Moe, Larry, and Curly. He had set up each of the computers to recognize voice commands, but it still amazed Carrie every time she watched him do it. It was like watching a great magician performing his tricks and not knowing how they did it.

"Moe," he commanded the other computer. "Pull up directory 'Carrie.' Pull up file 'Ramirez.'" A page of text appeared on the center monitor.

"Okay," Charlie said to Carrie. "Ramirez Excavation and Johnson-Dealy Construction both opened for business four years ago. Bell Electric's been around for eighteen years and is owned by Dorothy Bell, who took over the company after her husband died eight years ago. It'll take a little more digging to find out who actually owns the first two. I may have to do a little work from my house, but I'll find out."

"That's great. What about—" Carrie stopped as she heard her name being called overhead. There was a phone call holding for her at her desk.

She picked up the phone on Charlie's desk and answered the call. "This is Carrie." There was a short pause while she listened to the person on the other end.

"Oh, God," she whispered, her bottom lip beginning to tremble.

"I ... I'll be there as soon as I can."

Without saying good-bye, she hung up the phone. "I ... I've got to go," she stammered. Her voice quivered as she spoke and tears began brimming in her eyes.

"What's wrong?" Charlie asked.

Unable to hold back any longer, she burst into tears. "My grandparents were killed last night," she sobbed. After she grabbed her purse, she raced from the cubicle, her half-eaten burger left to go cold.

CHAPTER 24

Montana

It was late afternoon by the time they had finished gathering and photographing all of the evidence at the Joneses' cabin. The sun was beginning to dip behind the mountains to the west, casting ever-deepening shadows across the valley. George Greyhawk nodded at Deputy Johnson as he backed around to head back into town, taking the FBI agents with him.

During the day, George had sent Clayton back into town to a hardware store to purchase three sheets of plywood, a hammer, and a box of nails to board up the missing window.

Clayton and the FBI agents had all offered to stay and help, but George had sent them on their way, telling them that they had had a long day and that he could handle it without their assistance. Actually, he had his own reason for staying behind alone, one that he didn't care to try to explain to them.

After he boarded up the window, George stored the hammer and nails in the back of his Yukon and then lifted a Remington 870 shotgun from the rack along the side window. Using one of the keys on his key ring, he unlocked the padlock and opened the lid on a metal storage box bolted to the floor of the truck against the backseat. Inside were several removable trays of differing size that contained road flares, flashlights, batteries, and several boxes of ammunition of varying calibers.

The shotgun had an extended magazine. He pulled out eight shells from one of the trays and loaded them into the breach. He pumped the barrel and chambered the first shell. He then pulled out a large, black Maglite and closed the storage box.

After he shut the back gate of the Yukon, he returned to the front porch of the cabin, where he sat down in one of the wooden rockers and waited for true night to fall.

* * *

It was just after midnight when George first sensed it. He was sitting perfectly still—as he had been for the last four hours—listening to the wind as it soughed through the trees and scanning the darkness for any signs of movement. The moon was almost full, its silvery light quivering and dancing on the surface of the lake as the gentle waves lapped at the ice-crusted shore. In spite of the light from the moon, it was still impossible to see into the dark recesses of the forest, but that didn't matter to George. He knew something was out there. He could sense it.

Thoughts of his grandmother and the legend of the coyote filled his mind, but he quickly pushed them away.

He rose from the chair with such slow deliberation that it remained perfectly silent in spite of its tendency to creak and groan at the slightest disturbance. The floorboards remained quiet as he moved across the porch to the railing. His breath steamed in the frigid night air, momentarily disturbing his vision as the moonlight turned the vapor into a luminous, silvery cloud. Eyes narrowing, he scanned the darkness searching for the source of the disturbance.

Nothing moved except for a few dead leaves and pine needles blowing across the ground.

Remaining perfectly still, he closed his eyes. He could just sense it out there—something incredibly powerful and dangerous. It was not one with the forest. It did not belong, and thus, George was able to sense the uneasiness within the forest itself. The night had fallen silent. There were no ghostly calls ringing out as lonely owls hooted to one another, no rustling of limbs or scraping of claws against bark as tree squirrels scurried about. Nothing. Just the faint *shooshing* of the breeze passing through the treetops.

George was as still as the trees themselves, waiting for the thing to make its move. He could sense it out there just beyond the edge of his perception, as if it were sizing him up.

George pumped the shotgun, cracking the silence of the night.

He had hoped the sudden noise and movement and the threat it implied might startle the thing into action, but the night remained quiet.

Then suddenly, it was gone. To George, it felt as if he had been in the pressurized cabin of an airplane and one of the emergency exit doors had been suddenly opened, allowing the strange sensations to evaporate into thin air.

Knowing the encounter was over, George walked to the truck and got in. He laid the shotgun across the passenger seat within easy reach. It wasn't until he started the engine and looked in the rearview mirror that he noticed the beads of sweat on his forehead.

CHAPTER 25

Maryland

Anderson Colquitt was a man who liked order. Everything about him reflected this. His shirt was crisply starched and wrinkle-free, his tie perfectly straight. His dark suit was carefully pressed and free of lint. His shoes were polished with a spit-shine that made the black leather gleam like the surface of a new mirror. The only items on his finely polished mahogany desk were the blotter, the corners of which were lined up square with the edges of the desk, the telephone, which was also squared up with the desk, and the letter he was currently writing.

The walls of his office were uncluttered by calendars or dry-erase boards. The only picture that hung on the wall was not a piece of decorative art but a framed photograph of him shaking hands with the president of the United States. In the photograph, he wore his military parade uniform. He stood tall and erect, his head held straight and firm. The photograph had been taken years ago, before the wrinkles and gray hair and fading vision had forced him into retirement from the military.

The telephone intercom buzzed, and the voice of his secretary, Linda, came through. "General Colquitt, you have a call on line seven." Even though he worked in the private sector now, everyone still called him a general.

Without asking, he knew it was an important call. Their phone system was a digital one with hundreds of extensions. There was one special extension, however, that was accessed by dialing a number only a select few people had been given. Whenever a call entered the system through this number, he knew it had come from a remote switching station that had routed it through a series of transfers around the world to prevent anyone, including the phone company, from tracing the call or even backtracking through the records to determine the origin of the call. Before it was connected, it was patched through a digital encryption system and then routed to the decryption server hidden in a locked enclosure behind the wooden paneling in a corner of his office. Anytime a call came in through this server, an icon on the secretary's phone would light up, and she would inform the general of the nature of the call by informing him the call was on line seven.

"Ring it through," he said, putting the cap back on the black Mont Blanc pen. He adjusted the piece of paper he had been writing on, making sure it was square with the blotter. He placed the pen down on the blotter parallel to the paper.

He waited for the phone to ring twice before he answered. "General Colquitt," he said.

The expression on the general's face did not change while the person on the other end spoke.

"I see," the general said at last. "Yes, you were right to call. I'll take care of it from here. Continue on as before and call if there are any further developments." He hung up the phone. As he often did when he was thinking, he stepped to the window behind his desk.

He stood there with his hands behind his back, staring out the window at the long, four-story, mirrored building across the courtyard. Even though it was cold outside, there were still several people huddled together in the wooden gazebo in the middle of the tastefully landscaped space. All of them were smoking. Smoking within any of the buildings on the campus was strictly forbidden. It was a filthy habit. If he could have things his way, smoking by employees would be prohibited. Period.

After he pondered the situation for a moment, he returned to his desk to place a call. Before he dialed, he entered the code sequence that routed the call through the outgoing encryption system.

"Colquitt here," he said as soon as Nathaniel Brockemeyer answered.

"We may have another situation developing. I want you to be prepared in case we have to respond again quickly."

"Yes, sir," Nathan replied sharply.

With that, Colquitt hung up the phone. He leaned back in his plush leather chair and looked at the photograph of himself with the president. In the military, he had been taught to plan for every possible contingency. Before his arrival, his predecessor's failure to properly plan for every conceivable situation had nearly cost them everything. He was determined to see that nothing was overlooked while he was in charge.

Satisfied, he picked up the pen and began working on the letter once more.

CHAPTER 26

The flight from Denver to Kalispell seemed like the longest flight Carrie had ever taken. In the past, she had flown all across the country—from coast to coast and even to Hawaii—but none of those flights seemed to take half as long as the one she was currently on.

She sighed and took another drink of her Bloody Mary, which was really just a double vodka with a splash of V8. Her head throbbed dully against the backs of her eyes and around her temples. Reaching behind her, she pulled the rubber band farther down her ponytail in an effort to relieve some of the tension.

She felt exhausted, probably from the wine and sleeping pills she had taken last night, and yet, like last night, she found it impossible to sleep. Her mind just kept going around and around, thinking about her grandparents. Why would anyone want to kill them, and how was she going to get by without them? A profound sense of loneliness had settled around her like a thick fog. She felt alone and isolated like she had never felt in her entire life. This time, there was no one left to turn to. This time, she was truly alone.

Carrie stared out the window at the blanket of puffy white clouds drifting beneath the wings. She remembered Audrey Gran had always told her that God never gave people burdens that were more than they could handle, but that held little comfort for her now. She wasn't nearly as strong-willed as her grandmother had been.

"Would you like another drink?" the flight attendant asked as she pulled the cart next to Carrie's row.

"Uh, no. No, thank you," Carrie replied, looking down at the empty plastic cup in her hand. It wouldn't look good if she showed up at the sheriff's office reeking of booze.

As the attendant began to push the cart down the aisle, Carrie reached out for her. "Wait, I'm sorry, I ... let me have another Bloody Mary please."

CHAPTER 27

Montana

Morning found Kyle and Lewis back in the Justice Center conference room with Marasco and the sheriff. A rolling metal cart and monitor sat at the end of the table. They had been reviewing the taped interview with Bill and Audrey Jones from several weeks ago, looking at it again for any clues they might have previously missed.

Kyle's stomach gurgled.

They hadn't bothered to stop for breakfast. Instead, they had made do with a dozen donuts brought in by Deputy Johnson. Even though he had gotten little sleep the night before, Kyle drank water instead of the thick, black coffee everyone else was drinking.

On the table in front of them lay a copy of the *Kalispell Mountain Herald*. Printed across the top in big, bold letters, the headlines read, "NEW MURDERS AT HUNGRY HORSE. POLICE AND FBI BAFFLED."

Lewis hadn't said anything about it, but Kyle knew he was furious over the headlines. It was that reporter, Wallace Hipple, again, casting them all as a group of bumbling idiots.

To make matters worse, Deputy Johnson had informed them that the phone company had rebuffed his attempt at getting a copy of the phone records without a warrant. It was one thing to do it when an individual was suspected of a crime, they said, but there was just too much risk of exposure and potential liability if they were to do it against the local newspaper.

All of that topped off with the greasy donuts had given Kyle a queasy stomach.

It rumbled again as the sheriff hit *play* on the CD player.

"Nine-one-one, what is the nature of your emergency?"

No reply. Sounds can be heard in the background, as if the receiver is off the hook.

"Nine-one-one, hello?"

Still nothing. There are several seconds of faint rustling and clattering followed by a sudden gasp and two thunderous booms, undoubtedly the sounds of a shotgun being fired.

"Hello? Hello?"

In the background, there is a second or two of unintelligible gasps and groans along with a low, thumping, scraping sound.

Boom!

More noise. Then a woman's horrified scream of "Bill."

More noise, still indiscernible.

"Hello ... hello, can you hear me?"

A loud clattering, as if the handset was dropped.

Silence.

"Is that it?" Lewis asked.

"Yes," the sheriff replied.

"Goddammit!" Lewis stood up, his chair screeching across the floor as it was shoved into the wall. He started toward the door, as if he were about to storm out, but then he stopped, his hands on his hips. He let out a long, frustrated sigh. "I assume a copy's been sent to our lab for analysis?"

"Yeah," said Marasco.

"Did your people come up with anything on the Joneses?" Lewis asked.

The sheriff looked at the open the folder in front of him. "The fingerprints on the severed limb were a positive match for Mrs. Jones. We still have not heard word from your office regarding the rest of the evidence."

"I talked with them this morning," Lewis said. "It'll take them another day or two, but it's a top priority."

The sheriff continued. "Six years ago, they leased the land from the government for thirty years. Their lawyer told us they leased it with money from an insurance settlement with a trucking company they received about ten years ago. Their daughter and son-in-law were killed in a wreck when one of the company's drivers fell asleep and jumped the median."

That explains the lack of family photos at the cabin, Kyle thought.

"Did he say how much the settlement was for?" Lewis asked.

"About four million," George replied.

Marasco whistled.

"Did he say who inherits the Joneses' estate?"

"Their daughter was an only child. Their only surviving heir is their granddaughter, Carrie Daniels. We contacted her yesterday and informed her of what happened. She should be here this morning."

"Anything on her?" Lewis asked.

The sheriff flipped to another page. "She was eleven when her parents were killed in the wreck. She lived with the grandparents until she went off to college at Stanford. After graduating, she took a job in Denver with a small weekly newspaper."

"Did he say anything about her relationship with her grandparents?"

"Only that they were very close," the sheriff said and then added, "When the Joneses received the settlement, they put half of the money in a trust fund for the granddaughter, which she received when she turned twenty-one."

"She received two-plus million when she was twenty-one and still graduated from Stanford?" Kyle said. "Most kids coming into that much money would have never even considered going to college, and even if they had, it would have just been to party. They probably would never have graduated."

Lewis didn't seem as impressed. "Any idea what her financial status is now?"

"No," the sheriff replied.

"Sometimes when people come into a lot of money, it changes them," Lewis said, almost in an I-told-you-so manner. "She's known about that money since she was just a kid. Who knows how she really feels about it? Hell, for all we know she might have resented the grandparents getting half of it."

"I don't think that's the case here," Kyle offered.

"Why?" Lewis asked.

"The pictures at the cabin."

"Pictures?"

"Yeah, on the TV. They looked like a happy family. I just can't imagine that she had anything to do with their murder."

"Oh, come on," Marasco said mockingly. "Are you trying to tell us that we should rule her out as a suspect just because they looked happy in a few family photos?"

"I'm not saying we should rule her out, just that I don't think she did it. There *is* a difference." Kyle knew that it wasn't good investigative procedure to make judgments based on a few pictures above the mantel, but there had been something about the pictures that had struck him. He knew of all the stories of jealous lovers and greedy family members killing each other for money—there was one in the papers almost every day—but he hated to think that what appeared to have been a happy, loving relationship between the Joneses and their granddaughter might have ended that way. If that were true, how could anyone ever feel safe?

"Is there anyone else who stands to benefit from the Joneses' death?" Kyle asked. "Someone who wants their land? Maybe a dispute with a logging company or the Forest Service?"

"Not that we know of," said the sheriff.

"Maybe that's why we haven't come up with any leads on the Seattle men," Kyle thought out loud. "Maybe they were just in the wrong place at the wrong time. Maybe the Joneses were the target all along. Maybe they were just lucky the first time when they went into town because of the storm."

"It's possible," Lewis admitted. He sat back down at the table. "But what about the missing skier? What was his name?"

"Adam Peters," said the sheriff.

"Maybe Peters isn't tied in with the others," Kyle said. "Isn't it possible he had an accident or something?"

"It happens," said the sheriff. "He could have hit a tree, fallen into a snow well, or skied off the trail and broken a leg and then been covered up by the recent snows. If so, it might take another month or two for his body to turn up."

"But we can't assume that's what happened until we have evidence to back it up," Lewis said. "I want us to take a look at the files on the Seattle men again, see if maybe there's some connection between them and the Joneses we might have missed the first time."

A thought occurred to Kyle. "Sheriff, did the Joneses call in at any time between the first killings and now?" he asked.

"There were no other 911 calls," he replied.

"Not 911 calls but just a regular call like a complaint about someone intruding on their land or something."

"Or a certain poacher—say someone named Tucker?" Marasco offered.

"Right," Kyle agreed.

"Non-911 calls aren't stored on the system. We'd have to do a manual search of the phone records for the last several months," George said.

Kyle looked at Lewis. "It's not a bad idea," Lewis said. "Why don't you get with Deputy Johnson and see about getting a copy of the records. And I want to call the Joneses' lawyer back to ask him if there have been any inquiries by anyone looking to buy out the Joneses' lease in the past."

The sheriff nodded. "I'll check with the game warden to see if he received any calls from the Joneses and the Forest Service to see if they know of any reasons someone might want that land."

Lewis seemed less than optimistic, but Kyle was beginning to feel at least some encouragement with the new developments. He felt like he was actually contributing something, and for the first time in weeks, they had a new avenue to pursue.

CHAPTER 28

When Carrie Daniels stepped into the room, Kyle hardly recognized her as the same girl he had seen in the pictures at the Joneses' cabin. That girl had appeared youthful and exuberant, with a sparkle in her eyes in spite of what had happened to her parents. But the girl who sat across from him now looked older than her years and weary to the point of collapse. She wasn't wearing any makeup, and her skin looked pale and splotchy. Her eyes were red, but more than that, they appeared dull and lifeless. Kyle had seen that look before. It was the same look he had seen on Miss Vera's face after her son, Roberto, had been killed in a convenience store robbery. Kyle immediately felt sympathy for the girl.

When Lewis introduced him, the look in her eyes was one of near panic, and for a brief moment, Kyle thought she might turn and run. Instead, she tentatively shook their hands and sat down.

"Ms. Daniels," Kyle began. "First, let me say how deeply sorry we are for your loss and assure you that we are doing everything in our power to ensure that the perpetrators are brought to justice." He pulled out one of his cards and handed it to her. "My job is to act as a liaison between yourself and our office to make sure that you are kept informed about the ongoing investigation and eventual trial as well as to offer grief counseling and to provide assistance with any other needs you might have during that time." While Kyle spoke, she kept her head down, looking at the purse clutched tightly in her hands. "I know this is a very difficult time for you, and I want you to know that I'm here to help you through it."

Carrie nodded and quietly asked, "What happened?"

"We're not really sure," Lewis said. "It appears that someone broke in through the front window and killed both of your grandparents."

"Why would anyone want to do that?"

"We don't know yet," Lewis said. "We were hoping you might be able to help us with that. If you don't mind, we would like to ask you a few questions."

Carrie cleared her throat, trying to regain control of her tremulous voice. "Okay."

"Ms. Daniels, do you know of any reason why someone might have wanted to kill your grandparents?" Lewis asked.

"No, they were both incredibly kind, loving people." While Carrie spoke, she continued to look down at her purse, nervously twisting the thin straps around her fingers. It was painfully reminiscent of the way that her grandfather, Bill, had held his ball cap during his interview.

"Are you aware of any reason why someone might want to take over your grandparents' lease?"

Carrie sniffled and shook her head. "Not that I'm aware of."

Lewis nodded. "Just take your time and think. We're not in any hurry here. Do you know if there were any former business partners or associates who might have had a disagreement with either of your grandparents?"

"No, my grandfather was a ranch hand for years, and my grandmother was a schoolteacher. They didn't start the fishing-guide company until after I was away at college."

Lewis made a few notes in his pad and then asked, "Has anyone approached you about your grandparents land?"

"No."

"Do you know if they had any disagreements with any of the renters who stayed at their cabins?"

"No, at least nothing that they told me about."

"Did they ever say anything to you about the murders at their other cabin?"

Carrie looked surprised by this. "No, what other murders?"

"Four men from Seattle were killed at your grandparents' rental cabin in February. They never said anything to you about this?"

"No," Carrie said. "They never mentioned it."

"So you spoke to them between that time and now."

"Yes," Carrie said and nodded. "I talked to them all the time."

Lewis paused again, nodding. He was being careful not to push her too hard. "When was the last time you spoke with your grandparents?"

"I ... I don't remember exactly. About a week ago, I guess."

"And during this time, did they say anything that seemed unusual? Did they seem different? Like they were nervous about something?"

"No, but I'm not really surprised they didn't say anything. They were both so protective of me, especially my grandmother. I've been having a bit of a hard time lately, and I'm sure they just didn't want to worry me about anything else."

"What sort of trouble?" Lewis asked.

"I ... I've been having some trouble with one of my exes. But I don't see how—"

"Please be patient with us," Lewis said. "I know it may not seem relevant, but we need to gather all the information we can. Now, specifically, what kind of trouble were you having?"

Carrie bit her bottom lip. "I ... it ... he had been abusive, and after I broke up with him, he began stalking me," she finally blurted out. "I went to the police about it, but they said there wasn't anything they could do about it."

"Please understand ... we have to cover every possibility," Lewis said. "Did your ex-boyfriend ever make threatening statements against your grandparents?"

Carrie looked stricken by that thought. "He's made them to *me*, but he never mentioned my grandparents. You don't think—"

"We don't know," Lewis said, trying to keep her calm. "That's why we're asking you. Do you think he is capable of something like that?"

"I ... I don't know. I ... oh, God, if—" She paused as she struggled to maintain her composure. She bit her lip and squeezed her eyes shut in an effort to hold back the tears. "Can I see them?" she blurted out.

Lewis frowned. "I'm afraid that's not going to be possible."

"Why?"

Lewis sighed.

"Ms. Daniels," Kyle jumped in. He knew Lewis wasn't the most diplomatic person in situations like this. "This is not going to be easy for you, but I think it's better that you hear it from us rather than read it in the papers. Your grandparents' bodies were ... dismembered, and we have yet to recover all of their remains."

Carrie sat in stunned silence for a moment, unmoving, as if time had stopped for her. Then she suddenly burst into tears. She opened her purse and pulled out a crumpled bar napkin with the airline's logo on it but dropped it. It was as if that one small incident was the last straw. She dropped her purse, sending things spilling out and rolling across the floor. She buried her face in her hands as sobs racked her body.

Instinctively, Kyle stood up and moved toward her to offer support, but she flinched backward and held up her hand as if to ward him off. He stopped and stood there, unsure of what to do.

"Can I *please* go?" she cried.

"Yes," Lewis said. "Just let us know where you're staying so we can get in touch with you."

Kyle helped gather up the contents of her purse. She grabbed the purse and stood quickly, the chair scraping across the floor. She rushed out the door, her hand held over her mouth, tears streaming down her face.

They were both silent for a moment after she left.

Finally, Kyle asked, "Do you think the boyfriend might have done it?"

"I don't know," Lewis said. "He might have, or he might have hired someone to do it if he knew about the money."

Seeing something, Kyle knelt down and picked up a pen that had slid under the table. It was a silver Mont Blanc with engraving on the side: *We are so proud of you!*

He looked at the door, feeling terrible for the brokenhearted girl who had just run from the room.

CHAPTER 29

The white steeple rose high into the sky in stark contrast to the banks of low, gray clouds that shuttered the day. A few scattered snowflakes drifted down only to melt as soon as they landed on the hoods of the cars or the wet sidewalk.

Kyle turned up the collar of his overcoat and stuffed his hands in the pockets as he and a handful of local townspeople made their way into the church for the Joneses' memorial service.

He wasn't exactly sure why he was here. He had brought her pen with him, but he could just as easily have called her to let her know he had it. He had told Lewis he thought it might be worthwhile to attend in order to keep an eye on the girl and any possible suspects who might show up, but that wasn't really the reason. Nor was it anything as shallow as physical attraction for the girl. Sympathy, empathy, and even guilt were more accurate descriptions for the feelings that had drawn him here. He supposed it stemmed from his childhood experiences with Miss Vera and her son, but he had always been drawn to people in need. Deep down, he felt guilty about their situation in life, as if he were somehow responsible for their misfortune and it was his duty to make things right again.

In this particular case, Kyle's guilt was not totally unfounded. The hard truth of the matter was that if they had found the killer in time, Carrie's grandparents would still be alive.

Whatever his motivation, Lewis hadn't seemed to mind. The past few days had been spent following up on information about Carrie's ex-boyfriend, including any airline tickets he might have purchased to

Montana, substantial bank withdrawals, loans or credit card advances he might have made, or any other suspicious activity he might have been involved with in recent weeks. They were still waiting for the forensics report on the Joneses' place, which was due back today.

Halfway down the aisle, Kyle paused when he saw the elaborate stained-glass windows above the choir loft. They were reminiscent of the windows in the Highland Park Methodist Church in Dallas, bringing back a sudden flood of memories he thought he had put behind him long ago.

The last time he had been there had been for his father's funeral. He could still remember it as clearly as if it were yesterday. It was a cool day in late October, the sky a brilliant blue. The leaves on the long row of maples lining the walk had already turned, and the ground was awash in a sea of colors. The crisp, clean scent of fall was in the air, along with the musty smell of damp, decaying leaves.

As he thought back to that day, Kyle realized he hadn't been back to that church since. It wasn't because he wasn't a religious person; it was just that after his father died, there hadn't been anyone left who cared enough to take him anymore.

That was one thing he had in common with Carrie. Although the circumstances weren't exactly the same, he knew what it was like to lose one's parents. He had lost his father to a heart attack when he was thirteen, and even though his mother was still alive, for all intents and purposes, he had lost her to the bottom of a bottle years before that.

As he stared at the multicolored depiction of Christ on the cross, Kyle wondered if it was that similarity with Carrie that had drawn him here today, perhaps in hopes of finding someone he could commiserate with.

He took a seat at the back of the mourners. He wasn't a relative or a friend of the family, and he didn't want to be disrespectful. Besides, this way he would be able to see everyone else who was in attendance.

The front of the stage was lined with an array of flower arrangements. In front of the flowers was a large black-and-white photograph of the Joneses on their wedding day. It was a duplicate of the one Kyle had seen in the cabin.

When everyone was inside and settled, an elderly lady began playing the organ. After a few hymns, the minister stepped up to the lectern to deliver the eulogy. He spoke fondly of the Joneses and of their promised life in the hereafter before he turned the podium over to Carrie.

Kyle straightened up, trying to see over the heads of those in attendance while Carrie made her way up the red-carpeted steps. Her hair was pulled into a ponytail, the long, brown tresses spilling down the middle of her back. She wore a simple, dark blue dress, without any noticeable makeup or jewelry.

She appeared nervous as she adjusted the microphone to her height, flinching at the amplified creaking that rang out through the sanctuary.

After she cleared her throat, she paused for a moment as she unfolded a few sheets of paper and laid them on the platform before her.

"Please forgive me for reading this," she said, her voice trembling. "I'm not very good at public speaking. I'm much better at writing, and there were so many things I wanted to say I was afraid I would forget if I didn't write it all down.

"When I was eleven, my parents were taken from me in an automobile accident. It was the most horrible time in my entire life. I couldn't understand why something so terrible should have happened to me. What I had done to deserve such punishment from God? Fortunately, Grandpa Bill and Audrey Gran took me in. Without them, I'm not sure I would have made it through the next few years." At first, she was just reading aloud, but as she continued, she seemed to gain confidence, the words seeming to come easier.

"My grandmother was an incredibly strong lady. No matter what happened, she never lost faith. At my parent's funeral, she was the one who held us together. I remember her standing before the church, her chin held high as she spoke of how proud she was of her daughter and how she knew she was in a better place, waiting for her friends and family to join her one day. I remember Grandpa Bill pulling out his hanky to dab his eyes and holding it for me to blow my nose. And even though she was hurting as much, if not more than the rest of us, my grandmother never shed a tear. She was our backbone, our strength. Her faith was amazing."

Carrie paused to flip the page, and it appeared as if she might break down. She sniffled and wiped beneath her eyes with a shaky hand. A smile crossed her face. "Guess I could still use Grandpa's hanky," she said. A few in the audience laughed nervously, but Kyle wasn't one of them. The more he listened, the more guilt-ridden he became.

"Grandpa Bill and Audrey Gran lived on a small ranch in Montana at the time," she continued. "With Bill and a few hired hands running the ranch while Audrey taught third grade at the elementary school in Lewiston. I remember how strange it all seemed to me after moving from the city. My parents were gone, and I was in a new place without any friends. I began to withdraw, but it seemed like every time I began feeling sorry for myself, Audrey Gran would suddenly appear with milk and a plate of freshly baked cookies or an offer to go horseback riding to the far side of the ranch. It was as if she was gifted with clairvoyance. She was always there when I needed her most.

"Some of my fondest memories from that time are riding out late in the afternoon to watch the sun set behind the mountains in the distance. Although she never spoke about it directly, later I came to realize that this was Granny's way of getting me to look at life from a broader perspective, to see all the beauty and wonderment of life instead of focusing on the darkness and pain that was so prevalent in my life at that time."

She paused for a moment and bit her bottom lip. Tears welled in her eyes as she struggled to maintain her composure.

"I told myself I wasn't going to do this," she said, her voice cracking as the tears rolled down her face.

Kyle felt as if someone had stuck a dagger in his gut. And every time she threatened to break down, it twisted a little bit more.

It took a while for her to regain her composure, but she would not step down. The sanctuary was silent except for the scattered sobs and coughs and sniffles as everyone shared in her grief.

Finally, when she had gathered herself sufficiently, she cleared her throat and began again.

"Grandpa Bill was one of the kindest, funniest, and most loveable people in the world. While my grandmother showed me how to be strong, he showed me how to laugh again. He loved animals and the outdoors, and he taught me to love them as well. The first time he tried to teach me how to milk a cow, we wound up getting more on the ground and each other than we did in the pail. We both laughed so hard we cried, and I swear that from then on, every time I passed that cow, it ran from me." She smiled through her tears as people in the audience chuckled. "Even though he was busy with the ranch, Grandpa Bill always found time for me, and every few weeks, he would take a day off so the two of us could go hiking or fishing. I didn't have the heart to tell him how much I hated the smelly, slimy things, but I loved those trips."

She looked toward the ceiling and blinked several times. When she spoke again, her voice was thick with emotion.

"Now that they're gone," she said, "I don't have anyone else to rely on to help me through this. But I do have the lessons of courage and love that they taught me, and as long as I have that, I'll never be alone." Again, she paused before she managed to get out, "Thank you all for your kindness ... and prayers ... and for being here today." And then it was as if the emotional weight became too much for her, and she broke down again as she hurried from the podium back to her seat.

Kyle felt like a complete bastard. He couldn't have felt worse if she had called him up in front of everyone and pointed him out as the reason her grandparents were dead.

There was an uncomfortable silence, broken only by a few more coughs and sniffles as an older lady made her way up the steps. She shuffled over to a microphone on the right side of the podium. She sang as the organist played "Amazing Grace."

At the conclusion of the service, Kyle stayed back while friends of the Joneses gathered around Carrie to give their condolences. He didn't want to make her feel uncomfortable, as if she were being watched. Nor did he want to embarrass her by returning her pen in front of a group of people. He was contemplating if he should just slip out and do it at some other time when he noticed a tuft of red hair among the well-wishers at the front of the sanctuary. After he made his way to the far end of the row, Kyle slipped down the aisle behind Carrie to get a better look. It was the reporter, Wallace Hipple. Kyle recognized him from the press conferences and his photo in the paper.

He didn't think Hipple had known the Joneses. So why was he here other than to try and get something from her that he could write about in the paper like some over-aged TMZ reporter? The story had become the talk of the town, and Hipple had done nothing but increase the apprehension of everyone in the valley with his sensationalized reporting. Kyle wanted to hear what the reporter had to say.

The crowd around Carrie had dispersed for the most part, and Kyle got close enough to catch part of what Hipple had to say. He was the last to speak to her—no doubt in an effort to maximize the amount of time he might spend with her while minimizing the number of witnesses to his questions.

"... dear friends and I just wanted you to know how much they will be missed."

"Thank you," Carrie replied politely.

"Yes, well, it's the least I can do," Hipple said, doing his best to appear sympathetic. "Now I know this isn't really the best time for this, but I was wondering if—" He broke off as he glanced above Carrie's shoulder, his eyes meeting Kyle's.

Kyle arched his eyebrow, challenging Hipple to continue with his question.

"Yes, well, perhaps this is not the best time," said the pompous little reporter. "Maybe we can talk again some other time. In private," he added with a sneer toward Kyle. "Here's one of my cards. Please feel free to call me any time if there is anything I can do for you."

Hipple turned and walked away down the aisle toward the doors. Kyle was disappointed that he hadn't caught more of the conversation, but he was glad the little weasel was gone.

Apparently sensing Hipple's sudden change had been caused by someone behind her, Carrie turned around.

"Special Agent Andrews, isn't it?" Carrie asked.

Kyle was caught off guard. He hadn't planned on Hipple spotting him and bolting so quickly. "Uh, yes ... well, no. I'm a victim specialist, remember?" he explained, hating the way it sounded.

"Isn't it a little unusual for an FBI agent to attend the memorial of the victims?" she asked. It sounded like more of an accusation than a question.

"I can't really say," he said with a shrug. "I just wanted to offer my condolences and let you know how sorry I am. I met your grandparents, and they were both very kind."

"Thank you," she said. "Is that all?"

Kyle *had* been sincere, but she seemed suspicious of his motives.

"I was also curious to hear what that reporter had to say to you," he admitted.

"Why is that?"

Kyle didn't want to get into the details of the situation, so he simply said. "I don't trust him."

"I see," she said, her voice suddenly terse. "You don't trust reporters?"

Damn, Kyle thought as he remembered that she was a reporter with a small paper in Denver. "No, no, it's just that I—"

"Look," she said wearily, "I've had enough dealings with the justice system lately, and to tell you the truth, I don't trust you either. Instead of worrying about what some reporter has to say to me, why don't you go find who killed my grandparents?"

She turned and marched away, leaving him to stand alone at the front of the church. Now he felt like a complete asshole.

The final insult came as he started back down the aisle toward the door. When he stuffed his hands in his coat pockets, he found he had forgotten to return her pen.

CHAPTER 30

As Kyle walked down the aisle toward the exit, a shrill chirping emanated from inside his coat. It sounded unnaturally loud and horribly out of place in the sanctuary. He scrambled to pull his cell phone from his pocket. He had forgotten he had left it on. He was just glad it hadn't gone off during the service.

He looked at the display. It was Lewis. "Hey, what's up?" he answered.

"Where are you?"

"At the church. Why?"

Lewis spoke to someone in the background. There was a muffled reply in a deep voice that sounded like the sheriff's.

"Okay," Lewis said into the phone. "Stay there. Meet us out front. We're on our way."

"All right, what's up?"

"We're on our way back to Tucker's place. I'll explain the rest on the way." Lewis hung up without waiting for a reply, but Kyle knew from the sound of his voice that something big had come up.

Hardly two minutes later, a pair of county Yukons roared up in front of the church, lights flashing. The back door was flung open, revealing Agent Marasco on the far side. Kyle suppressed a smile as he noticed that Lewis was in the front passenger seat while Deputy Johnson drove. Kyle hurried over and climbed in. They took off as he slammed the door behind him.

"What's going on?" he asked.

Lewis tossed Kyle's overnight bag to him. "You'll probably want to change." Inside were his jeans, a long-sleeved blue T-shirt with the FBI logo on the breast, and his hiking boots. As he began shucking out of his clothes, Lewis filled him in.

"The forensic report came back from the Joneses' place," he said. "The lab was able to positively identify two different blood types at the crime scene. Both the blood on the floor and on the stairs matched that of Bill and Audrey, who are both type O, but blood on the log that was thrown through the window was type B, which is found in only about 10 percent of the population."

"So we've got a sample of the killer's blood," Kyle said excitedly.

"Looks like," Lewis said. "But it gets better. The lab checked it against Carrie's and her ex-boyfriend's type for a match, and it turned up negative. Carrie's type A, and her ex is type O. But guess who *is* type B."

"Tucker?"

"You got it, cowboy."

"Are we sure it's his?" Kyle asked as he pulled the T-shirt over his head.

"Not positive yet. We know his type from his medical records. Since there was no type-B blood found at the first murder scene and since we didn't identify any at his place, there wasn't sufficient evidence for a blood sample the first time we took him in. But the fact that he's type B and we've got type B on the log narrows it down a hell of a lot. We've got enough now to take him in and get a sample of his blood for DNA testing."

Kyle nodded. It was the most telling piece of evidence they had been able to gather so far, but along with it came the possibility that it might be Tucker's. They had had him in custody and let him go because of insufficient evidence, and by doing so, they may have set him free to kill the Joneses. Kyle knew that if that turned out to be the case, the media would crucify them in spite of the fact that they had been acting within the limits of the law. But worse than that was the thought of facing Carrie Daniels and trying to explain to her how they had let her grandparents' killer go free.

* * *

Hazy light filtered into the shack as Kyle and Lewis stepped inside. To the left beneath the window was the small, rusting sink. A metal plate and a fork sat in a couple of inches of water that had frozen solid. The rickety table and chairs still sat in the middle of the room. Behind it in the fireplace were the charred remains of a log gone cold. On the rack above the mantle, the M16 with the bayonet was missing.

"Looks like he bolted," said Marasco.

"Shit," Lewis muttered.

Across the small room, Clayton pushed the door to the curing shed open.

Zzzhing!

Everyone jumped as a thick chain that had been hanging from the ceiling slipped over a beam and rattled to the floor. As he looked into the room Kyle noticed that one of the carcasses hanging from the rafters when they had searched the place the first time was gone.

They searched the room again. The disgusting array of steel traps, rusted cans, chains, hooks, and hacksaws remained as before, as well as the large, finely honed knife with bleached bone handle that had been left on the workbench.

Kyle looked at the rafters where the chain had fallen. Something about the missing carcass bothered him. With the truck still parked beside the cabin, it appeared Tucker had fled on foot. It seemed crazy, but Tucker was, if nothing else, a mountain man and a survivor. But if he had fled into the mountains, what had he done with the carcass hanging in the shed? It didn't seem likely that he would have taken the thing with him, even if he had a sled. Wouldn't he have just cut the meat from the bones to reduce the weight? Then he remembered the garbage pit out back and decided to check it out.

The sheriff was just stepping into the shack as Kyle left the curing shed. The sheriff had to duck his head as he entered, and the room seemed suddenly cramped. Kyle squeezed past and told Lewis he was going to look around back.

Outside, Davidson and one of his assistants were making their way toward the cabin, the assistant lugging the heavy forensics case.

Around back, Kyle found the garbage pit—or what was left of it—covered with patches of snow and dirty ice. It had been scattered during their search when they had collected the charred bones. He picked up a small stick and poked around at the pit but saw nothing that appeared to be new amid the garbage and certainly nothing as large as the remains of the carcass he had seen hanging from the ceiling of the shed.

Kyle tossed the stick away and started back around to the front of the cabin. He was just coming around the corner when he was once again struck by the unnatural quiet of the forest. As he stopped to listen, he noticed that Sheriff Greyhawk had stepped back outside and was standing in front of the cabin. He stood there motionless, his head tilted forward slightly, staring into the woods with a look reminiscent of the one he had had at the Joneses' cabin.

Something at the edge of the porch had caught the sheriff's attention. He knelt down and picked up a clump of matted dog fur that had caught on a nail and was fluttering in the breeze. Curious, Kyle stepped back and peered around the edge of the shack. The sheriff was standing with his eyes closed, the clump of fur held to his nose like a bloodhound trying to pick up the scent, or was it more like someone savoring the scent of his lover's perfume?

Kyle watched, curious of the enigma that was George Greyhawk. Most of the time, he seemed like an ordinary man, strong and quiet, but nothing too far out of the norm. But then at other times, he seemed unlike any man Kyle had ever known. It was as if he could hear and see and sense things that others couldn't. Kyle couldn't help but wonder what was going on with him. Did he know something more than he was letting on, or was he just as confused as they were?

"You find anything?" Lewis asked, breaking the eerie silence as he stepped out front.

The sheriff shook his head. "No," he said, letting the fur drift away on the breeze.

"It looks as if he may have taken off on foot, assuming someone else didn't come and pick him up," Lewis said. "How long before we can have a party of search dogs here?"

"It will have to wait until morning," the sheriff replied without taking his eyes off the trees. "It will be dark soon. It is not safe to be in these woods after dark."

CHAPTER 31

Despite the cold, Carrie Daniels was standing outside in the loading and unloading zone of Glacier Park International Airport when Kyle pulled up in Marasco's Expedition. He had called her that morning to inform her that her grandparents' property, including the Hummer, had been released to her. To Kyle's surprise, she had asked him if he could help her with the return of her rental car and by giving her a ride to the cabin to pick up the H2. Kyle had said he would be glad to help.

"I appreciate you doing this for me," she said, looking out the windshield as they pulled away. "I ... I didn't know who else to call."

"No problem," Kyle said. "That's what I'm here for." He knew she was going through an incredibly difficult time. One of the most common feelings shared by victims after the sudden loss of a loved one was a sense of intense isolation and loneliness, even when they were still surrounded by other family. But in Carrie's case, there was no one else. The grieving process was likely to be a long and arduous one for her, and it was his job to help her through it as much as possible.

"I ... I also want to apologize for my behavior at the funeral the other day," she said. "I was upset, but that's no excuse. I was rude, and I'm sorry."

"There's no need to apologize," said Kyle.

"Yes, there is. It was kind of you to come."

They pulled out of the airport, and Kyle turned left onto Highway 2, which headed north toward Hungry Horse.

"Oh, before I forget again," he said. He reached into his pocket and pulled out the silver Mont Blanc.

"Oh, my God," she gasped. "Where did you find that?"

"It fell out of your purse when you were at the station the first time. I meant to give it to you at the funeral the other day, but—"

"I had no idea it was missing," she said, grabbing it and clutching it against her chest. "You have no idea what this pen means to me." She looked over at him for the first time. "Thank you," she said quietly.

Kyle nodded. "By the way, as far as we can tell, your ex-boyfriend didn't have anything to do with your grandparents. He was in Denver the whole time, and we haven't found any evidence that he hired someone else to do it."

"Oh, okay," Carrie said and looked out the passenger window. Just the mention of her ex seemed to make her uncomfortable.

"And just so you know, I don't think you'll have to worry about him bothering you anymore. The two special agents that showed up at his door made it quite clear that there would be serious consequences if he continues to harass you."

Carrie nodded, quietly thanking him without looking away from the window as if embarrassed by the situation.

They continued on in silence then, and Kyle left her alone with her thoughts. After a while, he turned on the radio and set it at a low volume so the silence wouldn't seem quite so oppressive.

A short time later, Carrie sniffed and wiped at her eye with the sleeve of her sweater. "Sorry I'm not very talkative."

"No, its fine," Kyle said. "I understand."

"You must get pretty tired of dealing with people like me," she said, idly running her finger through the fog that had formed in the bottom corner of the window.

"Not really," said Kyle. "At least not like you might think. I do get tired of it, but only from the standpoint that I wish there was some way to prevent bad things from happening to good people—like your grandparents—but I can't. No one can. I mean, we can try to prevent it, but no one can stop all the evil in the world, so ... well, I try to do what I can to try to help those left behind." Kyle had wanted to explain it in a way that she would understand, but instead, he wound up feeling like a babbling idiot. "I don't guess that made any sense, did it?"

Whether it did or not, she was kind enough to nod and say, "Yeah, it did ... actually."

A few miles farther down the road, Carrie asked, "So how did you get into doing this?"

Kyle looked over at her. "You don't have to try to make conversation if you don't feel like it. I understand if you just want to be left alone."

"No, I don't," she said. "We've still got a ways to go, and it helps me keep my mind off ... you know."

"All right," said Kyle, "But if I'm boring you, just let me know, and I'll shut up."

She smiled then and said, "I promise."

"When I was young, my father was away on business all the time, and my mother spent most of her time at the country club, so I was basically raised by my nanny, Valeria Sanchez. When I was little, I couldn't pronounce her name. It came out sounding something like 'Miss Vera,'" he said with a childlike lisp. "And I guess it just stuck. I've called her Miss Vera for as long as I can remember. Still do in fact," he admitted with a slightly embarrassed smile. "She's a sweet lady. She still takes care of my mother's house.

"Anyway, when I was nine years old, Miss Vera's son, Roberto—who was only fifteen—was killed in a convenience store robbery. He worked there after school, helping to stock the shelves, sweeping up, that sort of thing. He was working there one evening when two men came in and robbed the place. No one ever knew exactly what happened—the place only had one camera looking at the register—but the man behind the counter and Roberto were both killed, all for $137 and a couple of cartons of cigarettes. I was at home with Miss Vera when the police came to tell her about her son. It was awful. I can still remember how she wailed and collapsed in the foyer."

Kyle paused and glanced over in Carrie's direction. He hoped the story wasn't upsetting her more than she already was, but he thought it was important for her to hear it. She was sitting quietly and staring out the window at the mountains now looming before them.

"Afterward, Miss Vera changed," he continued. "Roberto was the only family she had. Roberto's father had never been around. He left them when Roberto was just a baby. I think he was a drunk. Anyway, for the longest time afterward, Miss Vera seemed to be like a zombie, just going through the motions day after day. It was as if the will to live had simply gone out of her. Sometimes, when she looked at me, she would start to cry. At the time, I didn't know why. I thought maybe it was something I had done. I wanted nothing more in the world than for her to feel better, but no matter what I tried, I just couldn't seem to make her happy again.

"It wasn't until my father died when I was thirteen that I realized what she had been going through." Carrie looked over at him then, perhaps in sympathy or commiseration, but she didn't say anything. "I guess my mother had always been an alcoholic and was probably into drugs too, but it got worse after Dad died. She was always gone, or else she was up all night and asleep during the day. It was like she wasn't even there. I started to get into trouble at school then, hanging out with the wrong crowd. We would skip class and go get stoned in the alley across the street. I didn't know it at the time, but I was desperate for attention. Fortunately, one of the teachers caught us. They threatened to expel me, and in order to avoid it, I was forced to start going to a counselor after school three days a week. My mother, Janet, wouldn't ever take me. Miss Vera always had to do it. The counselor's name was Mrs. Campbell, and she helped me a lot. If it wasn't for her, I don't know what would have happened to me. Anyway, each day after my sessions during the drive home, Miss Vera and I would talk about what Mrs. Campbell had told me and how it was helping me to deal with the loss of my father. Maybe it was just because enough time had passed or because she finally had someone to talk to about it, but I think it helped Miss Vera with the loss of her son too.

"Janet had always wanted me to be a doctor or a lawyer when I grew up, but after that, I realized that I wanted to be able to help people like Mrs. Campbell had helped Miss Vera and me."

It wasn't until Kyle finished that he realized how long he had been talking. They had already passed through the tiny burg of Hungry Horse and were on the road nearing the dam. He hadn't meant to go on for so long, but once he had started, it had just come out. He told himself it was because he wanted Carrie to know that he had been through similar difficulties and therefore might be better able to understand her situation and help her through it, but he realized it was more than that. It had been so long since he had had someone close to talk with that he had unconsciously taken advantage of the situation for his own benefit.

"Sorry if I got a little carried away there."

"No, don't be," Carrie said quietly. "I'm glad you did."

They crossed over the dam in silence. To their left, the glimmering water stretched away into the distance, its placid surface belying the incredible pressure that continued to build as the water rose with the spring thaw.

CHAPTER 32

Carrie watched as Agent Andrews pulled away and disappeared into the lengthening shadows the trees cast across the roadway. He had offered to stay with her, but she had told him she preferred to do this alone. "All right," he had finally conceded. "But the power's still off, so make sure you're gone well before dark."

"I will," she had promised. Part of her was intrigued by him. He seemed genuinely kind and caring, unlike most of the men she was used to dealing with. But then they all seemed that way at first.

Turning, she stood in front of the cabin and stared at the sheets of plywood where the big picture window had been. Her heart pounded in her chest in spite of the Xanax she had taken to help calm her nerves.

She walked up the steps to the front door, unlocked it, and stepped inside. Even though she knew better, a part of her still expected to smell the familiar scent of baking bread and to hear Audrey Gran humming merrily as she worked in the kitchen.

Instead, she found silence and darkness. The magnificent view of the lake was gone. Faint beams of light filtered into the room, which smelled of bleach and Pine Sol.

She closed the door behind her. She wasn't exactly sure what she was doing here, though she knew she had to come. She hadn't decided if she was going to sell the place or not; however, even if she didn't, she knew she would have to go through her grandparents' belongings sooner or later, and she figured it would be better to do it now and get it over with as opposed to prolonging the inevitable.

The coat closet's door was missing, and as she looked about the room, Carrie noticed the large hole where the sheetrock had been cut from the wall next to the stairs. She started toward the kitchen, trying hard not to let her imagination run away with suppositions of what might have happened in this room. She intended to sit down and make a list of things that needed to be done, such as calling a glass company to replace the front window and a carpenter to repair the wall and door, but as she passed the stairs and saw the broken baluster and the bleached-out spot on the floor where the blood had been cleaned up, it all became too much.

She rushed into the kitchen and leaned over the sink as her body was suddenly racked with sobs.

After she cried herself out, she turned on the faucet and splashed her face with cool water.

Then, with trembling hands, she took down a glass from the cabinet above the sink and went to the pantry, where her grandfather had kept the liquor on the top shelf. She grabbed a bottle of Bacardi and poured a large shot which she slammed down without the benefit of ice or a mixer.

She coughed and spluttered as the rum burned its way down her throat, but it wasn't enough. She knew she would never be able to get through this in her current state. She moved to the table and sat down. Grandpa Bill's fly-tying equipment was still scattered across its surface. *I can't do this*, she thought, nearly losing it again. She opened her purse and dug around in it. A growing sense of panic started to bloom in her chest before she finally found the bottle of Xanax. She jerked the top off the bottle and sent pills scattering across the table and onto the floor. Then she poured herself another shot, which she quickly tossed down along with one of the bitter pills.

She picked up one of the flies from the table and admired the details of her grandfather's handiwork. Then she noticed the black powder dusting it all like a layer of fine ash, and the fly disappeared in a blur of tears. She poured herself yet another drink and downed it as quickly as the last, desperately seeking to escape from the nightmare that had become her reality.

CHAPTER 33

Carrie woke with a start. Her blurry vision slowly cleared, revealing a large black bat, its wings spread wide against a blood-red background. The room around her was almost dark. She could just make out the Bacardi logo on the nearly empty bottle in front of her.

She lifted her head from the table and wiped away the thin streamer of drool from her cheek. Her head pounded, and her face was stiff with dried tears. She was momentarily disoriented, and then it all came back to her. She was at her grandparents' cabin on the lake. She had come to start the arduous process of going through their belongings but had fallen apart and passed out at the table. Now it was dark, and something had caused her to wake suddenly.

She sat still, listening. Outside, the wind had picked up, rustling the trees and moaning through the eaves. There was a *tick* at the window above the sink.

She jumped at the sound. She pushed away from the table, and stared at the window as she backed against the cabinets on the far side of the room. She was so dizzy she wavered, just managing to catch herself by grabbing the edge of the counter. Even so, she felt as if she might fall and spiral downward into a bottomless well.

There came another *tick*, and even though she tried to tell herself it was nothing more than moths or pine needles tapping the glass, it was a struggle to keep her imagination from running away with itself.

Outside, the wind picked up, suddenly howling and wailing. Inside, the cabin creaked and groaned.

Carrie stood there, frozen with fear. She was certain someone or some*thing* was outside. She could sense its presence. She could practically *feel* it clawing at the cracks between the logs, struggling to get inside.

Thunk!

Her heart lurched, and she barely stifled a scream. The sound had come from above, as if someone had just leapt from one of the trees and onto the roof.

She crept to the end of the kitchen and peered into the living room. It was even darker in there, but the boards over the window were still intact. She reached for the telephone that hung on the wall just above the counter and found the base unit, but the cordless handset was not in its cradle and the base had no speakerphone capabilities or keypad for dialing. She thought about her cell phone, but then remembered there was no cellular service at the cabin.

As she fought against the rising panic in her chest, she reached around into the living room, blindly feeling for the light switch on the wall. There was a faint *click* as she flipped it, but nothing happened. Then she remembered Agent Andrew's final warning as he drove off that morning. *The power's still off, so be sure you're gone well before dark.*

Without waiting for anything else, Carrie bolted around the corner and raced toward the stairs and the bedrooms on the second floor. The back bedroom had been used as an office for their business. It had a telephone, and perhaps even more importantly, it had her grandfather's gun locker in the back of the closet.

In the dark, she tripped over one of the steps and fell on the landing halfway up, cracking her shin in the process. The floorboards creaked loudly beneath her as she limped down the hallway and into the converted bedroom.

Just enough wan light filtered into the room for Carrie to see the computer desk with the printer/fax machine beside it. She rushed over, grabbed the handset, and punched in 911 before she realized the line was dead. At first, she thought someone must have cut the line like a scene in a bad horror movie, but then she realized the machine didn't work with the power off. Therefore, the telephone wouldn't work either.

"*Damn it!*" she cursed as she threw down the handset. Turning, she started toward the closet, her shin throbbing dully with each step.

Halfway across the room, she froze. She thought she had heard something downstairs. Motionless, she listened for any sounds that might give away the presence of an intruder: the squeak of a door, the creak of the stairs, or the sound of heavy breathing in the hall.

And then she heard it—a scratching, scraping sound on the roof, as if someone was dragging something across it. It went on for a few seconds, stopped, and then began again. There was no rhythm to the sound, just a random procession of thumping and scraping that pushed Carrie to the edge of hysteria.

Without taking her eyes off the window, she hurried to the closet and Grandpa Bill's gun cabinet. The cabinet was a heavy, sixteen-gauge-steel locker with a single door. And it was locked. There was a combination lock like a safe on the front and a keyhole in the latch handle, but Carrie didn't know the combination and had no idea where Grandpa Bill kept the key.

She hurried back across the room to the desk. Frantically, she searched all the drawers, pens and pencils and tiny boxes of paperclips spilling to the floor as she tossed them aside, all while continually glancing up at the window before her. Time was running out, and she knew it. At any moment, she expected to see a dark form come hurtling down from the roof and crashing through the window.

In desperation, she snatched up a gold-plated letter opener and raced back to the closet. She pulled on the cabinet's handle as hard as she could while she worked the opener into the crack between the door and the side in hopes of prying it open, but the opener bent and then snapped in two without even scratching the door.

"*Damn it*," she whimpered, hammering futilely at the cabinet before finally slumping to the floor.

Sitting there, she began contemplating her situation. Would it really be so bad to just give up and surrender to the inevitable? She had done all she could, and it hadn't been enough. She was so tired of being alone and afraid, and now that her grandparents were gone, she was *truly* alone—more alone than she had ever been before. What reason did she really have for going on anyway?

But even as those thoughts crossed her mind, she knew the answer. She owed it to her parents and grandparents who had loved her and had done so much for her, especially Audrey Gran, who had refused to let her give up after her parents' death. She owed it to them all to go on, to live a full life and continue their legacy, because that was what they would have wanted. More than that, she owed it to them to find out who had murdered them and why. They had never done anything to deserve the horrific deaths they had suffered.

Carrie knew then what she had to do. After she picked herself up off the floor, she shut the closet door. Then she moved around beside the gun cabinet and pushed against it. It was too heavy to slide across the carpet, which just buckled up in front of it, but she kept pushing, bracing herself against the wall and shoving with everything she had until the carpet ripped loose from the tackboard and the cabinet slid away from the wall slightly.

With renewed determination, Carrie slowly worked the cabinet back and forth until it blocked the closet door shut. There was just enough room between the wall and the cabinet for her to slip into. She squeezed herself into the small gap and sat down, her knees pulled up against her chest. Her only hope was that if someone did break in, they wouldn't search the house thoroughly enough to find her in the narrow recess behind the heavy cabinet.

It wasn't much, but at least she wasn't giving up.

And that, she thought, would have made her grandmother proud.

CHAPTER 34

Just sixteen miles beyond the town of Hungry Horse on Highway 2 at the western entrance to Glacier National Park lay the small town of West Glacier. While called a town, it was really nothing more than a collection of a few gift shops—all built to look like log cabins—a small grocery store, a gas station, and an Alberta Visitor Center for travelers interested in crossing the border into Canada. In the summer, West Glacier was the western entry point to Glacier National Park and the Going to the Sun Road. The narrow, two-lane road snaked its way through the park, offering grandiose views of the majestic, snowcapped mountains and numerous waterfalls that plummeted hundreds of feet down sheer stone escarpments into crystal-clear blue-green lakes. In the winter, however, from early October until late May of each year, the Going to the Sun Road was closed, buried beneath tons of snow and ice in drifts and slides up to eighty feet deep.

During that time, travelers wishing to reach the east side of the park had to continue on past West Glacier, following the route of Highway 2, which dipped around the southern edge of the park along the boundary between Glacier National Park and the Flathead National Forest. The highway, which followed the valley that had been cut between the mountains by the Flathead River, ran roughly parallel to the river that had been dammed up to form Hungry Horse Reservoir. At the southernmost point of the highway just past the tiny burg of Essex, the road extended about halfway down the reservoir's length before it turned back northward toward East Glacier, the Blackfoot Indian Reservation, and Canada. During summer and the peak of tourist season, the road was well traveled, but in the winter, hardly any traffic at all was found on the road.

It was at this point on the highway that a late-model Ford Taurus made its way along the lonely road. The sun had just dipped behind the mountains, the rosy glow of twilight slowly spreading across the sky. Snow chains on the tires made an awful clattering sound that echoed down the valley like the roar of a distant avalanche. The highway had been plowed, the snow piled in dirty mounds along each side of the road, but dangerously slick patches still lurked within the shadows of the mountain.

With the onset of night, the deepening cold pressed ever more insistently against the windows, but Tammy Knowles felt as warm and as cozy as she could ever remember having felt in her entire life. She looked over at Danny—as she had done countless times in the past two days—and in particular his left hand on the steering wheel. The shiny silver band was still there. Again, she felt the warm glow spread outward from the core of her being through her entire body—a tingling wave of absolute bliss from her fingertips to her toes.

Danny glanced over at her. He wasn't the greatest looking guy in the world. In fact, to be totally honest, he was more than a little pudgy, with unruly brown hair, plain brown eyes, and the remnants of acne scars on his nose and cheeks. But he was sweet and kind, and he loved her for who she was in spite of her big nose and small breasts. He smiled, looking a little shy and embarrassed and perhaps even a little nervous all at the same time, which only made her love him that much more.

They had gone a few miles farther when a sudden thumping came from the back of the car.

"Ah, fuck," Danny cursed as he looked in the rearview mirror.

Tammy rolled her eyes. He wasn't exactly Prince Charming either. "What is it?" she asked, looking behind them.

"I think we've got a flat," he groaned. He slowed and turned on the hazards. "I knew I shouldn't have put the chains on so soon."

"So what do we do?" Tammy asked, a hint of uneasiness creeping into her voice.

"Don't worry," Danny said. "There's a spare in the trunk. I'll just change it. We'll be fine. The roads aren't that bad, and we've still got the chains on the other three tires. Once we get to the next town, we'll find someone to fix it."

Just ahead was a scenic overlook complete with dozens of parking spaces and a little brick building housing the restrooms, which Danny pulled into. The rest stop had also been plowed, although not as thoroughly as the highway. Snow still clung to the asphalt in slick, frozen patches that made loud, crackling sounds as they drove over them.

Tammy looked out the window. Across the valley, an elevated train trestle crossed a deep gorge cut by the rapidly flowing Flathead River. To the right, in stark contrast to the rest of the dark mountain, a large white flank stood out in the gathering gloom.

Just in front of the car was an angled metal plaque detailing the area for tourists. Tammy opened her door and gingerly made her way across the icy macadam.

The marker was titled, "the Salt Lick." The location was a favorite of mountain goats, which, in the summertime, came to the spot to lick the salt from the exposed stone.

Intrigued, Tammy looked at the Salt Lick, but there were no goats to be seen. The trees across the river rustled in the rising breeze, and the tiny hairs on the nape of her neck stood on end as the cold knifed across it. A shiver slid down her spine. She pulled her coat tighter around her and carefully shuffled back to the car.

She adjusted the rearview mirror in order to watch while Danny banged around in the trunk and pulled out the jack and the spare tire. He moved to the passenger side, and after a few moments, the back of the car began to rise. Tammy looked at the rearview mirror on her side. She could see his dark silhouette, which was lit up intermittently by the hazards as he worked the crank. *At least the flat's on the passenger side of the car*, she thought. That way she didn't have to worry about him getting run over, which she would have if the flat had been on the other side, even though there was hardly any traffic on the highway.

Danny had the car jacked up in almost no time. With the rear of the car in the air, Tammy could no longer see him in the mirror. She thought about adjusting it to see better, but it was electric, and the controls were on the driver's side armrest. Plus, Danny had them adjusted so he could see while he drove, and she didn't want to mess them up for him.

A sudden knock at the window caused Tammy to jump. She turned and saw Danny grinning sheepishly. She rolled down the window.

"Sorry. Didn't mean to scare you," he said. "But would you mind turning off the car, I'm about to choke to death on the fumes back here. You can leave the stereo on. It's not gonna take me that long."

"Sure," she said. After she rolled the window back up, she leaned over and switched off the ignition, leaving it in the accessory position. She turned the stereo back up to keep her occupied until Danny was finished.

Outside, it had started to snow. The first big flakes blowing against the windshield began to melt almost immediately, but with the heater off, it didn't take long for them to begin to accumulate. It was beautiful, but it also concerned her. They still had a fair ways to go to the Prince of Wales Hotel in Canada, and now that one of the tires was flat—

Thunk.

The car shook as if it had been hit by something. Tammy looked at the mirror, but it was obscured by the snow. She couldn't see anything out the window either, except for the white ground, which lit up intermittently with the flashing red light of the hazards. She figured it was just Danny putting on the spare. Then she thought she heard him call out.

She turned down the music. It was silent except for the *blink* ... *blink* ... *blink* of the hazards. She rolled down the window and stuck her head out. "Honey, did you call me?" He wasn't beside the car anymore; she could see his silhouette behind it. It looked as if he was hunched over something on the ground, but it was too hard to see amid the brief flashes of red light.

"Danny?" she called out louder this time.

When he didn't respond, she got out to see if he needed help. The wind whipped her hair into her face. She pulled it back out of her eyes and looked at the ground, making sure not to slip.

The red light flashed on the snowy ground.

Blink. Blink. Blink.

The dark form huddled behind the car raised as she approached.

It wasn't Danny.

It took a moment for her mind to grasp the horrific scene before her.

Danny lay on the ground, unmoving, his midsection a bloody mess that spilled onto the pavement, glistening in the light of the hazards.

Blink. Blink. Blink.

Tammy screamed.

The dark form turned in her direction.

She ran.

She didn't even think about trying to get back into the car. She *couldn't* think. Rational thought was gone. She didn't know where she was running or if she might slip and fall or how long she could survive outside in the cold. She just ran as fast as she possibly could. She ran past the open door and the front of the car, across the beam of the headlights, and into the middle of the highway, her breath coming in harsh, raspy gasps, the cold air burning her lungs.

Blink.

Twenty feet in front of the car, a sudden, sharp pain pierced her shoulder as if she had been stabbed.

Blink.

She tried to scream, but all that came out was a faint, wheezing gasp as she was driven to the ground.

Blink.

CHAPTER 35

The faint glow of colored lights glimmered in a wet smear across the windshield. It was snowing, and the best the defroster could do was melt it into a half-frozen slush that the wipers smeared back and forth. From out of the darkness came the red and blue flashers of a police cruiser and a line of pink-white flares. Still bleary-eyed, Kyle watched from the backseat as a highway patrol officer used his flashlight to direct them forward.

The abandoned car had been found in the rest area off Highway 2 overlooking the Salt Lick, which would not normally have been such a big deal. In this country, because of the severe weather, it was not uncommon for stranded motorists to get a ride to the nearest gas station or back to town, where they could call for help or wait until morning. It was *not* common, however, for the hazards to be left on, the trunk open, and the passenger's door left ajar.

The patrolman was bundled up in a thick, nylon parka, the hood pulled up and tightened until only a small portion of his face was exposed. He looked at the truck, and seeing the light rack and the county sheriff's seal on the door, he waved them through.

Just ahead, the sheriff's Yukon and the coroner's Suburban sat beside a state trooper's vehicle and a flatbed wrecker. Behind them was Marasco's Expedition. No one had said anything about it, but Kyle wondered why Clayton had picked them up instead of Marasco.

The spotlights on all the vehicles were aimed at a maroon Ford Taurus. A group of three or four men huddled about the abandoned vehicle. Long, black shadows cast by the spotlights swept across the car as the men moved about.

Deputy Johnson pulled in behind Marasco's truck and stopped. The police radio crackled as someone was dispatched to an unrelated call. Clayton reached under his seat and pulled out a big Maglite which he handed to Lewis. They stepped out into the blustery wind and blowing snow. Clayton pulled up the hood on his parka, and Kyle found himself wishing the FBI coat he wore was as well-equipped for such an environment.

As they made their way toward the car, the largest of the dark figures turned toward them. It was Sheriff Greyhawk.

"What've we got?" asked Lewis.

"Abandoned car with large amounts of blood in front and behind the vehicle." He led them to the back of the car and pointed at the ground where a section of the pavement had been marked off. A large dark stain spread across the asphalt. A wide smear of blood trailed off toward the edge of the lot as if a body had been dragged through it. Small numbered tags had been placed on the ground beside the spots. A technician took snapshots of the area, the strobe causing the blood to flash bright red. Snow blew about, and occasionally, the technician had to stop and clear away some of the accumulation before he continued.

"Any chance they hit a deer or something?" Lewis asked.

"There's no damage to the car," said the sheriff, his deep voice carrying easily through the wind. "It looks as if someone was changing a tire. At first, the trooper who came across the scene thought that whoever was changing it might have been hit by a passing car, but the flat was on the passenger side. Then he found blood in front of the vehicle. We found this just beyond it." The sheriff held up a small plastic evidence bag. Inside was a female's wedding ring.

Lewis pointed his flashlight at the bag. "No bodies?" he asked as he looked at the ring.

"No, we searched the surrounding area as well as we could in the dark but didn't find anything. From everything we've seen, it looks like there were two victims. In both cases, there are trails leading away from the area, as if the bodies were dragged part of the way. Then the trail just stops, as if they were picked up and carried away."

"Any footprints?"

"If there were, they've been covered by the snow. But look at this." The sheriff pointed his flashlight at the front of the car.

Mounted to the bumper was a metal trailer hitch that could be raised and lowered to enable the vehicle to be towed.

"You think it was being towed?" Lewis asked.

"It could explain where the bodies are," George offered.

Lewis nodded and handed his flashlight to Kyle. Lewis pulled out his little black pad and made a few notes, including the number of the Idaho license plate.

"So you think someone had a flat on the car they were towing, and when they stopped to change the tire, someone came along and jumped them, stashed their bodies in the back of the motor home, and took off."

"Maybe," the sheriff replied.

"So we're looking for two vehicles," said Lewis.

"That's assuming it wasn't a hitchhiker," said Marasco. "He could have caught a ride somewhere along the way, maybe even with the people in this car. Then when the car had a flat, he might have gotten nervous that a trooper might come along and decided not to wait."

Clayton chimed in, "You know, people are a lot more likely to pick up hitchhikers in bad weather."

"And who else would be more desperate for a ride than our old buddy Tucker?" noted Marasco.

"But how could he have gotten this far?" Kyle asked. They were at least forty or fifty miles from Tucker's cabin.

"Hungry Horse Reservoir is just on the other side of that mountain," the sheriff said with a nod. "And Jewel Basin is just beyond that. There are trails through the backcountry all the way from there to here. It's a long way, but he could have made it."

"There's been plenty of time for him to get here from the Joneses' cabin. And if anyone knows these mountains, it's Tucker," said Marasco.

"Okay," Lewis said, "we don't want to jump to any conclusions here, but we need to get a message out to all the border stations along the Canadian border, telling them to be on the lookout for anyone fitting Tucker's description just in case. And run the plates through the DMV to see if we can find out who owns the car."

"I've already contacted the border agents," said Marasco. "The car's registered out of Idaho. The office is trying to contact the Idaho DMV."

Lewis nodded as he took more notes. "Tell Davidson to get us any information he can regarding the blood types, fingerprints, footprints, hair samples, anything that can confirm or clear his presence at the scene as fast as possible. We don't want to go running off half-cocked. The press'll have a field day if we make the wrong call on this."

Lewis took the flashlight back from Kyle and stuffed it and his notepad back into his coat, which he quickly zipped back up. "Damn, it's cold," he growled. "Any chance there's any hot coffee around here?"

"Yeah," Clayton replied. "In a big Thermos in the back of my truck. It's hot, and it's strong."

"Just what I need," Lewis said.

Kyle followed them back toward the truck. They were going to be here for some time still, and even though he usually didn't drink coffee, he was tired and cold enough at the moment that he was willing to drink just about anything if it would help him stay warm and awake.

CHAPTER 36

Carrie was surprised to see sunlight sneaking beneath the closet door when she woke. She didn't remember falling asleep again, and she was oddly surprised to find that nothing had happened. Her head was pounding, and her neck was stiff from the awkward position she had slept in. As she tried to stand up, needles of pain shot through her left arm and hand, which had fallen asleep. She groaned and began shaking and rubbing her hand in an effort to restore some feeling. Gradually, the tingling numbness faded away, and she was able to pull herself out from behind the gun cabinet.

She opened the closet door slowly and cautiously peered into the room. Everything appeared to be as it should. She listened for a while and heard nothing but the whistling of a bird perched in the tree outside the window. She slipped from the closet down the hall to the bathroom. There were no obvious signs that an intruder had been upstairs. She wasn't sure what signs she might have been able to pick up on, aside from the fact that things just *felt* right.

In the bathroom, she turned on the cold water and splashed her face to help wake up and to relieve some of the painful throbbing of her head. She fumbled through the medicine cabinet until she found a bottle of extra strength Tylenol. She popped the cap off and took four of the caplets, washing them down by drinking straight from the faucet.

Standing back up, she looked at herself in the mirror. Her hair was a tangled mess in spite of being pulled back in a ponytail, and her face was red and splotchy. Her eyes were even worse. They were puffy and red and underscored by dark, half-moon-shaped blotches, but more than that, the irises looked glazed and unfocused like ...? Like a drunk, she forced herself to admit. She didn't think she was a full-blown alcoholic, but she had certainly been too dependent on booze and pills of late.

As she stood there, taking stock of herself, she found she was ashamed of her behavior last night and, in fact, for the last several months. She should never have put herself in the position of being alone in the cabin after dark. She had been warned, and she knew better; however, her little drinking binge had caused her to lose all sense of rational thought. And this time, it could have cost her her life.

Though she would never have admitted it before, she realized that in some sense, that was exactly what she had been trying to do. Ever since things with Bret had gone bad, she had been doing nothing but going through the motions, waiting for her life to hurry up and be over so she wouldn't be subjected to the possibility of being hurt again. She had never openly contemplated suicide, yet somewhere, deep down inside her in a place she hadn't been willing to look, a part of her had been trying to attain the same result in a much more subtle manner.

And, in fact, that deepest, darkest part of her had already succeeded to some extent. She had withdrawn so much that she had stopped living, for all intents and purposes. The vibrant and confident Carrie that her grandmother had worked so hard to resurrect after the death of her parents was gone again, leaving nothing more than a shell of the person she had been, an automaton passing through the days, waiting for the end.

It was that part of her that had hoped that something would happen last night, that she would be put out of her misery by someone else. But when she had thought that someone was actually breaking in, she had been much more terrified of dying than she would have ever thought. Down in that deepest of dark places, along with the fear and despair, hope still lurked as well, waiting for just the slightest ray of sunshine to come into her life so that it might blossom.

Perhaps she *had* inherited more than just hair and eye color from her mother's side of the family. That was certainly the way Audrey Gran had seen things.

Carrie made her way downstairs, still on the lookout for someone who might be lurking within the house. In the kitchen, she nearly became sick at the smell of rum that permeated the room from the open bottle on the table. She picked up the bottle and poured the remains down the sink. Standing there, she noticed the other bottles still on the top shelf. She stood there a moment, staring at the bottles. Then, she grabbed three of them and emptied them in the sink as well. By the time she was done, there were eight empty bottles on the counter. She found the garbage bags in the cabinet under the sink and filled one with the empty bottles.

She took the bag, the bottles clinking nosily as they bumped against her leg, and dumped it on the porch outside the back door. She was about to close the door when she noticed the tip of a tree limb hanging just over the edge of the roof. She couldn't quite reach it, so she went back inside and dragged one of the kitchen chairs back outside with her. When she stood on the chair, she was just able to reach up and pull the limb down. It was larger than she had expected, and it made a hideous noise as it scraped across the roof before it fell over the edge.

Tears welled in Carrie's eyes as an unexpected realization came to her. She bit her lip, struggling to keep from breaking down as she stared at the cause of her night of terror—a harmless tree limb.

Something within her snapped. Heedless of the cold, she stomped out into the snow, grabbed the limb, and dragged it away from the landing. With a loud scream, she tossed it toward the trees, where it tumbled and bounced into the undergrowth. She tilted her head back and yelled again as loud as she could, the veins on her neck standing out and her face turning red as all of the hurt and anger and frustration surged forth.

Breathing heavily, she listened with satisfaction as the yell echoed down the valley. The cold air in her lungs felt good, and her head felt clearer. After she brushed off her wet cheeks, she turned and marched back inside.

She still hadn't decided what she was going to do with the place; however, she *had* decided on one thing she was going to do, and she started back upstairs with a renewed sense of purpose.

In the office, she began going through all of her grandparents' paperwork that hadn't been taken away by the feds, looking for anything unusual, relying on her reporter's nose for the suspicious in an effort to find out why someone might have had a reason to kill her grandparents. The computer and appointment books for the trips they had booked for the coming year as well as the two previous had been confiscated, which didn't leave her much. She went through all of the invoices, letters, tax returns, and any other paperwork for the last two years that had been filed away in boxes in the closet, but she didn't find anything that seemed out of the ordinary.

After an hour of fruitless digging, Carrie decided there was nothing of significance to be found. Undaunted, she had already decided on her next course of action. Going downstairs, she found the keys to the Hummer hanging on a pegboard on the wall next to the phone in the kitchen—right where she had known they would be.

As she lifted the keys from the peg, she was almost overcome by emotion once again. Grandpa Bill had always been bad about misplacing his keys, and so at Christmas one year just after Carrie had moved in, she and Audrey Gran had given the little pegboard to Bill as a gift. The board was painted yellow, the varnish old and crackled. There were little squiggles that Carrie had painted to look like flying birds across the top, and *Grandpa Bill's keys* painted in colorful letters across the bottom.

Clutching the keys in her hand so hard they dug into her skin, Carrie bit her lip and hurried out the door.

CHAPTER 37

Maryland

A cold drizzle fell on Baltimore. Splashing through the puddles in the rutted roadway, a black Lincoln rolled slowly past row after row of warehouses along the waterfront. The Lincoln's brilliantly polished surface and mirrored windows reflected the lead-gray color of the sky and the bay, which caused the car to appear more silver than black.

The car slowed and then turned and pulled up to the concrete wall of the loading dock in front of warehouse number thirty-seven. Two closed-circuit cameras mounted innocuously on each corner of the warehouse pivoted toward the car.

A security guard wearing a vinyl rain slicker stepped out from a door to the left of the car. Unlike most contract security employees, old men, or washed-up police officers with big guts hanging over their belts, this one was young and built like a linebacker. He was tall, at least six foot two, with broad shoulders and a thick neck. The small amount of hair that could be seen beneath his hat was cropped short on the nape of his neck and above his ears. He didn't slouch or waddle or tug on his belt to hike up his pants as he walked toward the car but remained perfectly upright, moving with a self-assured precision learned only in the military.

The driver's side window slid down. Warm air smelling of cinnamon spilled out. Inside, Nathan nodded at the guard, who bent down to look inside the car.

"Welcome, general," the guard said with a tip of his hat to the passenger in the backseat. Satisfied, he returned inside the warehouse. Moments later, a steel ramp tilted up in front of the car, and the loading dock door slid open. The Lincoln pulled up the ramp and disappeared inside.

On the outside, the warehouse had looked as old and weather-beaten as all the others along the wharf, but inside was another matter. Inside, the cinder-block walls, structural steel, and underside of the roof were all perfectly white. Row upon row of high-intensity, mercury-vapor lights ran the length of the building, reflecting off the highly buffed, clear-coated seal on the concrete floor. The overhead door, which had appeared to be old and rickety from the outside, actually consisted of three large sections of one-inch-thick plate steel with weathered and paint-chipped wood bolted to the outside to give it the desired effect.

Inside, three steel barricades operated by hydraulics in the floor had been raised, one on each side of the car and one in front, allowing just enough room for it to pull into the warehouse. Nathan put the car in park and killed the engine as the overhead door slid shut behind them.

A six-foot-long aluminum tube with evenly spaced holes along its length descended from the ceiling. It looked like one of the attachments at an automatic car wash that might spray down the car with soap or wax. From somewhere overhead came the high-pitched whine of a large fan and motor building up speed. Then the arm began slowly making its way around the front, sides, and rear of the car. There was a loud sucking sound as the arm passed the windows on each side of the car.

The general recognized the device as a sniffer—a high-powered vacuuming system that took air samples from around the car and passed it through an analyzation chamber where the air was checked for minute traces of explosive chemicals other than those found in gasoline.

In the year and a half since he had accepted his new position, General Colquitt had prided himself on the new security measures he had instituted at his company. In fact, some people had claimed they were so extreme as to seem paranoid, but this was so far beyond anything they had implemented—or anything even currently available on the open market—that it made their system seem archaic. And that was something the general did not like.

After the sniffer retracted, the barricade on the left side of the car lowered to the floor with a *boom* that echoed throughout the cavernous interior of the building.

"Stay with the car, Nathan," General Colquitt said as he got out. "Make sure no one gets near it."

"Yes, sir, general," Nathan replied.

The general paused, taking the time to adjust his tie and straighten the wrinkles from his jacket before stepping across the lowered barricade. Once across, the hydraulics lifted it back into its upright position.

Across the warehouse in the right-hand corner of the building, two brand new, black Kenworth semis with long, silver trailers sat parked side-by-side. They looked like something that might be seen on the NASCAR circuit were it not for their obvious lack of company logos plastered over every square inch or, for that matter, any identifiable markings whatsoever.

In front of him, two chain-link fences topped with razor wire ran the length of the building. The guard escorted the general to a golf cart sitting in the wide aisle between the fences. Rows of cameras hanging from the ceiling in domed enclosures tracked the golf cart as it made its way down the aisle toward the far end of the warehouse.

Behind the fences were row upon row of steel racks, stacked to the ceiling with various containers. There were large wooden crates and pallets of cardboard boxes tightly shrink-wrapped with heavy-gauge plastic and woven, hundred-pound sacks of rice and flour and sugar.

Colquitt knew that nothing stored on this level was out of the ordinary. This level was for the tents and blankets, building materials, tools, water and food rations, and nonsensitive medical supplies, such as Band-Aids, bandages, cotton balls, tongue depressors, Q-tips, splints, crutches, and wheelchairs—everything that an incredibly well-funded humanitarian relief group would have.

The *really* interesting stuff was stored several stories below in a cavernous vault filled with containers of every imaginable size and shape, ranging from as small as a shoebox to as big as a railcar. There were industrial-size refrigerators, freezers, hundreds upon hundreds of unmarked black fifty-gallon drums, and even farther below in a specially sealed vault, row upon row of gleaming, vacuum-sealed, titanium canisters. All of this, much of which were items developed by his own company, were kept where they were safe from prying eyes or—though highly unlikely—an ill-intentioned intruder who might somehow manage to make it inside the warehouse.

At the end of the long aisle was a single door. Colquitt's escort inserted his hand into the boxy palm reader beside it. The general smirked. At his facility, they had already moved beyond the old-fashioned readers. Then he noticed the mirror above the reader, no doubt concealing a thermal-imaging camera behind, and the smirk slipped from his face. There was a *beep*, and the door in front of them slid open, revealing an elevator cab. Inside, the guard pressed the bottom one of three unmarked buttons.

There were no lights to indicate the direction of movement or what floor they were on, but the general knew they were going down. After several seconds, the doors slid open again. It was as if they had been magically transported onto the executive level of a Wall Street brokerage firm. The walls of the corridor, unbroken on each side by doors, were covered floor to ceiling with panels of dark mahogany. Gold sconces housing halogen lamps spaced evenly along the walls lit the expanse in soft blue-white light. At the far end, a pair of mahogany doors with gold hardware awaited. Colquitt had never been here before—in fact, very few people even knew of its existence—but he was suitably impressed.

Neither spoke as they strode toward the doors, their heels clicking sharply on the polished marble floor.

At the end of the hall, the escort opened the door on the right, waited for the general to step inside, and then shut the door behind him.

General Colquitt found himself in a large conference room. A long polished mahogany table ran the length of the room, with burgundy leather chairs at each end but none in between. Across the room, opposite the general, another set of double doors led into the room.

The general sat down in the nearest chair and tugged his jacket taut to remove any wrinkles. After five minutes, the general began to feel agitated, but he refused to let it show. He knew he was being monitored. He remained seated, his posture perfect.

After fifteen minutes, he was furious, but outwardly, his appearance remained unchanged.

Then after twenty minutes, the door at the far end of the room swung inward, and Thomas Wade stepped into the room.

Thomas Wade was a tall and lanky man with a dark complexion, dark brown hair streaked with strands of gray, and a thin, crooked nose. It was the middle of winter in Baltimore, but he had a deep bronze tan. His face was ruddy with acne scars still clearly visible in spite of the store-bought tan. His hair was slicked back, and he wore an expensive, custom-tailored suit that hung on him like a pair of baggy warm-ups. He might have been trying to look like a high-toned NBA coach, but to Colquitt, he came off looking more like a low-budget porn star.

A cigarette with a long ash dangling precariously at the tip hung from Wade's thin lips. Smoking was not allowed in any public buildings these days, but Thomas Wade and his organization were not subject to such petty rules. They were above the law—or so Wade thought. The only laws his organization obeyed were the ones they made for themselves.

General Colquitt despised Thomas Wade, but like any good soldier, he kept his opinions to himself. Everything about Wade annoyed him, not the least of which was the fact that he demanded that everyone call him "Thomas," as if that made him more respectable. He was loud, brash, arrogant, cocky, and rude. But worst of all, he was a civilian. He had no military training and no discipline whatsoever. He was full of himself and full of shit, which meant he fit right in with the movers and shakers in DC. And it was through his connections with those people—some of the most powerful and influential political figures in the country—that he had managed to wheedle his way to the top of his organization. And now the general was forced to deal with him.

Wade carried a black plastic ashtray with him, which he sat on the table and knocked his ash into. It was the only thing he had brought with him to the meeting.

That was another thing about Wade's organization that irritated the general. Nothing was ever written down, taped, or otherwise documented. It was just one of the ways they were able to maintain complete deniability. There was never any incriminating evidence to worry about, and the few witnesses who might exist were always easily persuaded or simply eliminated.

"Anderson, this is some fucked-up shit you've got us into," Wade said as he sat down.

The general bristled. Even though he had retired from the military, everyone still referred to him as "General Colquitt." Everyone except for Wade.

"I would remind you that the situation existed before I took over," the general said, doing his best to hide his indignation. "That is why I was brought in—to ensure that mistakes were eliminated."

Wade leaned back and pursed his lips as if he were considering whether or not to accept the general's statement. "And you think the only way to clean this one up now is by sending in one of my teams again."

"Yes." *Believe me, you sack of shit,* thought Colquitt, *if Nathan could handle this by himself, he would already be on his way, and I wouldn't be here listening to your ignorant ass.*

Wade blew out a cloud of smoke and squinted at the general. "How certain are you about what's going on? This is a damn risky operation you're proposing. I've already hung my ass out for you on this. Do you have any idea the strings I had to pull to get the forensic evidence suppressed?" he asked, pointing at the general with his cigarette. "I practically had to get on my hands and knees and blow the director myself, and that's not something I care to repeat anytime soon. I'm in the business of granting favors, not asking them. *I* collect the IOUs, not the other way around. I don't like owing people. And now you're asking me to lay my dick out on the chopping block again. I'm not sure I want to risk exposing my organization, if you know what I mean," he said with a wry grin.

You think you're so clever, don't you? You fucking moron. The general struggled to maintain his composure as he spoke. "The risk is nothing compared to the disaster this situation could become if nothing is done in time."

"What are we talking about here? What do you need?"

"Four to six of your best men and equipment. Transportation to and from. I'll provide one of my scientists, Myles Bennett, along with the necessary specialized equipment. He can brief them in route."

"How much time are we talking about here?"

"Not counting transportation, twenty-four to forty-eight hours max. Anything beyond that and we risk further exposure."

Wade leaned back and took another drag of his cigarette. Colquitt sat perfectly still, his hands flat on the conference table, looking straight ahead at Wade. He knew the *son of a bitch* was reveling in his little power trip, but the general was determined not to give him the satisfaction of seeing him squirm.

Wade blew out another cloud of smoke. "It'll take seventy-two hours to put it together. Make sure your man's ready."

"He'll be ready," said the general.

"All right," Wade said as he stood to leave. "But if this operation goes to shit, it's *your* ass, not mine," he said, crushing his cigarette in the ashtray.

CHAPTER 38

Montana

Carrie took the Hummer—which was legally hers now—into town. Compared to her Lexus, it felt like she was driving a semi, but she was glad to have it. Last night's storm had dumped four to six inches of new snow on the ground and littered the roadway with pine needles and broken tree limbs. None of it was a problem for the truck. Grandpa Bill had equipped it with a custom off-road package. It had a heavy-duty suspension and four-wheel drive with specially designed snow tires—which caused it to ride even higher than normal—as well as aftermarket pipe bumpers on the front and rear, a roll bar behind the cab with four floodlights, and last but not least, an electric winch on the front.

It took a little longer than usual, but when she reached Kalispell, she stopped at her motel to take a quick shower and change clothes. With her hair damp from the shower, she simply combed out the tangles and pulled it back in a ponytail. Other than eyeliner, Carrie hadn't worn makeup in months, and today, she didn't even take the time for that. She slipped into a pair of jeans and was about to pull on a sweater when, on second thought, she decided to wear her gray Stanford University sweatshirt. After she pulled on her boots and ski jacket, she gathered up her purse and satchel before she headed out the door.

After she climbed back into the Hummer, Carrie headed for the next place on her agenda. As she drove, she couldn't help but think about the case. The odds of so many murders occurring in such a small town over such a short period of time had to be astronomical. It had to be more than just coincidence. Call it reporter's intuition or a logical assumption based on the facts, but she felt certain that something strange was going on. The events taking place hinted at something much larger—perhaps even a conspiracy of some sort—something she was familiar with. In her career as a journalist, she thrived on such cases. She had always thought of them as similar to one of Audrey Gran's needlepoints. Intricately woven, it all started with the first thread. Once you found that thread, you followed it to the next one, and from there, you moved to the next until a pattern began to emerge. If you kept at it long enough, the entire scene would finally come into view. It was how she made her living—and she was *damn* good at it.

There was *something* that tied it all together, and regardless of what the police and the FBI were doing—or weren't doing—she was determined to find that thread.

After she parked in one of the visitor's spots, she got out and strode into the offices of the *Kalispell Mountain Herald*, where she asked to see Wallace Hipple.

* * *

"Ah, Miss Daniels," Wallace said with insincere aplomb as he stepped into the reception area. "How can I help you?"

"Well," she said, "if it's not too much of an imposition, I was hoping I might take a look at some of your back issues."

"Why, certainly," he replied. "Always glad to help out a fellow reporter." Carrie was a little taken aback by the comment. They had only briefly met once at her grandparents' funeral, and the fact that he knew of her occupation was somewhat unsettling, even though it wasn't all that surprising. After all, he was a reporter who had recently done a story on her grandparents. Like any good reporter, he had obviously done his homework.

"Here, let me help you with your coat," he said, reaching out for her sleeve. Carrie's chest tightened much like a skittish dog might react around a stranger. As she fought against the rising anxiety, she turned about and allowed Wallace to take her coat. He hung it on the rack in the corner. As he turned back around, he noticed her sweatshirt.

"Stanford, eh?" he said with an approving nod. "Fine school. Good journalism program. After I graduated from Cornell, I almost went to graduate school at Stanford," he said as he led her into the back. "But I had to return to Oregon for my mother's sake—God rest her soul."

After their first meeting, Carrie had pegged Wallace Hipple as a stuffy pseudo-intellectual, and her hunch had been correct. She had worn the shirt, thinking it might help her curry favor with him when she asked to use their computers, but now she was beginning to have second thoughts about it.

"I'm glad you're in," she lied. "I thought you might be down at the police station."

"Yes, well, that's what junior reporters are for, isn't it?" he said with a smug grin.

Carrie tried to humor him by smiling back. Hopefully, it didn't appear as fake to him as it felt to her.

"Besides," Wallace said. "In a town this size, one tends to make some very good contacts over time. Everyone knows who I am. I don't have to go digging for information like I did in the early days. These days, the information comes to me."

The man's pomposity was nauseating. "How nice for you," Carrie said.

In spite of her polite attempts of refusal, Wally gave Carrie the full tour of the offices, showing her virtually every square inch of the place before finally leading her to the research and archives department.

"I know we're a little behind the times, but we just converted to a computerized archival system a few years back," Wally explained as he pointed at the workstation. "The computer is tied to our in-house network and has access to any of the stories run during that time. They're all stored on our server under the 'P' drive. Just think 'Past' issues if you can't remember. It also has an Internet connection, so you can access any of the online information sources, including Nexis. If you need it, just let me know, and I can log in to it for you. If you need anything further back than about ten years, I'm afraid you'll have to do it the old-fashioned way. All of our microfiche issues are stored in the filing cabinets by year, going back to 1965. And if you're looking for anything before that, you'll have to go to the old hard-copy volumes in those binders on the bookshelves. If you need to print out or copy anything, the printer and the copier are just around the corner."

"Thanks," Carrie replied.

Wallace nodded and remained silent for a moment, as if in anticipation of an explanation. When she didn't offer one, he finally said, "Yes, well, I've got an important story I need to get back to. You know where my office is, right?"

"Yes, you showed me."

"Yes, well, I'll leave you to it then," he said before he finally walked away.

With a sigh of relief, Carrie sat down in front of the computer, laying her satchel on the table next to her. She pulled out the ragged notebook in which she kept all her notes and her pen, the Mont Blanc her grandparents had given her and that Agent Andrews had been kind enough to return to her. She gazed at it momentarily, grateful to have it and the fond memories it triggered still in her possession.

Before her emotions could overcome her, Carrie quickly pushed those thoughts from her mind and logged onto the computer to begin her search.

CHAPTER 39

Kyle was miserable. He had been out of the cold for hours, but he was still shaking like a leaf thanks to all the caffeine racing through his system. He had been so hungry that he had even eaten a couple of greasy, leftover donuts, but the sugar rush had just added to his misery.

Marasco suddenly burst into the room. He had been in and out all morning, checking the fax machine every five minutes in hopes that the Idaho DMV might have finally forwarded the information on the abandoned car. Everyone looked up anxiously. This time, he held a piece of paper in his hand. "Got it," he said.

The entire room seemed to come alive. "The car's registered to a Mr. and Mrs. Roy Lattimer of Pocatello, Idaho," Marasco said. "He's sixty-eight, and she's sixty-four. Fortunately, they both had their licenses renewed recently. The DMV's e-mailing us their license photos. They also ran a cross-check for us. It turns out that the Lattimers are also listed as the owners of a '91 Winnebago. License number BCK-779."

"All right, just like we thought," Lewis said, a hint of excitement creeping into his voice. He turned to look at the dry-erase board of the wall. During the wait, they had put together several course-of-action lists to be followed depending on what information they did or didn't get back. Lewis began to tick off the items under the "RV" list. "Kyle, contact our office and have them get to work on the credit card records. Tell them to check everything, not just the big ones. I want 'em all—gas cards, Diner's club, Sears, I don't care."

"I'll put the word out to my men," said the sheriff. In addition to sending the information to all the deputies on patrol, the sheriff had called in four additional officers who were going to begin checking all the privately owned campgrounds and RV parks in the area.

"Remind them not to approach the Winnebago if they come across it," said Lewis. "Tell them to call us and not to let it out of their sight until we get there. I'll call the Forest Service. Marasco, you call the border patrol. And since you did such a fine job hounding the Idaho DMV, why don't you call the police in Pocatello and ask them to check the Lattimers' residence."

Without another word, the sheriff and Marasco scattered, leaving only Lewis and Kyle in the conference room. Two extra phones had been brought in, their lines trailing across the floor and into the center of the conference table. While Lewis used one, Kyle pulled the other in front of him and began dialing the Seattle field office. With the renewed activity, the caffeine-induced jitters and racing heart that had caused him to feel so miserable only moments earlier now made him feel alive and alert, crackling with energy and anticipation. *No wonder cops get hooked on the stuff*, he thought as the phone began to ring.

* * *

It wasn't long before information began to come in. The first came from the Canadian Border Patrol, which reported that they had no records of a Winnebago, either with or without Idaho plates, crossing the border in the last forty-eight hours at either of the two nearest border stations. They promised to call immediately if such a vehicle was spotted.

The next report was from the Pocatello Police Department, which had gone to the Lattimers' house. No one was at home, but that was what they had expected. The police questioned the neighbors, who knew surprisingly little other than the fact that they had been gone for several days and who confirmed that they had taken the motor home and the car. More and more, as the pieces began to fall in place, it was beginning to look as if their theories about Tucker might be right.

It was the FBI's turn next, and when Kyle took the call, he knew they were on to something. He waved at Lewis to get his attention. He repeated the information out loud as he wrote it down. "Right. You got charges on a Visa from the Lakeshore RV Park and the IGA Market in Lakeside on the twenty-seventh … and the Stone Creek Cafe on the twenty-eighth. Right," Kyle said. Even as he was writing down the addresses, the others in the room were already preparing to head out. As soon as he hung up, they were on their way. Marasco stayed behind in case any new information came in.

In the truck, the sheriff got on the radio and coordinated with his deputies. Two of them were to meet them at the RV park, while two others were to follow up with the IGA Market where the charges had been made.

* * *

Lakeside was a small community of private houses, motels, lodges, and a few RV parks nestled along Highway 93 about fifteen miles south of Kalispell on the northwest side of Flathead Lake. When they arrived, a pair of deputies was already there, waiting just outside the entrance to the RV Park. They had talked with the manager and verified that the Lattimers had rented a space. According to the records on file, they had been driving a '91 Winnebago, Idaho plate number BCK-779 and a maroon Ford Taurus, Idaho plate number TJM-426.

"That's them," Lewis said.

"They're in space A-16. The manager says they're still here. Said they've rented the space through the weekend," said the deputy.

"They're still here?" Lewis asked, surprised. They had been working on the assumption that the RV would be gone.

They pulled into the park, taking care to stop before coming into view of space A-16, where a cream-colored Winnebago sat.

Kyle and Lewis got out and quietly slipped across the snow-covered road, taking up positions next to the door while the sheriff and Clayton watched from across the way. Even though it was unlikely that Tucker would have returned to the same location, they weren't taking any chances.

Lewis reached under his coat, placed his hand on his gun, and nodded to Kyle. They had decided to knock on the door to see if anyone answered. If not, the sheriff would call downtown to get a search warrant.

As he stood to the side of the door in case Tucker *was* in there and decided to greet them with a blast from his shotgun again, Kyle rapped on the door.

Inside, they heard the sound of muffled voices. The RV rocked slightly as someone within moved. Lewis raised his gun.

The door opened, revealing a pleasant-looking man with gray hair and glasses. He wore a blue terry-cloth robe over a white T-shirt. His thin, white legs were bare down to the wool slippers he wore on his feet. Kyle recognized him from the driver's license picture.

"Mr. Lattimer?" Lewis asked.

"Yes," the man replied, looking confused.

"Sorry to disturb you, sir," Lewis said, flipping open his badge. "I'm Special Agent Edwards, and this is Agent Andrews. Do you mind if we step inside? We have some questions to ask you."

"Uh, no, I guess not—" the man stammered as he backed away from the door.

Lewis stepped up first, looking in both directions inside before entering the camper. Until they were certain, Kyle knew they had to be leery of someone lurking in the RV, but the fact that Mr. Lattimer had been so quick to let them in seemed to dispel that possibility. If there *had* been a kidnapper inside, he most likely would have instructed Mr. Lattimer to try to get rid of them as quickly as possible. And unless he was a master thespian, Mr. Lattimer did not seem to be acting like a frightened kidnap victim.

The smell of coffee filled the air as Kyle stepped into the camper behind Lewis. It was accompanied by the mouth-watering scent of cooking bacon.

"Please, have a seat," Mr. Lattimer said, motioning to the small dining nook beside them. "This is my wife, Jean," he said, indicating the short, silver-haired lady standing over the gas range where the bacon popped and sizzled.

"Hi there. You fellows in that Airstream next door? Sure is a nice rig. Can I get you some coffee?" she offered.

"No," Kyle blurted. That was the last thing he needed. Lewis politely declined as well.

"Are you sure? It's—"

"Honey," her husband interrupted. "These men aren't staying here. They're with the FBI."

"Oh," she said, suddenly falling silent. An unpleasant look crossed her face like a dark cloud slipping across the sky.

"Do you own a maroon Ford Taurus?" Lewis asked.

"Yes," Mr. Lattimer replied anxiously.

Mrs. Lattimer raised a hand to her mouth, "Oh, no, what's happened?"

"We're not sure," Lewis replied. "But your car was found abandoned along Highway 2 around 1:30 this morning."

"Oh, dear God," she gasped and collapsed to the floor.

CHAPTER 40

Carrie began her search with the paper's online archive system. She started by searching for the word "murder" in any news stories within the last year. The system returned forty-three entries, each sorted by date from most recent to oldest. She scrolled to the end of the list and began reviewing the oldest ones first. She wanted to try to follow the chain of events of the last year chronologically, but she also knew that the majority of the articles within the last ten days would be about her grandparents, something she wasn't ready to deal with yet.

As she made her way through the list, she was able to eliminate many of the items simply from the titles of the articles, such as one regarding the local high school's production of *Dial M for Murder* or a book review of the latest murder mystery by Carole Nelson Douglas. Others, including several regarding a drunk driver charged with manslaughter, she skipped because they didn't fit the pattern she was looking for.

Several stories, however, did register a blip on her mental radar. As she read them, she wrote down her thoughts regarding the possible relevance of each before she went on to the next one. There was a series of articles covering the trial of a young man accused of killing his friend in a dispute over drugs and then burning down his house but not before removing all of the chemicals used in the production of crystal meth.

Then she came across the stories regarding the murder of the four Seattle men in her grandparents' rental cabin.

She knew of the murders from her discussions with the police, but she had never known any of the details until now. She was appalled by the ghastly nature of the murders. Her insides knotted up as she read, and for a moment, she thought she might get sick, but she forced herself to continue.

She filtered on through several more stories, including one about a local man, Adam Peters, who had disappeared while he was skiing. A major search had been launched, and his car had been found, but he had not. She wrote down the man's name, the date of his disappearance, and the location where his car had been found. He was an insurance salesman, which caught Carrie's attention. There were countless stories of people being murdered for insurance money, and while she knew that wasn't the reason for her grandparents' murder, it could have played a role in the murder of the Seattle men. It was at least something worth checking into, so she printed out the story before she continued on through the others.

Then she came to the first of the stories regarding her grandparents. These, she printed out without reading. She knew she would have to read them at some point, but not now, not here.

"Are we doing all right?"

Carrie jumped, a surprised squeal escaping from her.

"Pardon me," Wallace chuckled. "Didn't mean to startle you, but I was going to step out for lunch, and I thought you might want to join me."

"Oh, uh, that's very kind," Carrie replied, trying not to sound too repulsed. "But I'm not really hungry, and I'd like to finish this up before I leave. Thanks, anyway."

"Yes, well, maybe some other time then," he said with a slight bow and a polite nod. The prissy, sibilant sound of his voice and the way he moved reminded Carrie of a snake, sneaky and slithery. She shuddered in disgust as he walked away.

After she waited long enough to be sure he was gone, she made her way to the break room, where she bought a Diet Coke and a bag of pretzels.

With her lunch taken care of, she returned to the computer. This time, she tried a new angle, searching for the word "killed" instead of "murdered" to see if it came up with any different hits.

For the most part, the only stories that came up different were several stories involving people killed in various automobile accidents and one involving a couple of extreme skiers who died in an avalanche while they were attempting to ski down one of the glaciers the previous winter. There was also an unusual story from the previous summer regarding the number of goats visiting a particular location known as the "Salt Lick" just south of Essex. The appearance of the goats had been such a common occurrence in the past that a lookout had been built next to the site just off the nearby highway. But over the last year, almost all of the goats had disappeared. Carrie would have dismissed the article as simply a human-interest story and thought nothing more of it, but one item in particular caught her attention. The article speculated that poachers or illegal trappers might have killed the goats, which caused her to think of Jeffrey Wayne Tucker. Even so, she still couldn't imagine how the disappearance of a bunch of wild goats could be related to the murder of her grandparents.

Another story was a follow-up piece regarding the death of two men killed in a plane crash eighteen months earlier. Before she called it up, Carrie checked her watch and decided it could wait unit tomorrow. It was already 2:25, and she had a meeting with her grandparents' lawyer at 3:00 to go over some of the details involving the transfer of her grandparents' estate.

As she was packing up her things, Wallace appeared once again. "Oh, leaving us so soon?"

"I, uh, have a meeting to get to," Carrie said, focusing on the papers she was placing in her satchel in order to avoid eye contact. "But if it's all right, I'd like to come back tomorrow, I mean, if I wouldn't be in the way or anything."

"No, certainly not," Wallace replied. "Be our guest."

"Thank you," Carrie said, pulling her satchel over her shoulder. Ducking her head, she slipped past Wally and into the hall.

"Allow me," Wallace said, attempting to lift Carrie's satchel from her shoulder.

"Oh, no, it's fine, really. I've got it. Thank you, though," she said as she pulled away. Quickly, she made her way to the front. She knew he was there, watching her the entire way. She could practically feel the heat of his gaze warming the nape of her neck. It was everything she could do to keep from running.

* * *

Wallace Hipple watched as Carrie hurried away, amused by how flustered she became around him. *Like a schoolgirl with a crush on her professor,* he mused. He watched until she was out of sight and then went to the computer she had been using. He logged on, pulled up the Web browser, and page-by-page began scrolling backward through the links to see what she had been viewing.

CHAPTER 41

Kyle and Mr. Lattimer helped Mrs. Lattimer up from the floor. While Kyle helped her sit in the dining nook, Mr. Lattimer turned off the range and wet a dishtowel in the sink. When he returned to the nook, he sat next to his wife, who leaned her head against his shoulder. He put his arm around her and gently placed the cool cloth across the back of her neck to help calm her.

Mr. Lattimer looked up, his face twisted in misery. "Our grandson, Danny, was married last week," he began, his voice was low, thick. "We … we drove here with him and Tammy and let them borrow the car to go into Canada for their honeymoon. They were going to spend two nights at the Prince of Wales Hotel and then drive back."

"You said their names were Danny and Tammy?" Lewis confirmed as he pulled out his notepad. "And their last names?"

"Knowles," Mr. Lattimer said, a hint of disgust creeping into his voice. "He's our daughter's son. He's a good kid. His father's a worthless bastard, but Danny's a good kid. He's never been in any trouble."

"And what was Tammy's maiden name?" Lewis asked.

"It was … uh," Mr. Lattimer paused, trying to remember.

"Taylor," Mrs. Lattimer said as she looked up, taking the damp cloth from her neck and using it to dab at her puffy eyes. "She's a sweet girl. They both work at the Walmart in Pocatello."

"Do you know about what time they left yesterday?"

"Not exactly," Mr. Lattimer replied. "Around two or three, I guess."

"Were they going anywhere first? Going to meet someone? Anything like that?"

"No," said Mr. Lattimer. His wife shook her head.

"Was anyone opposed to them getting married? Parents, former lovers, anyone like that?"

"No," he answered firmly.

"Not even Danny's father?"

"The only thing he cares about is his next drink. I doubt he even knew Danny was getting married." The comment reminded Kyle of Janet. *My mother and Danny's father would make a hell of a couple*, he thought.

"Do you happen to have a picture of them?" Lewis asked.

"I took some pictures at the wedding," Mrs. Lattimer offered. "The camera's in my purse."

"I'll get it," Mr. Lattimer said. He slipped out of the booth and stepped to the small bedroom at the back of the RV.

While he was gone, Mrs. Lattimer looked at Lewis. "Their life is just starting," she said, a beseeching tone to her voice.

Lewis nodded in response.

"You have to find them," she said, the tears gathering in her eyes. "Please tell me you'll find them. Tell me they'll be okay."

A strained look came over Lewis's face. His jaw muscles tightened as he clenched his teeth. In spite of the pleading looks from Mrs. Lattimer, he remained silent. His lack of response was so noticeable it became uncomfortable. The silence was almost palpable, like a wall of glass between them.

Mr. Lattimer returned with the camera, diffusing the uncomfortable situation. Lewis took it from him.

"It's one of those digital ones," Mr. Lattimer explained, and Lewis just nodded.

"We'll get you an evidence receipt for it," Lewis said. "But we won't need to keep it long. Once we download the images, I'll have Agent Andrews call you to return it."

The Lattimers both nodded, looking helpless and lost as he and Lewis stood. Kyle got a number where they could be reached and then handed Mr. Lattimer one of his cards, assuring him that he would call as soon as they learned anything new. Then they stepped from the RV.

Neither of them spoke as they marched back across the lot into the rising wind. Tiny pellets of ice peppered him in the face, but Kyle hardly noticed. Because of their failure, a young couple was almost certainly dead. And the guilt brought on by that realization left him numb to everything else.

CHAPTER 42

Carrie woke to a bleak day. It wasn't the weather but her attitude that had changed overnight. Yesterday, she had been motivated, determined to find out what had happened to her grandparents in honor of their memory and in an effort to extract at least some small measure of vengeance. But this morning as she lay in bed, it occurred to her just how foolish her little quest really was. What did she expect to find when the FBI, with all of their vast resources, had been unable to come up with anything more substantial than rumors and wild speculation? Besides, what did it matter? Nothing she did would change the fact that her grandparents were gone. Her meeting with the attorney had only confirmed what she already knew. There were no other surviving family members, which meant that she inherited everything. But to Carrie, it also meant that she had no one left to call when she needed someone to talk to, no one to spend the holidays with or to lean on in hard times, no brothers or sisters or grandparents, aunts or uncles, or even distant cousins. There was no one.

She was alone—utterly, totally, alone.

At ten o'clock, she was still lying in bed, trails of dried tears on her cheeks. All of the notes and articles she had printed the day before lay scattered across the bed, some spilling onto the floor. She had read everything at least three times, but none of it made any sense. It was nothing but a collection of articles with the word "murder" in the text—nothing more, nothing less. She was completely at a loss as to what to do, so she just lay there.

As inevitably happened when she was in a funk like this, her thoughts began to turn toward alcohol. She knew that wasn't the answer, but as a quick fix, it would at least numb her enough so that she might be able to make it through the day without breaking down every few minutes. And she still had the bottle of Xanax in her purse.

Her cell phone rang. It was a number she didn't recognize.

"Hello," she answered, her voice low and raspy.

"Ms. Daniels, this is Agent Andrews. I'm returning your call from yesterday."

"Yes?"

"I apologize for not getting back to you sooner, but there was a lot going on at the time. I just wanted to let you know that I followed up on the return of your grandparents' computer for you."

"Oh, okay—" she said, surprised.

"Unfortunately, I don't have anything good to tell you. It's being held as evidence, and as you know, the case is still open, so I'm afraid it will have to be kept until the case is resolved and, if necessary, until the trial is completed."

"So in other words, never," Carrie growled. There was no response, and she suddenly felt guilty for taking out her frustrations on him.

"I'm sorry, Ms. Daniels, but it's really out of my—"

"I know. I know," Carrie sighed.

"Is there anything else I can do for you?"

"No, that's fine," Carrie sniffled.

After she hung up, she forced herself to get up and shuffle into the bathroom.

She felt better after a shower. It was good to be up and moving about. It helped to keep her from dwelling on her grandparents too much.

It was 10:45, and because she hadn't eaten yet, she decided to stop at the diner in front of the motel to get breakfast before she went downtown. Before she went inside, she bought a paper from the machine out front.

After she ordered, she opened the paper. The headlines announced, "IDAHO COUPLE MISSING, PRESUMED DEAD." Intrigued, she began reading. The article was by Wallace Hipple, and once again, Carrie found herself irritated by the tone of the story. But as she read on, her pulse quickened. There were elements of the story that seemed eerily familiar to her. The missing people were two young newlyweds on their way to Canada for their honeymoon. The couple's car had been found abandoned on Highway 2 just past the Salt Lick overlook. While there were signs of foul play, including blood at the scene, no bodies had been found.

The thing that jumped out at Carrie was the mention of the Salt Lick. Just yesterday, she had read about the strange disappearance of goats from that same area. And now this? The proximity and similarity of the incidents caused Carrie to wonder if something more than coincidence might be involved.

When her food arrived, she ate quickly, anxious to get back to her room to compare her notes to the article in the paper.

Back in her room, Carrie sipped from the coffee she had gotten to help motivate her as she leafed through her notes from yesterday. Finally, she found what she was looking for. She hadn't printed out the article on the goats, but she *had* noted the date the story had run, so it would be an easy matter to recall it from the archives.

She stuffed the newspaper and her notes into her satchel, grabbed the keys to the Hummer and was off.

At the newspaper, Carrie was pleased to find that Wallace Hipple wasn't in but had apparently anticipated that she would be back. He had already cleared it with the receptionist, who told her to just go on back.

Sitting in front of the computer once again, she pulled out her notepad and got to work.

She performed a search for the story with "goats" that had appeared on August 16th of the previous year and was able to retrieve the article about the Salt Lick. It had been written by a staff reporter who had interviewed Amanda Johnston, a local game warden. Part of the warden's duties had been to monitor the health of the mountain goats that came to the Salt Lick. Over time, the warden had become so familiar with the goats that she had named them—names like Gramps for the one with the long beard, Shaggy for the one with the thick, ruffled mane, and Daisy for the female that liked to eat flowers. The warden had become troubled over the last year, however, as almost all of the goats had inexplicably vanished. Ms. Johnston had been personally saddened by the loss, as well as the many tourists who came to the overlook only to find the site vacant.

The author had gone on to note that according to the game warden, there had also been an alarming increase in the number of mutilated deer and elk and even bear remains found in the surrounding areas. The State Wildlife Federation had asked for additional funding to help catch the responsible parties.

Carrie found it odd that the missing couple's car had been found in the same vicinity, and though she tried to think of any possible connection between their disappearance and those of the mountain goats, she couldn't come up with anything plausible.

Frustrated, she flipped to a new page in her notebook, turned it sideways, and with her pen, drew in a number of columns. At the top of each of the columns, she wrote, "Name, date of death, location, home, occupation, record, and motive." Then she began to methodically go back through each of the stories, filling in the columns with the pertinent information in hopes of finding a connection. If the information she needed about a specific person wasn't in the story, she tried to pull it up from other Internet sites she was familiar with like 411.com and CriminalBackground.com. It wasn't an exact science; however, it had worked for her in the past, and now more than ever, she was determined to find the common link, if one existed.

As she filled up the page, she found that she kept writing down Hungry Horse as the location of many of the incidents. Of course, a number of the deaths had happened at her grandparents' cabins, but there were several others that had occurred in the vicinity of the lake as well. Curious, she used the browser to pull up a map of the area on the computer. Her grandparents' cabins were about halfway down the lake, whereas the insurance salesman's car had been discovered near Swan Lake, which was almost due south of the cabins on the other side of the mountain range. The location of the Salt Lick was almost directly north, again in line with the cabins. The thing that leapt out at her as she looked at the map was the relative proximity of all the locations. She began ticking off the incidents in her mind: the missing goats, the honeymooning couple, the insurance salesman, the men from Seattle, her grandparents.

With the exception of the intervening mountain ranges, they had all occurred within a radius of about thirty miles.

With this new information, Carrie went back to the archives and began searching again. Only this time, she searched for stories involving Hungry Horse. There were not nearly as many, and most of them involved the cases she already knew about. There were two, however, that fit the pattern she was looking for. She read the articles chronologically in reverse, simply because that was the order in which they were listed.

One involved a teenage boy who had been staying in the cabins at the Diamond R Ranch last summer. He had gone out four-wheeling along Beaver Creek Trail late one evening and had never returned. The next day, the search-and-rescue team had found the four-wheeler covered in blood. Though rare, it was assumed that the boy had been mauled by a bear and dragged off into the woods. His body was never found. The Diamond R Ranch was located at the southern end of the reservoir, near the Spotted Bear Ranger Station. It was about twenty miles from her grandparents' cabin.

The other stories involved the plane crash that Carrie had come across yesterday. At the time, she hadn't thought there could be any relevancy to her grandparents' deaths, but now that it had come up again in the same vicinity as the other murders, she began to think about it. It seemed odd that such a flurry of murders would have taken place in such a small and sparsely populated area, especially when all of them had occurred within eighteen months after the crash.

Curious, she expanded her search to include any stories involving Hungry Horse for a four-year period prior to the crash. About a dozen articles came up, but as she read them, she found that none of them involved mysterious deaths or murders.

Suddenly, she wanted to know more details of the events surrounding that plane crash and what might have been on it.

The first story she read indicated that the final results of the NTSB's investigation into the exact cause of the crash had been inconclusive. There had originally been several theories as to the cause of the accident, including wind shear and mechanical failure, but the NTSB had been unable to conclusively pinpoint any one event as the exact cause for the crash. The NTSB's investigator-in-charge, Jack Kleister, noted that the investigation had been hampered by the fact that the plane's black box had never been recovered, and because the plane had gone down in a remote and heavily wooded area of Flathead National Park, the recovery operation and accurate reconstruction of its condition at the time of the crash had been "very difficult."

Carrie made a note of the investigator's name, printed out the story, and then began reading the earlier article.

Just under eighteen months ago on October 3rd, a corporate jet had gone down in Flathead National Forest during an ice storm. Flight records indicated the plane, which was owned by the multinational conglomerate NorCorp, had been in route from Baltimore to Seattle when it disappeared from radar approximately forty miles east of Kalispell. Search-and-rescue efforts that had been coordinated by the Montana Aeronautics Division, Flathead County Sheriff's Department, and the US Forest Service had been hampered by darkness and a blizzard, with winds up to seventy miles an hour accompanied by lightning and freezing rain that had turned to snow during the night.

Three days later, rescue workers located the wreckage in a rugged, remote area near the summit of Shadow Mountain, approximately fifteen miles east of the Spotted Bear Ranger Station, which, Carrie noted, placed it within the thirty-mile radius of the other incidents. Despite the fact that portions of the fuselage were relatively intact, there were no survivors.

The three men killed in the crash were: the pilot, James Laidlaw, age forty-eight; the copilot, Derrick Hughes, age twenty-six; and the passenger, Dr. Phillip Sandefur, age fifty-four. The article noted that the official coroner's report would be held pending positive identification of the three men by the state crime lab in Missoula.

Carrie left the paper's archive system, pulled up the Web browser, typed www.ntsb.gov and hit enter. She knew the NTSB's report would give a much more detailed account of the crash and the investigative findings than were included in the paper. The screen filled with the home page of the NTSB's website, which included postings of all its final reports of investigations into accidents involving virtually any mode of mass transit in the United States.

The site had its own search engine, which allowed her to search for all crashes within a certain date range by state and if there were any fatalities, which made it easy to find the one she was looking for. The final report was nine pages long, so instead of reading it from the screen, she printed it out and began reading as soon as the pages were spat out.

On October 3rd, a Gulfstream V-SP, number N9712E, had taken off from Baltimore International Airport in route to Seattle. At 23:18 MDT, the aircraft was contacted by the Salt Lake City Air Traffic Control Center and instructed to climb from ten thousand feet to twelve thousand feet to allow for the terrain as it crossed Montana. At approximately 23:32, the Salt Lake ARTCC lost radar contact with the plane.

According to the report, the accident occurred at 47 degrees 54.75 minutes north and 113 degrees 10.33 minutes west, which, Carrie knew from the earlier article, was on Shadow Mountain, approximately thirty miles from her grandparents' cabin.

She scanned down to the section detailing the personnel information. There had been three people killed in the crash. Two were the pilot and copilot, and the third was an employee of NorCorp. Both the pilot and copilot had originally received their training during service in the US Air Force. The pilot had flown for Delta Airlines for seventeen years before he had retired to fly on a part-time basis as a private pilot for NorCorp. The copilot had just left the air force two months prior, and this was his first commercial flight. There was an extensive investigation into the background of both men, including interviews with family and coworkers as well as the most recent medical records. The conclusion of the report was that there was no evidence to indicate that the crash had been caused by pilot negligence or error.

Of the single passenger, nothing more was mentioned aside from the fact that he was an employee of NorCorp. While this wasn't necessarily anything suspicious, it did leave Carrie to wonder about who he was and why he was being flown to Seattle on the company's private jet.

The report also contained a section detailing specific information on the plane, a Gulfstream V-SP, including its empty and maximum weight capacity, last annual inspection, and maintenance records, but again, it wasn't much help with any information that Carrie thought might be relevant, such as a description of any cargo the plane might have been carrying in addition to its mysterious passenger.

Switching tactics, she tried to go another way, namely through the website of the company that owned the plane. The NorCorp website itself was impressive, with an overview of the numerous companies that made up the giant conglomerate and products ranging from cosmetics to pharmaceuticals to medical equipment and specialty plastics.

Carrie spent over a half an hour navigating the site, scrolling through company overview after company overview and countless pages of mission statements and corporate financials. Not surprisingly, she was unable to find a single mention of the plane crash.

Undeterred, her next approach was to call up the *Baltimore Sun's* website, where she did a search through the obituary pages for the three days following the plane crash. Then on second thought, because it had taken three days to find the wreckage, she expanded her search to six days. After she printed out the results, she began reading through them, looking for any that mentioned the plane crash. The first one she found was for Derick Hughes, the copilot. As she continued through the list, she was disappointed to find that there were no other obituaries related to the crash. Next, she repeated the process with the *Washington Post's* and *Seattle Post Intelligencer's* online obits for the same date range, but again, she came up empty-handed. Because NorCorp's headquarters was located in Atlanta, she tried the *Atlanta Constitution* site as well, where she found the obituary for James Laidlaw, the pilot, but still nothing on the passenger, Dr. Sandefur.

Frustrated to the point of giving up, Carrie decided to call in someone who was better in the ways of electronic information retrieval than she could ever hope to be.

She took her cell phone from her purse and punched in the two-digit speed-dial number for her office in Denver.

"Hi, Sandy," she said to the receptionist. "Is Charlie in?"

CHAPTER 43

The day was clear and bright. The sun shone in a brilliant blue sky, the dazzling white of the snow-covered landscape almost blinding him in spite of the mirrored sunglasses he wore as he drove from Flathead Lake and the Lakeshore RV Park back to Kalispell. But Kyle was in no mood to enjoy the day. He was becoming accustomed to living in a world that was eternally cold and gray.

He rode in silence. There were no Jimmy Buffet CDs in the rental, and even if there had been, he wouldn't have played them. His taste for the music had soured. Instead of reminding him of good times, it now served as a painful reminder of yet another of his many failures.

He had just left the Lattimers after he had returned their camera. They had anxiously asked if there had been any more news about Danny and Tammy, and Kyle had told them no. He hadn't even bothered to take off his shades. He had been too ashamed to look them in the eyes.

His cell phone rang. He frowned when he saw the caller ID. It was Janet again.

He wasn't in the mood for her, but he had been putting her off for days. *Better to get it over with now while I have some privacy*, he thought.

"Agent Andrews," he said just to see if she would say anything.

"Kyle, it's your mother."

"Hello, Janet."

"Have you told them yet?" she asked.

"No, I haven't. I'm in the middle of a case. I can't just quit in the middle of it."

"Why not? I'm sure they can find someone to take your place." Normally, Kyle would have been irritated by her constant trivialization of his chosen career, but as she spoke, her voice quivered as if she were about to cry, which was something that was completely out of character for her.

"I need you here with me," she added shakily.

"Why?" Kyle asked suspiciously. He could tell something was wrong.

"I'm supposed to start chemo next week," she said and began to cry. "The cancer's spread to my lymph nodes."

CHAPTER 44

"Hey, Carrie," Charlie Weisman said as he came on the line.

It was comforting to hear a familiar voice. "Hey, Wise Man."

"I wasn't expecting to hear from you for at least another week or so," he said. "Is everything okay?"

"I've been better," she admitted. "How's it going there?"

"We're gettin' by," he said, and then, whispering where no one else could hear him, he added, "Just between you and me, Allan's freaking out. He's afraid you're not going to come back."

"Are you kidding me?" she said. It felt good to know that she was missed.

"You know how he is."

"Yeah, I know. But listen, the reason I called is I wanted to see if you can dig up some information for me."

"Sure, what do you got?"

Carrie looked out the door to make sure no one—meaning Wallace Hipple—was eavesdropping on her conversation. She closed the door. "A year and a half ago on October 3rd, a plane crashed in the mountains near my grandparents' cabin. The only thing I've been able to find out about it is that it was owned by a huge multinational conglomerate called NorCorp. I found some information on the NTSB's site but not what I was looking for, so I went to the company's website. Of course, there wasn't even a mention of it there. I wanted to see if maybe you could dig up something on it."

"Sure. Anything in particular you want me to look for?" Charlie asked.

"I don't know," Carrie replied. "You know how I am. I'm probably just overreacting, but something just doesn't seem right about all this. There was a passenger on the plane. The NTSB's report hardly mentions him. It didn't even give his name. I searched the obituaries in all the papers—Baltimore, Washington, Seattle, even Atlanta, where NorCorp's headquarters is located—and came up with nothing. I want to know why he was being flown across the country to Seattle on the corporate jet but wasn't important enough to be mentioned anywhere after the fact. And see if you can find out if the plane was carrying anything. There's no mention of any cargo in the report, but it doesn't specifically say there wasn't any either. Just see what you can find out about any of it. I'm going to call the NTSB myself and see if I can come up with something more that way. If you come across anything that jumps out at you, let me know."

"You got it," Charlie said. In the background, she could already hear the furious clicking of his keyboard. That was one thing Carrie loved about Charlie. He was always eager to do anything she asked without ever questioning why. Aside from Allan, Charlie was a big reason why she had never considered leaving the paper. She knew she wouldn't be half as good a reporter without him.

"You got your laptop with you?" Charlie asked.

"No," Carrie replied. "Just my phone. I didn't plan on doing any work while I was here. I've been using the local paper's computer."

"No problem. I'll call you if I find anything. Give me the name and address of your motel, and I'll FedEx your laptop to you. I wouldn't recommend using the paper's computer anymore if you want to scoop them. They might be watching what you're doing."

Carrie hadn't thought of that, but it was exactly the sort of cheap ploy she would expect from Wallace Hipple.

"That would be great. Thanks, Wise Man. I owe you big time," she said. "And I don't mean just a burger and shake. This one's worth dinner at Morton's at least."

"Nah, don't worry about it," Charlie replied. "I'd have to get dressed up for that. Just make it a steak burger from CityGrille, and I'll be happy."

Carrie smiled. "Deal! But you're selling yourself short there, Wise Man."

CHAPTER 45

Carrie's next stop was downtown, only this time her destination was across the street from the justice center at the old yellow county courthouse.

Inside, she checked the building directory and then proceeded downstairs. She followed the directions on a sign posted on the wall and made her way down the drab corridor to the door with "County Clerk" stenciled on the glass in gold letters.

She opened the door and entered into a small reception area. Across from her, an old oak counter ran across the width of the room, its surface worn smooth from years of paperwork being shuffled back and forth. An elderly lady at one of the desks behind the counter looked up at Carrie through thick, silver-framed glasses. The nameplate on her desk read Marjorie Mays.

"Can I help you, dear?"

"Yes, ma'am," Carrie replied. "I need to get a copy of the death certificates for several men who were killed in a plane crash on October 3rd of the year before last."

"Are you related to one of them?" the old lady asked as she stood up and shuffled over.

"No, I'm researching their deaths for a newspaper article," Carrie replied.

Marjorie looked at Carrie over the top of her glasses and frowned as if trying to decide whether or not to help her.

"You have their names?"

"Yes," Carrie said, pulling out a sheet of paper with the information.

Marjorie pulled three 5x8 index cards from a stack on the counter and slid them in front of Carrie. "I need you to fill out one of these for each of the copies you are requesting, including your name and address, employer, and a phone number. There's a three-dollar charge for each copy."

Carrie filled out the information, paid for the copies, and then waited impatiently while Marjorie printed out the certificates. Using a small silver tool, she imprinted the county seal on each of the certificates before she returned to the counter.

Outside in the hallway, Carrie shuffled through the documents, anxious to review the new information. The first was the copilot, which she skipped. The second one was the one she was looking for, the mysterious passenger. The death certificate showed his name as Dr. Phillip Keith Sandefur. He had been fifty-eight at the time of the crash. His "occupation" on the form was listed simply as "technician," and under "business or industry" was printed "medical."

Carrie frowned and blew a strand of hair from her face. She had hoped the death certificate would give her more information than that. Was he a medical doctor, or did he just have a PhD? If he *was* a medical doctor, would his occupation have been listed simply as "technician?" And if that's all he had been, what could be so important that the company would fly a technician across the country? Some special surgical equipment that had broken down and required immediate repair? That seemed unlikely. It was frustrating that his listed occupation and industry were so generic. There wasn't really enough information for her to even speculate as to what he did. But it hadn't been a complete waste of effort. She thought she had found the thread she was looking for. Now it was just a matter of following it.

She made her way upstairs and hurried back out to the Hummer. In spite of the clear, bright day, it was cold, with patches of fresh snow still on the ground. She started the truck to get the heater going and then called Charlie to give him the passenger's name and occupation and, perhaps more importantly, his social security number.

After she hung up with Charlie, Carrie glanced at her watch. As so often happened when she was researching a story, she had lost all track of time. It was after two o'clock now, and she hadn't eaten lunch. She remembered seeing a combination KFC/A&W a few blocks north on Main Street, so she drove through and picked up a cheeseburger and large fries.

Back in her room, she flipped through her notes while she ate, heedless of the greasy prints she left on the pages. When she found what she was looking for, she picked up the phone and began to dial.

After three rings, a stern-sounding receptionist answered, "National Transportation and Safety Board, how may I direct your call?"

"Jack Kleister please," Carrie replied.

"May I ask who's calling?"

"Yes, Carrie Daniels. I'm a reporter with the *Denver Inquirer.* I have a few questions regarding an accident investigation Mr. Kleister was in charge of."

"Just a moment please," the receptionist said as she sent the call through.

"Kleister here," came the sudden response. He sounded older and his voice was deep and nasally, as if he might have spent a good portion of his life smoking.

"Hello, Mr. Kleister, my name is Carrie Daniels. I'm a reporter with the *Denver Inquirer,* and if I could, I would like to ask you a few questions regarding a plane crash you were the lead investigator on about eighteen months ago."

"Accident."

"Excuse me?"

"Airplane 'accident.' We don't refer to them as 'crashes.'"

"Oh, I'm sorry."

"What paper did you say you were with?"

"*The Denver Inquirer.*"

"I'm not familiar with that one."

"It's a weekly paper," Carrie said. "We typically focus on local political stories, but I'm currently working on a special report into the crash—I mean accident—of—" Carrie glanced at her notes to get the number correct. "Flight N9712E that crashed in northwest Montana on October 3rd about eighteen months ago."

"The final report regarding that is posted on our website, I'm—"

"Yes, sir, I know," Carrie interrupted politely. She didn't want to make the man angry, but she didn't want him to think she was an idiot either. "I reviewed the report. But there were some additional questions I had, and I was hoping you might be able to answer them for me."

There was a pause, and Carrie cringed. Here it was—the moment she always hated, when she was told, "No," or "I'm sorry. I can't help you," and she was forced to find another way to get the information she was after. It happened almost every time, and while it never stopped her, it just made things more difficult and time-consuming. Fortunately, she already had Charlie working it from another direction.

There was a long, rumbling cough from the other end of the phone. "Excuse me," he said as he sniffed and snorted. "I've got a bad chest cold. Now what sort of questions did you have?"

Surprised by his acquiescence, Carrie grabbed her notepad. She wished she had a recorder, but pen and paper would have to do. "Well, sir, the report states that the plane was owned by NorCorp, but there are a number of companies owned by NorCorp. Do you recall which company was using the plane?"

"Can't say that I do. The plane was registered to NorCorp, and all of the records and maintenance information I recall seeing were in NorCorp's name." He paused to cough again before he continued, "Our investigation focuses on the cause of the accident, not on the company or passengers using the plane unless they are suspected of criminal activity."

"I see." Based on that answer, Carrie's hopes for her other questions began to fade, but she decided to try them anyway. "There was a third person killed in the cra—uh—accident, a Dr. Phillip Sandefur."

"Don't remember his name for certain, but go on."

"Is it possible that you might have the name of the company that Dr. Sandefur worked for on file somewhere?"

"It's possible. But if the passengers are not suspected to have had any impact on the accident, then more than likely, there is going to be very little information on him in our files."

"Could you please check that for me?"

"It's not that simple," he wheezed and coughed as he spoke. "After the final report is issued, all of the pertinent hard-copy records are sent to our storage warehouse. You're talking about a pretty big undertaking to pull all of those files just to look up where the guy worked. Can I ask why you are so interested in this person?"

"I'm not sure I'm as interested in the person himself as I am the company he worked for." Carrie didn't want to have to explain the whole situation or the rationale for her thought process, so she just simply said, "I'm trying to determine if that company might have been involved in any illegal activities."

"I see." There was a pause as Kleister cleared his throat. "What kind of illegal activities?"

"That's what I'm trying to find out," Carrie replied. "But there was no information in the NTSB report indicating what kind of cargo might have been on board at the time of the crash."

"Again, that is not a part of our investigation unless it was determined to have contributed to the accident. If there *was* any cargo, I can assure you that nothing carried was against FAA regulations. Nor were there any illegal substances found at the site."

"I see," Carrie sighed. "I don't suppose there was anything about the accident that you can remember as odd or out of the ordinary? Anything at all?"

"No, ma'am, I'm afraid I don't," he sniffed. "Our job is to investigate the cause of the accident and to report the facts that we are able to determine from that investigation. We're not allowed to publish any suppositions about what might have happened or why, only facts that we can prove through scientific investigation."

"I understand," Carrie replied. "I certainly appreciate your time. If you do remember anything or you have the time to retrieve those records, I would really appreciate it if you would call me."

"Sure, I can do that."

"Thanks," Carrie replied. She waited while he found a pen and then gave him her cell phone number along with a final plea for assistance.

After she hung up, Carrie sat there for a while, thinking. She had hoped to get more information than that. Now she had to try to figure out where to go next.

She decided to try the direct approach. She flipped through the ever-growing stack of pages she had printed out until she found the pages from NorCorp's website. She picked up the phone and dialed the number for the corporate headquarters. When the receptionist answered, she requested the human resources department.

Carrie spent several frustrating hours trying to get information regarding the plane crash from NorCorp, but no matter whom she talked to or what approach she tried, the answer was always the same: They were not allowed to give out that information over the phone. It was as if the entire company had been trained very specifically in regards to nondisclosure. But Carrie was determined. She was on to something. She just *knew* it. And with every call that ended abruptly or with someone hanging up on her, she became more and more certain of it. This had become her own personal David and Goliath, and she wasn't going to stop until she got what she wanted.

She continued to play the corporate runaround game, trying person after person, prodding and poking, digging for bits and pieces of information like a forty-niner panning for flecks of gold, until the NorCorp offices on the East Coast closed for the day. Even then, she continued until after she got her fourth voice mail in a row when she finally conceded that she wasn't going to get what she wanted today. For now, she was forced to wait and hope that Charlie came up with something in the meantime.

But tomorrow, she would begin again.

CHAPTER 46

Kyle parked the car in the lot behind the justice center and sat there, thinking. He was more disturbed by the news about Janet than he would have expected. From what he had been told by her doctor, he had been led to believe that her breast cancer wasn't that serious. He figured she had just been looking for attention like she always had. He had been putting her off in hopes that the report would come back with good news and he wouldn't have to deal with it anymore. Now he had to consider the very real possibility that it might be life-threatening. He wasn't sure how he felt about that.

For a long time now, he had done everything in his power to distance himself from Janet in an effort to escape her constant belittling and because he wouldn't have to bear witness to her self-destructive behavior. He wouldn't have cared if they hadn't spoken for years.

But the possibility of her death and his being left alone without any parents wasn't something he had given much thought to before now. And it was unsettling.

Suddenly, he had a new perspective on the emotional struggles that Carrie Daniels had to be going through.

When Kyle walked into the conference room, Marasco and Lewis were sitting there, a pile of paper and file folders spread out before them. They had spent the remainder of the day yesterday checking into the background of the Lattimers to make sure there was nothing suspicious about them, like a recently purchased insurance policy or an amended will, but they had found nothing. They had released the photographs of the young couple to the media, hoping that someone might have seen them, but that had yet to provide any significant leads either.

"Anything?" Lewis asked, putting down his coffee.

"No," Kyle said, shaking his head. Facing a dead end, they had hoped the Lattimers might have some further ideas as to who might have wished harm on the newlyweds.

Lewis's brow knitted as he looked at Kyle. "What's wrong?" he asked, a concerned tone to his voice.

"I just—" Kyle was cut off by the ringing of the phone.

Lewis hit the button on the speakerphone. "Agent Edwards here."

"Lewis." It was SAC Geddes.

"Something come up?" Lewis asked hopefully.

"No. Still no hits on any of the credit cards or bank accounts. But that's not why I'm calling. I'm calling to let you know the governor of Montana called the director this morning, raising hell about our handling of this case. Says all this attention is bad for tourism, and he wants some answers now. So tell me … do we have any?"

"Not any he wants to hear," Lewis replied flatly.

The other end was silent for a moment, and Kyle tensed in anticipation. He imagined Geddes taking a long drag of her cigarette, the tip glowing red as her temper flared.

"Do I need to send in Kendrick and Thomas to help?" she asked.

"No," said Lewis. "We'd just be tripping over each other."

"Are you sure?" she asked again, sounding suspicious. Kyle knew it was directed at him.

"I'm sure," Lewis said. "Manpower's not the problem. Kyle's busting his ass just like the rest of us, and the locals have given us everything we've asked for."

"So what's the problem?"

"I don't know," Lewis admitted. "There's something strange about this case. We haven't had any breaks go our way yet. But they will. Things'll turn."

"They'd better, or you know what will happen. We're under the microscope now."

"Yeah? Well, tell the director he might want to start by looking in his own backyard. This might have been over by now if we had gotten any help from the lab. With all the evidence we've sent them, we haven't gotten shit for leads."

"I don't think that would be beneficial to either of our careers," said Geddes. "Just come up with something. *Soon.*"

Lewis seemed to be more irritated than anything as he hung up, but the knot in Kyle's stomach that had started with Janet's phone call had just tightened. He had worked hard to get this chance, and he didn't like to think about what would happen if they failed. This was his one shot. If he blew it, he would never get a second chance. The problem was it had become political now. It didn't matter if they were making progress or not. It was all about perception. The rug could be pulled out from under them at any minute, if for no other reason than the appearance that SAC Geddes was taking steps to correct the situation.

Kyle hoped Lewis was right about their luck changing soon, because if it didn't, the agents assigned to the case would be.

CHAPTER 47

Tick.

It starts slowly, a faint disruption of the darkness, like the ripple of a raindrop in a calm, dark ocean.

Tick.

Tick.

The tapping of a tree limb blown against the cabin's window.

She sits in the chair at the table, frozen by fear, her eyes fixed on the empty bottle of rum before her.

Tick … tick … tick.

It grows louder, the tempo increasing with urgent persistency as if in warning.

Tick. Tick. Tick.

Knocking against the pane harder, harder. Faster, faster.

Escalating into a deafening crescendo.

The blare of a truck horn. A blinding white light.

With a scream, the window shatters. Jagged splinters of light tear her face and hands.

She runs from the cabin, desperate to escape, but the shadow is lurking, waiting for her. Darker than the night, it disengages from the inky blackness to pursue her.

She flees into the forest, seeking shelter among the trees. Limbs grab at her, tugging and clawing, slowing her down. Thorns cut like shards of glass.

The shadow is right behind, bearing down on her.

A shrill cry pierces the dark. Echoing out, it rings in her ears.

Ringing—

Ringing—

Ringing—

The ringing of a telephone.

Alone in the dark, Carrie slowly surfaced from the depths of her nightmare. In a confused state of semiconsciousness, she groped about the nightstand, nearly knocking off the alarm clock before finally finding the phone.

"Hello," she answered, her voice thick with sleep.

"Carrie?"

"Yeah."

"It's Charlie. I think I've got something for you."

"What time is it?" she groaned, the last tendrils of her nightmare slowly slipping away like fog.

"It's uh ... oh, shit, it's 3:43," he said with a giggle. He sounded giddy. "Man, I didn't realize it was that late. Sorry about that. Guess maybe I shouldn't have had that last Red Bull. But I think I've got something for you, and I figured you'd want to know as soon as I found out." He was talking so fast that Carrie could barely keep up with him.

"No, that's fine. Hang on a second." She sat up and flicked on the lamp. Squinting in the harsh glare of the light, she picked up her notebook and pen. "Okay, what have you got?"

"You remember how you told me that the plane that crashed was owned by NorCorp and it took off from Baltimore, right? Well, I looked up all of NorCorp's subsidiaries and found there were seven of them in the DC-Baltimore area alone. I thought I'd try that first to see if I got lucky, you know. So I tried the websites of the ones that had websites but didn't find any mention of the crash or a Dr. Sandefur. Anyway, when that didn't work, I had to resort to other alternative methods, which I'd rather not disclose at this time, but let's just say that using the social security number you gave me, I finally managed to obtain a copy of Dr. Sandefur's final tax return. And guess who's listed as his employer."

"Who?"

"NorCorp."

"What do you mean?" Carrie asked. "I thought NorCorp was nothing more than a holding company for a bunch of other companies. Are you telling me he was an officer or on the board of directors?"

"No, especially not based on what he made his last year. But what I noticed that seemed funny to me was that the address listed for NorCorp was a post office box, so I ran a search on the post office's website, and it turns out the zip code is in Baltimore, Maryland. But I didn't remember seeing a listing for NorCorp's headquarters in Maryland, so I went back through the list and found that only two of the companies in the area have that zip code. One is DynaPlate, which is this small electroplating company. But the other one's a different story. The other one's a company called GenTech, which is in NorCorp's pharmaceutical and bioengineering division. You need to check it out in the morning. These guys are into all kinds of drugs and stuff—prescription allergy relief and cold medicines, vaccines for smallpox and anthrax, and they're even working on one for AIDS. Can you imagine how much that would be worth? They're into research for a cure for diabetes and—dig this—schizophrenia. Can you imagine them being able to cure someone like Charles Manson with just a shot?"

"No," Carrie admitted.

"Yup, and that's just the public side. I haven't even gotten in to their intranet side yet, but when I get a look at their HR records, I'll bet you anything we'll find our mysterious Dr. Sandefur listed as a former employee—and there's no *telling* what he might have been involved in."

Carrie's mind was now beginning to race with the implications of this discovery. It seemed as if every effort had been made to hide the connection between Dr. Sandefur and GenTech. Now the next question to be answered was why. "Charlie, this is great. This is exactly what I needed, but don't go hacking into their site. I don't want you getting into trouble if this turns out to be a wild-goose chase."

"Don't worry about it. It's not like I'm going to crash their system. All I want to do is get in and snoop around a little bit, just look at things, you know. I'll be in and out without a trace. No one will ever know I've even been in there."

"No, Charlie, I don't want you doing that, at least not yet. Get all the info you can from their website but don't go breaking into anything, you understand?"

"All right," Charlie groaned.

"And get some sleep," she added.

"And waste this buzz? No way! I'm up for the duration. Besides, right now is prime surfing time."

Carrie started to say something more but then thought better of it. It wasn't like she was his mother. Instead, she just said, "Thanks, Wise Man."

"No problemo," he said.

Maybe it was because of the dream she had just had or perhaps it was just an instinctual reaction, but for some reason, Carrie felt an overwhelming compulsion to offer one last admonition before she hung up.

"And Charlie, *be careful.*"

* * *

Afterward, Carrie sat in bed, contemplating what Charlie had told her. Was it possible that there had been something on that plane that was responsible for all the recent murders? Could there have been some experimental drug on board, some biological or chemical agent used for research purposes that, once released, was causing people in the area to react unpredictably, perhaps even to the point of murder? That was certainly something the company would never admit to, and anyone would be prone to take steps to cover it up.

She wished she had her laptop with her now so she could do some more investigating; however, it wouldn't arrive until midmorning, and it was too frustrating to try to do any serious research with her phone. Even so, she knew she wouldn't be able to get back to sleep. There were so many things she wanted to check out, so many more avenues to pursue. Like this GenTech company. She wondered about the research they were involved in, the symptoms and behavior of schizophrenics, and the type of drugs used to treat them. She also wanted to talk to Jack Kleister again and ask him about the first rescuers to come across the wreckage as well as the members of the NTSB's "go" team that had investigated the crash site. Had there been any unusual incidents involving any of them after the investigation? Any sudden or strange illnesses or odd behavioral changes? Any mysterious deaths? Or murders? But it was almost 4:00 in the morning, and as far as Carrie knew, Kalispell didn't have a twenty-four-hour FedEx Office she could go to in order to gain Internet access at this time of the night.

She jotted down her thoughts and questions in her notebook so she wouldn't forget in the morning. Once she had written down everything that came to mind, she tried to think of other possibilities, but the longer she sat there in the dimly lit silence, the more bits and pieces of her nightmare began to creep into her thoughts.

She blinked and shook her head as if that could somehow dislodge them from her thoughts. She didn't want to take a sleeping pill this late because she had things to do in the morning, so she turned on the TV to try to keep her mind occupied. Aside from infomercials, the only movie she could find was *Sleepless in Seattle*, so she settled for CNN.

As usual, the news was anything but uplifting. There were stories of the ongoing troubles in the Middle East and Iraq, but to Carrie, that was better than the alternatives. While most people found the news depressing, it had the reverse effect for Carrie. To her, it served as a reminder that no matter how bad things seemed, there were always others who had it much worse. And if they could manage to get through it, then surely she could too.

Even so, it was a long time until dawn.

CHAPTER 48

The Flathead County Library was located in a two-story limestone building on First Avenue East, five blocks north of downtown. Carrie parked in the lot across the street and paused long enough to gather her satchel and purse before she stepped out into the cold again.

As she climbed the steps and entered the library foyer, a rush of warm, musty air smelling of old books washed over Carrie. It was a familiar scent, one she had become accustomed to during years of research. It was comforting, like returning to one's house after a long vacation. That was how she felt as soon as she walked in. She was in her element. She was home.

She made her way through the library, enjoying the familiar sights and sounds of the place. She checked the signs, and then headed upstairs to the reference section and a cluster of six computers that offered Internet access.

After she called up the browser, she started her search by accessing NorCorp's site once again. From there, she followed the link to the medical subsidiaries division of the mega-corporation. She scanned the page for a while, highlighting several menus and other links before finding the one that directed her to the GenTech site. On it, the company's mission statement was displayed with a collage of diverse employee photographs in the background.

The research-and-development page heralded GenTech's cutting-edge research into drug and gene therapy for the treatment and cure of a number of diseases, including AIDs, cancer, Parkinson's, and schizophrenia, as well as the prevention of congenital birth defects. At the bottom of the page was a small blurb heralding their pride at being one of the companies selected by the US government to assist in the manufacture of a national supply of anthrax and smallpox vaccines, which immediately caught Carrie's attention. Smallpox and anthrax were two of the most highly anticipated agents for use in biological weapons. If the company was working with the government on those, it was possible they might be working with other more dangerous biological agents as well. And if they were involved with biological weapons, then might they be researching countermeasures for chemical weapons or even the development of the weapons themselves?

She frowned, looking at the screen and trying to think if there could realistically be any connection between GenTech and the string of murders that had occurred over the last eighteen months. She took a moment and tried to look at the situation from a more objective viewpoint or, more precisely, from Allan Dilbeck's point of view. He was always good at telling her when he thought she was on to something and when she "had a big bag of horseshit," as he was so fond of putting it.

She pulled out her notepad and began brainstorming, jotting down little notes about her thoughts, following them wherever they carried her, and trying to shoot holes in her suppositions about where the story was leading.

First, if there had been any chemical or biological weapons on the plane, wouldn't they have been required to be logged prior to the flight, and wouldn't they have been housed in some sort of indestructible containers similar to the flight recorder's black box? There was no mention of any such material or cargo in the flight manifest, and although she had not talked to Jack Kleister again to confirm it, he hadn't mentioned any ill effects experienced by any of the search-and-rescue or investigation teams.

But supposing there *was* something on the plane that wasn't listed, was it possible it had survived the initial crash but had been damaged enough that it finally leaked out over time? Even she had to admit that was a stretch. The investigative team had scoured the crash site and would almost certainly have found any such cargo and removed it. Besides, they were dealing with murders, violent, grisly murders and not death from some chemical or biological agent. She could practically hear Allan's voice in her head: "horseshit."

She took a deep breath, leaned back and blew it out in frustration, even though her hair was still firmly pulled back in a ponytail. What could have been on that plane that would have caused people to react in such a violent manner? What would drive people to murder? Make them act insane like they were ... Charles Manson or something?

And then something Charlie had said last night sprang to mind: "Can you imagine them being able to cure someone like Charles Manson with just a shot?"

GenTech performed research into schizophrenia. What if, instead of a chemical agent like mustard gas or nerve gas, it was something they had developed through their research into schizophrenia, some sort of hallucinogenic agent that caused people to go on murderous rampages? Hadn't there been one man from Seattle who hadn't been killed but had run into the forest and been found frozen to death later? What if he was the one who had killed them, not because of any real motive but because of an imaginary one, a hallucination?

Thinking she might be back on track again, Carrie called up WebMD and did a search for "schizophrenia." "Schizophrenia," it said, "is a severe and disabling brain disease ... a type of illness that causes severe mental disturbances that disrupt normal thought, speech, and behavior." The article went on to state that, "The first signs of schizophrenia usually appear as shocking or radical changes in behavior ... and it is widely believed that neurotransmitters, brain chemicals that allow communication between brain cells, play a role in causing schizophrenia."

She printed out the article and then did a search for "chemical weapons." There were hundreds of sites that contained information on the topic. After she scanned the summaries, she selected several and began reading. She read several that didn't contain anything of much interest before she came across a site that purported to list all of the known chemical weapons from various countries around the world and their effects. She called up the site and began skimming through the list. As she read, she became appalled at the various horrific methods mankind had come up with to kill one another. There were agents, such as Sarin, Tabun, and Soman, which were powerful nerve gases that caused wildly thrashing, choking deaths. Then there was a section dealing with what were called glycollates, including agents with names like BZ, Agent 15, and Agent 16X. It went on to mention that there was little public knowledge regarding the agents, except for a reference to a statement made to the House of Commons by the British secretary of state regarding the existence of Agent 15 in Iraq's arsenals prior to the start of the Iraq War. Even less was known regarding the mysterious Agent 16X other than unconfirmed rumors from unnamed sources in the intelligence community that it was an extremely powerful hallucinogenic agent that caused extremely violent and unpredictably aggressive reactions in subjects.

Another article she read was one in which declassified Pentagon reports confirmed that the United States had secretly tested chemical and biological weapons during the 1960s and '70s. The tests involved releasing deadly nerve agents in Alaska and Hawaii as a part of Project 112, a military program to test chemical and biological weapons and defenses against them. In one incident in the Utah desert, the military was forced to reimburse ranchers and agreed to stop open-air testing of agents after some 6,400 sheep died when nerve gas drifted away from the test range.

Immediately, Carrie thought about the Salt Lick and the missing goats, but then another thought came to her. All the information she had seen indicated that the original flight plan of the plane had been from Baltimore to Seattle. But what if its final destination wasn't Seattle? What if its final destination had been Alaska or Hawaii? In the article she had just read, the United States admitted to having tested chemical weapons in Alaska and Hawaii in the '70s, so it was obvious they had a facility there then. And if that was the case then, why not now? So the question now became more shocking: What would happen if a plane carrying something like Agent 16X crashed into the mountains of Montana?

Now that she seemed to have more possible evidence to back up her theory, she desperately wanted to talk to Jack Kleister again, not only to ask about the investigators but also to inquire if the flight plan filed had included a second leg to Alaska or Hawaii. Even though she wasn't too worried about eavesdroppers, she preferred to do it somewhere private, so she logged off the computer, gathered up her things, and made her way back to her truck.

She started up the Hummer and turned the heater on high to cut through the chill in the cabin. Then she pulled out her cell phone and dialed the number for the NTSB.

The same stern-sounding receptionist as before answered. She must have recognized Carrie's voice, for when Carrie asked for Jack Kleister, she was put through without having to explain who she was or what she wanted.

She didn't have as much luck with Mr. Kleister, however. After the line rang several times, his voice mail picked up. Disappointed, she left him a message requesting that he call her back on her cell phone at his earliest convenience.

Even without confirmation from the NTSB, Carrie felt she had at least enough circumstantial evidence to warrant further investigation. And that was exactly what she intended to see happen.

CHAPTER 49

When they arrived at the police station, the sheriff and Deputy Johnson were already there, going over last night's reports and assigning the most recent leads to the deputies for follow-up.

"Boy," Clayton said when he saw the box of donuts in Lewis's hand. "Krispy Kreme *and* store-bought coffee. You feds really know how to do it up right."

While the deputy helped himself to breakfast, Lewis asked if anything had turned up. The sheriff answered with a disappointed frown and a shake of his head as he handed a stack of paperwork to Lewis.

Marasco arrived after eight only to report there still had been no sightings of Tucker or the couple by the border patrol.

Several hours later, they were still struggling to come up with a plausible explanation for the disappearances when Lydia interrupted them to inform Kyle that Carrie Daniels was there to see him.

Marasco looked up, his eyebrow arched, a smug grin on his face. Kyle frowned back at him. He knew what Marasco was thinking, but he was wrong. Kyle had no idea why she would be back, unless it was to ask for the return of her grandparents' computer again. She *was* a reporter. She probably intended to check on it every day until she got what she wanted.

With a weary sigh, Kyle rose and went up front to tell her it was out of his control and he had no idea when she might be able to get it back.

When he got there, he found her standing at the counter with a

211

black leather satchel in her hands. Her hair was pulled back in a ponytail again, and she still wasn't wearing any makeup. He noticed the light sprinkling of freckles across the bridge of her nose. But there was something about her that looked different today. Instead of the sad, depressed girl he had seen before, she had a determined look about her. Instead of brief, sideways glances, she looked directly at him. Her dark brown eyes shone with an intensity he hadn't seen before.

"I have something to show you," she said, a hint of anxiety in her voice. "I would have just called, but I didn't think it would make sense unless I showed you. Is there somewhere we can go?"

"Sure," Kyle said as he pulled open the swinging door at the end of the counter. He led her into the interview room and shut the door behind them. When he turned back around, she already had her satchel open, pulling out pages of computer printouts with notes scribbled on them and all around the margins.

"I know this may sound crazy, but please just hear me out."

"All right," Kyle said, curious.

She went on to explain to him that she had decided to do some investigating of her grandparents' murders on her own and how she had begun by reviewing all of the newspaper articles over the last couple of years that involved murdered or missing people in and around Kalispell. Then she told him about the three men killed in a plane crash.

At first, Kyle had listened out of respect but with no real interest. She hadn't told him anything they didn't already know, and he could see no reason to consider the deaths of three men in a plane crash as relevant. But he felt that her staying busy researching was probably serving as a therapeutic release for her, allowing her to gradually come to grips with the loss of her grandparents, and he didn't want to do anything to dissuade her as long as she didn't carry it too far.

She showed him the article she had printed out about the disappearance of the goats from the Salt Lick and related to him her reading about the missing newlyweds and how it had triggered a memory of that story. She pulled out a map on which she had marked all of the locations of the murders and spread it out before Kyle. He leaned over and looked at it as she pointed out the proximity of all the locations.

Again, it wasn't anything they hadn't already noticed themselves, and she was missing the location of Tucker's cabin, which also fell within the perimeter of the other sites. But as she continued, he began to listen more intently. What her map included that they hadn't considered was the teenage boy who had vanished from the Diamond R ranch and the location of the plane crash. She told him that all of the murders and disappearances had occurred within the last eighteen months after the plane crash and that there had not been any other similar deaths in the vicinity for four years prior to that.

Kyle sat there a moment, unsure what to say or do. Could it be that she had actually stumbled across something they had missed? Perhaps it was possible, because none of the projected profiles they had received from Quantico had included anything about the plane crash. But it was also just as likely that she was making things fit into a certain pattern because she so desperately wanted to find one.

"Miss Daniels—"

"The company that owned the plane is NorCorp," she hurried on, pulling more papers out to show him. "The passenger worked for a subsidiary called GenTech. It's a pharmaceutical company that does chemical and biological research into hundreds of diseases, including schizophrenia. There's also information in there regarding their development of vaccines for the government in case of chemical warfare. The question is … what if the plane that crashed—"

"Miss Daniels," he interrupted.

"Carrie," she said, looking at him imploringly, as if she sensed that she was about to be dismissed without any further consideration.

"Carrie," he said gently. "Leave the information with me. I'll make sure that it's followed up on."

She stopped and nodded and then began to gather up the stack of papers. "These are yours to keep," she said. "I've already made copies of everything." Then she looked at him as she handed him the papers. "Just please don't let this get swept under the rug. Innocent people are being killed, and we deserve to know why."

"Trust me. We all want this to be over," he said. "I promise you this information will be followed up on, even if I have to do it myself."

Carrie continued to look at him, as if trying to judge whether or not to trust him. Kyle locked eyes with her and held his there, unflinching. Then, as if their gaze had continued for too long, she quickly looked down. After she grabbed her satchel, she paused just long enough to say, "Thank you," before she hastily left the room.

For several moments afterward, Kyle just sat there, looking at her notes and wondering about what had just happened.

CHAPTER 50

Kyle was conflicted as he walked back to the conference room. On the one hand, he was excited by the possibility of a new lead in the case, but he was hesitant to put too much stock in it. More than likely, it was nothing more than the creation of a distraught survivor desperately grasping at straws in hopes of finding a reason for her loss.

But it went further than that. Kyle wasn't sure how to define what had happened in that interview room, but he was certain of it nonetheless. He had seen it in Carrie's eyes. Something about the way she had looked at him had touched him in an unexpected yet familiar way.

As a child, Kyle had often felt alone and unwanted in spite of doing everything he could to gain his mother's favor. She had always been too busy with her social life to have time for him, and the few times he had been around her when she was with her friends, she had acted as if she were embarrassed that he was her child. With the death of his father and the rapid decline of Janet immediately thereafter, he had virtually become an orphan at the age of thirteen. Because of that, Kyle knew the struggle that Carrie was going through. He had been able to identify it by the look on her face despite the fact that she had tried to keep it hidden. Kyle knew firsthand of the desperation and the loneliness that she felt and how badly she needed to trust in something or, more importantly, some*one* again.

He had told her she could trust him. It wasn't something that came easily for her, but the look in her eyes told him that she had done so in spite of the dangerous consequences.

As he opened the door to the conference room, he found himself fervently hoping that he wasn't setting her up for another letdown.

* * *

Lewis didn't say anything as he flipped through the pages. He looked up at Kyle, his eyebrow raised skeptically.

"I know it seems far-fetched," Kyle said. "But what if she accidentally stumbled onto something? Even you've said that's how some of the hardest cases are finally broken."

"She's a reporter," Lewis growled. "The last thing we need is another pain-in-the-ass reporter spreading wild-ass rumors and making us look like a bunch of jackasses."

"That's a lot of asses," Marasco muttered with a smirk.

"That's not what she's doing," Kyle said. "She never mentioned anything about doing a story on this."

"Did you ask if she was?"

"Well, no," Kyle admitted.

"And by accepting this, you have just given her confirmation of her story," Lewis said, his voice rising. "Now she can write that the FBI has received information regarding a possible connection between the plane crash and the murders, and we won't be able to deny it. She knows it's true, because she's the one who fucking gave it to us!"

Kyle flinched. "She wants to find out who killed her grandparents," he protested weakly. "She's trying to help us." But after what Lewis had just said, he was beginning to have second thoughts himself.

Lewis muttered something under his breath and shook his head as if disgusted with Kyle's naiveté. Marasco just sat there, watching the show with a shit-eating grin on his face. All he needed was a little popcorn. Kyle wanted to tell him to go fuck himself.

Lewis banged the papers hard on the table to straighten them and then shoved it all back at Kyle. "Fax it to Seattle," he growled. "They can follow up with the NTSB and GenTech, and we'll follow up on the local aspects. And you'd better hope like hell this doesn't show up in the papers."

CHAPTER 51

Washington, DC

The streetlights were just coming on as dusk settled across the city, reflecting in the curbside puddles and causing the wet streets to shine as if they were made of obsidian. The earlier showers had cleared, leaving a cool air that smelled crisp and clean as it spilled into the back of the limousine. If only the city's soul could be cleansed so easily, Thomas Wade thought as they passed by the Capitol building. He took another drag on his cigarette, letting the smoke billow out through the cracked window. Although, it would take more than a gentle shower to wash away the stink and decay that was slowly eroding Washington's once-proud status as the capital of the greatest nation on earth. What was needed was more like a fire hose to flush out all the withering old farts and left-wing liberals. Wade smiled at the thought of himself in front of a big red pumper truck, hose in hand, blasting the old farts off their feet and rolling them down the gutter into the sewer.

Wade took a drink of his scotch on the rocks, relishing his vision almost as much as the taste of the liquor as it mixed with the lingering smoke and nicotine. He held it there for a moment, letting it roll across his tongue. He savored the warm, tingling burn as it slid down his throat.

He checked the time on his gold Rolex Presidential and frowned at the tightness in the shoulder of his jacket. He hated wearing tuxedos. They were too tight, too constricting. It was like wearing a straitjacket.

He much preferred the loose-fitting jackets of his custom-tailored suits. But on occasion, as was the case tonight, when he was attending a fund-raiser for one of his more important supporters in the Senate, he was forced to put on the preferred costume of the politico in order to ensure that his organization would continue to be well funded. It was a necessary evil and a minor inconvenience compared to what he gained in return. Besides, the fund-raisers themselves were almost always entertaining. He enjoyed watching all the old farts strut around as if they were the president-elect, pretending to be all chummy and committing their support to one other, all while secretly planning to stab each other in the back, each of them desperately craving more power and prestige than the man next to him.

But what Wade found especially amusing was that most of them had no real idea of who he was or what he did, yet he held more power than any of them. Knowledge, as everyone knew, was the real power. And Thomas Wade knew things that none of them, including even the president himself, knew. It was better that way. Just like the suits Wade preferred to wear, it gave his organization a freedom of movement that would have otherwise suffered from the constraints of the governmental tuxedo.

And then there were the young wives and interns in their slinky, low-cut, designer gowns with glittering sequins and silicone implants. Wade had enjoyed more than one of the senators' wives or mistresses at similar functions before. Perhaps he would do so again tonight, he mused with a sly grin.

Wade's reverie was interrupted by the ringing of the limo's telephone. After he set his scotch in the drink holder, he picked up the phone, waited for the tone, and then entered in the day's code. Like all of the phones Wade used, this one was secured with built-in encryption and decryption circuitry that required the entry of the proper code before the system would accept the call.

"Wade here."

"The picnic basket is packed and ready," said the deep voice on the other end. Wade recognized it as Mitchell Ainsworth, leader of the recon team. "Meet me at the park in the morning."

"I'll bring the potato salad," Wade replied and then hung up without further comment. He dialed the code for an outgoing call and punched in another number. He took another drag off his cigarette while he waited for the connection.

"Colquitt here," came the answer.

"The party's a go," Wade replied, smoke billowing from his nostrils. "Make sure your man Bennett is there bright and early."

"He'll be there at 0600, as we discussed."

Wade rolled his eyes at Colquitt's use of military time. The poor bastard just couldn't let it go.

"Just remember, this is your party," Wade said. "If it rains, you're the one who's going to get wet, not me."

"It won't rain," Colquitt replied confidently.

"That's what the weatherman said this morning," Wade replied ominously before he hung up.

CHAPTER 52

Montana

Sheriff Greyhawk listened while Kyle went over the information he had received from Montana Fish, Wildlife & Parks regarding the disappearance of the goats around the Salt Lick. "I finally got a hold of the ranger who was interviewed for the article," Kyle was saying. "I asked her if they had ever found out what had happened to the goats, and she said, 'No, it was as if they just disappeared.' I asked if she thought poachers might have killed them, and she said it was possible but doubtful, since there wasn't really anything valuable about them. I then asked her if they might have died from some disease or poison. She said it was possible but that from the number that appeared to be missing, she thought it was odd that none of their carcasses had been found like those of the deer."

"Deer?" Lewis asked.

"Yeah, she mentioned that there have been several cases of mutilated mule deer being found around Hungry Horse. She said the carcasses had been hacked up pretty bad, as if a hunter had taken a big knife or machete to them, but that none of them showed any gunshot wounds."

"Do they know what killed them?" Lewis asked.

"That's the odd thing. She said she wasn't sure. She said most of them were torn up pretty good, like they had been mauled and partially eaten after the fact, but they don't think they were killed by other

220

animals. They also checked them for chronic wasting disease, but none of them showed any signs of it."

"Did they check for any other diseases?" George asked. "It's possible that after they died, the carcasses became bloated and split open, making it look like they had been cut up."

"I didn't think about that," Kyle said. "But I did ask if they had run any other tests or samples from the animals and she said no. She said they tested for chronic wasting disease by taking a sample of the animal's brain and that afterward the animals and all the tissue samples were destroyed as a precaution."

"So it's possible they were killed by some other biological agent and they just didn't know it," said Lewis.

"It's possible," Kyle agreed.

"Did she mention anything about any of the people who performed the tests getting sick?" Lewis asked.

"She didn't say, but I didn't think to ask about it either," Kyle admitted.

"Call her back and tell her if they find any other animals like that not to touch them and to call us immediately," Lewis said. Then he quietly added, "I hope to hell we don't have a gotdamned biological disaster on our hands."

George nodded in agreement, but something about this new possibility concerned him. From the time he had first investigated the Joneses' cabin, he had sensed that something had been wrong with the forest. He had spent enough time traveling through it when he was younger that he could tell when something was wrong. He had first noticed it standing in front of the Joneses' cabin on the night after their murder. The woods had been unnaturally silent. But there had been something else—a darker, forbidding presence that had hung over the valley like smoke from a forest fire. He had felt it again when they had returned to Tucker's cabin after his disappearance.

For the first time in the investigation, they seemed to be pursuing a direction that fit with what his instincts had been telling him.

There was a knock at the door, and Lydia stuck her head in. "Sheriff, there's a call for you. He says he's your cousin."

George's brow lowered in a mix of confusion and concern. The only reason he could think of for the call involved his grandmother. "I should take this," he said.

He went to his office to take the call in private. As he sat down, he looked at the picture of himself and his mother. Though taken so long ago, the pain and bitterness still seemed fresh. He took a moment, steeling himself before picking up the phone.

"Sheriff Greyhawk," he said slowly.

"Uh, hello, sheriff," the boy on the other end stammered. "It's Joseph. I ... I wouldn't have called, but I didn't know who else to call."

"What is it?" George asked.

"It's Grandmother. I don't know what's wrong with her. I think she's dying."

George remained silent. He had closed the door on that part of his life so long ago that the boy's pronouncement failed to affect him. To him, he had been without a family since the death of his mother.

"And what would you have me do?" he asked. He had not meant to seem callous, but his deep voice made it seem so anyway.

"I ... I think she's having fever dreams. She sleeps almost all the time, but then sometimes she starts thrashing about and babbling, something about monsters in the mountains and calling out for Little Hawk, over and over. I try to talk to her, tell her it's just a bad dream to try to settle her down, but she just keeps calling out for Little Hawk, saying, 'It's time. It's time,' over and over. You were the only one I could think of who might know what she was talking about."

"I cannot help her," George replied bluntly, anxious to end the call. "She clings to the old ways and refuses to allow anyone to treat her with modern medicine. Call the medicine man and see if he can help," he said, even though he knew it wouldn't do any good, just as it had failed to help in his mother's case. "There is nothing I can do for her," he said and then hung up.

He sat there a moment, taking several deep breaths to clear his head. He ran his hand across the back of his neck beneath his hair and found it damp with perspiration. He didn't know why he was allowing himself to be affected by this now, when he thought he had put it behind him years ago. If the foolish old lady was seeking to clear her conscience before she died, she would have to find some other way to do so. In all the years since his mother's death, he had not found it necessary to forgive her, and he felt no compulsion to do so now.

He pushed away from his desk and started back down the hall to the conference room.

As he passed Clayton's office, he noticed that the deputy's door was closed but appeared to have slipped open a crack. It was unusual for Clayton to close his door unless he had someone in his office. George knocked lightly on the door before he stuck his head in. He happened to catch the last of Clayton's conversation: "Don't worry. I said I'll take care of it."

When Clayton looked up and saw him, he hung up quickly. "Uh, hey, sheriff," he said. "Something come up?"

"No," George replied. "Who was that?"

"It was uh, Billy. He, uh … he's feeling a little under the weather, and I told him if he needed to stay home, I'd cover for him."

George nodded, but he wasn't convinced. Clayton seemed to be hiding something, which was completely out of character for him. He remained silent for a moment, waiting to see if Clayton would say anything more, but the usually talkative deputy remained silent.

George nodded and pulled the door shut. Whatever it was, it would have to wait. At the moment, they had more pressing matters to deal with.

CHAPTER 53

Montana

In the kitchen of his small trailer house "Big John" Morris cracked open another Black Star and took a big swig. The trailer was located just south of Route 209, on the eastern side of Highway 83, a few miles north of Swan Lake. There wasn't anything special about its location as far as Big John was concerned. It had just been the cheapest place he could find when he had been looking for somewhere to stay.

He slammed the door shut on the old refrigerator and hobbled back into the living room where a rerun of *Wheel of Fortune* was blaring on the TV. He plopped down with a groan, the worn out springs of the brown Lay-Z-Boy creaking in response. Beside the chair was a rickety TV tray, its wooden surface marred with cigarette burns and water rings. He shoved aside the bag of Doritos and the plastic tray caked with the remnants of refried beans from his enchilada dinner. He sat the beer down, wiping the condensation on the belly of his dingy undershirt before he grabbed another handful of Doritos.

He took a look at the board on the TV. "G!" he called out, as if the contestants could hear him.

The lady currently up, a frumpy schoolteacher named Helen, guessed, "P."

"Dumb bitch," John muttered, showering Doritos crumbs down his chest.

"Sorry, no P," said Pat Sajack.

Big John nodded in satisfaction and took a big swig of his beer.

The next man spun. Before his guess, Big John shouted out, "G!"

Larry, the realtor from Spokane with a bad comb-over, guessed, "R."

"Dumbass," Big John said, shaking his head in disgust.

"There are two Rs on the board," Pat replied as the audience cheered. "Spin again."

"Huh," Big John's forehead scrunched up in concentration as he took another swig. Then it came to him.

An eruption of angry barking suddenly came from out back. "Shut up, Butch!" he yelled, but the dog continued its frenzied barking. There was a crashing sound, like that of a garbage can being knocked over.

"Stupid dog," Big John grumbled as he hefted himself from the recliner. The harsh winter had forced some of the bears down from the mountains. At least one had been rummaging through people's garbage lately. He limped into the kitchen, flipped on the back porch light and peered out into the darkness. He couldn't see more than about twenty feet out back. Beyond was nothing but blackness.

He opened the door, the cold air prickling his stubbly beard, and stood there listening. He didn't want to have to go out there, not because he was afraid of bears, but because he was tired and the cold made his left knee ache. The damn thing had never been the same after the accident. But at least his disability payments were enough for him to live off of, and it *sure* as hell beat working for the highway department, sweating your ass off in the summer and freezing it off in the winter.

There was a sudden yelp, and the dog fell silent.

"Butch?" Big John called out, but the dog had stopped barking. The damn thing was constantly running off, chasing after every damn rabbit and squirrel it saw. A couple of times it had come back all scraped up and bedraggled, like it might have tangled with a coyote or a bear.

The sound of applause came from the TV in the living room. Big John slammed the door and hurried back into the living room to see if he had been right.

"All right," said Pat Sajack. "Time for the next word after we come back."

"Goddamn it," he growled. He had missed the answer and he was sure he had known it.

While the commercial was on, Big John pulled on his shoes and lumbered to the closet. He put on his old coat and pulled out the shotgun he kept there. On his way back through the kitchen, he reached into the pantry and took down the battery-operated lantern he used whenever the power went. He stepped out back.

"Butch?" he called out, but there was no sound of the dog.

He hobbled through patches of snow and dead grass, past the rusting carcass of a '54 Ford pickup that had been there when he bought the place, and into the darkness beyond the reach of the porch light. Thirty yards ahead loomed the dark wall of trees.

Big John had never been afraid of anything. He had always been big and strong enough that no one ever messed with him much. That wasn't to say that a few hadn't tried, but they had all learned their lesson quick enough. But tonight, something about the pitch-black forest seemed foreboding, as if something lurked within its depths, something big and mean enough that it spooked even him.

He held the lantern over his head and tried to see past the edge of the tree line while he kept the shotgun at the ready in his right. But the darkness remained impenetrable. Cast by the porch light behind him his shadow stretched across the ground but fell short of the woods, as if it too was afraid to enter.

His hands and feet were beginning to get cold. His left knee ached. "Butch, get back here," he called again, but the forest had fallen silent.

And then he saw the amber reflection from a pair of eyes glaring at him from amid the trees. They were up high, staring down at him like an owl stalking a mouse. Maybe it was just an owl, but it didn't look like any owl he had ever seen before.

He lifted the gun and fired a shot off into the trees.

When the smoke cleared, whatever it had been was gone.

Big John turned and hobbled back to the trailer as fast as his stiff, achy legs could carry him.

Inside, he laid the lantern and the shotgun on the table. He jerked open the refrigerator and grabbed another Black Star. He popped the top and slammed half of it. With his nerves sufficiently settled, he shuffled back into the living room and sank into his easy chair once more, all thoughts of the dog and the ruckus out back already put out of his mind.

"Doris, it's your spin," said Pat.

"G!" Big John shouted. Against his advice, Doris guessed, "T."

"No, I'm sorry, no Ts," came Pat's reply.

Big John just nodded and shook his head. *Stupid bitches never learn,* he thought as he slammed down the rest of the beer.

CHAPTER 54

Denver

Charlie Wiesman stared at the monitor, anxiously waiting while the latest in a series of programs he had tried continued to run. "Come on, baby. Come on," he coaxed, rubbing the side of the CPU tower.

He picked up one of the last fries from amid the pile of grease-stained take-out sacks, pizza boxes, and Red Bull cans that littered the dining table next to his computer desk. The desk was in the dining area because the light was better and there was more space than in his apartment's tiny bedroom. He took a bite of the fry, made an awful face, and tossed the remainder back. The oil had congealed. They had moved beyond the point of no return.

He pushed his glasses back up from the end of his nose and continued monitoring the latest program's progress. He was getting close. He just *knew* it. He had been going at it for almost thirty-six hours straight, slowly worming his way deeper and deeper into GenTech's intranet, until now he felt certain that once he managed to gain access to this current node, which had been the hardest to crack by far, he would find what he was looking for.

Getting into the system initially had been easy enough. It was amazing how many people would give out their access ID and password when called by someone who professed to work in the IT department and who needed their info to test out a new user-verification program they were installing. It really didn't matter what the excuse was. Virtually

228

every time, all it took for the ruse to work was to keep calling until you got a hold of someone who wasn't all that familiar or comfortable with computer networks—most often women—and bombard them with technobabble until they gave you what you needed.

Once into the company's intranet, Charlie had run a program that mapped out the network and then gone in search of those systems that appeared to be associated with research and development and had the most security protecting them. Those were the ones most likely to contain important company data. Once identified, he began breaking into them one by one and examining their contents. It would have been much faster if he could have used Moe, Larry, and Curly—his systems at the office—where he could have had all three processors working on different nodes at the same time, but that was strictly forbidden by the boss for any activity like the one he was currently conducting, so he was forced to tackle them one at a time.

So far, he hadn't come across anything he thought was useful, at least not to him—just a bunch of scientific data regarding some of the drugs they produced, including the formulas and clinical trial results. If he had been an industrial hacker, it might have been of great value, but he knew it wasn't what Carrie was looking for, so he had kept at it until he had come across the node he was trying to hack now. He had almost skipped it without even trying to access it, because the mapping program he used had identified it as an unknown processor type. Looking at the settings for the system, Charlie figured it was one of the company's old, outdated mainframe systems that had been tied into the network during the conversion and then never removed from the network. But when he tried to access the node to see what it was, he hit a firewall. And not just any generic, off-the-shelf variety, either. This one was custom-designed, and a kick-ass one at that. Charlie had been trying to gain access for the last day and a half, without even the slightest hint of success. He had been totally stumped to the point that he was forced to ask some of his hacker friends for help. One of them said it sounded similar to one he had run across when he hacked the Department of Defense's network prior to their upgrade and had e-mailed Charlie a copy of the program he had created to crack that one.

The first few attempts had failed, but this time, it had already run twice as long without getting kicked out, which was a good sign.

He decided to risk taking a bathroom break. He hated leaving the room while a program was still running. It seemed like every time he did, something happened while he was gone. And if he missed any information that scrolled up the screen or the system locked up on him, he would wind up wasting time having to backtrack.

He hurried down the hall, took care of his business with all possible haste, and rushed back. He was still zipping up when he returned to the dining nook only to find that—as usual—something had happened while he was gone. The screen was now filled with a menu of eight numbered items, below which the computer's command prompt blinked patiently while it awaited his input.

He was in.

With a whoop of delight, he plopped into his chair and began his exploration of the system. He spent the next several hours downloading everything he came across that he thought might be pertinent without taking time to go through any of it. It was nearing 6:00 a.m. on the East Coast, and he didn't want to be online when the company's IT people started showing up to work. He worked as long as he could safely before he backed out of the system, making sure he hadn't disrupted any of the files and removing all evidence of his intrusion from the system logs. Lastly, he inserted a small block of code that created a back door for him in case he needed to reenter the system later and then severed the connection.

Bordering on delirium but fueled by adrenaline and copious amounts of Red Bull, Charlie began the tedious task of sorting through the immense amounts of data where he would find all of the answers that he and Carrie had been searching for, although what he found was more incredible than either of them could have ever dreamed.

CHAPTER 55

After he dug through the data for over an hour, Charlie was confident he knew what had happened. It was improbable and unbelievable, and yet there it was on the monitor before him. He had waded through gigabytes of information, most of it confusing and far beyond his level of comprehension, but he felt certain there was enough hard evidence contained therein to blow the story wide open.

He grabbed the phone and dialed Carrie's cell. It was just after seven now, and she was probably still asleep, but he couldn't wait to tell her what he had found. This was the kind of shit that made national news. It was like Woodward and Bernstein and Watergate. It was the kind of shit that won the Pulitzer Prize, for God's sake. It was fucking unbelievable!

There was no answer.

"Carrie!" he practically yelled into the phone as her voice mail picked up. He was so exhausted and wired and excited that he was babbling, but he couldn't help it. "I've found it. I know you told me not to do it. But I couldn't help it, and it was worth it 'cause I found it and you're not going to believe it. Call me as soon as you get this. I have to talk to you ASAP. Call me."

After he hung up, he tried to think of how else to get in touch with her. He had to get the information to her as soon as possible, but there was so much of it he couldn't send it via e-mail. The e-mail server for the paper's network would kick it out as being too large even if he compressed it. Instead of sending it all to Carrie at once, he wrote her an e-mail summarizing what he had found and attached a couple of what he considered to be the most important files as proof. Hopefully, she would check her e-mail and phone for messages this morning and call him back. In the meantime, he would copy all of the information to a flash drive and FedEx it to her. Just to be safe, he would make another copy to take to the paper.

* * *

Montana

Carrie stared at her face in the mirror. It was as if she were looking at a stranger. It had been so long since she had worn makeup that she had almost forgotten what she looked like with it on. Now, standing there, eyeliner still in hand, she looked at the results and began to reconsider. Her plan was to go to the Hungry Horse Reservoir Control Station to ask if they had noticed anything unusual regarding the fish and wildlife in the area, and if she got lucky, obtain a copy of the water analysis reports for the last two years. She knew it was a long shot, but she also knew from past experience that men would do just about anything if you played them right, which meant makeup, her red V-neck sweater, and a little flirtation.

After the problems with Bret, she had done everything she could to avoid drawing attention to herself, which included eliminating makeup. She had taken steps to make herself unattractive and undesirable and therefore—in her mind—as safe as possible.

Now she was intentionally doing just the opposite. She hated what she was doing. It made her feel cheap and manipulative, but she knew her chances of success increased greatly if she played the game. And that was all that mattered to her now. More than anything, she was determined to find the answers she was searching for, and if it wound up costing her a little self-respect, then self-respect be damned.

Once finished with her makeup, she plugged in the blow dryer. She was going all out today, which meant no ponytail. She had worn her hair pulled back for as long as she had been going without makeup, but today, it was coming down. She flipped the switch, and the whistling drone of the blow dryer continued her uneasy transformation.

Across the room, the ringing of the cell phone in her purse went unheard.

CHAPTER 56

Maryland

Nathaniel Brockemeyer marched down the long mahogany and marble corridor with the steady stride and stone facade of a soldier on parade. Only the slight limp and lack of a uniform gave away the fact that he wasn't. He opened the thick oak doors into the plush reception area and slowed just enough for Linda to inform him that the general had no visitors and was expecting him.

There was a sucking sound as the doors to the general's office swung inward, breaking the soundproof seal on the room. The general didn't look up from the stack of papers neatly arranged before him until Nathan had come to full attention before the desk. Neither of the men wore uniforms anymore, which might have made the formality of their behavior seem unnecessary, perhaps even pathetic to some. But to Nathan, it was a sign of mutual respect they shared for each other, even if their country had decided not to show them any of its own.

Both of them had been released from duty after the War in Iraq, the general because of his age and Nathan because he was seen as damaged goods. He had blown out his knee jumping from a rooftop in Bagdad, and it had never fully recovered. Still worse, there had been allegations of inappropriate behavior involving female prisoners in Iraq. The army had taken the easy way out, using his injury as an excuse to discharge him without having to prove anything regarding the sexual misconduct. The general had not had any difficulty finding a respectable position almost immediately, whereas Nathan, saddled with a bum knee and rumors of impropriety, had struggled to survive. In fact, had it not been for the general calling and offering him a job as an industrial security specialist, Nathan knew there was a good chance he might have followed a path of destruction similar to that of other disillusioned soldiers with nowhere else to go.

As it was, Nathan had been saved, and in an ironic twist of fate, he had even been given a chance to serve his country again, albeit in a much more covert role. He had tremendous respect and admiration for General Colquitt, who, in his eyes, had saved his life. So it was no wonder that he was willing to do anything the general asked of him without questioning.

After a few moments, the general took off his reading glasses and looked up. "Any problems with Dr. Bennett this morning?" he asked.

"No, sir," Nathan replied. "He seemed a little nervous about the deployment from the Hawk, but during the briefing, he seemed excited about their prospects."

"Good." The general nodded. "I have another mission for you. I received a call from our informant yesterday. It seems that reporter is beginning to dig in places she shouldn't. And this morning, I was notified that our intranet was breached overnight. Some very sensitive data was downloaded. The perpetrator, it seems, was quite talented. He did an admirable job of covering his tracks, but fortunately for us, we managed to track him back to the source."

The general handed him a piece of paper with a name and address.

Nathan looked at the information, carefully memorizing it as he had been trained, and then handed it back to General Colquitt to be shredded and incinerated. Nothing that might link them to the infiltrator was to leave the office.

"A private plane is waiting for you at the airport," the general said. "Once you have finished there, report back to me through the usual method for additional instructions."

"Understood," Nathan replied.

"Very well," the general said. "You are dismissed."

Even though it was not necessary, Nathan saluted the general and then turned and marched from the room, silently repeating Charlie Wiesman's name and address over and over in his head.

CHAPTER 57

Montana

Kyle listened as the sheriff gave them a rundown of the leads that had come in overnight. They had been doing it long enough that it had almost become routine, but today, there was something different about the sheriff. His normally clear, gray eyes now seemed dull and flat, with dark circles beneath them as if he hadn't slept well. The deep timbre of his voice seemed tempered with uncertainty, as if something had shaken him.

Perhaps their failure to resolve the case was finally taking its toll. It was something Kyle was well acquainted with—the gnawing guilt that slowly ate away at him with every passing day. Kyle could imagine how much worse it must have been for the sheriff. This was his jurisdiction, and it was his job to protect the people within it.

After he watched and listened to him a while longer, Kyle decided that George Greyhawk had taken on the appearance of a man haunted by something. It was an unpleasant realization. Kyle found it disturbing that the seemingly rock-solid sheriff might be starting to crumble. It reminded Kyle of other glimpses he had caught in which the sheriff's persona had seemed to suddenly shift right in front of him, as if he had become someone else entirely. He had seen it happen outside the Joneses' cabin when the sheriff said he sensed something wrong with the forest and then again outside of Tucker's cabin after his disappearance.

Carrie's comments regarding chemical or biological agents triggering hallucinogenic schizophrenia suddenly came to mind, and while Kyle wanted to dismiss it as ridiculous, a part of him couldn't help but wonder if that might be the cause for the sheriff's odd behavior. What if the flurry of murders was being caused by a biological phenomenon that was beginning to affect the entire population of the Flathead Valley like the flu or something, only instead of feeling achy and running a fever, you gradually became delusional to the point of murder?

Kyle's thoughts on the matter were cut short as the telephone intercom beeped. It was the overnight operator informing them that SAC Geddes was holding.

Lewis punched up the call on the speakerphone. "Morning, JoAnne. You guys come up with anything?"

"Nothing to get your hopes up over," she replied. Her raspy voice sounded even harsher than usual over the speakerphone. "On first pass, GenTech appears to be clean, at least on the surface. Since they're involved in the manufacture of vaccines for chemical and bioweapons, they're subject to intense screening and monitoring procedures for how the stuff is handled. It's all thoroughly documented. They've even hired a retired four-star general to help ensure their compliance with the military's requirements. But we're just getting started. There could still be a big ugly hidden in their closet, and if so, we'll find it."

"What about the plane crash?" Lewis asked. "Is it possible that there was something hazardous onboard?"

"Don't know about that yet," said Geddes. "Apparently, there's still an ongoing civil suit between GenTech and the families of the victims. Needless to say, GenTech's officials are all being tight-lipped about it. They referred us to their lawyers. The NTSB's official report on the incident didn't tell us anything either. We've requested copies of all the NTSB's investigation records. I'll forward a copy of everything to you as soon as we receive them. And make sure Ms. Daniels knows she's not to print a word of this until we clear it first. Tell her we'll give her first shot at anything we come up with before releasing it to the press."

Lewis looked at Kyle, who nodded and said, "I'll call her."

"I've got the lab in DC going back through all the evidence sent to them to see if they can find any traces of foreign agents in the blood samples," Geddes continued. "The guys in the lab want you to contact the people in charge of Hungry Horse Reservoir to get copies of their water quality analysis for the last twenty-four months to see if something might have contaminated the water supply. Same for the Montana Fish, Wildlife & Parks.

"What about the guy who had the heart attack in the forest?" Lewis asked. "Larry—"

"Henderson," Kyle finished for him. Even Lewis wasn't his normally sharp self this morning.

"Yeah, Henderson," Lewis said. "Have they checked to see if he might have been affected by anything?"

"They're working on it. There wasn't anything that came up in his original autopsy," Geddes replied. "They ran a toxicology, but it came up negative for any of the usual drugs. The lab's going to run more tests on his samples to see if they find anything that fits with this new information. Anything new on your end?"

"Not yet," Lewis said.

"All right, keep me posted."

"Will do."

CHAPTER 58

Denver

Charlie's stomach growled. He hadn't eaten since … he couldn't remember when exactly, sometime late last night when he had gone to the all-night burger joint a few blocks away. He looked at the clock in the corner of the screen and was glad to see it was after 11:15, which meant he could order take-out.

He pulled open a drawer to his right and shuffled through the collection of colored menus until he decided he was in the mood for Chinese. He had yet to have Chinese during the marathon, and it was less likely to make him sleepy than pizza was. He called in his order for Kung-Pao chicken with fried rice and then offered the driver an extra five-dollar tip on top if he would stop at the 7-Eleven a few blocks away and pick up a couple of Red Bulls on the way.

He was still sitting in front of the computer, copying the data to the second flash drive when the doorbell rang. He jumped up and hurried to the door, anxiously grabbing the sack with the cardboard cartons of food and the Red Bulls from the startled Middle Eastern deliveryman. The Red Bulls were even cold. Awesome! He hated it when they brought the warm ones. Red Bull over ice just wasn't right.

After paying, he slammed the door and checked on the computer. The hard drive's led was still blinking as the data was transferred. *Time for a bathroom break*, he thought. Leaving his lunch on the table, he had just starting down the hall when the doorbell rang again.

Must have forgotten the fortune cookies or something, he thought as he went back to the door. But when he opened the door, it wasn't the deliveryman. Instead, a large, hulking man with short-cropped, reddish blonde hair was standing there. He held a small silver aerosol can in front of his face. Charlie had just enough time to notice that it looked like a can of mace or pepper spray before the mist hit him in the face. Only it didn't burn his eyes or nose at all. It just made everything go instantly black.

* * *

The darkness faded slowly, gradually shifting to a blurry gray before coalescing into the speckled white of the ceiling. He had the bed-spins, as if he had been up all night drinking, but he didn't remember any of it. Charlie's head lolled to the right. He looked for the clock beside the bed, but it wasn't there. Instead, he saw a long, low brown table with his gaming magazines and a couple of oddly shaped white things with neon green in the middle of them. They looked scary but strangely familiar. Then it came to him—*Xbox controllers.* That's what they were. *On the coffee table, but why is the coffee table in the bedroom?* Then he noticed the entertainment center beyond and realized he wasn't in his bedroom. He was on the couch. He must have stayed up too long and crashed on the couch.

He tried to sit up to shake the cobwebs from his head, but his body didn't respond. It was as if all his limbs had turned to jelly. A warm, floating feeling suffused his body, radiating from the inside out, but something wasn't right. Nothing moved.

The only true discomfort came from his right arm. He looked down, struggling to focus through the kaleidoscopic haze until the three arms slowly merged into one. There was an ugly red spot and small trail of dried blood in the crook of his arm.

There was a noise behind him. He tried to turn his head enough to see into the dining area, and in the process, he wound up falling off the couch. He landed with a *thud*, but he didn't feel a thing. Except floaty. And warm. He felt warm and floaty.

As he lay with his face against the carpet, he giggled as he realized that this was what the world looked like from a roach's point of view. He could see just enough to notice a man sitting at the computer.

His computer. And he was doing something to it. Charlie stopped giggling.

The man ejected a CD from the drive. He must have been loading something onto his computer. Something about it seemed wrong, but his thoughts were all muzzy, as if his head were full of warm molasses, and he couldn't seem to remember why.

The man picked up the flash drives from the table, dropped them into his pocket, and then walked over to Charlie. Squatting down in front of him, he held up the CD. Incredibly bright, silver-white light reflected into Charlie's eyes. He squeezed them shut, but the light kept bouncing around inside his head like a disco ball in a spotlight.

A steady tapping on his forehead caused him to open his eyes. Had he passed out? The man rapped the disk against his head a few more times. "Who are you working for?"

Working for? Couldn't the idiot see he wasn't working? He was lying on the floor. He giggled at his cleverness and then realized he was drooling onto the carpet. Oh, well, he'd just make a little lake for the roaches. He giggled some more.

"Who are you working for?" the man asked again.

His tongue was thick, and the words came out slurred like after he went to the dentist. "Ithss for Cair-eee."

"Who else knows about this?"

"No uhn, jus Caireee."

The guy held up a slip of pink paper. "Is this where she's staying?"

Charlie tried to focus. His eyes burned from the sweat seeping into them. With great effort, he managed to make the swirling colors slow enough to make out the FedEx receipt from when he shipped Carrie's laptop. "Caireee," he mumbled pleasantly. She was going to be so happy when he told her what he had found. He should call her. But he felt so sloshy, like he was getting seasick. Maybe the man with the silver disc would help him.

But the man didn't seem interested in helping him at all. He just pulled out his cell phone and began punching in a long string of numbers. Maybe he was calling 911.

"I'm done here," he said. "Yes, sir, I'm on my way there next."

The man flipped his phone shut. Without another look in Charlie's direction, he walked out the front door and closed it behind him. It was then that the sickening realization of what had happened finally dawned on Charlie.

He puked as a massive black wave came crashing over him, washing away the light.

CHAPTER 59

Montana

Carrie had just turned off Highway 2 onto the road leading to Hungry Horse Dam when her cell phone rang. As she dug it out of her purse on the passenger seat, she was careful not to drive off the road into the deepening valley on her right.

It was Agent Andrews. Carrie felt an unexpected thrill of excitement. "To what do I owe this pleasure?"

"I just wanted to call you to let you know we're following up on the lead you gave us," he said.

"Have you found anything?"

"Not yet," he said. "But there's something else I need to ask you."

"What?" she asked, excited by the prospect.

"This isn't something you're working on for a news story is it?"

"What do you mean?"

"There's concern from within the bureau that you're working on this for your paper. I told them you weren't, but I have to be sure."

"No," she said. "You know why I am doing this." She was disappointed and a little hurt that he had even asked.

"Good," he said. "That's what I told them. If anything comes of this, I promise you've got first rights to the story, but I have to ask that you not print anything in the paper about any of this until then."

"Fine." She knew he was just doing his job, but that didn't mean she had to like it.

"Also, I have to ask that you stop investigating on your own. Now that the bureau is looking into this, they want to make certain that no one does anything to tip anyone off."

Carrie was silent for a moment. She didn't like where this was going. She began to get an uncomfortable feeling in the pit of her stomach. If she had uncovered something that the government was trying to cover up, it would make sense that the FBI would know about it. She thought she could trust Kyle, but she wasn't sure about the people he worked for.

"Okay, fine," she said, even though she had no intention of doing it.

"Thanks," he said. "I'll be sure to keep you informed of our progress."

She hung up and flung the phone onto the passenger seat.

A few miles ahead, she pulled off the road onto the narrow asphalt lot alongside the visitor center overlooking Hungry Horse Dam. The lot was vacant except for a couple of cars, so she pulled in sideways, afraid the rear end of the Hummer would stick out into the road if she didn't. She sat in the truck for a moment, gathering herself, but she couldn't shake the growing sense of dread she felt after Kyle's phone call. Was the FBI really investigating it, or were they just putting her off while they worked to help cover it up?

The only way she could be certain of the truth was if she found it out for herself.

She flipped down the mirror on the back of the visor and ran her fingers through her hair as she checked her makeup. She hadn't worn any in so long that it was jarring to her at first, but she had to admit that she *did* look better with it on.

The main visitor center overlooking the dam, which had been recently renovated, did not open to the public until May. Carrie continued past it to the smaller building housing the dam's operational offices. Inside the front office, she was greeted by a middle-aged secretary with mousy, gray-brown hair.

"Hi there, how can I help you?" she asked.

Carrie looked for a nameplate on the desk, but there wasn't one. "Hi," she said with a pleasant smile. "Is the facility manager in?"

"Yeah," the secretary replied with a suspicious tone. "Can I ask what this is about?"

Thanks to Charlie, Carrie had picked up her laptop from the motel office yesterday. Last night, she had used it to search for more stories involving Hungry Horse Reservoir and had come across an interesting one that had prompted her trip here today. According to the article, early last year, the US Department of Energy had begun a program designed to conserve the genetic purity of the Westslope cutthroat trout in Hungry Horse Reservoir and upstream of it in the south fork of the Flathead River. What Carrie had found curious about the story was that part of the program included the introduction of fish toxins, piscicides, into the reservoir and streams in order to kill off hybridized species of fish that had been introduced into the area and threatened the native cutthroat population. The piscicides, it said, had been applied through the use of aircraft, boats, and in some cases, packhorses had been used to reach some of the more remote streams and lakes.

The story had grabbed Carrie's attention for several reasons, the first being that it could have been used as a way of explaining a sudden appearance of large numbers of dead fish in the lake, and secondly, it gave a reason why aircraft might have been seen flying over the lake and up the valley, dumping large clouds of chemicals.

Carrie saw it as a convenient method of covering up the fact that the government had been trying to mitigate the damage caused by whatever had been on the GenTech plane.

"I'm Wanda Hipple with the *Kalispell Mountain Herald*," she lied, hoping the name might at least sound familiar enough to work. "I'm working on a story about the cutthroat trout conservation program currently underway, and I was wondering if I might have a few minutes of his time."

"Do you have an appointment?" the secretary asked, her eyes narrowing.

"No, I—" Carrie stopped as a dumpy man with a big potbelly walked into the room. He was wearing gray polyester pants and a short-sleeved dress shirt with a burgundy tie that barely reached more than halfway down his belly.

"Can I help you?" he asked as he hitched up his pants. He had thinning hair combed over the top of his head and beady little eyes behind horn-rimmed glasses.

"I hope so," Carrie said, trying to sound demure as she walked over, holding out her hand as she introduced herself again. Apparently, she pulled it off, for the man smiled and shook her hand.

"Bob Kellogg," he said, his eyes drifting down to her chest. "Why don't you come on back to my office?" She wasn't disgusted by him half as much as she was with herself for what she was doing.

Like the secretary's up front, Bob's office was also furnished with an old metal desk along with a row of metal filing cabinets against one wall. The wall behind him was covered with large, complex-looking mechanical diagrams that Carrie assumed were representations of the plant's systems. The computer monitor behind him was covered with a number of readouts in varying colors. Carrie surreptitiously glanced at the display, but she was unable to make out anything useful.

Bob motioned to an old chair with a brown vinyl seat in front of his desk. Carrie took a seat and began to pull her notebook from her satchel. Instead of returning to his chair, Bob remained on the side of the desk with Carrie, casually sitting on the front edge with one foot still on the floor, giving him an even better vantage point from which to look down her sweater.

Carrie could feel her face beginning to flush. It was going about as well as she could have hoped, but now she found herself having second thoughts. She didn't see any family photographs on his desk, which made her feel a little better, until she noticed the gold wedding band on his pudgy finger.

"Now what can I do for you?" Bob asked cheerfully.

"Well," Carrie said. "I'm working on a follow-up story about the cutthroat trout mitigation program that was begun last year, and I was wondering if you could give me an update on the status of the program."

Carrie feigned interest, dutifully taking notes while Bob towed the company line, raving about the success of the program. She even asked a couple of follow-up questions before she got to the real reason she had come. "And what about the water quality after the application of the piscicides?" she asked.

"Well, of course, there was a temporary situation after the application," Bob said. "But the water was detoxified through the use of potassium permanganate."

"So you're saying the water is safe for human consumption?" she asked.

"Oh, certainly," Bob said. "No concerns whatsoever."

"I assume the toxicity levels were carefully monitored throughout the process?"

"Of course, constantly," Bob said. "Your readers can rest assured that there are no reasons to be concerned about the water quality downstream of the dam," he said with a placating smile.

"That's good to know," Carrie said, forcing a smile in return. "I don't suppose you would happen to have copies of those toxicology reports for say … the last two years or so, would you? It would *really* alleviate their concerns if we could tell them that we were given copies of those reports to verify the accuracy of the DOE's claims." She placed her hand on his knee as if emphasizing the point.

"Well, of course, we do," he said, glancing down at his knee and then over at the filing cabinets. "But—"

"I would *really* appreciate it," Carrie purred as she leaned forward.

Bob leaned forward as well, his eyes inexorably drifting to her chest. He was so close Carrie could smell his sour breath as he spoke. "I don't see why that would be a problem," he said. "I just need to make a call first to get approval." He got up off the desk and began walking back around to his chair. "Funny thing is … the FBI called just this morning asking for the same information and instructing me not to give out any records to the media without going through them first. Still got the number right here. If you don't mind waiting, I'll call 'em right now."

"I really don't have time for that," Carrie said as she stood up. "I'm … up against a deadline."

"Oh, it won't take but just a minute," Bob said, reaching for the phone.

Carrie leaned across the desk and put her hand on top of his, holding the receiver down. "Bob, can't you just give me the records without calling. I promise I'll make it worth your while."

Bob had a confused look on his face as she leaned across his desk.

Tiny pinpricks of sweat began to bead on his greasy face. He licked his lips.

"No. I'm afraid I can't," he said as he lifted the receiver.

Carrie turned in a huff and quickly stormed from the office before he could make the call.

"If you'll give me one of your cards, I'll be happy to bring 'em to you," Bob called out to her as she left.

Back in the truck, it was all Carrie could do to keep from crying. She took several deep breaths to try to calm down. She felt … *dirty* … and sick to her stomach. She had made a fool of herself—and all for nothing.

After she mentally berated herself for a few moments longer, she began to slowly regain her composure. As she thought about her setback, she knew what she had to do next.

She started up the truck, threw it in gear, and with a spray of gravel started across the dam toward her grandparents' cabin and the far end of the reservoir.

CHAPTER 60

Highway 83 heading east through the tiny town of Swan Lake was wet and slushy as the snow of the previous few days slowly melted away. The roads at the southern end of Flathead Valley had gradually worsened as they neared the mountains. Kyle rode along with the sheriff and Lewis as they headed toward the Jewel Basin area in order to follow up on a complaint that had come in overnight. The place belonged to a Mr. John Morris.

The complaint had come in around 9:00 p.m., with reports of gunfire heard in the area around Mr. Morris's residence. When the deputies arrived to question Mr. Morris, he admitted to having fired a shot into the woods behind his trailer because, as he said, "I seen something out there, and my dog's gone missing." That coupled with the location of his trailer, which was just over the mountains from Hungry Horse Reservoir as well as within a few miles of Jeffrey Wayne Tucker's cabin, was enough to warrant further investigation. Marasco, of course, had thought differently, telling them in no uncertain terms that he thought they were wasting their time.

Just past the sweeping curve where Highway 83 headed south toward Swan Lake, the sheriff turned left onto an unmarked, gravel road. The tall, thin evergreens and the white-barked trunks of the aspens were plastered with numerous neon yellow and orange signs stating, "No trespassing" and "No hunting." The addresses for the residences along the way consisted of wooden planks with reflective numbers nailed to trees or fence posts next to each drive. They had nearly reached the end of the road when they came to the lot for Mr. Morris.

The mobile home was in disrepair, the once-white siding riddled with dents and brown streaks of rust. A cord of firewood stacked against the left side of the place was covered with blue plastic sheeting to keep it dry, and it was held in place with an assortment of boards and rocks. A rusty, metal-pipe carousel used to dry clothes creaked as it slowly turned in the breeze.

A man about five foot nine and weighing at least 320 pounds opened the door. His dirty, stained undershirt was worn thin, and his thick, wiry black hair and beard looked as if it hadn't been trimmed in years.

"John Morris," the sheriff said in the deep, commanding voice of his.

"Yeah," Morris replied. "What'd I do now?"

"In the report filed by my deputies, you claimed there was someone or something in the woods behind your place last night. We'd like to take a look around back to see if we can find any evidence of trespassing."

"Yeah, sure. Help yourself."

"Have you found your dog yet?" Lewis asked.

Morris looked at Lewis and appeared to frown, although it was hard to tell with the overgrown beard. "Nah, I still ain't seen him."

"Thanks," Lewis said. "We'll let you know if we need anything else."

They proceeded around back and began a careful examination of the area behind Morris's trailer. They found no noticeable footprints either on the soft, damp ground or the patches of crusty snow lying in the shadows. Foot by foot, they worked their way deeper into the woods, scouring every inch of the needle-strewn carpet of wet, decaying leaves and rotting bark.

The sheriff called to them and knelt down, pointing. When he reached the sheriff's side, Kyle was able to see the dark, blood-spattered leaves.

"Do you think he might have hit someone?" Lewis asked.

The sheriff moved forward and picked up a small clump of dark fur. The fur was matted with blood.

"Probably his own dog," said the sheriff. The disappointment in the tone of his voice was obvious. Once again, a potential lead appeared to be gone.

Kyle sighed. "So do we keep looking?" he asked, looking farther into the woods.

The sheriff didn't reply. He just continued to crouch there, his eyes narrowing as he looked at a tree five yards in front of him. Kyle followed his gaze. The rough bole of a tall pine stood before them, but the real item of interest was the freshly cut, eight-inch-long gash in its trunk about three feet above the ground.

As one, they moved forward, carefully scanning the ground in front of the tree. There were no footprints, but there was an abundance of dog prints. And more blood.

"I'll call forensics," said the sheriff.

Kyle couldn't explain why, but like the sheriff, he felt certain that the cut in the trunk of this tree had been made by the same weapon that had severed the body parts of the previous victims. Perhaps it was just a hunch like all good agents claimed to have from time to time, but perhaps this time, it was more than that, similar to the way Sheriff Greyhawk seemed to sense things. It was as if he *knew* they were getting close, that somewhere there *was* an answer to all of the murders and the key to it all was right in front of them.

CHAPTER 61

The Hummer hit a deep rut, sending snow and frozen mud flying. The front end lurched to the left toward a drift of hard-packed snow and ice. Carrie yanked the wheel back to the right. The left front tire clipped the bottom of the mound. The truck bounced in front. It lurched again as the rear tire struck the drift, and then, miraculously, it straightened back out and continued to barrel down the road as if nothing had happened.

Carrie glanced at the Styrofoam cooler in the floorboard of the passenger seat. In spite of the rags and old T-shirts packed around them, the glass jars within *clinked* against each other as she made her way down the rough stretches of road.

She knew she was probably wasting her time, but after her setback that morning, she hadn't known what else to do. A growing sense of dread had begun to bloom in her chest, threatening to overwhelm her if she didn't keep moving. So she had gotten the water samples herself. She had filled one of the jars in front of the cabin before she had driven to the far end of the reservoir, where she had filled the other jar in the freezing river just upstream of where it fed into the lake. Allan would know of somewhere she could send them for analysis.

She had made it almost all the way back to Hungry Horse Dam when her cell phone, which was still lying in the passenger seat, beeped, indicating it was back within the service area. She had been out of range since crossing the dam earlier that morning. She slowed down to pick up the phone and looked at the display to see if she had any messages. But the message waiting display didn't work when she was

253

roaming. She hit the button with the icon of an envelope to retrieve her messages. The digitized voice informed her that she had one message. She frowned when she heard it had come in at 7:13 a.m. Somehow, she had missed it.

"Carrie!" came Charlie's unmistakable, high-pitched voice. He always sounded that way when he got excited, just like a little kid. "I've found it!" he practically squealed with delight. "I know you told me not to do it, but I couldn't help it. And it was worth it, 'cause I found it and you're not going to believe it. Call me as soon as you get this. I have to talk to you ASAP. Call me!"

"Charlie," Carrie growled at the phone. She hated it when he left her messages like that. She had told him time and time again to just leave the info on her voice mail, but he never did, preferring instead to build the suspense before giving her the information himself.

She punched in the two-digit speed-dial number for the office in Denver. When Sandy answered, she told Carrie that Charlie hadn't come in all day.

"He told us he was doing research for you," Sandy said. "Did you try his cell phone?"

"Not yet, but I will. Thanks." Carrie hung up and called Charlie's cell. After five rings, his voice mail picked up. The greeting was a digitized sample of the Three Stooges singing, "Hello ... hello ... *hello*," followed by Charlie imitating Curly Neale saying, "Nyello, leave a message."

"Charlie, it's Carrie. I've been out of range all day, and I just now got your message. Call me back as soon as you get this. And if you get my voice mail again, just tell me what the hell you found. This is important. I don't have time to fool around." In frustration, she tossed the phone back onto the seat. Carrie knew Charlie well enough to know that he had probably been up all night again, for the second night in a row. He had probably hit the wall and crashed out about midafternoon. It was now a little after 5:30, which meant he probably wouldn't come to again until around midnight.

Then she remembered her laptop at the motel room. Hopefully, Charlie had thought to send her an e-mail before he had hit the sack. Heedless of the rugged road, she stepped on the gas.

CHAPTER 62

The drive along Highway 2 heading into Kalispell was a scenic one. The afternoon sun spilled through the snow-dappled evergreens along the side of the road, the frozen flakes sparkling in a dazzling kaleidoscope of light and color. The natural splendor, however, was lost on Nathaniel Brockemeyer, whose sole focus was on the twin ribbons of gray slush in front of him. He made sure to stay under the speed limit, carefully watching the road signs for directions. Every car that passed him on either side on the road was watched warily until it was safely out of range. He couldn't afford to get a speeding ticket or be involved in an accident. Even though the Xterra he drove was a rental and he was traveling under an alias, any documentation of or, more importantly, any witnesses to his visit were to be avoided at all costs.

On the outskirts of town, Nathan pulled to at a stop at the light. He reached into his jacket pocket and pulled out the pink FedEx receipt. The address read:

Carrie Daniels
c/o Mountain View Motel
640 E. Idaho
Kalispell, MT 59901

There was no unit number on the receipt. Apparently, whatever had been delivered had been sent to the main office for her to pick up.

He only had a disposable phone without any GPS, so using the paper map that came with the rental, Nathan made his way through town until he came to the motel. Across the street on one side was a McDonald's, which wouldn't work, because it had too much traffic for his purposes. On the other corner, however, was an old drive-in burger joint that had gone out of business and had been turned into an unofficial used car lot for the local residents. Two cars were parked there, handmade signs and shoe polish on the windshields that announced, "For sale," along with the phone numbers. He pulled into the lot next to the two cars and carefully positioned the Xterra so that he could keep watch on the motel across the street without being suspicious.

Nathan shut off the truck, and without taking his eyes off the motel, he pulled off the glove on his right hand. He reached inside his jacket pocket and removed the photograph of Carrie Daniels. He had studied it intently on the plane from Denver to Kalispell, looking at it for long moments until her face was forever imprinted in his memory. He should have destroyed it before now, but something had prevented him.

The photo was a typical headshot printed from the *Denver Inquirer's* website, but something about her smile and the look in her eyes struck Nathan. She was beautiful, and he wanted her. On his last assignment, he had been forced to keep his desires under control, but this time, the situation was set up perfectly for him—the girl, alone in her motel room. He thought of the possibilities, the images playing through his head until he shuddered with desire. He could hardly wait for the opportunity to explore each and every nuance of his hunger.

Fortunately, that time would come sooner rather than later. And he would take his time with her. He would be much more deliberate than he had been in the past, allowing himself to savor each and every exquisite moment until her very last breath. He stroked her photograph with his thumb, becoming hard in anticipation of how he would use her.

He placed the photo on the dash where he could see both it and the motel, and then reached into his jacket pocket again, this time removing a Plen-T-Pak of cinnamon-flavored gum. After he unwrapped a stick, he thrust it in his mouth, savoring the hot, sweet flavor as he settled in to wait.

CHAPTER 63

It was late afternoon by the time Carrie made it back to the motel. The Hummer was so big it practically took up two parking places, but it was the off-season, so the lot was virtually empty. After she parked, she went around to the passenger side and took the cooler out of the floorboard before she hurried into her room.

Inside, she sat the cooler on the dresser next to the TV. She sat at the small table beneath the window, pulled open her laptop and turned it on. Next to it was a portable printer—which Charlie had been thoughtful enough to send along with the laptop—a sheaf of blank paper, and the pile of her collected notes. She drummed her nails on the table as she waited for the machine to boot up. Surely, Charlie had thought to e-mail her the information.

Once the desktop came up, she double-clicked on the icon for Internet access. Her heart was pounding as she pulled up her e-mail. There were two messages from Charlie.

She retrieved the first one. As he often did when he was talking to her, Charlie went on to explain in minute detail—none of which Carrie understood—how he had managed to hack into GenTech's system. She skimmed on down through the text:

Carrie,

You aren't going to believe this. But I think I found it. GenTech has an old Unix server tied onto their intranet.

There was so much data it took a while for me to figure out what I was looking

257

at. But now, I'm certain that these guys have been experimenting with genetic manipulation to create some sort of new species. But not like Dolly, the sheep, or anything like that—more like a monster of some sort. And a mean-looking mother at that! There are digitized sketches of this thing with wings and claws and big-ass teeth. And there are hundreds of photos of these gross-looking things—you can hardly tell what they are—with a bunch of scientific gibberish superimposed over them. It looks like something straight out of Alien or The X-Files. I've attached some of the files, but there's just too much of it to send via e-mail. I'll copy it to a flash drive and FedEx it to you.

You may think I'm crazy, but I know this is it. There was just too much security around that thing for it not to be it. Let me know if you need anything else.

Can you say "Pulitzer?"

Charlie

For long moments, Carrie just sat there staring at the screen. Could that be it? It seemed so ridiculous. The idea that it might have been some chemical or biological agent that caused hallucinations and murderous rampages in people had seemed somewhat plausible, if far-fetched. But this just seemed too unbelievable. Charlie was right. It *was* like something out of *The X-Files*.

She had heard of recombinant DNA applications in plants and animals used to create hardier strains of corn that were resistant to pests, and there were those cows that produced more milk than normal. She had even heard stories of human ears being grown on the backs of mice and predictions that within a few years, kidneys and livers might be grown in pigs to be harvested for organ transplants. She knew genetic engineering was making things possible that had been thought to be inconceivable just a few years ago, but how was it possible to create a completely new species like Charlie was talking about? And even if it *was* possible, why intentionally create a monster? All of the developments she had heard of had positive applications. But where was the market for this? The idea that a company would spend millions, perhaps even billions on research to create a monster fit for nothing more than the lead role in a horror film seemed preposterous.

But then she opened the attached file.

And she believed.

The photographs were unlike anything she had ever seen. There were gruesome, hideous, malformed *things* on stainless steel examination tables, some still whole, others split open and dissected like frogs in a high-school biology class, its insides held open with clamps and pins. Overlaid on many of them was white text and arrows pointing to specific areas with explanations of the results of "X" gene on the growth of the subject or "Y" gene on the cranial development. There were dozens on them, each one more graphic and disturbing in its own way. Carrie's stomach turned at the sight of them. If she had eaten recently, it might have wound up on the screen of her laptop.

Finally, she had to stop looking. She had to get this information to Kyle as soon as possible. But she didn't know his e-mail address, and she knew if she tried to explain it to him, she would sound like some loony conspiracy theorist. She printed out Charlie's e-mail and then began printing out the first of the digital pictures. With only the portable printer, the print quality of the photos was poor and grainy, but she hoped it was good enough to back up her story and get the FBI moving without having to wait for the flash drive to arrive.

Printing out the photos was incredibly slow. The third one was only halfway done when she got tired of waiting and opened the other e-mail from Charlie. The text simply said, "More information." Another file was attached. She clicked on it to open it.

The progress bar appeared, and the hard drive hummed as the file was downloaded. Once complete, the progress window disappeared. The LED indicators at the top of the keyboard blinked in a dizzying display, and the hard drive growled as a new program started.

The printer froze and began beeping incessantly. She tried to click on the printer icon to see what the problem was, but the screen of her laptop had frozen up as well.

The hard drive continued grinding away.

She hit CTRL-ALT-DEL to bring up the task manager, but nothing happened. She tried it again. Still nothing.

Shit. The damn thing was locked up. The data file she was trying to open must have been too big and crashed the system. Frustrated, she hit the reset button. Nothing. Except the lights continued to blink crazily and the hard drive kept on grinding. She hit the button again and again, but nothing changed. She didn't know what else to do to get the damn thing to stop, so she unplugged it and pulled out the battery. The system died instantly. All the LEDs went out, and the screen went blank. The hard drive stopped. The cooling fan wound down with a fading *whirr.*

She snapped the battery back into place, plugged in the AC adapter, and then hit the power button. The LEDs blinked, and the system beeped at her as the fan started up again. The screen blinked and then went blank except for a line of text across the top that read, "No bootable media present. Insert boot disk to begin."

Carrie sat there a moment, confused as to what had happened.

And then it hit her.

The second file had been a virus that had crashed her system and wiped her hard drive.

Which meant that they knew their system had been infiltrated and that they had taken steps to cover their tracks. No doubt they were already destroying all the evidence on their own system as well.

Carrie's heart began racing. The clock had started ticking, and time was running out. If something wasn't done fast, there would be nothing left to prove what had happened. She had to get to Kyle before it was too late. She grabbed the printout and photos from Charlie's e-mail, jerked the half-printed one from the printer, and stuffed them all into her satchel.

After she slung her purse and satchel over her shoulder, she threw open the door and nearly collided with the man outside.

CHAPTER 64

The chuddering roar of the helicopter rolled down the valley like thunder as the large Blackbird, flying at full tilt just above the treetops, raced toward its destination. The chopper, a specially modified MH-60G2 Pave Hawk, was complete with radar-jamming equipment, night-vision capability, and anti-icing systems for the instrumentation, engines, and rotors, making it perfectly suited for this particular mission.

Even though he couldn't hear the helicopter through the noise-canceling headset built into his helmet, Dr. Myles Bennett felt the vibrations all the way down to his bones. That and the fact that his entire body was trembling in fear caused them to rattle about inside him like a skeletal marionette dancing at Halloween.

Even with the doors closed, it was frigid inside the cabin of the helicopter. But inside his suit, Myles was sweating profusely, which caused the system's internal cooling system to kick on and only worsened his shivering. Again, fear was to blame for his condition. In spite of that minor malfunction, Myles was suitably impressed—and proud—of the suit's features. After all, GenTech had played no small part in the development of them. The armor plating woven into the suit and helmet was incredible. Constructed of a special nano-composite—made in part from the silk of spiders genetically engineered in GenTech's labs—it was waterproof, chemical-proof, and bio-proof, lightweight and flexible yet stronger than Kevlar while leaving no areas of its wearer unprotected. The helmets were sleek models that looked like something out of *Star Wars*, complete with built-in cameras, GPS sensors, and a computerized, heads-up display on the flip-down visors.

The communications system was digitally encrypted and controlled through the use of an eye-tracking system. Across the top were six rectangular blocks displaying the radio frequencies of each of the other men. By simply looking at a particular block and winking, you could select the individual you wanted to speak to, or by selecting the public icon, you could speak to everyone at once. In daylight, the information visor displayed in color, while at night, it offered either infrared or night-vision capability.

The big bird lurched. The bottom fell out from beneath them and dropped twenty or thirty feet in an instant. Myles's insides lurched as well, and for a moment, he thought he might be sick. He looked around the cabin to check the reactions of the five other men. None of them acted as if they had even noticed it. They were all dressed in identical black suits and helmets with no name or insignia anywhere. Had it not been for the briefing he had given them prior to donning the suits, it would have been virtually impossible to tell any of them apart.

To his right, Mitchell Ainsworth checked his watch. The mission commander reminded him of a drill instructor with a graying, blonde buzz cut and square-jawed face. Next to him, Javier Ramirez was calmly praying the rosary as he had been doing for a good portion of the flight. Across the cabin, Dietrich was asleep. His head lolled to the side in such a way that a portion of a brightly colored tattoo of a serpent-reptile-dragon thing could be seen on his neck. Bill Handley, the big farm boy from Kansas who everyone called "Busey" because of his uncanny resemblance to a young Gary Busey, and the stout black fellow, Johnson, were sitting side-by-side, talking through their helmets and giggling like a couple of school kids on a thrill ride.

The icon indicating Ainsworth's frequency lit up on Myles's display. "Peaches, what's the ETA to the drop point?" Peaches was Patricia Donaldson, a tall, busty blonde from Georgia who, aside from being one hell of a chopper pilot, was self-confident and beautiful, and she didn't take any crap from the "hard dicks" she worked with. Myles was terrified of her.

"ETA in twenty-five minutes, sugar," she replied in her syrupy-sweet, Southern drawl.

Along with all the innovations the suit had to offer, Myles suddenly wondered if it had any special features to deal with a soldier soiling himself.

CHAPTER 65

Carrie yelped in surprise.

The fat, bald man on the walkway outside her door was so startled he nearly dropped his Dr. Pepper and bag of Cheetos.

"Sorry," Carrie called out as she dashed past him toward the Hummer.

The man muttered something under his breath and glared at her indignantly, but by then she was already opening the door. The truck started with a roar that further startled the poor man, who schlepped off toward his room, shaking his head in disgust. Carrie threw the truck in gear and tore out of the lot with an even louder roar.

She tried to remain calm as she raced down the street, weaving in and out of traffic. Overhead, lumpy, blue-black clouds were gathering, forewarning of bad weather and killing off the day more rapidly than normal. The streetlamps lining both sides of the street had come on, but they offered faint illumination against the growing darkness.

* * *

Kyle peeled the paper farther back, pulled two of the Rolaids from the roll, and popped them into his mouth. *I've become a living cliché,* he thought as he chewed up the dry, chalky tablets. Even so, it was better than the agonizing heartburn he had been suffering through. *I don't know how they do it,* he thought as Lewis came walking back in, accompanied by the lingering scent of cigarette smoke. He had a fresh cup of coffee in his hand. He had refilled it at least four or five times today, twice

263

before the trip out to the Morris place and at least twice, if not three times since.

"Marasco still hasn't shown up?" Lewis asked.

"No," said the sheriff.

Just as well, Kyle thought. He wasn't in the mood for any smart-assed comments right now.

The phone beeped, and Lydia's voice came over the intercom to tell them that Al Crowe was on the line. They had been waiting on the coroner's report on the blood samples from behind Morris's place.

"Put him through," said the sheriff.

The phone rang once as the call was transferred.

"Hello, can you hear me?"

"We hear you, Al," said the sheriff. "What have you got for us?"

"Don't know if I've got good news or bad. I guess it all depends on how you look at it, eh? Anyway, I ran the hemoglobin test on all the samples first, and they all came up negative, so we know it's not human blood. The three I've tested so far have all turned out to be dog blood. I'm testing the last two right now."

"How long before you get those back?" the sheriff asked.

"About another half hour, assuming it's also from the dog or it matches one of the antiserums we've got on file. If not, it may be days before we can identify it. Either way, I'll call you as soon as we know."

"Thanks, Al," the sheriff replied and then punched off the speakerphone.

"Shit," Lewis growled.

"You really think he shot his own dog?" Kyle asked.

"Yeah, I do," Lewis said. "We know he was drinking last night. The son of a bitch probably got crocked, and when his dog started barking, he got pissed off and blasted it from his back porch."

"But what about the cuts on the trees?" Kyle asked. He wasn't ready to write off the possible connection as fast as Lewis seemed to be.

"We won't have anything back from the lab for days, if not weeks, but I'm not holding my breath. Those could have been from anything. Besides, even if they do match, they don't give us—"

Lewis stopped as the conference room door opened. It was Clayton.

"Uh, 'scuse me, sheriff, but Miss Daniels is here again. Says she needs to talk to Agent Andrews immediately. Says she's got something important to show him."

Lewis looked across the table to Kyle. "Don't ask me," Kyle said with a shrug. He had no idea what she was doing here.

"Send her in," Lewis said.

Carrie came rushing in with a handful of papers clutched in her hand, shaking them in their faces like a teacher scolding her students for their bad test scores. Kyle just sat there, his mouth agape. But it wasn't her behavior that caught him off guard. It was her appearance. For the first time since they had met, her hair was down, and she was wearing makeup. In spite of appearing windblown and dismayed, she looked absolutely stunning.

"You've got to do something fast," she said. "I've got information that proves that GenTech is to blame for all the murders—only now they know about it, and if you don't do something fast, they'll get away with it, and I—"

"Wait a minute," Lewis said. "Slow down. What the hell are you talking about?"

"GenTech," she said, throwing the papers onto the table in front of them. "This proves that they're running a genetic research project, and I think that whatever was on that plane is what's been killing all those people."

Lewis picked them up and began looking at them. "What do you mean this proves that?" he asked. "Where did you get this?"

"From Charlie. He downloaded it from one of the servers on their network."

Kyle looked up at Carrie. He didn't like what he was hearing.

"Who's Charlie?" Lewis asked.

"Charlie Wiesman, the IT guy at the paper. He hacked into GenTech's network and—"

"He what?" Lewis barked.

Carrie stopped, her eyes widening. "He ... he downloaded a ton of stuff like this from one of their servers," she continued hesitantly.

"Goddammit." Lewis looked at Kyle. "I thought you told her to stop sticking her nose in where it didn't belong."

"I did," Kyle said. He looked at Carrie. "I told you we were handling this. You told me you would stay out of it."

"I ... what does it matter?" Carrie said. "At least I got it."

"Yes, it does matter," Lewis said. "This doesn't do us a *damn* bit of good!" he said as he slapped the papers onto the table.

"How can you say that?" Carrie replied. "You haven't even looked at it."

"It doesn't matter," Lewis shot back. "It was obtained illegally. It can't be used as evidence. We have to get a search warrant before we go in there for any of this to stand up in court. Now all they'll say is it was planted."

Looking at Carrie, Kyle noticed the tears beginning to shimmer in her eyes.

"I know how the system works," she said, her voice trembling. "Believe me. I've seen it in action enough to know. You guys'll screw around waiting for some judge to tell you it's okay to go look for something, and by the time you get there, it'll be too late."

"That's not true," Kyle said, even though a part of him knew she was right.

"Yes, it is," Carrie said. "That's what I was trying to tell you earlier. They already know they've been hacked. Charlie sent me two e-mails with files attached. The first one had this information and a lot more, which I started to print out. I assumed there was so much information he had to send two files. But when I opened up the second file, it crashed my computer. I think it was trying to wipe out my hard drive. I couldn't get it to shut off, so I unplugged it and pulled the battery."

The room was silent. It was as if all the air in the building had suddenly been sucked out, leaving them in a giant vacuum.

Kyle found it hard to breathe, as if the air had been sucked out of him as well. She had lied to him. He had trusted her, and she had betrayed him. Just like always, he had been too trusting, too naïve. Now it was all falling apart. Carrie looked at him, trying to gain his support with the same beseeching look he had seen in her eyes before, but he wasn't going to make that mistake again. He turned away and looked to Lewis.

"Gotdamned reporters," Lewis growled, his jaw clenching in anger as he shook his head. "Fuck!" he shouted, slamming his fist to the table.

Carrie turned and ran from the room.

CHAPTER 66

Lewis was on the phone immediately.

Focus, Kyle thought. *Stay focused.* He picked up the printouts from the table and looked at them. There was the e-mail from Charlie and two complete photos and a part of another. The print quality wasn't great, but it was still good enough to make out what looked like photographs taken during the early stages of development of a strange, monstrous-looking beast with leathery wings, sharp, talonlike claws, and a long, toothy snout. A yardstick had been placed beside the creature to show that it was a little more than two feet long. It was impossible to tell how far along in its development the thing was or how large it might become. The second page was what appeared to be a computerized design sketch of the creature, complete with measurements and notes with arrows pointing to different areas of interest. According to this, the thing was over seven feet tall. Structurally, it was much larger than the one in the photograph, and it had large, batlike wings extending from its torso. The main trunk of the thing was reminiscent of a crocodile, as was its long, toothy snout, but it stood upright on thick, powerful-looking hind legs. Behind it trailed a long, whiplike tail. As Kyle looked at the thing, it reminded him of something out of a science-fiction or horror movie like *Predator* or *Alien*, and it occurred to him just how useless this information was without actual proof of the existence of such a creature. Who would believe that such a monster could be created in a laboratory, especially when it looked more like something created in a special-effects studio in Hollywood?

He understood why Lewis was so upset. Even with him on the

phone to Seattle now, it would take time for SAC Geddes to get in contact with Washington and then even more time for them to show sufficient evidence to a judge to get a search warrant. And search warrants were required to be very specific about what was being looking for and where. There was no way for them to pin that down yet, and even if they could, now that the intrusion had been uncovered, it was certain that the people involved at GenTech were already hard at work removing or destroying any evidence that might remain.

Lewis was right. They were fucked.

"I know. I know," Lewis's voice rose as the conversation became more heated. "It's not his fault. He told her. Some hacker at her office did it. Yeah, the guy's name is Charlie Wiesman. We don't have an address. He's the IT guy who works at the paper with her. Yeah, get a team over there ASAP."

Realizing his job was on the line in spite of Lewis's defense, Kyle's attention remained locked on the phone conversation.

"No," Lewis replied. "There are some notes and a couple of photographs she printed out. But then she opened the virus, and it wiped out her hard drive."

But that wasn't exactly right.

"Wait a minute," Kyle said. "Carrie said that when her computer locked up, she unplugged it and disconnected the battery."

"Yeah, so?" Lewis said, not understanding the significance of that statement.

"So maybe the program didn't finish running. There might still be some data on her computer that can be retrieved, but we've got to get it from her before she tries to do anything with it."

"Did you hear that?" Lewis said into the phone. "Yeah, okay, we're on it. I'll call you as soon as we have it." He hung up and turned to the sheriff. "Do you have the address of the motel she's staying at?"

"It's in her file," he said, already rising to get it.

To Kyle, Lewis said, "You still have her cell number?"

"Yeah." Kyle pulled out his phone and dialed the number. Her voice mail picked up. "Carrie, it's Kyle Andrews. Don't do anything with your computer. Don't try to boot it up again or anything. There still might be something on it that we can retrieve. We're on our way to your motel to pick it up, so if you get this, just wait for us there. If you have any questions, call me at this number."

"I hope you're right about this," Lewis said as they hurried out. "Or both of us might be looking for a job."

CHAPTER 67

The helicopter settled into the clearing, sending up great clouds of whirling snow. The side door slid open. As lithe as panthers, four black-clad men leapt from the chopper and fanned out and set up a perimeter. Inside, Myles shuffled toward the door, afraid of tripping over something. He reached out for the wall to steady himself. It was difficult to see in the cargo bay with his helmet on. He wasn't used to the night-vision display, which turned everything into shades of luminous green and severely reduced his field of vision, not to mention that it painfully mashed his glasses against the bridge of his nose and forehead.

As he stood in the doorway, Myles could make out the shapes of two of the men about twenty yards out. They lay flat on the ground, facing outward, their weapons at the ready. His knees nearly buckled and he grabbed the door frame even tighter as snow swirled into the chopper. His body was wracked with shivers as icy spiders scurried down his spine.

"Jump!" Ainsworth's voice crackled in his ear as he was shoved from behind. He tumbled from the helicopter, arms windmilling about wildly. He landed awkwardly and stumbled forward a few steps before he fell face-first onto the hard, frozen ground.

A hand grabbed the collar of his suit and hauled him back upright. "You all right?" Ainsworth's voice came again, lighting up the small icon at the top of his display. It sounded sincere, but Myles could imagine the laughter and jokes being cracked over the private links.

He was afraid his voice would fail him, so he just nodded. He returned to the doorway of the chopper along with Ainsworth, and with the help of the copilot, unloaded the rest of the gear, including two large equipment trunks and two eight-foot-long-by-two-foot-diameter cylinders, which contained twenty carbon-fiber/titanium rods and twenty flat panels that would be assembled into a transport cage. In spite of the lightweight composites, the cylinders were still incredibly heavy.

Once offloaded, Ainsworth saluted the copilot as the door rolled shut. "All clear," he reported.

"Happy huntin'," Peaches radioed as the chopper lifted off. "You boys call when you need a lift. And don't keep me waitin' too long now, you hear? Blackbird out."

Myles watched forlornly as the dark helicopter disappeared into the night.

"Damn, I'd love to bang the shit outta that," radioed one of the men over their private link.

"Dream on, Busey," Johnson's frequency lit up. "Just 'cause she's from Georgia doesn't mean she'd waste her time with a big-eared country dick like you."

The radio crackled, and the display lit up as the others joined in on the laugh. Then Ainsworth's voice came through loud and clear: "All right, let's get set up."

Pentagon cabin was a small, one-room way station located just off the Spotted Bear River trail. Situated in a small meadow, it was normally open from late June through August, providing a remote campsite for anglers fly-fishing along the Spotted Bear River or an overnight stop for the hikers and backpackers traversing the trails along the Limestone and Chinese Walls. About twelve miles from the Spotted Bear Ranger Station, the trail leading to it was closed the remaining nine months of the year because of the heavy accumulations of snow, which brought with it the threat of avalanches and, during the spring thaw, mudslides. During the off-season, the cabin was sealed, windows shuttered and the front door barred and locked with a thick padlock.

It took only seconds for Ramirez to unlock the door with the small laser cutting torch he pulled from his pack.

A short while later, the two large trunks were unpacked, and their remote ops station was up and running. Ainsworth unpacked the field tactical data unit, a highly ruggedized computer and display that everyone simply called the FTU, and set it up on the wooden table in the middle of the room. The FTU communicated with small transmitters built into each of the men's helmets. The unit displayed telemetry readings from each of the suits up to three miles away, including distance and direction in relation to the base unit, a live video feed from the small, helmet-mounted camera, which was capable of viewing in night-vision and infrared mode, and the wearer's vital signs—heart rate, blood pressure, respiration, and body temperature.

Outside, six tripods were located in a circumference around the cabin, stakes driven through the eyelets in each of the feet to hold them in place. A dish-shaped antenna that was similar to a miniature satellite dish was mounted to each of the tripods and switched on. The units were extremely sensitive ultrasonic receivers capable of detecting the slightest sounds at a range of up to five miles, although that range was severely reduced in mountainous terrain like the kind they were in now. For this mission, each of the units had been attuned to detect the emanation of one very specific frequency.

Inside the cabin, Dr. Bennett moved in close to Ainsworth, struggling to see the FTU's screen. A series of beeps emanated from the unit's speaker, and the row of icons across the top of the screen switched from red to green as each of the transponders came online.

CHAPTER 68

Tears blurred Carrie's vision as she drove back to the motel. It was always the same whenever she needed help from the authorities. It had been the same way when she had gone to the police about Bret. All they did was sit around and make excuses for why they couldn't do anything. And to think, she had actually trusted Kyle when he had told her he would help. He had seemed sincere, but when push came to shove, he was just like all the rest of them.

She felt so stupid, rushing in there all made-up like a cheap whore, raving about what she had found only to fall apart and go running out in tears. After all she had been through recently, she thought she had become tougher because of it, but obviously, she had been wrong. When Agent Edwards had yelled at her, she had crumbled just like the old Carrie. Nothing had changed.

Sitting at a stoplight, she noticed a convenience store on the corner across the street. Brightly colored, neon beer signs lit up the night, calling to her like the bright lights of Vegas. Only these lights didn't offer riches. They offered something even more enticing to Carrie. They offered a means by which she could escape into a haze of numbness, a momentary sanctuary from the cruel reality of the world. It was so much easier to simply wash away the pain instead of enduring it.

She switched on the left-turn blinker.

As she did, she thought of her parents and grandparents and how disappointed they would have been if they were still around, especially Audrey Gran, who had always given her credit for being stronger than she really was. But now that her grandmother was gone, there was no one left who believed in her, no one left to prop her up when she needed it most. She hated that they were gone, but worse, she hated the fact that she was all that remained of their legacy. They had been such special people. They deserved better.

A sob escaped her. The red light across the intersection shimmered as fresh tears gathered in her eyes.

The turn signal continued its steady *tink ... tink ... tink*.

The light turned green.

Tink ... tink ... tink.

Biting her bottom lip so hard that it hurt, she drove on through the intersection without turning.

* * *

Carrie opened the door to her room, flipped on the light switch, and tossed her purse on the table as she stepped inside. She felt wrung out, like a dirty dishrag left to dry out in the sink. She thought about soaking in a long, hot bath to try to forget about what had happened. At least she hadn't gone into that—

Something smelled odd. She sniffed, trying to place it. It was slightly sweet ... like cinnamon. That's what it was. It smelled like—

A hand clamped down over her face, pressing a noxious-smelling rag against her nose and mouth.

She tried to turn, but her attacker was strong. He held her tightly against him. She kicked and clawed, trying to break free, trying to scream. But it was no use.

Her mind raced, fear pounding through her veins. She felt light-headed. The corners of her vision grew dark.

In desperation, she reached behind her between the attackers legs and grabbed a handful of his manhood.

She squeezed—hard.

The man grunted and moved back, trying to escape the death grip she had on his testicles. She threw her other elbow behind her, slamming into his gut just below his ribs. His grip faltered, and she broke free. He blocked the door, so she raced for the bathroom, screaming for help as she ran.

He reached her before she made it. Together, they slammed into the far wall.

The breath was knocked from her. His big hands crushed her arms as he slung her about and slammed her into the other wall. Her ankle turned, and she fell. They tumbled to the floor between the bed and the dresser.

The man pulled his way up her body. She kicked and punched and clawed at him, but he was too strong. He crawled on top of her and pinned her arms to the floor. Behind the black ski mask, his pale blue eyes were electric, charged by the excitement of the struggle. As he crushed her arms beneath his knees, he pressed the rag over her mouth again. She whipped her head back and forth, struggling to keep from breathing in the fumes, but she could already feel herself beginning to slip away. Dark shadows gathered around her.

Fighting against the darkness, she managed to wriggle her left arm free from the elbow down. Her hand was growing numb. She flopped it about, desperately grabbing for something—anything—that might keep her from going under.

Beside the dresser, her hand closed around a thin plastic cord.

Her vision faded around the edges, the light shrinking to a distant circle as if she were falling down a well.

Clinging to the wire, she pulled with everything she had left.

The lamp tumbled to the floor with a crash, plunging the room into darkness.

CHAPTER 69

Thanks to the thermal warming feature of the suit and the fire in the cabin's fireplace, Myles had stopped shivering, but he knew it was only a temporary reprieve. He could already feel them returning—tiny tremors that started low in his spine and radiated upward through his shoulders and into his hands.

Having already assembled the cage, the rest of the team waited patiently. Busey and Johnson stood behind Ainsworth, watching the FTU and quietly offering an occasional comment or suggestion. Sitting in one of the rough wooden chairs, Ramirez calmly cleaned his handgun while Dietrich sat on the edge of the wooden bunk bed, passing the time by balancing a large knife with the point down on the back of his knuckles.

"There it is," Ainsworth said, startling Myles as the computer began to beep. The target was located approximately four miles southwest of their current position, moving at about thirty miles an hour in a westerly direction. Ainsworth switched to the mapping screen, which showed their location in the center of a topographic map and the location of the target as it sped across the screen before it disappeared from view.

"Damn," Ainsworth growled. "All right, men. We're in business. Time to go hunting. Johnson, I want you and Dietrich to head north. You've got Shadow Mountain. Busey, you and Ramirez take Bungalow Mountain to the south."

The plan was for the men to head in different directions from their current location, setting additional transmitters as they went in order to increase the coverage area. Then, when the creature returned to its roost, they would be able to pinpoint its location and go in after dawn to tranquilize it while it slept. If they were unsuccessful the first night, they would repeat the process each successive night until they were successful. When they were ready for pickup, Ainsworth would use the satellite radio system to call Peaches.

The only real risk involved came from the fact that they were tracking the creature while it was hunting. There was a chance it would see the men as prey and attack, but with all of their specialized equipment and training, the threat to the team had been determined to be minimal.

"And remember," Ainsworth continued, "we want this thing alive, so no weapons other than the tranq guns unless it's a matter of life and death, and then you'd better think twice about it. Got it?"

"Yes, sir," the men replied in unison.

"All right," Ainsworth said. "Move out."

The men helped one another quickly shrug into their gear. Each of the black, hard-shell packs contained three transponders, a half-dozen tranquilizer darts, rope, rock hammer, carabineers and other repelling equipment, first-aid kit, thermal blanket, two MREs, and other necessary survival equipment along with a pair of small, lightweight snowshoes strapped to the outside of it. Each of the men carried a black, oddly angular air rifle capable of firing the tranquilizer darts at a velocity of 1,200 feet per second. The darts contained 30 cc's of a potent tranquilizer made from curare, which would paralyze the creature almost instantly without killing it. The weapon was fired from the shoulder but was also designed for use when the men were wearing their helmets. It had no scope attached to the top of the barrel. Instead, sighting was accomplished from a miniature digital camera mounted at the front, where the sight would have been located. The camera transmitted the image via a wireless link to the helmet's visor, which displayed a barrel's eye view as if one were looking through a typical scope, including targeting overlay. The system was capable of 20X optical and/or 30X digital zoom.

Each man pulled on his helmet and performed a quick systems check to verify his video and vital signs were being properly transmitted. Once these were cleared, they opened the door. Frigid wind swirled in from outside. Flakes of snow and ice sizzled and hissed as they landed in the sputtering fire. Then, like shadows on a moonless night, the men disappeared into the darkness.

Even after the door was closed and the fire had regained its strength, Myles found it did little to quell the shivers that racked his body.

CHAPTER 70

"Okay, there it is," Kyle said, pointing at the blue neon "Mountain View Motel" sign ahead on their right.

Lewis didn't say anything as he pulled into the lot. The units themselves were set back from the street about a half a block, with the motel office and a diner sitting out front. Lewis drove past the office and around behind the diner.

"That's her truck," Kyle said. The big, black Hummer was unmistakable. There was a car next to it on the passenger side, so Lewis passed the Hummer and pulled into a spot on the far side. A light snow had begun to fall, the flakes dotting the windshield momentarily before melting.

"Why don't you wait here and keep the car running. I'll get it," Kyle said. He wanted to talk to Carrie, and he was afraid if Lewis went in, he would just upset her again.

Lewis gave him an I-know-what-you're-up-to look and said, "Okay, cowboy. Go get it. Only you'd better not leave my ass sitting out here in the car more than five minutes, or else I'm coming in," he said, pulling out his pack of cigarettes.

"What's that supposed to mean?"

"I saw you gawking at her when she came in earlier."

Kyle got out without responding. "And don't smoke in the car," he snapped as he slammed the door.

Lewis looked at him through the window as he stuck a butt in his mouth.

Kyle shook his head and walked off.

He turned right and made his way along the walk in front of the Hummer, trying to think of what he would say to her. He didn't intend to apologize for Lewis, but he wanted to make sure she understood that he hadn't meant it as a personal attack.

Then he heard the crash. It had come from the room just ahead. *Carrie's room.*

He ran for the door.

He grabbed the knob and slammed into the door with his shoulder, expecting it to be locked. But it wasn't shut. The door flew open, banging into the wall as he stumbled inside.

The room was dark. The glow of the parking lot lights spilled in through the doorway, providing faint illumination.

A dark shadow rose before him, swinging. Kyle tried to duck, but the attacker's forearm cuffed him on the ear and stunned him. Another blow caught him in the gut. His breath exploded in a ragged cough as he was driven to his knees.

The attacker raced out the door.

Kyle tried to call out to Lewis, but all he could manage was a wheezing moan.

From out of the darkness came a muffled *whump ... whump, whump.*

Rising, Kyle staggered to the door. The walkway was deserted.

Still struggling to catch his breath, he slipped along the walk and scanned the backside of the diner for movement among the shadows of the dumpsters and AC units. He passed around the front of the Hummer. The interior lights were on in the car.

"Lewis?" he called out.

Lewis was nowhere to be seen. He must have chased the perp on foot. Kyle almost felt sorry for the poor bastard if Lewis actually caught him. Lewis hated chasing suspects. That was something cops did, not the FBI.

The driver's side door was open. The interior chime rang ceaselessly, a hollow, mournful sound like distant church bells on a foggy night. Then he saw the spiderweb of cracked glass in the front windshield.

Kyle crept around the car, approaching the open door. A faint groan and a haggard wheezing came from the other side.

Lewis lay on the asphalt, clutching at a bloody mess on his right side. He looked up. "Son of a bitch ... shot me," he groaned in disbelief. Beside him, amid the broken glass and beer can tabs, lay his cigarette, a thin tendril of smoke trailing away into the darkness.

"Oh, shit," Kyle gasped, kneeling next to him. "How bad is it?" he asked stupidly.

"Bad, I think," Lewis moaned, lifting his hand. Fresh blood burbled from the hole in his gut.

Oh, shit.

Kyle's concern for the attacker disappeared immediately. He had to get Lewis to the hospital—and fast. It wasn't far—he knew where it was from their trip to the morgue—and he didn't know how long it might take for an ambulance to arrive. "Hang on," he said. "I'll be right back."

He raced back to Carrie's unit and collided with someone as he barreled into the room, nearly bowling them over.

It was Carrie.

Thank God. "Are you okay?" he asked. Without waiting for a reply, he ran to the bathroom and grabbed all the towels from the metal rack above the toilet.

When he came out, Carrie was leaning against the open door, taking deep breaths of the cold night air. "Are you all right?" he asked again, rushing to her side.

"I ... I feel dizzy—"

"Hold these," Kyle said, handing her the towels. He put his arm under her knees, picked her up, and carried her. He hurried back to the passenger's side of the car and put her in the backseat.

After he grabbed a towel from her, he raced back around to Lewis and placed it over the wound. Lewis groaned as Kyle pressed down.

"Hold that," Kyle said, placing Lewis's hand on the towel. As gently as possible, he slipped his arms under Lewis and lifted him. Lewis groaned and spewed curses as Kyle slid him into the backseat.

Despite her grogginess, Carrie seemed to understand what was happening. She helped pull Lewis into the car, scooting back into the far corner and laying his head in her lap.

Kyle grabbed another towel from Carrie and put it over the first one, which was already soaked with blood. "Help him hold that."

Kyle jumped in and threw the car in gear. Tires squealed and smoke boiled from under the car as they rocketed from the parking lot.

They raced through town with the hazards flashing and the horn blaring. There was little traffic on the streets after dark, which was good, because Kyle had no intention of stopping. He flew through one intersection after another, heedless of the traffic lights.

In the backseat, Lewis coughed weakly.

Kyle glanced in the rear-view mirror.

Specks of blood dotted his lips and colored the corners of his mouth. His eyes, half-closed, met Kyle's in the rear-view mirror.

"Keep your eyes on the road," he wheezed. "It won't do us any good if you kill us before we get there." He coughed again, a wet, rattling one that sent fresh blood dribbling from his mouth.

"Hang on. We're almost there," Kyle said, "Just three more blocks."

He looked back through the bullet-riddled windshield. They were coming to the intersection with Main Street. Tires squealed as they slid through the turn. A hubcap flew off and shot across the median to the far curb.

They were heading north now.

Two more blocks. Just two more blocks.

The car bounced through the last intersection. Ahead, the sign for the emergency entrance came into view. Tires shrieking, he pulled beneath the porte cochere and slammed on the brakes, stopping just outside the entrance.

"We're here," he said, throwing the car into park. He leapt out and yelled for help as he ran around the car.

There was no one outside. The automatic glass doors swung open in front of him, and he raced inside. The reception desk was to the right. A lady holding a small child wrapped in a pink blanket stood there talking to the receptionist.

"I need help," Kyle interrupted. "I've got a gunshot victim in the back of that car."

The nurse looked up from the computer monitor. "Is it serious?" she asked.

"Yes, it's serious," Kyle shouted, holding up his bloody hands as proof. "There's a federal agent in that car with a bullet in his gut."

The receptionist's eyes grew wide. She jumped up and hurried through the door behind her, calling out to someone as she went.

Two emergency-room technicians came rushing out with a gurney and raced to the car. Kyle watched helplessly as one of the men leaned inside the backseat. The tech began giving rapid instructions to the other, but Kyle was unable to make out any of it. The other tech squeezed in beside the first, and together, they lifted Lewis from the car. Once on the stretcher, one of the men cut Lewis's sleeve and began working to get an IV into his arm while the other pushed the gurney, shouting out orders to the staff as he went.

Kyle watched as they rolled through the vestibule, sharp voices and clattering wheels echoing off the tile surfaces. Past the reception desk, a set of doors leading into the trauma area swung open. A nurse and a young man in blue scrubs rushed out to meet them. As one, the swarm disappeared through the doors, which whisked shut, swallowing them like a Venus flytrap.

Kyle was left standing alone in the driveway.

He heard something behind him. When he turned around, he found Carrie tottering beside the car. Her face was streaked with mascara, her sweater and jeans covered with blood. She held out one of the bloody towels as if unsure what to do with it. A bright red drop dangled perilously from one of the folds. It trembled in the blustery wind for a moment before it was blown loose. It fell and spattered the pavement.

As Kyle reached for her, Carrie collapsed into his arms.

CHAPTER 71

Javier Ramirez whispered a quick Hail Mary and crossed himself as he and Busey made their way out of the clearing. He always asked for the protection from the Blessed Virgin before he went on any mission, but this one in particular concerned him more than any he had been on before. There was something about the creature they were tracking that seemed unnatural, perhaps even demonic, and it was that element of the supernatural that spooked him more than any bomb-toting terrorist ever had.

"Man, I could sure use a piss right now," came Busey's voice over the radio. "I bet it'd freeze before it hit the ground."

Ramirez didn't bother to offer a response. That was just Busey being Busey. He was a good team member who could be counted on in a tight situation, but at times like this, his incessant babbling tended to get on Javier's nerves.

His display suddenly lit up in alarm. Javier dropped to his knees, the tranq gun at the ready. The visors weren't large enough to allow a digital map to be displayed. The only indicators they received were direction and distance. The signal had emanated 4,213 yards to the southwest from their current location and was moving away from them. He watched the numbers scroll upward until it passed out of range again. They waited for several more moments, but when the alarm remained clear, he gave the signal to begin moving forward once again. This time, Busey remained silent.

A few hundred yards farther up, they came to a steep drop off of about ten to twelve feet. During the summer months, when the river was at its peak, this would have been the bank of Beaver Creek, but at this time of year, it was hardly more than a small stream just beginning to emerge from the winter freeze. Each of them took turns making their way down the incline while the other one stood watch.

After they forded the creek, Ramirez checked their coordinates on the visor. They continued upstream for another half mile before they reached the junction with Wall Creek Trail. Here, they left the river's edge, turned right, and took the trail upstream along the ridgeline of Bungalow Mountain. They would deploy the transponders at various intervals along the climb.

Even with night-vision capabilities, the thick growth of spruce and fir reduced their visibility significantly. The bright green images devolved into dimly glowing shapes that shifted and faded like ghostly apparitions dancing amid the shadows.

Two hundred yards into the ascent, Busey called for a halt. "Fuck this," he said, reaching behind him to pull the snowshoes from his pack.

Ramirez stood watch while Busey struggled with the shoes. Under the current conditions, they proved to be considerably more difficult to put on than they had been during the training exercise.

A shrill buzzing went off inside the helmet as one of the transponders detected the creature.

Ramirez looked to the sky. Busey dropped and rolled onto his back, tranq gun in hand. Again, the display indicated that the creature was still several miles away. Ramirez watched the readout, but this time, instead of continuing until it was out of range, it simply stopped. It must have landed in a tree or on some rocky perch.

After several moments, Busey rolled back over and finished putting on the snowshoes. He stood up and stomped around a little to test them out.

"Hey, this is actually—" The alarm sounded again.

The display showed the same distance and direction as before, but then it suddenly jumped from several miles to several hundred yards and back again almost instantaneously. At first, Javier thought his eyes were playing tricks on him, but then it happened again, flickering between several miles and several hundred yards before stopping at 3,760 yards to the west.

"Did you see that?" Ramirez asked.

"See what?" Busey asked, still stomping around in his snowshoes.

"The display jumping back and forth."

"I didn't notice nothing wrong with mine."

Ramirez just shook his head. He looked up at Ainsworth on his visor and radioed back to camp. "Team One to base."

"Go ahead."

"Hey, chief, you notice anything strange about that last reading?"

"Yeah," Ainsworth replied. "We're trying to figure it out now. We picked up two signals, but the one that came in near your position was very weak. Team Two didn't pick it up at all. The doc here thinks we must be picking up an echo from the mountains. He's working on it now, trying to isolate the primary signal and filter out the rest so that shouldn't happen again. We'll let you know when we've got it fixed."

"And in the meantime?" Ramirez asked.

"Proceed as planned."

"Roger," Ramirez replied. He switched his com channel back to Busey. "Keep watch while I put on my shoes."

"Got it," said Busey.

Ramirez pulled the snowshoes from his pack and dropped them in the snow in front of him. He slipped the tranq gun over his back to keep it out of his way and then knelt down to snap on the shoes.

The alarm went off again.

"What the fuck?" Busey muttered, slapping the side of his helmet with the palm of his hand.

Ramirez stood up. "What?" One foot broke through the crust and sank into the snow, throwing him off balance. Before he could right himself, something slammed into him from behind and sent him flying.

He clipped a tree. Sharp pain shot through his leg as he went tumbling through the brush and into the snow. His display blacked out except for the personal icons, which lit up like a Christmas tree. An intense ringing filled his ears. He gasped for air, the ragged, wheezing sounds reverberating within his helmet as the buzzing alarm blared. It was like he had stuck his head in a beehive. He thought he heard the sound of tiny voices yelling at him from far away, but they were impossible to make out amid the chaos.

He tried to move, but something was wrong. It was as if his arms were being held down by someone. Everything seemed incredibly heavy.

After a brief moment of near panic, he realized he was upside down in a snow well beneath the tree. He kicked and flailed, struggling to right himself, but it was virtually impossible. The snow kept shifting around him, and the heavy pack weighed him down.

His display was partially covered with snow, and the rest of it was fogged up from his heavy breathing, making it difficult to see the icons and apparently impossible for the sensors to pick up his eye movement. No matter how much he tried to radio Busey, he got no response.

The buzzing alarm finally stopped. "Damn it. Someone answer me!" Ainsworth's voice crackled over the radio. "What the fuck is going on?"

Ramirez continued to struggle. It was getting more difficult to breathe by the moment. Had it not been for his helmet, he would have probably already passed out.

"What the fuck? Someone answer me!" Ainsworth continued to scream.

Ramirez finally managed to contort his body enough to shrug out of his pack. No longer restrained, he reached inside his visor to clear the snow. Once he could see the icons he radioed Ainsworth. "Chief, I'm here," he wheezed.

"Ramirez, what the fuck is going on?"

"I don't ... know," Ramirez said. "I got ... knocked off the trail. I'm ... buried ... in snow," he grunted as he continued to struggle.

After several more long moments, he managed to dig and claw his way out of the hole. Standing up, he opened his visor and began sucking in deep breaths of the cold air.

Around him, the forest seemed unnaturally still and quiet. It was pitch-black, the moon and stars obscured behind the thick veil of clouds that had rolled in.

With his glove, he wiped off the inside of his visor and flipped it back down. The forest sprang to life in a sea of green, but there was no sign of Busey. He tried to radio him but got no response.

"Ramirez, you there?" came Ainsworth's disembodied voice.

"Yeah, chief."

"Busey's locator shows him to be twenty yards northwest of your position. I'm not picking up any vital signs."

Ramirez grabbed his pack and scrambled back down the trail, scanning the area for Busey.

"Stop," came Ainsworth's voice. "You're right on top of him."

Ramirez looked around, but there was no sign of Busey. He began searching off the trail in the brush and under the larger trees in case Busey had been knocked into a hole like himself. Then he spotted something beneath a nearby huckleberry bush. He slogged through the deep snow, sinking to his knees with each step until he was able to reach it. As soon as he felt the hard, smooth surface, he knew it was Busey's helmet. He picked it up, terrified of what he might find. He whispered a quick prayer to the Virgin Mother before he looked inside.

It was empty. He sighed with relief, but at the same time, his fear of the mission had suddenly risen to new heights. He turned in a slow circle, watching the forest around him as if it were alive, a dark and malevolent spirit waiting to snatch him up without notice.

Ainsworth's disembodied voice came to him out of the darkness. "Did you find him?"

"Just his helmet, sir."

"Come again?"

"He's gone, sir," Ramirez replied. "He's just … gone."

CHAPTER 72

Kyle lifted Carrie in his arms and carried her into the emergency room. She seemed so light, almost frail.

As soon as the nurse at the reception desk saw him, she called for help. The two technicians who had just wheeled Lewis in came rushing back out with a second gurney.

"Was she shot too?" one of the techs asked.

"I ... I don't think so," Kyle said, but he wasn't sure. There was so much blood it was impossible to tell. It had all happened so fast that he hadn't even thought about that. Before he could look, the techs were over her, checking her vitals and rolling her off through the automatic doors.

Numb, Kyle stood there for a moment, unsure of what to do.

He reached for his cell phone but stopped. His hands and clothing were covered with blood.

"There's a restroom over there," the receptionist offered. "When you're done, I'll need to get some information from you."

"Yeah, okay," Kyle said and nodded.

The restroom was unisex, with enough room for a person in a wheelchair to maneuver within. Kyle engaged the lock on the door. Leaning over the sink, he looked in the mirror. He was shocked by his own reflection. He had a two-day beard growth, and his eyes appeared sunken, with dark circles beneath them.

Without waiting to clean up, he pulled out his phone and called the sheriff's department. The sheriff said that he would get Clayton and a forensics team over to the motel immediately and that he was on his way to the hospital.

Kyle called Seattle next. It was after six, but as expected, SAC Geddes was still in the office.

"Andrews, what are you doing calling me?" she asked. "You guys come up with something?"

"No, I'm … it's … Lewis has been shot."

"What? Jesus Christ, what the hell happened? Is he all right?"

"I don't know. We just got to the hospital," Kyle said.

"What the hell happened?" she asked again.

Kyle began to explain what had happened when he had gone to Carrie's room.

"Wait a minute," she interrupted. "You went to the room alone?"

"Yes," Kyle said. "Lewis was in the car. Someone inside was attacking Carrie. He hit me and took off. I tried to warn Lewis, but—"

"Damn it! I knew it was a bad idea. I should have never let Lewis talk me into it." It was as if she was talking to herself. She didn't even seem to care that Kyle was listening—or maybe she wanted him to hear it.

"All right," she sighed heavily. "Have the sheriff set up guards inside the ER or outside their rooms if they're checked into one. They're not to let anybody in unless it's a doctor, and then only with an officer present. Got it?"

"Yeah, got it," Kyle replied.

"All right. I'll get a pair of agents there just as soon as I can, but it probably won't be before morning."

"The sheriff and I can handle it until then," Kyle assured her.

"You don't do anything. You've already fucked up enough for one day. Where's Agent Marasco?"

Kyle flinched at the comment. "I don't know," he said. "He's been gone all afternoon."

"All right. I'll call him. Don't do anything until he gets there. And Andrews," she added, "the boys in Denver found Charlie Wiesman dead on his sofa. Said it was made to look like a heroin overdose, but his computer's hard drive had been wiped. Someone's serious about covering this up, and they're willing to do whatever it takes to do so. So stay put and watch your ass. You understand?"

"Yeah, I got it." Kyle replied.

"All right. I'll get Joan to call Lewis's wife and let her know—"

"No," Kyle interrupted. Joan Thompson was the other victim specialist in Seattle. "I'll call her."

"You sure?"

"Yeah, I should do it."

"All right," she said. "And call me the minute you know anything more about Lewis."

"I will," Kyle said and then hung up. It was obvious that Geddes didn't think he could handle the situation. He knew that as soon as the other agents arrived, he would be relieved of his duties ... and probably his job.

Kyle sighed. Maybe she was right.

He washed his hands in the sink. He scrubbed and scrubbed with water so hot it scalded. Even then it wouldn't all come off.

When he stepped out of the restroom, an elderly woman from housekeeping was cleaning up the blood on the waiting room floor. The strong smell of ammonia filled the room. Outside, a man was mopping the drive.

Kyle gave the receptionist the information she needed for Lewis and as much as he could on Carrie. He asked if there was any word on Lewis's condition.

"No, sir, not yet. He's been taken into surgery. It may be a while. There's a waiting room down the hall to your right that's a little more comfortable if you'd like to wait there."

Kyle nodded. "What about Ms. Daniels?"

"There didn't seem to be any serious injuries, but the doctor wants to keep her overnight for observation. I'll let you know as soon as she's checked into a room."

"She needs to be in a private room," Kyle said. "Let me know before she's transferred. We'll be posting officers outside her room for security."

The receptionist's eyes widened. "Oh. Yes, sir."

"Thanks," Kyle said.

He went outside. The car was still running, steam billowing from the exhaust before disappearing into the cold night air. He pulled into a spot facing away from the hospital and sat there for a moment, dreading what he had to do next. The wind moaned as it swirled through the hole in the windshield. The snow fell in fat, wet flakes that stuck to the glass, gradually obscuring the view. Blurry, yellow-white halos ringing the parking lot lights slowly disappeared behind the thickening mantle.

Shivers wracked his body. He turned up the heater but left the defroster off, preferring the privacy the snow offered.

He took a deep breath, and then pulled out his cell phone to call Rochelle.

CHAPTER 73

When Busey came to, he knew he wasn't in Kansas anymore. He knew, in fact, that he was in Montana, but it took him a few moments longer to figure out just how he had come to be where he was now, which was completely in the dark. His neck was stiff and sore, and his head was pounding. He reached up and felt his throat, which was badly abraded and sensitive to even the slightest pressure. He remembered his display going crazy just before he was struck from behind, and he seemed to remember the sensation of choking, but everything else was a blank. He *did* remember the briefing about the creature and its lethal tail, and he realized he was lucky to still have his head at all.

His helmet was gone, which made it impossible to see in the dark without the night-vision visor, but he could tell enough to know he was in some sort of cave or cavern. There were no stars overhead and no frigid winds blowing across his face. From somewhere far away, he thought he could hear the slow *plink ... plink ... plink* of dripping water. He reached back for his pack and flinched from the pain that wracked his entire body. His left leg was pinned beneath him in an awkward position that told him it had suffered a serious break. He tried to roll over, and the shooting pain in his right ankle told him that it was broken as well.

A strange clattering sound like that of sticks and twigs being dislodged accompanied his movements. The ground beneath him was spongy and wet. The entire place was permeated with the smell of limestone, but the overriding odor that burned in his nostrils was the scent of ammonia mixed with the sickening, rotten smell of what he assumed was a dead animal.

Gingerly, he managed to work his pack free from beneath himself, and he dug about blindly within it until he managed to put his hands on several of the flares and the transponders. He almost laughed out loud with relief. Even without his helmet and its built-in locator, there was still a good chance that Ainsworth and the others would be able to pick up the signal from the transponders and rescue him.

He shoved all but one of the flares into a pocket on the leg of his suit and then snapped off the end of the other one. A dazzling, blue-white light sprang to life, hissing and crackling. He tossed it a few feet away to illuminate as much as the area around him as possible. He squinted, momentarily blinded by the sudden light. As his eyes adjusted, he began to take stock of his situation.

As he had expected, he in was in some sort of cavern. He could make out the rough stone surface some fifteen feet away, which rose above his head. He was in the center of the room lying on top of a mound of stones and branches, decaying leaves, and pine needles, all of which was covered with a layer of putrid, black sludge. But then he saw more.

Bones.

What he had thought were sticks were bones in most cases. There were shattered tibia and fibula and femurs, exposed pieces of crushed rib cages, fractured and broken skulls, antlers and horns and claws and teeth and countless other shards and splinters too small to identify. There were black clumps of matted fur and wool and hair, the remains of dogs and goats and deer.

And humans.

He nearly puked at the sight of a severed arm, its bloated, purple flesh covered with writhing maggots. A silver wedding band was still on the ring finger. He tried to push himself away, sending paralyzing currents of pain shooting up his leg and throughout his body.

He rolled over to take the weight off his left leg, and with his arms and his right knee, he began clawing and scrabbling across the pile of bones and feces, desperately struggling to escape the carnage, but everywhere he looked, death and decay awaited him.

Grunting and groaning and verging on panic, he crawled across the mound. In spite of the cold, sweat poured down his face, burning his eyes, but he didn't dare try to wipe it away. His hands were covered with the putrid muck. At one point, he wondered if he had already died and gone to hell, fated to crawl across this hideous landscape for all eternity.

His hand came down on something hard and cold. He recoiled, but when he looked at it, he was amazed to find an old M16 with a severed strap lying amid the ruins. The large bayonet was still attached. Buoyed by his luck or perhaps divine intervention, he pulled it from the slime and used it to help lever himself across the floor. He checked the cartridge. It was empty. But at least the bayonet might provide him with some measure of defense until the others could reach him.

His left hand came down on something soft and leathery like a rotten melon, and he pulled away in horror, afraid of finding a severed head, its sightless eyes staring back at him. Instead, he found it was an oblong, gourdlike thing slightly larger than a football. It was split open down its length, as if something had exploded from within. A strange, yellowish puss oozed from it, as if a dozen rotten eggs had been cracked and poured inside.

Something moved in front of him. The flare behind him was beginning to die, filling the cavern with flickering shadows and making it difficult to see. He pulled out another flare, snapped the end from it, and tossed it before him.

A hideous, reptilian-looking creature about two feet tall stood before him, mewling and snapping. Its long snout, which was lined with hundreds of tiny, razor-sharp teeth, was covered in blood. It flared its wings open and shook them and hissed in warning before it turned back to bury its teeth in the ripped-open underbelly of what had once been a dog.

Busey snapped.

As he shoved himself forward, he screamed at the monster. "Get away from him. Leave him alone!"

The creature turned to face him, flapped its wings, and snapped angrily. Busey stabbed the thing with the bayonet, driving it through its belly and out its back. It screeched in agony, its tail writhing and twisting about wildly. Busey stabbed it again and again until the thing finally stopped moving. The only sound left to be heard was Busey's ragged, grunting breathing as he drove the bayonet into the mangled carcass again and again until at last, shaking and sobbing, he collapsed.

A rustling came from above. When he looked up into the darkened recesses of the cavern, Busey could just make out the shape of something large and black against the ceiling.

Then he realized something. There was more than one. There were two. No, there were three of them barely discernable amid the shadows in the flickering light. But during their briefing, they had been told that only one of the creatures had survived the plane crash.

And he knew they had made a terrible mistake. They had assumed there was only one of the creatures. But they were wrong. Somehow, it had managed to reproduce. Now there were as many as two or three generations of the things ravaging the wilderness and slowly spreading outward as their need for food increased during the harsh winter months. It also explained why he hadn't been killed right away. He must have been attacked by one of the offspring without the titanium blade on its tail.

One of the shadows on the ceiling moved again. Its leathery wings fluttered, as if it were just coming awake. He had to get out of there—fast. He began crawling across the pile, struggling to reach the side of the cavern, where he hoped to find a connecting tunnel or at least a low-lying overhang to hide beneath until help arrived.

Then he remembered the transponders. He looked behind him, where his pack still lay atop the pile of bones and guano some twenty feet away. He looked up at the ceiling. Nothing moved.

He looked at his pack again. It was almost directly beneath the creatures. He had no choice but to go back. Without the transponder signal, the others would never find him, and he knew he wouldn't survive the night if they didn't.

He began working his way back, making every effort to be as silent as possible. He would cautiously scrape and slide forward and then pause to look at the ceiling before he repeated the process. Each time he looked up, he was certain he could perceive more movement among the shadows than he had previously. Sweat poured from him. His body shook with exhaustion. The pain in his leg was so overwhelming he nearly puked.

When he put his hands on his pack, he almost cried out in relief.

He switched on one of the transponders, and a barely perceptible, high-pitched whistle filled his ears as the unit powered up.

Above him, there was movement again. He wasn't sure if it had anything to do with the transponder, but he left it where it was in the hope that it might serve as a decoy. As quickly as possible, while still trying to be quiet, he began clawing his way back across the grotesque landscape, inch by agonizing inch.

The flapping of wings above him broke the silence and stirred the air within the cavern. He froze. Slowly, he turned his head just enough to look to the ceiling.

A pair of malevolent, yellow eyes stared back at him.

It spread its wings and then dropped toward him. Busey rolled and brought up the rifle. The beast slammed into him, impaling itself on the bayonet. It screeched furiously, an ear-piercing wail that echoed throughout in the cavern. It snapped at him, razor-sharp teeth mere inches from his face. Claws tore and ripped at his midsection as it sought to disembowel him.

Busey screamed and rammed the bayonet farther into the beast's belly. The thing clamped down on his arm with its long snout, tearing through the protective suit and into his flesh. He ripped the bayonet sideways with all his strength. Gouts of thick, black blood erupted from the creature, slathering his arms and chest. Its grip on his arm loosened as its entrails spilled out.

With a final, mewling cry, it collapsed on top of him, its last few breaths blowing hot across his face. He gagged from the putrid stench.

He shoved the monster off to the side and began working to pull the bayonet free, but his hands were slick with blood, which prevented him from getting a good enough grip.

There was movement above.

He stopped and looked up.

And had just enough time to raise his arms in a futile act of defense as the shadows fell upon him.

CHAPTER 74

"Hello?" It was a child's voice that answered.

Shit.

"Hey, Lincoln, it's Kyle," he said, trying to sound upbeat. "Is your mom there?"

"Yeah," the boy replied sheepishly. He then turned away from the receiver and yelled, "Mom, phone!"

There was a brief pause. Kyle could hear wacky cartoon music playing in the background.

"I've got it, son. Hang up now," came Rochelle's voice.

"'Kay, bye, Kyle," said the boy as he hung up.

"Kyle?" Rochelle asked. The tone of her voice was laced with concern.

"Yeah, it's me, Rochelle. I—" He had done this hundreds of times before, but now that it involved someone close to him, he found himself struggling to get the words out.

"Oh, God, something's happened, hasn't it?" Rochelle asked.

"It's—" He wanted to tell her that everything was going to be all right, but he couldn't. "Lewis has been shot."

"Oh, God, is he all right?"

"I don't know," he replied. "We're at the hospital. They've taken him into surgery."

Rochelle's voice quivered as she asked, "Where was he shot?"

"In the stomach."

"But that's good, isn't it? I mean, it shouldn't be life-threatening, right? He'll be okay, won't he? Tell me he'll be okay, Kyle."

"I ... I honestly don't know, Rochelle." He felt like shit for saying it, even though it was the truth. But he couldn't bring himself to tell her that it was his fault, that if he hadn't let the bastard get away, then her husband wouldn't be in surgery with a bullet in his gut. "We got to the hospital real fast. I wish I could tell you more, but I just don't know."

Rochelle started crying, and Kyle stayed on the line with her, unsure of how else to support her. "I'm sorry," she said, sniffling. "You'd think that after all these years, I'd be ready for this, but I'm not. How can you ever be ready for something like this?"

"You can't," Kyle agreed.

"So what do I do?"

"I don't know all the details yet, but the bureau's flying out two more agents in the morning. SAC Geddes will get in touch with you about flying in with them, but I thought ... I thought I should be the one to call you."

"Thank you, Kyle. I appreciate that," Rochelle said as she struggled to regain her composure.

"Do you want me to have someone come over?"

"No, not yet—" She didn't finish the thought. It just hung there in the silence—the one possibility that neither of them were willing to speak of, as if saying it might make it a reality.

"I'll call as soon as I find out anything more," he said.

"Okay," she said and then hung up quickly as if she might break down again.

In spite of the heater, the temperature in the car had fallen to the point that he could see the silvery mist of his breath. As he grit his teeth to keep them from chattering, he pushed against the steering wheel and drove himself back into the seat until his arms shook. He wanted to scream.

It was cold. So *fucking* cold.

CHAPTER 75

His own panting breath reverberating within his helmet was all that Ramirez heard as he slogged his way down the steep trail. He constantly scanned the forest around him, struggling to differentiate the movement of the wind-blown evergreens from a possible bogey in the neon-green display. He no longer trusted the alarm system to give him adequate warning—it had already failed them once—and having lost his partner, he no longer had the benefit of an extra lookout. Several times already, his scrutiny of the surroundings had caused him to stumble. On one occasion, he had nearly fallen down a steep ravine just off the trail.

Even with the snowshoes, it was a constant battle to remain upright. In some areas, the snow was deep and soft, causing him to bog down, while in other areas, it was hard and icy. His toes were jamming into the ends of his boots with each step until he was certain he would lose a few of the nails. The throbbing pain in his knee from his earlier collision with the tree continued to worsen, which caused him to hobble like an old lady as he fought his way down the trail.

When his radio went off, he nearly dove for cover.

"Team One," came Ainsworth's voice. "We've just received a signal from transponder 403. It's one of Busey's. I want you down that mountain on the double. Team Two will meet you at the base before proceeding on to the transponder location."

"Roger," Ramirez replied. In spite of the pain, he picked up the pace, more than happy to comply with the order. His spirits were lifted with the hope that they might be able to rescue Busey and that he would no longer be facing the menace of the forest alone.

Ramirez was making his way through the lower elevations near the point he would meet up with Team Two when his alarm went off. He ducked immediately and then checked the alarm coordinates. It was within a mile of him and closing. He watched the display as it counted down the distance. It was heading in his direction—and fast. With a sinking feeling, he realized it wasn't just coming in his direction, but it was coming directly at him. He quickly surveyed the area, looking for a place to take cover. To his left, the mountain dropped off precipitously, to his right, it rose sharply, and the tree cover was sparse. About twenty yards ahead, he spotted a fair-sized boulder lying halfway across the trail. He began running as best as he could manage while the alarm continued to buzz and the counter dropped.

"Team One," Ainsworth's voice cut through the alarm. "You've got a bogey bearing down on you."

"I'm on it," Ramirez replied. The display rolled below twelve hundred yards. He ducked behind the boulder, unshouldered the tranq gun, and turned to face the incoming target.

"Hold your position. Team Two is within a mile and closing."

"Roger," Ramirez replied. The counter continued to wind down

One thousand yards. He raised the gun and activated the targeting system in the visor.

Eight hundred yards.

And then, suddenly, it veered off course, turning almost ninety degrees to the east, continuing on for a few hundred yards before stopping.

Ramirez waited for several long moments, his eyes glued to the alarm indicator on his visor, before he finally relaxed. He stepped from behind the boulder and radioed back to camp. "We've lost it, sir."

"I know," Ainsworth replied. "Continue on down to the rendezvous point with Team Two."

"Roger," Javier replied. Instead of reshouldering the tranq gun, he decided to carry it in case the bogey began moving again. He turned and started back down the trail.

Wham!

Something big slammed into him from out of nowhere, knocking him across the trail. There were no buzzing alarms or shouted warnings this time, but fireworks still erupted within his head as his helmet cracked against the trunk of a tree.

He struggled to rise, but his body seemed unwilling or unable to respond. Everything seemed far away, as if he were at the end of a long tunnel or the bottom of a deep pool. He tried to call for help, but the faint lights of the display kept fading in and out of focus as he struggled to maintain consciousness.

The monochromatic green display flickered as there was movement to his right. He turned his head in time to see a clawed foot crunch into the snow next to his head.

No amount of debriefing could have prepared him for such a sight. What stood before him was a vision straight out of hell. The thing was massive, much larger than they had expected, at least seven feet tall with thick, sinewy legs that looked like those of the raptors in the *Jurassic Park* movies, along with the eight-inch claws. Unable to move, he could only watch in horror as the thing spread its large wings and fluttered them. Its long, thin head reared back as it issued a squealing, screeching cry, its razor-sharp teeth glimmering green as they reflected the ambient light.

Knowing his time had come, Javier begged the Virgin Mother for mercy. He began praying the rosary, the litany of words barely a whisper inside his helmet as the demonic presence of El Diablo loomed over him, blocking out the last of the faint green light.

* * *

From somewhere far away came the sound of voices calling to him, telling him things were all right. And above him in the distance, the merest hint of light—a beautifully twinkling luminescence like stars on a foggy night or perhaps angels come to carry him home.

"Mama?" he whispered as he fell into darkness once more.

CHAPTER 76

The surgery waiting room walls had a pastel, rose-colored wallpaper above a dark-paneled wainscoting. The thick carpet was a lush green inlaid with patterns of pink roses. The harsh overhead fluorescents were recessed into the ceiling with reflective grids that softened and dimmed the light. The entire room was designed to be soothing, but Kyle found no comfort in its appearance. He just sat there, staring at nothing, replaying earlier events over and over in his head, and wondering if there was something he could have done to have prevented it, while each minute dragged interminably on into the next.

Sheriff Greyhawk sat beside him, eyes closed, as still and as silent as a mountain. But he wasn't asleep. When the sheriff had arrived, he had been accompanied by two of his men, who were now standing guard outside of Carrie's room. He had told Kyle that Clayton and the forensics team were at the motel searching for evidence and dusting for prints, but it didn't look good. Even worse was the news that Carrie's computer was gone, a fact that had only fueled SAC Geddes's anger when Kyle had called her back.

Marasco came marching into the waiting room and straight at Kyle. "What the fuck did you do?" he shouted, grabbing Kyle by the collar and jerking him from the chair. "You killed him, didn't you?"

"Fuck you," Kyle shouted, shoving Marasco back. "You weren't there."

Sheriff Greyhawk pulled Marasco off.

Something came to Kyle then. "Or were you? Where the hell have you been all afternoon?"

"Aay, fuck you!" Marasco lunged at Kyle again, but the sheriff held him back. Marasco struggled to escape the sheriff's grasp, but it was pointless. He finally gave up, jerked free, and stormed off to the counter at the back of the room, where a stack of Styrofoam cups sat beside a glass coffeepot on a hot plate.

Sheriff Greyhawk followed Marasco to the back of the room. He poured himself a cup of coffee and one for Marasco. The two spoke in hushed tones for a moment. Marasco raised his voice and glanced in Kyle's direction several times, but the sheriff continued to talk to him until he finally seemed to settle down.

A television was suspended from the ceiling above the sheriff's head. The latest reality show was on. *Reality TV.* It was about as far from reality as one could get. The only thing real about it was the shallow and greedy nature of the contestants. Kyle knew about reality. He saw it up close and personal every day. Reality was alcoholic and drug-addicted parents, abused children and battered wives, corrupt CEOs and politicians, violence and terrorism. Reality was sitting in a surgery waiting room while a friend fought for his life. *That* was reality.

Kyle's thoughts were interrupted by the appearance of one of the surgeons, a harried-looking older man with silvery hair. He was still in his scrubs, with his blue-green cap and booties. His surgical mask was pulled down around his neck.

The sheriff and Marasco came back up front. Kyle stood and joined them.

"Sheriff, I'm Dr. Bayless," he said. The sheriff nodded.

"You're the one who brought him in?" the doctor asked, looking at Kyle.

Kyle nodded.

"I ... uh." The doctor paused to clear his throat, and in that moment, Kyle knew what was coming. He had done it enough himself to know the telltale signs. "I'm sorry to be the one to have to tell you this, but, uh ... Agent Edwards died on the operating table. We did everything we could, but it appears the bullet ricocheted off his pelvis and the bottom of his rib cage. There was just too much damage to his internal organs. I am truly sorry for your loss."

Kyle stood there, too stunned to move. The death notification. It was normally his job to deliver such news to loved ones. He was the one who counseled them on how to deal with their grief. And while he had always felt sympathy for the families of the victims when he informed them of their loss, he had never fully realized just how cold and hollow those words coming from him must have sounded … until now.

Kyle took a step backward and slumped into his seat, suddenly faced with the harshest reality of them all.

CHAPTER 77

"Team Two, come in. Goddamn it," Ainsworth yelled into the radio.

"Team Two here," came the reply. It was Dietrich. "Sorry about that, cap," he said through ragged breaths. "We were a little busy for a moment there."

"What the hell is going on?"

"Don't know how, but the dragon got to Ramirez without the alarm going off. We got here just in time. The damn thing was right over him when we bagged it."

A cold lump formed in the pit of Myles's stomach as Ainsworth glared at him. After he called up the detection system's software, he began backtracking to try to find out what had happened.

"You got it?" Ainsworth asked.

"That's affirmative. The damn thing's a hell of a lot bigger than we were told. Took three darts to drop it, but we got it."

"What about Ramirez?"

"Not sure. He's unconscious."

"His breathing and pulse are slow," Ainsworth replied as he studied the display on his terminal, "but it doesn't appear to be critical. Can you move him?"

"I think so. Johnson's rigging up a travois right now. Once we truss up the dragon, we'll start back. But it's going to be a bitch with each of us having to pull one."

"Fuck," Ainsworth growled, causing Myles to flinch. The big man rubbed his hand across the stubbly hair of his burr cut. To Myles's surprise, Ainsworth actually seemed to be torn between the mission and his men.

After a moment's hesitation, Ainsworth keyed the radio. "Team Two, come in."

"Team Two here, sir," Dietrich replied.

"Continue as you were and get back here on the double. If one of you can't manage the creature alone, shoot it with another tranquilizer to make sure it doesn't come to—but don't kill the damn thing, or it'll be our asses. Then get Ramirez back here on the double. The doc can look after him while you go back for the dragon. I'm going after Busey. We aren't leaving without him."

"Roger that," Dietrich replied emphatically. "We'll join you ASAP."

While Ainsworth gathered his gear, Myles replayed the data from Ramirez's helmet, but it was next to impossible for him to concentrate. He was terrified by the prospect of being left alone in the cabin and in charge of the command center.

He backed it up again, watching the video and the data stream for the fifth time—or was it the sixth? He had lost count. The video feed was a grainy, monochrome green with poor clarity. It appeared that Ramirez had just moved from cover and was starting back down the trail when the feed suddenly went haywire and blacked out. It was reestablished a few seconds later, capturing what appeared to be the dragon's clawed foot coming into the frame and then disappearing again. There were several more seconds, and then a shot of Johnson and Dietrich rapidly approaching.

Myles was still unable to ascertain anything useful from it.

The wailing of the alarm system suddenly filled the room.

Oh, God, now what? Myles thought in horror as Ainsworth jumped to the table.

"What the fuck is that?" he shouted.

"I don't know—" Myles stammered. *There shouldn't be any alarms!* The dragon was knocked out. The only time it utilized its echolocation was when it was in flight. Unless the tranquilizer was wearing off, but Team Two would have noticed. *Unless— Unless—* Something else suddenly came to mind, but it was impossible. He tried to ignore it, too terrified by the implications to consider it as a viable possibility, but it was the only answer that made sense. *Unless there was another dragon.*

Or dragons?

A sudden chorus of grunting and shouting was transmitted over the radio. The static-filled video feeds were erratic as the men ran. It was impossible to tell what was happening. There was the muffled *poof, poof* of the tranq guns firing and more shouting. Myles frantically pulled up the tracking system and turned off the frequency filter, all the while praying that he was wrong.

"Team Two, report," yelled Ainsworth.

There was a burst of static and shouting, "Under attack ... everywhere—" and then a scream blared in his ears as Myles reinitialized the system.

"What the fuck is going on out there?" Ainsworth shouted.

The tracking system came back online, and suddenly, there were four red blips on the screen, all whirling and circling within a hundred yards of Team Two.

"What the fuck is that?" Ainsworth asked as he pointed at the display.

"I ... I don't know how—" Myles stammered. "But somehow, I think it's managed to reproduce."

"What?"

"I don't know how... There were two on the plane. Maybe before it crashed they managed to mate—"

Ainsworth grabbed the microphone. "Team Two, there are multiple bogeys. I repeat—there are multiple bogeys. Take any actions necessary to defend yourselves."

There was another scream, and the sound of automatic gunfire erupted over the radio. Johnson's vitals suddenly went black.

Ainsworth grabbed his tranq gun from the table, ripped open the door, and raced out. The door flopped back and forth, snow swirling through the cabin. The fire spluttered and died.

Terrified, Myles crept toward the door. Without night-vision goggles, it was impossible to see anything outside, but as he neared, he thought he saw a shadow sweeping down from the darkness beyond, sailing through the open doorway to pounce upon him. He fell to the floor with a cry of alarm, his arms crossed before him.

* * *

Myles found himself back in front of the FTU. He didn't remember doing it, but the door was closed and latched from the inside. Terrified beyond all rational thought, he just sat there alone, twitching and shivering in the darkness. Sweat trickled down his forehead and dripped onto his glasses unnoticed. He stared blankly at the video screen, watching the flurry of little red dots circling and capering as they closed in on their prey. His mouth moved, as if trying to speak, but nothing could be heard over the shrieking of the alarm system.

CHAPTER 78

Kyle stepped from the noisy, brightly lit corridor into the quiet solitude of the hospital's small chapel. The room was bathed in lambent red and yellow light, filtered through the backlit stained-glass windows lining each side. Three short rows of pews were evenly spaced on each side of the room, each one capable of holding only three or four people, although at the moment, they were unoccupied.

Still stunned by the news of Lewis's death, he slumped onto the bench to his left, leaning forward until his head rested on the back of the one in front of him. Even now, SAC Geddes and Joan Thompson were probably on their way to the house to give Rochelle the news.

Of course, the minute the car pulled up out front she would know. *I should be there,* Kyle thought, *I should be the one to tell her. If only I hadn't let that son of a bitch get away. If I had just managed to grab his leg and bring him down or at least trip him up—*

But he hadn't, and now Lewis was dead because of it.

This isn't the way things were supposed to happen. He could feel himself beginning to slip back into his old pattern of despair and self-doubt. He struggled against it, trying to focus on what needed to be done. *You're a counselor for God's sake. You know how to deal with this.* But it was as if everything he had ever learned had suddenly left him the minute he was told of Lewis's death. He couldn't remember a thing. Now that it was happening to him, he didn't know how to deal with it. He just sat there, thinking, *this can't be happening,* over and over again.

He sat up and looked to the front of the room. On the wall behind the altar hung an image of Jesus nailed to the cross, a bloody crown of thorns upon his head. As he looked at the crucifix, the only thing that kept running through his head over and over was the question *why*. All he had wanted to do was help, and now Lewis was dead because of him. *And for what?* He hadn't even managed to save the computer. What little evidence they might have salvaged was now gone, his career along with it.

At least Janet will be happy, he thought bitterly, resigned to the fact that there was nothing preventing him from returning to Dallas now. He could hear her now, speaking in that condescending tone of hers, appearing to be concerned about him when all she had ever really cared about was herself. "I knew that job wasn't right for you. Such a waste of time," she would cluck. "If only you had followed my advice, you could have already been well on your way to being a doctor or a lawyer. Then maybe Angela wouldn't have left you."

An agonized gasp escaped him, and he ducked his head, squeezing his eyes shut against the tears that threatened to come.

After several long moments, he slowly lifted his head. He stared at the crucifix, desperately seeking some sign of divine inspiration, if not absolution. But there was none to be found.

CHAPTER 79

The dark green Xterra sat in the far corner of the parking lot, carefully positioned to give its occupant a clear view of the hospital entrance without drawing anyone's attention. A fine layer of snow covered the vehicle. Delicate crystals were beginning to form on the inside of the windows, but the truck and its heater remained off. Nathan's gloved hands tightened around the steering wheel, his knuckles cracking as two more police officers wearing thick blue coats and carrying steaming cups of Starbucks made their way into the building. The place was crawling with them.

Nathan knew Colquitt wouldn't be happy with the latest developments. His shooting of the FBI agent had definitely complicated matters. Things were getting messy, and the potential for discovery was rising dramatically; however, they weren't out of control yet. He needed to find out what had happened since the encounter at the motel before he made his next move. He knew the girl was almost certainly still alive. She would have to be silenced—and soon—but he wasn't ready to give up on his plans just yet. It would be disappointing if he wasn't able to take his time with her. Unfortunately, if the FBI hadn't believed her story before, they were more likely to now that she had been attacked.

At least he had managed to retrieve the laptop after the idiot had taken off and left the room unattended. Nathan had wiped the hard drive clean again for good measure and then taken a little trip about twenty miles south of town to dispose of the computer, which now lay at the bottom of Flathead Lake.

Having finally decided he would have to risk it if he was going to learn anything more about the situation, Nathan tucked his gun under the seat before he headed inside.

The emergency entrance had been crawling with police, so he had parked on the other side of the hospital. The main lobby was deserted at this time of night with the exception of a man from housekeeping swinging the buffer back and forth across the marble floor. Nathan walked down the corridor, limping slightly as he favored his right knee, which had stiffened up in the cold. He passed the entrance to the chapel and then turned right, following the overhead signs that pointed the way to the emergency room. Next was the cafeteria, which had already closed for the night. The only sound was the low hum emanating from the row of vending machines just outside the cafeteria.

As he neared the end of the hall, he heard the crackle of a police radio coming toward him from around the corner. He had planned to go to the ER to see what information he could ascertain without drawing too much attention to himself, but another idea suddenly came to him. He hurried back down the hall and stopped in front of the vending machines.

As the cop rounded the corner, Nathan began to dig in his pockets for change. He nodded politely and fed change into the machine as the officer stepped up beside him. The officer was an older man who was almost completely bald with glasses and a large paunch. It was ridiculous that a fat slob like that could keep his job when he had been turned down for duty simply because of his bad knee. He could still outrun half the men on any police force in the country and then kick the other half's asses.

"So what's all the commotion about?" Nathan asked as he punched the button for a Diet Coke.

"Some FBI agent was killed," the cop growled as he bent over and picked up his package of powdered donuts.

Nathan's pulse quickened. The agent had died. That was both good and bad. It was good in that it would slow down the investigation into the Hungry Horse situation, but bad in that it would only serve to bring more agents in. The place was sure to be crawling with them by morning. He needed to finish off the girl and get the hell out. But the image of her that kept playing through his mind caused him to consider other options.

Nathan pulled the Diet Coke out of the slot. "Sorry to hear that."

The officer's response was drowned out by the crackle of his radio. "Hey, Weatherby, can one of you guys come up here to 312 and relieve me for a while? I need to take a leak, and the sheriff wants two men on watch at all—" The chatter was cut off as the officer turned down the volume on his radio.

Damn, Nathan thought. They had placed guards outside her room. Of course, it only made sense. It appeared the sheriff had more sense than the agent he had tangled with earlier.

"Well, good luck finding the guy," he said to the officer as he turned and started back toward the lobby. With the girl under guard, it would be more prudent to wait and see if a better opportunity presented itself. Now that he knew her room number, he could take care of her at any time with nothing more than the little canister he carried in his pocket, even with the guards. Of course, that would also serve to confirm any suspicions they might have had regarding the validity of her story, which would make an already messy situation worse, and General Colquitt hated messes. He would wait. For now.

Nathan had just turned the corner when a man stepped from the chapel at the far end of the corridor and began walking in his direction. He walked slowly, more of a shuffle, head down and slump-shouldered as if—Nathan stopped. Something about the man seemed familiar—the size, the build, the clothes. It had been dark, and things had happened so fast he hadn't gotten a good look, but Nathan was almost *certain* this was the man he had grappled with at the motel.

He glanced down the hallway behind him to make sure no one was following. As they neared each other, Nathan reached in his pocket for the silver canister he carried. Unlike the one he had used on the kid in Denver, this one was a powerful neurotoxin that would kill immediately upon inhalation. Nathan had been inoculated prior to leaving Baltimore, so it would have no effect on him.

They were no more than ten feet apart when the man suddenly looked up. Their eyes locked. It was him. There was no question about it. This was the man who had prevented him from taking the girl.

Was that recognition in his eyes?

Still concealed within his pocket, Nathan flipped open the canister's lid. He would never have a better chance to get rid of him than he had right now.

The sound of whistling came to him from down the corridor as the janitor rounded the corner, pushing the buffer.

Nathan hesitated. If he took out the agent, he would have to take out the janitor as well, and that would increase the possibility that he might get caught.

Then he was beside him. His finger on the nozzle, he was ready to use it at the first sign of trouble, but the man just walked on by as if he had never seen him.

Nathan flipped the lid shut and relaxed his grip on the canister. He would wait. He was used to waiting. It was something he did often. Despite his knee, sitting in the cold didn't bother him either. He had spent months in far more inhospitable conditions in the desert during Operation Iraqi Freedom.

Back in the truck, Nathan opened the Diet Coke. Because he had handled it without gloves, he made a mental note to dispose of it once he was done. Had he known he was going to be waiting some more, he would have gotten himself something to eat as well.

As he drank the soda, he took out the photo of the girl, his pulse quickening in response. At first, he tried to push down his thoughts of her and remain focused on his mission, but his urges grew until he was no longer able to control them. He closed his eyes as he leaned back against the seat.

A lascivious grin slowly spread across his face as he surrendered to the deviant images playing within his head.

CHAPTER 80

The wind railed against the cabin, tugging and prying at every joint and seam and rattling across the roof like a thousand ghosts seeking entry. Inside, Myles Bennett huddled in front of the FTU, trembling.

The alarms had gone silent. Dietrich's and Ainsworth's vitals readout was flatlined, and although their helmets were still communicating, the video displays showed nothing discernable. Ramirez's and Johnson's displays had blacked out completely. He had tried to radio each of them countless times with no response.

He had tried to radio out for help as well, but the satellite communication system was encrypted, and only Ainsworth had the codes necessary to radio the outside world. There was no way to contact anyone. His conscience told him that he should go out and try to find the others. Some of them might still be alive and in need of his help. But if the dragons had gotten them, what chance did he have of finding any of them and making it back to the cabin alive?

Not knowing what else to do, he just sat there, staring blankly at the FTU and waiting for the dragons to come.

There was a loud *thump* as something slammed against the door. Startled, Myles jerked backward and fell from his chair. They were here.

But there was no alarm. There should have been an alarm. Maybe it was just the wind.

On hands and knees, he scrambled across the floor to the bunk in the far corner. He grabbed his pack and yanked it open, desperately searching for something he could use as a weapon, but it was all emergency medical equipment—bandages, inflatable splints, an oxygen canister and mask, blood pressure cuff, several meal rations, flashlight and batteries, and a small plastic case with tranquilizer syringes.

Thump. Thu-thump. The pounding came again, rattling the door in its frame. It wasn't the wind. There was definitely something trying to get inside.

On the verge of panic, Myles grabbed the syringes and crawled beneath the lowest bunk. He reached out, grabbed one of the chairs by a leg, and tipped it over. He then pulled it against the bottom of the bed. It was pitifully inadequate protection against the creature, but it was all he had.

Another blow and the door flew open, slamming into the wall. Snow and frigid wind swirled in. A shadowy form fell into the room. Myles wedged himself farther back into the corner, a high, thin whimper escaping him.

The door slammed shut and bounced open again, swinging back and forth in the howling wind. Without his helmet's night-vision visor, he couldn't see a thing, but he knew it was there—a deadly, hulking presence across the room. And then he heard it—a low, rumbling growl that was quickly carried away by the storm.

He was about to die, alone and forgotten in this godforsaken cabin in the middle of nowhere. It was ironic but perhaps fitting that he was going to be killed by the very creature he had helped to create. Few, if any, would notice his disappearance, and even fewer would mourn his passing. His remains—if there were any—would probably never be found. No one would ever know what had happened to him.

As he held the syringes tightly in his hand, Myles considered simply stabbing them all into his leg before the dragon could get to him. At least it would be quick and painless—

As preoccupied as he was with the contemplation of his own death, it was several moments before he realized the creature wasn't moving. *Could it have been hit by one of the darts?* Dietrich had said it had taken three to down one. Maybe it was just slower acting than they had anticipated, or maybe one of the men had hit it with regular weapons fire. If so, was it dead or just wounded? He certainly didn't want to go anywhere near the thing, especially if it was wounded, but he couldn't continue to cower under the bunk for the rest of his life either. Sooner or later, he was going to have to do something.

After he gathered what meager amount of courage he still retained, Myles pulled the protective plastic caps from the tranquilizer syringes. He grasped them in his right hand like the hilt of a knife and then, with his left hand, rattled the chair against the bed, hoping the noise would lure the creature to him and give him the opportunity to stab it with the syringes as it tried to get at him.

Expecting it to pounce, he tensed in anticipation, but nothing happened. He rattled the chair again, more blatantly than before, but there was still no movement. Could it be the thing was actually dead? Surely, it wasn't smart enough to play possum. The dragons possessed rudimentary intelligence, and there was no way to anticipate what they might have learned during their time in the wild; however, it was still hard to imagine it being that clever. The prospect of capturing one of the offspring alive was especially exciting. The knowledge they could gain from such a creature and its value to the program was incalculable.

Cautiously, he slipped from beneath the bed. He picked up the chair and held it before him in a poor imitation of a lion tamer. He crept around the table. The faint illumination from the FTU bathed the upper reaches of the cabin in a ghostly blue light. He could just make out the outline of the dark form lying in the doorway. It was smaller than he had anticipated. There was no spiny ridge along its back, and instead of the large, leathery wings, it had ... arms.

Myles's heart leapt as he realized one of the men had found their way back to the cabin. He quickly stepped over the inert form and closed the door. The latch bolt was bent, and the wood around the catch plate was cracked and splintered. Leaning into it, he managed to force it back into place, but it was a loose fit at best. It would never hold up against an attack. He took the chair and wedged it between the floor and the door's wooden crossbeam. It was the best he could do.

He knelt over the body. There was a large gash in the helmet. It would have taken an incredible amount of force to cause that much damage to the specially constructed helmets. In spite of its protection, it was likely the wearer had at least suffered a concussion, if not a contusion. Taking every precaution, Myles carefully rolled the body over and removed the helmet. It was Ramirez.

"Javier, can you hear me?"

Ramirez groaned. His eyes fluttered and then opened. Frightened, he began to thrash about. Myles called out his name over and over, struggling to hold him down while reassuring him he was safe. Gradually, he seemed to recognize where he was and that he was no longer in danger. The terrified look on his face slackened, and his arms fell to his sides.

Myles grabbed the medical kit. After he pulled out the flashlight, he lifted each eyelid and checked the pupils. They appeared slightly enlarged but were responsive to the light, which was a good sign. Ramirez even lifted his hand in an effort to shield his eyes.

"Javier, it's Myles. You're safe now, okay? Do you understand?"

Ramirez looked at him and nodded slightly. His eyes appeared more focused than earlier.

"Can you stand?"

"I ... think so," he managed to whisper.

Myles helped him to his feet. Ramirez leaned heavily on him, swaying unsteadily with each step like a punch-drunk boxer. It was a long, slow process, but they eventually managed to reach the bunk. Concerned with the amount of blood flow to his head, Myles propped Javier up in the corner instead of letting him lie down. A fine sheen of greasy sweat covered the young man's face. Because he feared Ramirez might have a subdural hematoma and because the suit's internal monitoring system was no longer transmitting, Myles checked his pulse and blood pressure manually. His pressure appeared to be elevated but not alarmingly so. He made a mental note of the readings for later comparison.

Not taking any chances, Myles dug through the medical equipment again, pulling out a portable oxygen canister and mask, which he placed over Javier's nose and mouth. By maintaining cerebral perfusion, he hoped to reduce the effects of shock and to minimize the potential of brain damage. But the fact was that he had no way of knowing just how extensive Javier's injuries might be or how quickly his condition might deteriorate. The young man needed to be transported to a hospital as soon as possible.

Once Ramirez appeared to be resting comfortably, Myles returned to the FTU, hoping for signs of survival from the others. The display remained black. Without Ainsworth's passcode, they still had no way to radio for help, but at least there was no activity by any of the creatures at the moment. Hopefully, they had managed to tranquilize or kill them all.

Suddenly, he found he didn't care about the success or failure of the mission. He was not devoted to his work to the point that he was willing to risk his or Javier's lives in an attempt to retrieve one of the creatures. Nor did he care about the response of General Colquitt, who at one time had terrified him to the point that he would never have considered crossing him. All of that had changed. He had seen things infinitely more frightening than the general tonight. At this point, all he cared about was making it back home alive and in one piece.

But as he looked over at Ramirez, he feared even that was a long shot.

CHAPTER 81

Maryland

The geisha filled the tiny porcelain cup with sake and handed it to General Colquitt, careful to make sure that none was spilled. She wore a pink kimono adorned with purple nightingales in flight up and over her shoulder and a gold satin obi around her waist. The obi, embroidered with gold thread in an intricate pattern of cherry blossoms and pine branches, hung down to her feet, upon which she wore the traditional white *tabi* socks with six-inch-tall, wooden *okobo* sandals.

The general bowed in appreciation as he took the cup from Miko. It was a taste he had acquired—both for the sushi and sake as well as the geisha—during his time stationed in the Pacific. He admired the attention to detail and dedication to perfection that personified the geisha, ranging from the ritualized *chanoyu*, the tea ceremony, to the formal social interactions of an *ozashiki* to the precise, structured movements of the *mai*, the traditional dance of the geisha.

Fortunately for the general, the Kyoto Rose was one of the finest establishments found anywhere outside of Kyoto. On the outskirts of Annapolis, the Rose—as it was affectionately known by the regulars— was frequented by many of the professors and officers from the naval academy who, like Colquitt, had served extended tours of duty overseas. The décor was authentic, with dark teakwood beams and rails and a pine floor polished to a brilliant white. The bamboo walls were festooned with brightly painted scrolls, each one a highly stylized depiction of Japan during each of the four seasons.

Downstairs, the common dining area was a large, open space with a bar and a stage for public performances. Above, colorful paper lanterns hung from the rafters of the high ceiling. Upstairs, a balcony ran around the room, off which the private ozashiki were located. Unlike the typical Japanese *ochoyas*, however, the partitions between each of the ozashiki as well as the *fusuma*, the sliding entry doors, were of solid, soundproof construction instead of merely linen or rice paper.

The ozashiki was lavishly decorated in the style of the Gion Kobu District of Kyoto, with *tatami* floor mats and short, square tables with linen cushions to sit upon. In the corner was a small rock garden with a gently gurgling fountain, the water trickling over layers of carefully arranged stones before lightly splashing into a shallow pool stocked with colorful koi.

Colquitt took a bite of sashimi, savoring the exquisite flavor of the raw tuna and wasabi. The cell phone in his pocket began to vibrate, shattering his blissful reverie. *Who the hell could be calling me at this late hour?* he wondered as he checked the display. It had been transferred to his cell from his secure line, which meant that it was encrypted but offered no caller ID information. As much as he hated to, he had to answer it. As he held up his hand for the geisha to wait, Colquitt answered the phone.

"Anderson, are you intentionally trying to fuck me up the ass?" It was Wade. The man spoke so loudly even Miko heard him, her eyes widening in shock before she could look away.

Colquitt's face flushed.

"Miko, would you excuse me for a moment?" he asked, struggling to maintain a pleasant facade.

"Yes, general-san," she replied courteously as she bowed. With little, shuffling steps, she made her way out.

"*Arigato.*"

As the fusuma slid closed, the general spoke. "How dare you talk to me like that," he snapped. He was sick of Wade's vulgar bullshit. He could just imagine what kind of pervert the man must be, probably an ass-fucker himself.

"Don't give me any of that righteous indignation crap, Anderson. I know how you boys in the military talk to one another."

The bastard was intentionally trying to piss him off. And he was doing a damn fine job of it. "What do you want?" the general growled.

"Do you even know what the fuck is going on in Montana? I just got a call from our contact raising hell because one of the agents out of Seattle got whacked. Said he didn't sign up for that. The bastard actually had the balls to threaten to go to the feds with the whole story. So do you know what the hell he's talking about?"

"No, I don't," Colquitt replied. "But if there was collateral damage, then I'm certain it was unavoidable. My man is very conscientious. He would not complicate things unnecessarily."

"Well, he *has* complicated things. Considerably. And now he's going to have to clean up his own mess."

"Meaning?"

"Meaning that he needs to take care of the mole—that's what. And I want it done by the time my men get back with your little present. I want this thing over and done with, do you understand me? My balls are in a vise right now, and if that son of a bitch gets cranked any tighter, I'm coming after yours for replacements. You got me?"

"I'll take care of it," the general responded flatly.

"You'd better, or it's your ass," Wade replied and then hung up.

The general snapped the phone shut. The moron couldn't even be consistent with his anatomical threats. But that didn't mean they were to be taken lightly.

The general slammed down his sake and then poured another, allowing time for his anger to wane while thinking the situation through. He would not be hasty in regard to this matter. Hasty decisions led to mistakes. Mistakes led to casualties.

In the end, however, as much as he hated to admit it, the general came to the same conclusion as Wade. With one *minor* exception.

Colquitt opened his phone again and dialed into his secure system. Once it connected, he had it forward the call to Nathan's phone.

When Nathan answered, the general didn't question him about what had transpired—that could be handled later. He simply gave him the information about the new target and told him to call back after he was finished with the job. There was one more person for him to visit before his return.

The general slammed the remaining sake, imagining Wade's surprise when Nathan showed up on his doorstep. *I wonder if he'll be worried about his balls then*, he mused, a satisfied grin slowly spreading across his face.

He clapped his hands twice, signaling for Miko's return.

The fusuma slid open, and she shuffled back into the room, her head bowed respectfully. "General-san is happier now, yes?" she asked.

"Yes, much happier," he replied. "But I seem to be out of *sake*."

CHAPTER 82

Montana

Carrie jerked awake. Confused, it took her a moment to get her bearings. She was in the dark, but she felt safe. She was in a bed of fresh cotton sheets. To her right, a thin strip of light from the hallway slipped beneath the bottom edge of the door. Beyond, other sounds filtered into the room: muffled voices, the squeak of rubber-soled shoes on linoleum, and a persistent, steady beeping from down the hall.

The hospital, she thought as fragments of the night before began to come back to her. She remembered being attacked at the motel, and she seemed to remember riding in a car, but it was all such a blur it seemed less real than the dream that had just awakened her.

It must be near morning. Her bleary eyes slowly adjusted to the wan glow bathing the room in a palette of muted blues and grays. She looked to the window and was startled to see someone slouching in the chair next to her bed, asleep. Her heart leapt and thumped against her chest. She grabbed for the call button, but before she could press it, she recognized who it was.

It was Kyle. He was too tall for the chair. He had slumped down in it until he was in danger of falling to the floor. His head leaned against his left shoulder in what appeared to be the most uncomfortable position imaginable. His clothes were rumpled and filthy, his hair stuck out in every direction. The sight of him caused a relieved smile to cross her face. It was both touching and comforting to have him there beside her. It was something she hadn't felt in a long time.

He mumbled something, his head lolling about as he spoke in his dreams. This continued for several moments, and he gradually became more and more animated, his head tossing back and forth and his voice rising until he suddenly woke with a start.

"Bad dream?" Carrie asked softly.

Kyle shook his head to clear the cobwebs and blinked several times before his eyes appeared to focus on her. "No," he muttered. "God, how I wish that were true." He leaned back, looked up at the ceiling, and sighed deeply.

"What's wrong?" Carrie asked, although she was suddenly afraid of the answer.

Without answering, Kyle asked, "How are you?"

"Fine, I think, aside from a splitting headache."

"Hangover from the chloroform, I guess," he said. He took a deep breath and leaned forward, looking at her through the bed rails. "How much of last night do you remember?"

"Not much," she admitted. "I remember someone grabbing me in my room and then … you in the car. That's about it."

Kyle nodded. "I got to your room just as you were being attacked. The guy hit me and took off. As he ran, he shot Lewis."

Carrie struggled to piece together the events of last night, but there was nothing there. "I don't remember any of it," she said. "Is Lewis all right?"

Kyle shook his head and looked at the floor. "Lewis is dead."

Oh, God, no.

"I am so sorry," she said, her voice trembling. Tears welled in her eyes, blurring her vision of him, but he didn't respond. He just sat there, staring at the floor.

She slipped her left hand, the hospital's plastic ID band on her wrist, between the bed rails. After a brief moment, Kyle took her hand. She squeezed it gently and held on as he squeezed back. Neither one spoke.

Carrie's heart broke for him. It was obvious he had been hit hard by the loss. She wished there was something more she could do for him, but all she could think to do was to keep holding on to him.

"After I brought you and Lewis to the hospital, I called the sheriff and told him what had happened. When the men got to your room, your computer was gone."

Carrie felt horrible. It was as if he was confessing his failures to her. "It's all right," she said. "It had already been wiped out. Kyle, if you hadn't come to my room, I wouldn't be here now. You saved my life." But then she remembered that if it hadn't been for her, Lewis wouldn't be dead. "Oh, God, Kyle, I didn't mean—"

"It gets worse," Kyle interrupted. "Agents found your friend Charlie dead on his sofa. A syringe was found next to him. They say it looks like a drug overdose."

No, no, no. Not Charlie. Her heart caught in her chest. "Charlie *never* did drugs. They killed him just like they tried to kill me. Those bastards," she cried. "He was just a kid. A sweet, innocent kid." Racked with guilt and full of anger, her grip on Kyle's hand tightened until the muscles in her arm trembled from the effort. Kyle held on, his grip strong and firm without ever hurting.

She reached out with her right hand. Kyle stood and leaned against the rail. As she reached around him, he put his arm around her and held her while she cried into his shoulder.

It felt good to be held like that. She never wanted to let go. She wished time would stop so she could stay there forever, sheltered from all the pain and loss and loneliness of the outside world. But she knew it couldn't last. It never did.

After she cried herself out—and even though she didn't want to— she forced herself to let go. Leaning back, she asked, "What now?"

Kyle looked at her without speaking. He just looked into her eyes. She began to feel warm inside. Maybe she was wrong. Even if it wasn't forever, maybe having someone to hold on to just for now was good enough. Someone to help shut out the rest of the world for even a short time. She was about to reach out for him again when he pulled several tissues from the box next to the bed and handed them to her.

"I don't know," he said.

CHAPTER 83

Myles Bennett woke with a start, the remnants of a scream echoing in his head. Somehow, he must have dozed off. He looked around the cabin. Things appeared unchanged. Ramirez was still propped up in the corner. The FTU's alarm system remained silent.

He got up to check on Ramirez. The sound of the chair scraping against the wooden floor woke the young man. Wide-eyed, he looked at Myles and then settled back down when he recognized him.

"How's your head?" Myles asked.

"Hurts. Bad," Ramirez whispered. His eyes closed sleepily.

He checked Ramirez's pulse and pressure again and frowned at the readings. Not good. They were elevated from the last time, which could indicate a subdural hematoma. He needed medical attention immediately. But how?

Myles returned to the FTU and called up the operating system. For almost half an hour, he tried to find a way to bypass the code, but it was no use. He was locked out.

Outside, it was nearing dawn, the cracks around the boarded windows slowly fading from black to purple. It should be safe now. If any of the creatures still remained, they would have returned to their roost by now. But it was a long way to the Spotted Bear Ranger Station. There was no way he could make it with Ramirez.

Quickly, before he could change his mind, Myles began gathering the items he would need for the trip, hastily shoving them into his pack—medical supplies, water bladders, and a couple of MREs. He would have to travel light. It was a long way, and if he didn't make it out of the wilderness by dark—

He zipped up the pack and was reaching for his helmet when he heard a sharp *cha-click* behind him.

"Where you think you're goin'?" Ramirez asked, his voice slurred.

Myles turned around to find a Glock 9mm pointed at him, which nearly caused his bowels to let go right then. "I, uh ... I was just going to try to get help," he stammered. "I've tried everything. There's no way to override the com system."

"Not without me," Ramirez said.

"It's a long hike. I ... I don't think you can make it in your condition," Myles said, his eyes never leaving the gun. In Ramirez's state, he feared it might go off at any moment.

"You're going to help me."

"But it would be much faster if I went alone," Myles said. "I swear I'll come back with help."

"Not without me," Ramirez repeated.

"Okay, okay," Myles conceded, trying to remain calm. He didn't dare risk antagonizing him further. "Just let me get some more supplies, and we'll be on our way."

Myles gathered up a few more water bladders and MREs and added them to his pack. When he tried to lift it, he winced. It was so heavy. He had never been the athletic type, and now, not only was he going to have to try to lug it for miles in the snow, but he was going to have to help Ramirez as well. He would never make it. In an effort to reduce the weight, he took out most of the water bladders. As he did, he saw the case with the tranquilizer syringes. He snuck a glance over at Ramirez, who was carefully watching him.

"It's too heavy," Myles explained nervously as he zipped up the pack. "If we have to, we'll eat snow."

Ramirez nodded. He sat up slowly and then weakly dropped his legs over the side and sat there, clutching the edge of the bed.

There's no way we're going to make it, Myles thought. If Ramirez's injuries were as bad as he feared, Myles wondered just how far they would get before he faltered. And if he did, he would have to leave him behind. He just hoped Ramirez retained enough of his senses to let him go. If not, then he would be forced to try using the syringes—an option he did not relish.

As Myles helped Ramirez to his feet, he tried not to think about what lay ahead. It was going to be a long, painful day. Progress would be slow at best, and the chances of making it to the ranger station by dark were slim, with dire consequences awaiting them if they failed.

But Ramirez had left him with no other choice.

CHAPTER 84

There was a light rap on the door. It opened, and Sheriff Greyhawk stepped into the room.

Good thing he didn't arrive about two minutes ago, Kyle thought.

The sheriff greeted them with a nod and then looked to Carrie. "How are you?" he asked.

"Okay, I guess," she replied.

Not one for small talk, the sheriff just nodded and turned to Kyle. "Hank Gullickson with the Forest Service called me this morning," he said quietly. "He told me an unidentified helicopter was flying down Hungry Horse Reservoir just after dark last night."

"Do you think there's any significance to it?" Kyle asked.

"It's suspicious. It was blacked-out and flying fast at low altitude. Hank tried to radio them but got no response. He said it was big, probably military. He thought it might be a Blackhawk."

"Has anyone tried to verify this?" Kyle asked.

"I informed Agent Marasco, but he didn't seem concerned about it," the sheriff replied. The tone of his voice made it clear he didn't agree with Marasco.

"I'll call SAC Geddes and let her know," Kyle said. "We'll see what she wants to do."

Carrie kicked the sheets off her legs and got out of the bed. Holding the back of her hospital gown closed, she stepped over to the small closet by the bathroom.

"What are you doing?" Kyle asked.

"I'm getting dressed. Don't you see? This is our chance to get the proof we need. We've forced their hand. They know we're on to them. That's why they killed Charlie and came after me. And now they're trying to retrieve their monster and get rid of it before anyone can prove it exists. Why else would the military be in the area?"

"There could be a lot of reasons," Kyle replied.

"Yeah, like what?"

"I don't know," Kyle said, exasperated. "That's why I'm calling Seattle."

"But by then, it will be too late."

"And just what would you suggest be done differently?" Kyle asked.

"I say we go up there and catch them red-handed."

"What? Just how do you think you would do that?"

"By getting photos, evidence, eyewitness accounts. I don't know—something." She pulled out her suitcase, which had been brought to the hospital by Deputy Johnson, and started digging through it.

"Carrie, you're not thinking this through," Kyle said, trying to reason with her. "You can't just go marching up there, hoping to take a few pictures and solve everything. This thing, if it really exists, has already killed a lot of people. What makes you think the same thing won't happen to you?" He didn't want to seem callous, but she was making no sense at all. He looked to the sheriff for support, but the sheriff remained stone-faced.

"Because we know what we're dealing with," she replied, pulling out a pair of jeans. "And even if we don't manage to get pictures of it, at least we can document the military's involvement in the area. Anything we find will be better than what we've got now. I'm not just going to sit here and let them get away with this."

"Even if you did manage to find out what they're doing up there, do you really think they would just let you walk out with the proof?" He couldn't believe he was even arguing with her.

"That's why we have to be careful," she replied.

She had said it several times already, but this time, it caused Kyle to stop. "We?" he asked, his brows knitting with suspicion. "What do you mean ... *we*?"

Carrie looked at him, a hurt expression on her face. "I just assumed you would go with me. Don't you care about what they did to Lewis?"

"That's unfair," Kyle said. He knew what she was trying to do, and he was determined not to let her guilt him into a foolish decision. "You know I care, but running off into the forest isn't going to solve anything. Besides, there are agents coming in from Seattle. I can't just run off like that."

"So what do you expect me to do? Just sit here while they sweep it all under the rug?" she shouted. "I'm not going to do that. First my grandparents, then Charlie, and now Lewis are all dead because of these people, and I'm not going to let them get away with it!" Her bottom lip trembled as she struggled to keep from breaking down again. Tears filled her eyes as she grabbed her clothes and ran into the bathroom, slamming the door behind her.

Kyle sighed, running his hand through his hair in frustration. He knew Carrie was reacting emotionally, but he didn't know how to stop her. She wasn't a suspect, so there was no reason to detain her. He couldn't just ask the sheriff to cuff her to the bed. Nor could he let her go alone. If she persisted in going without him and something were to happen to her, he would never forgive himself.

"What do *you* think?" Kyle asked the sheriff.

"I think she is a very determined young woman," the sheriff replied stoically.

"No kidding," Kyle agreed. "But what do you think about her plan?"

"It's risky, and I don't think the chance for success is very high. But I agree with her. Something must be done. That's why I will go with you."

"You?" Kyle said, shocked by his response. "Why?"

"Because I have seen what this thing has done to the people of the Flathead, and I, too, have reasons for not trusting the government. I think it is better to learn the truth oneself than to have it told to me. Besides, it is obvious that she is going, and you are going to go with her. The two of you would not survive alone. I'm familiar with the area and the dangers involved. If you are to have any chance of success, I must go with you."

Kyle sat there for a moment, stunned. *Am I that transparent?* he wondered. *Or is the sheriff really that perceptive?* Either way, it didn't really matter. The sheriff was right. Kyle just hoped he wasn't that transparent to Carrie.

The bathroom door opened, and Carrie stepped out. "Well?" she asked.

Kyle looked at the sheriff, who nodded his approval. "All right, but the sheriff is coming with us."

"Oh, thank you," Carrie said as she hurried across the room and gave him a big hug.

CHAPTER 85

It was nearing dawn, the skies lightening just enough to reveal the mottled, steel-gray clouds hanging low over the valley. The weather forecast called for three to six inches of snow in the valley with accumulations of one to two feet in the mountains. It wasn't a major concern for Nathan, but it was something to stay aware of. If it snowed enough to shut down the airport, he might be forced to stay a few days longer than he planned—a complication he'd just as soon avoid. He didn't like staying in town any longer than absolutely necessary. It gave the authorities more time to organize a search, increasing his chances of being caught.

Nathan watched as several more people emerged from the hospital. It was hard to make a positive ID from this distance. He took what looked like an oversized, soft-grip Bic pen from his pocket. He then pulled off the cap, unscrewed the tip, and held it up to his eye. Inside, it was a night-vision monocular with six times magnification. With it, he was able to identify the men as a couple of local cops and an unknown deputy. Following close behind were two other men: Deputy Johnson and FBI Agent Marasco.

"Bingo," Nathan whispered when he saw the mole.

He watched patiently. They might just be stepping out for a smoke or heading home to catch a few hours of sleep and a shower. Hopefully, they weren't both on their way to the justice center. The mole would be easier to handle if he were alone. If necessary, he would do them both.

They paused under the porte cochere, talking among themselves and looking out at the overcast skies. Nathan wished he had a shotgun microphone with him, but he had been forced to travel light.

The two cops left while Johnson and Marasco continued to speak with the other deputy. Marasco pulled out a pack of cigarettes and lit up. A short while later, the unknown deputy went back in the hospital. Johnson and Marasco began making their way toward the parking lot.

Damn. It appeared as though they were leaving together.

But when they reached the first row of the parking lot, which had a half-dozen spaces reserved for law enforcement, they split up, Johnson getting into a Flathead County Yukon, Marasco into a black Expedition.

Nathan drove slowly, watching as the two vehicles wove through the lot to the exit onto Highway 93. The vehicles pulled up to the stop sign, the Expedition in front and the Yukon behind. Both vehicles signaled left, toward downtown.

Nathan pulled up to the stop sign a block north. He waited until both vehicles had turned, and checking both directions to make sure it was clear, he turned left as well. A block ahead, the taillights of both vehicles, now beside each other, were just disappearing over the crest of the hill leading down into town.

As he checked his rear-view mirror, Nathan signaled with his blinker and then calmly switched lanes and began following the mole.

CHAPTER 86

Sheriff Greyhawk's Yukon was sitting behind the justice center when Kyle and Carrie returned from the sporting goods store. They had picked up supplies from an extensive list the sheriff had given them, including thermal underwear, snowsuits, gloves, waterproof boots, food, and water. Carrie had also purchased an expensive digital camera with a high-powered, telephoto zoom lens. She had put it all on her credit card, explaining that if they got the evidence they were after, her boss would happily reimburse her in exchange for the story.

The sheriff got out and opened the back gate. Kyle went around back to help the sheriff transfer his gear to the Hummer, while Carrie unloaded the groceries from the backseat. They were taking the H2 because it was unmarked but still equipped for the trip down the reservoir road. The sheriff handed Kyle three large backpacks already partially loaded, three waterproof and hooded sleeping bags, and several pairs of lightweight, plastic and aluminum snowshoes. As Kyle was loading the equipment, his cell phone went off.

He pulled it from his pocket and checked the caller ID. It was the Seattle office. He let it ring. After they had discussed the issue, he and the sheriff had agreed not to tell anyone of their plans, including Deputy Johnson and Agent Marasco. There had already been too many suspicious leaks for them to trust anyone. It had occurred to Kyle that the sheriff could be the one who was leaking the information—it would certainly explain why the mole hadn't been discovered yet—and that his only reason for offering to accompany them was so he could eliminate both of them in the mountains, where they would never be

338

found. Kyle didn't put much stock in this thought, but he intended to keep a close eye on the sheriff just the same.

He checked his watch. It was probably SAC Geddes calling to ask where he was. The agents from Seattle were due to be arriving at any time now. Marasco was supposed to pick them up from the airport. When they arrived at the hospital, they would find that Kyle along with the sheriff and the only other witness to Lewis's shooting had disappeared without telling anyone about their intentions—behavior that was certain to cost him his job and any chance of ever working for the FBI again, a thought that bothered him considerably. It was ironic that he was going to get himself fired just when he had decided to stay. In spite of what he had told his mother, he had never really had any intention of resigning and returning to Dallas. He had just been putting her off, telling her what she had wanted to hear, partly out of guilt but mostly because it had been easier than telling her the truth.

The sheriff seemed to sense his indecision. "I will take her. You do not have to go."

Carrie came around the back of the truck then, arms loaded with bags of food and water, hair blowing across her face. As she walked from the shadow of the raised gate and into the sun, her eyes seemed to light up as she looked at Kyle.

"Yes, I do," Kyle replied.

"Do what?" Carrie asked.

"Nothing," Kyle said, taking the groceries from her and stowing them in the back.

Without further comment, the sheriff handed him two long, leather gun cases along with several boxes of ammo.

As Kyle stowed the gun cases, the true gravity of the situation struck him. Not only was he ignoring his superiors, he was placing himself in a situation that could get him killed. But like Carrie, he was determined to see it through. It was the right thing to do.

"Have you ever fired a shotgun?" the sheriff asked Carrie.

"A rifle but not a shotgun," she replied. "Grandpa Bill used to take me out on the ranch to plink cans from time to time. But it's been a long time. Why?"

"In case we have to defend ourselves," Kyle said, looking at her. He wanted to make sure that she also understood the dangers involved in this little excursion of theirs.

"I'm better with a handgun. I got one after my ex—" She suddenly trailed off and looked away.

The sheriff went back to the Yukon and then returned with a small handgun case and several more boxes of ammo.

"What is it?" Carrie asked.

"A Glock 17 9mm," the sheriff replied.

"I have a Smith & Wesson revolver," Carrie replied. "It's a little bit smaller, but I can handle that."

"Hopefully, it won't come to that," Kyle said.

The three climbed into the Hummer. Carrie let Kyle drive.

They pulled out of the parking lot onto Main Street and headed north. As they did, they failed to notice the green Xterra across the park from the courthouse as it pulled away from the curb and turned onto Main behind them.

CHAPTER 87

The Hummer bounced and lurched, rocks and chunks of slushy ice banging against the undercarriage as they made their way along the last mile of Hungry Horse Reservoir's West Road. It had been a rough trip. Where the road hadn't been covered in snow, it had been rutted and pockmarked. Banks of dirty snow lined both sides of the road where plows had cleared the way, but recent snows and strong wind had undone the work and created drifts that reached across the road in places while others had been covered with patches of black ice hidden among the shadows of the tall evergreens.

In the backseat, Sheriff Greyhawk looked out the window, the dreary, leaden skies reflecting the color of his eyes and the feeling in his soul. As he had feared, there had been a noticeable lack of wildlife visible during the ride. There was normally an abundance of deer and elk crossing the road and bounding into the woods this time of year, but all he had seen were a few birds and small squirrels.

He remembered the conversation in his grandmother's trailer. He had dismissed it as the senseless ramblings of an old woman, but now it appeared she had been right all along. As he recalled the moment, it was as if the inside of the truck became stuffy with the musty smell of urine and the cloying scent of incense. He became dizzy, a strange feeling washing over him. The hairs on the nape of his neck stood on end. He could hear the soft rattling of the bead curtain behind him and her raspy voice as clearly as if he were there now.

"Coyote came to me in a dream," she said. "He came to tell me the monsters have returned to the mountain."

He could see her lying there, the deep lines creasing her weathered face, her dark, piercing eyes boring into his. *You must become Coyote, Little Hawk. But beware, for unlike the hawk, the coyote cannot fly.*

What had she meant by that? he wondered. Now, as they were heading into the mountains, her ominous statements seemed vitally important. He wished he could speak with her again and ask her to explain, but the time for that had already passed.

Ahead, the ranger station came into view. At the southern end of Hungry Horse Reservoir, Spotted Bear Ranger Station was some fifty-five miles from the dam. It consisted of the main building, a large, single-story log cabin that housed the visitor's center and the Forest Service offices, with a couple of small storage and support buildings behind, including the barn-shaped cookhouse, the diesel-generator shed, and a half-dozen cabins operated by the US Forest Service during the summer months. Next to the visitor's center rose the new, forty-foot-tall lookout tower that was being built to oversee the site and to house new radio and cellular relay equipment. A small forest of antennas, miniature satellite dishes, and lightning rods sprouted from the roof of the tower.

They pulled around back and parked beside a pea-green-colored Forest Service Suburban with an empty trailer behind it. Two large snowmobiles sat beside the truck.

George checked his watch. It was already after 9:30, and they still had a long way to go. Kyle had done a good job driving, pushing the pace at every opportunity while not endangering their safety. It was doubtful they could have gotten there much faster. Even so, it had taken them over an hour and a half.

Whether from wrung-out emotions, anxiety, or simple exhaustion, a pall seemed to hang over the group. Hardly anyone had spoken during the ride. The somber mood lingered as George opened the back hatch to gather part of the gear. What little communication there was came in short, clipped sentences.

They followed a pair of footsteps in the snow that led around to the front. Next to the walk in front of the visitor's center stood a covered directory with a Plexiglas display case that contained a faded map of the Spotted Bear Ranger District, which ran from the southern end of Hungry Horse Reservoir far into the Bob Marshall Wilderness. A flyer stapled next to the map indicated that the station was "closed for the season."

The front room of the cabin served as the main office area and visitor's center for the station. The interior looked like a display for a hunting lodge. All along the wall just below the ceiling's exposed beams were numerous mounted animals, including a mountain lion, big horn sheep, mountain goat, and the head of a giant moose with its massive rack of antlers. Two wooden counters ran across the room with an aisle between them that ran down the hall to the back. The wall behind the counter was covered with large geographical survey maps of the area.

The steady thump of boot heels on the hardwood floor could be heard as someone made their way up to the front.

"Morning, sheriff," the man said as he appeared.

"Morning, Hank," the sheriff replied. "Thanks for meeting us on such short notice."

"No problem," Hank said. "Saved me from having to listen to the wife nag me about her 'honey-dos' all day."

George introduced Carrie. Kyle and Hank, who had met during the briefings after the first murders, exchanged greetings.

Hank stuck his hand in his pocket. "Here's the keys," he said, tossing them to George. "The two big ones are for the snowmobiles. The little silver ones are for the padlocks on the gate and Silvertip and Pentagon cabins."

Hank then reached beneath the counter and pulled out a pair of two-way radios. "These are good for about eight to ten miles from here, depending on the weather and your location," he said. "They're fully charged, and I checked 'em both to make sure they're working. Wish I could give you a little better range, but that's the best we can do 'til the new tower is complete."

"Thank you," the sheriff said. He handed one of the radios to Kyle.

"The snowmobiles are out back, all gassed up and ready. There's a bathroom in back you can use to change."

Taking turns in the bathroom, they each stripped out of their regular clothes and put on their thermals, snowsuits, and insulated boots.

While Kyle and Carrie were in back changing, Hank looked at George. "You sure you don't want me to go with you?" he asked.

"Thanks but no," George said. "It's better that you stay here. If we're not back by tomorrow night—"

"I'll come get you," Hank interrupted.

"No," George said. "That would be pointless. If we're not back, call Clayton and Special Agent Marasco. Tell them where we went. They'll know what to do."

After Kyle and Carrie had changed, they said goodbye to Hank, and then headed back outside. On their way back to the Hummer, Carrie asked, "Wouldn't it be good to have Hank with us? I mean, he is a ranger. Who would know the area better than him?"

George looked sideways at her. "I know where we are going," he said. After I left the reservation, I worked for a trail boss for several years. I know this forest well."

"Oh," was all she said.

They opened the back gate to gather the rest of their gear. George took the two Remington 870 shotguns out of the cases and began loading them. Each had extended magazines that would hold eight shells. Finished with the first one, he handed it to Kyle and loaded the second one. He then took out the Glock, slapped in a clip, and handed it to Carrie along with an extra clip. They filled the zippered pockets on each or their snowsuits with spare ammo. The rest was distributed among the three packs.

"Jesus," Kyle muttered. "I hope to hell we don't need all this."

"I do too," George said, but the words of his grandmother kept running through his head.

Once finished, George helped Kyle and Carrie shoulder their packs to make sure they were well balanced and adjusted properly. Because there were only two snowmobiles, George would drive one and Kyle the other, with Carrie riding behind him. The sheriff took Kyle's pack from him and strapped it along with the shotguns to the back of his snowmobile.

Kyle seated himself on the vehicle, and George gave him a few short instructions on its operation. "Got it," Kyle said, pulling down his ski goggles. "Don't worry," he called over his shoulder to Carrie as he started it up. "I used to ride an ATV on our ranch when I was a kid. I only turned it over on myself twice."

"I feel safer already," she said as she pulled on her goggles.

George shrugged into his pack and started the snowmobile. He looked up, checking the sky one last time before donning the tinted goggles. Banks of low clouds were scudding quickly overhead and appeared to be thickening. To the northwest, the skies above the snow-covered peaks looked dark and angry.

George looked at Kyle and pointed to the sky. "We must hurry," he shouted. "A storm is coming."

CHAPTER 88

Myles Bennett winced in pain with each trudging step. He could barely lift his legs anymore. His toes felt as if they had been smashed with a sledgehammer. He wasn't sure he could keep going, but somehow, he did, like a machine on automatic, his legs moving without thought, one foot in front of the other. His lower back had knotted up, nearly spasming from the strain of having to help keep Ramirez upright. Javier had held his own at first, but he had slowly begun to slip into a state of delirium, stumbling and weaving and requiring more and more assistance the farther they went.

Myles felt as if he had been cast into hell—only hell had frozen over—and he was being forced to march for all eternity while wearing snowshoes and carrying the weight of the world on his back. The otherworldly feeling was only heightened by the helmet, which blocked out all sounds other than his own whimpering, gasping breath and the incessant ramblings of Ramirez coming over the radio. *"Por nosotros pecadores, ahora y en la hora de nuestra muerte. Santa María, Madre de Dios, ruega por nosotros—"*

Ramirez said it over and over, a sort of litany with various deviations that included occasional cries of *"El Chupacabra es aqui!"* Myles didn't understand Spanish, but he understood enough to get the gist of it, and it wasn't good. He wished Ramirez would stop. He was terrified enough on his own without Ramirez adding to it.

When he felt he could go no farther, Myles finally stopped to rest. He found a spot just off the narrow trail where a large boulder leaned against a tree. He led Javier over and sat him down and then collapsed beside him like a turtle on its back.

After he rested for only a precious few moments, Myles realized that Ramirez had stopped praying. "Javier?" he asked over the radio.

"Yeah." His reply sounded thick, groggy.

"Just checking."

With extreme effort, Myles sat up. After he pulled off his helmet, he rolled over and slipped off the pack. He opened it and dug around until he found the first-aid kit. As he took out the kit, he saw the case containing the tranquilizer darts.

Now was his chance. Javier seemed to be worsening. There was no way the two of them were going to make it before dark. He could simply stick Javier in the neck with one of the darts, and he would be paralyzed before he could draw his gun. Then Myles could go on alone and send back help. In reality, though, Myles knew there was little chance that anyone could make it back before dark. He would essentially be signing Javier's death certificate. But if he didn't, he might as well sign one for both of them.

Leaning over, he removed Javier's helmet. Ramirez lay back against the rock, his eyes closed.

Myles lifted Javier's right eyelid. He squinted and tried to look away. "Damn, doc," he groaned.

Myles reached into the pack and took out a small package of smelling salts from the first-aid kit. Myles had a PhD in biological engineering, not medicine, so he wasn't actually a doctor in the manner most people thought. He had never taken the Hippocratic Oath. Even so, he couldn't bring himself to abandon the young man, no matter how small his chance of survival was.

He cracked open the ammonia capsule and waved it under Javier's nose. At first, there was no response, but then the young man's head suddenly jerked to one side, his eyes open wide.

"Sorry," Myles said.

"No, it's all right," Ramirez said.

Myles thought he sounded a little better, but that could have just been wishful thinking. They each drank a little of the water then. As Myles was putting it back in the pack, Ramirez suddenly spoke. "I'm dying, aren't I, doc?"

Myles paused, caught off guard by Javier's apparent lucidity and by his own hesitancy to answer the question. "I don't know," he finally said.

"Do me a favor, will you?"

"What's that?"

Ramirez pulled open one of the Velcro pockets and removed his rosary beads. He held them out to Myles. "Make sure these get back to my daughter."

Myles didn't know what to say. "I … I can't. I mean, you can return them yourself. We're going to make it."

"But if I don't, take these to her. Let my wife know what happened."

Myles suddenly felt ill. He hadn't even considered the fact that Javier might have a family. And what about the others? What about Busey and Johnson and Dietrich and even Ainsworth? What about their families? Who would tell them what had happened to their loved ones. Suddenly, everything he had worked so long and so hard for, everything he had sacrificed for the program all just felt … wrong. *How had it gotten to this point?* he wondered. *How had it all gotten so far out of control?*

He looked at the small silver cross dangling before him. His hand was shaking as he took the beads.

CHAPTER 89

Carrie held on tightly to Kyle's midsection as the snowmobile rocked and bounced down the trail. A short while after leaving the ranger station, they had come to a Forest Service road that was closed for the season. The road had been blocked by a steel gate that was secured with a loop of heavy chain and a large padlock. George had unlocked the gate with one of the keys Hank had given them. They had been traveling along the road for almost an hour now.

Unfortunately, they had been delayed for almost half of that time when they had come across a section of road that had been buried in a small slide of snow and mud. Before they could pass, they had been forced to remove a few of the tree limbs and smaller trunks that had spilled across the roadway. Finally, after they cleared enough of the obstacles, they managed to get the snowmobiles across the debris field.

The hood of the snowsuit and the monotonous drone of the snowmobiles effectively drowned out all other sounds, which caused Carrie to feel a certain sense of isolation in spite of being accompanied by Kyle and the sheriff. The ranger station was well behind them now, and with it the last remnants of civilization.

Carrie felt relatively safe with Kyle and the sheriff, but she kept scanning the sky for any signs of activity, natural or otherwise. The range of peaks on the far side of the river appeared to be little more than hazy shadows. What light there was filtering through the clouds cast an eerie, silvery glow across the valley. Through a break in the

349

trees, she caught a brief glimpse of the river below them to their right. They were still climbing.

It was getting colder as well. She thought it might be starting to snow, but it was hard to tell if that were the case or it was just chaff being thrown up by the sheriff's snowmobile. Either way, she was glad they had purchased the snowsuits, gloves, and boots. Even with the fur-lined hood up and her goggles on, her eyes were watering, and her face felt as if it was beginning to chafe in the frigid wind.

They hit a small bump, and Carrie was bounced from the seat, the weight of her pack pulling her backward. Her gloved hands slipped across the slick nylon of Kyle's suit, and for a frightening moment, she thought she was going to lose her balance. She grabbed at Kyle, clutching him tighter, her arms around his chest and her knees pressed against his thighs.

"You okay?" Kyle shouted over his shoulder.

"Yeah, fine," she shouted back, a little embarrassed, but she didn't loosen her grip on him. Kyle made no further comment, so she assumed it didn't bother him. It certainly didn't bother her. It felt good to be this close to him, even with the gloves and thick layers of clothing between them. In spite of the freezing conditions, Carrie felt a growing warmth inside her that had nothing to do with the insulated suit she wore.

A short while later, the sheriff slowed in front of them. He raised his arm, signaling to them before coming to a stop. Kyle guided their snowmobile around to the right and pulled up beside him. In front of them, a wooden barricade stretched across the trail, which ceased to exist beyond it. It was a dead end.

"What now?" Carrie asked.

"We walk," said the sheriff. He stood and began unstrapping Kyle's pack from the snowmobile.

"But where?" Carrie asked as she looked around.

"The Spotted Bear River Trailhead is just behind us," the sheriff said with a nod toward the trees. "It will take us past Silvertip Cabin and on to Pentagon Cabin, but we must hurry," he said, looking at the skies once again. "We must travel another ten miles before dark, and the most difficult part of our journey is still before us."

Carrie started to ask the sheriff if he had meant for that last comment to sound as ominous as it had, but she decided against it. She was afraid she already knew the answer.

Regretfully, she let go of Kyle and got off. Her boots broke through the top layer of icy crust and sunk halfway up to her calves in the unpacked snow beneath. Leaning over, she stretched her back, which was already feeling the effects of the pack she wore.

"You all right?" Kyle asked.

"Yeah, just stretching out the kinks," she replied.

The sheriff made his way over, his boots crunching in the snow. He handed Kyle's pack to him. "You should put on the snowshoes now," he said. "The snow is firmer here where it has been in the sun, but on the trail, it will be much softer and deeper."

After the prolonged droning of the snowmobiles, the valley seemed preternaturally quiet as they readjusted their gear and strapped on the snowshoes. The sheriff picked up one of the shotguns and pumped it, racking a shell into the breech before handing it to Kyle. The sound echoed eerily down the valley.

They made their way back up the road a short distance to the edge of the trees. A post with a small wooden plaque was mounted in front of a small gap. The letters TH inside a square with rounded corners was carved into the sign, marking the Spotted Bear River Trailhead. A narrow trail cut through the trees and angled down the mountain toward the river a short distance before it veered off to the left.

With the sheriff leading and Kyle bringing up the rear, they started down the decline and into the shadows.

CHAPTER 90

Nathan made his way up the walk in front of the Spotted Bear Ranger Station. The prolonged exposure to the cold had caused his knee to stiffen, which forced him to walk with more of a limp than normal, but it was a minor nuisance. It would all be over soon.

Following the girl and the others all the way up from Kalispell, he had been careful to keep his distance to avoid being spotted. When he had reached the ranger station and spotted the Hummer, Nathan had turned around and then pulled into the Diamond J Ranch, a privately owned campground with a collection of small cabins tucked away about a half mile back up the road. There, he had watched as the girl, the sheriff, and the FBI man had all left on snowmobiles.

They were playing right into his hand. It would be much easier to eliminate them out here. He could have done it in town, as he had with the mole, but this was better. Here, he would be afforded the luxury of uninterrupted privacy. And if things worked out right, he would still be able take his time with the girl.

Ignoring the wooden sign out front, Nathan stepped onto the porch and walked inside. The creaking door announced his presence to anyone within. The front room was empty except for a strange menagerie of stuffed wildlife mounted around the walls.

"Hello?" a man's voice called out from the back, followed by the sound of boot heels thumping on the wooden floor.

Nathan waited until the ranger stepped into view and then raised his gun and shot him twice in the face.

The man dropped like a stone. Nathan stepped around the counter, ready to finish him off, but the man was already dead. He pressed himself against the wall and then peered around the corner down the hall to see if anyone else was in the building. Even with the silencer, the thump of the body hitting the floor might have roused their suspicion.

The hallway was empty. A faint, spluttering hiss came from one of the back rooms.

Nathan slipped down the corridor and checked each room to make sure no one was hiding under a desk or in a closet. In back was the break room. The spluttering sound he had heard came from an old Mr. Coffee that was just beginning to brew, the dark liquid trickling into the glass pot beneath it.

Confident he was alone, Nathan went back to the first office he had checked. Against the wall to his left was an old roll-top desk. The roll-top had been pulled back, revealing the shortwave radio and microphone. He walked over to the desk and pulled the radio off into the floor. Sparks jumped from the electrical socket as the plug was jerked from the wall. With a nearby coat rack, he smashed the equipment until there was no chance it would ever be used again.

Nathan went back to the break room. He had been up for several days now, only catching brief catnaps here and there, and he was beginning to feel the effects. He opened the cabinet doors until he found a shelf with several coffee cups. After he took one down, he picked up the tan canister of Imperial sugar from the counter and poured it into the cup, letting it sift out until the bottom was covered with a large, white mound. He filled the cup with coffee and mixed it with a plastic stirrer he found in one of the drawers. He then took out a small pillbox from his pocket. Inside were pills of various sizes, shapes, and color. He took out one of the small red capsules and washed it down with three big gulps of coffee. The pill was another of GenTech's many innovations for the military. It allowed soldiers to go for days without sleep with only minimal diminishment of their mental faculties.

While he was drinking the coffee, Nathan noticed a box of Little Debbie honey buns sitting on the counter. His stomach rumbled in response. He tore open the box and was happy to find there were still two honey buns left. He ripped into the cellophane and inhaled the first one in four bites.

He then went back up front and checked the ranger's pockets. He found a set of keys, which he took with him as he went back through the break room and out the back door. Beside the Hummer was a pea-green US Forest Service Suburban.

And there, in a gun rack in the rear side window was just what he had been looking for—a shotgun.

Moments later, Nathan stepped back inside with the loaded shotgun. After he laid the gun down on the table, he poured himself a fresh cup of coffee and picked up the remaining honey bun. He then sat down at the table and enjoyed the rest of his breakfast while images of the girl, bound and gagged, danced within his head.

CHAPTER 91

With each huffing breath, the air in front of Kyle fogged briefly before it was quickly whisked away. The wind had picked up, whispering its warning of the coming storm through the treetops that swayed back and forth as if bowing before an angry God.

The sheriff paused, looked at the trunk of a tree, and then moved on without comment. They had been traveling for hours now, stopping only once to take a quick break at Silvertip Cabin, where they had gone inside for a brief rest and a quick meal. As he passed the tree, Kyle noticed what looked like an upside-down exclamation mark carved into the thick bark. He had noticed similar markings on other trees along the way and had assumed it was a method of marking the trail. While the trail might have been visible in the summer, it was virtually impossible to make out with the snow cover. Kyle realized that without the sheriff, he and Carrie would have become hopelessly lost within minutes of entering this vast wilderness.

Carrie turned and looked back at him. And though it was hard to tell behind the goggles and fur-lined hood, Kyle thought she smiled at him, and he found himself grinning stupidly in return. He was glad she was in front of him. Even with the snowsuit and the large pack, he couldn't help but notice her shapely figure as she walked, but more importantly, it made it easier for him to keep an eye on her. He was determined to stay close enough to make sure nothing happened to her.

A short while later, they emerged from the hall of trees and came to a strip of undisturbed snow in their path. The sheriff held up his hand for them to stop. After he handed the shotgun to Carrie, he snapped a limb off a nearby spruce and then moved forward, kneeling down here and there, carefully testing the depth of the snow. The stick sank up to his hand in several places before he finally struck something solid. Using the limb as a broom, he cleared away enough snow to reveal a portion of two logs buried beneath.

"This is Dean's Creek," the sheriff said. "Cross as I do, with your feet sideways to the logs so you don't slip off."

In the distance to their left, Kyle could see the racing torrent of frigid water roaring down the mountain before disappearing beneath the snow. It would be disastrous if they stepped in the wrong place and fell through.

After they each crossed the creek, the trail began to rise again. Kyle's thighs and calves burned with every step as they made their way up the slope. It was hard to tell how far they had gone, but he was afraid it wasn't nearly as far as it felt. Regardless of the distance, the trek was already taking its toll on him. He watched Carrie in front of him and wondered how she was holding up.

At the top of the climb, the trail leveled off onto a rocky, windswept bluff clear of the trees. Barely visible through the misty clouds, they were just able to make out the upward-canted cliffs of the Limestone Wall across the valley to the south. The snow-covered bed of the Spotted Bear River was now far below them. "We're about halfway to Pentagon Cabin," the sheriff said over the rising wind. He pointed to their left, where a wooden sign nailed to a tree marked an intersecting path. "That trail follows Elk Ridge up to the peak of Shadow Mountain."

"Shadow Mountain? That's where the plane crashed," Carrie said.

"Yes," said the sheriff.

Kyle looked up, his eyes following the craggy ridgeline as it zigzagged up the side of the mountain before it disappeared into the growing bank of dark clouds that obscured the peak. Despite the snowsuit he was wearing, Kyle shivered as the frigid wind gusted across his neck and down his spine.

"The storm is growing," the sheriff said, looking back to the west. "We must hurry."

Ahead, the trail ducked back down into the cathedral of trees, momentarily sheltering them from the worst of the wind. They trudged on, twisting and snaking through the thick undergrowth before coming to a narrow, snow-clogged defile.

The sheriff stopped. Kneeling down, he examined the deep snow in front of them. "Others have been here," he said, pointing to several irregular depressions the wind had not managed to completely erase. They all knew who the "others" were.

"Can you tell how many?" Kyle asked.

"It is hard to be certain," the sheriff said as he examined the marks. "But it looks as if two came this way and then returned."

The sheriff turned back to them. "We must be careful. If I signal, get off the trail. Duck behind whatever cover is available and wait for me. I will come back for you. If I don't return in ten minutes, turn around and head back to the ranger station as fast as you can."

"But—" Carrie started to protest.

The sheriff looked at Carrie. "Do *not* come after me," he reiterated and then looked at Kyle. Kyle nodded in confirmation.

They continued on through the swale, forcing their way through the deep snow for another half mile or so. Even with the snowshoes, they still sank up to their knees in the soft powder, and more than once, they had to help each other to keep from getting bogged down. It was the perfect place for an ambush, which forced Kyle and the sheriff to take turns moving forward while the other kept watch.

By the time they cleared the bog, Kyle and Carrie were spent. The sheriff seemed no worse for wear, but thankfully, he suggested they take a break. While the sheriff kept watch, Kyle and Carrie ate one of the bland protein bars, which had already become hard and brittle from the cold. No one spoke, afraid that any sounds might give away their presence.

A narrow break in the trees to their left provided a view of Dean Falls in the distance. The icy cataract plunged hundreds of feet down the steep cleft, the craggy stone bearded with crystalline frost from the frozen spume. Even now, with much of the falls still locked away in snow and ice, it was a breathtaking sight. Its beauty, however, was lost on the three, whose sole focus was the shadowy confines of the surrounding forest.

CHAPTER 92

Every muscle and joint in Kyle's body ached as they continued to slog their way along the trail. Even though he worked out regularly and thought he was in pretty good shape, nothing could have prepared him for this. The backs of his knees burned, and his right hip had developed a catch that would pop occasionally, sending currents of pain shooting down his leg. His lower back and shoulders were cramping up beneath the weight of the pack. His forearm burned from carrying the shotgun. Everything hurt.

In front of him, Carrie seemed to be doing all right, but Kyle knew she had to be struggling as much as he was. Even so, he felt certain she would never admit it. She continued to trudge forward without complaint.

The sheriff stopped. He stood motionless, staring at the trail ahead of them. He cocked his head as if listening for something and then signaled for them to get down.

They clambered off the trail and ducked behind an old, splintered stump. Kyle crouched next to Carrie. He scanned the forest, but the fading light made it impossible to make out anything against the backdrop of swaying brush and trees. When he looked back at the trail, the sheriff was gone.

Kyle assumed the sheriff had either hidden alongside the trail or had gone farther up to investigate, but he wasn't taking any chances. He pulled off the glove on his right hand with his teeth and then released the safety on the shotgun. The shotgun's metal stock was so cold it practically burned. Trying to remain as quiet as possible, Kyle slowly pulled back his hood and strained to listen for any telltale sounds. He could hear Carrie's rapid breathing beside him and the haunting moan of the wind overhead, but nothing more.

Neither of them dared to move or even whisper as they huddled next to the tree. One by one, the seconds crept by, each one feeling like a minute, every minute an hour. Kyle could feel himself sweating within the snowsuit, and had it not been for the cold, his forehead would have beaded with perspiration.

Next to him, Carrie shifted slightly, the weight of her body leaning against his. It felt good. Kyle remained still, taking pleasure in her closeness while he could. As he watched, a few stray strands of her hair danced in the rising wind.

He waited for as long as he felt prudent before he finally checked his watch. Eight and a half minutes had gone by and still no sign. The sheriff must have encountered someone. *Or something*, he thought, his worries rapidly ascending toward fear. Surely, he wouldn't have been gone this long otherwise. He looked at Carrie, who stared at him with wide-eyed concern.

"*I know*," he mouthed back at her silently. They had to do something. But what? The sheriff had expressly forbidden them to come after him, and Kyle respected his instincts enough not to second-guess him.

Kyle flexed his right hand, which had grown stiff from the cold, trying to keep it ready in case he had to use the gun. *What the hell is going on?*

A brittle *snap* came from behind them. Kyle whirled around, his finger on the trigger, but there was nothing there. He scanned the area, straining to see amid the muted shadows, looking for signs of movement, but there was nothing. *Just ice … falling from a frozen branch*, he told himself, but he continued to watch just the same.

And then he felt Carrie grasp his arm in alarm.

He looked back at her and then in the direction she pointed. There, a large, dark figure was moving rapidly up the trail in their direction.

Kyle hefted the gun, leaving his finger outside the trigger guard. His fingers were stiff from the cold. He didn't want to accidentally shoot the sheriff if it was him.

The figure continued up the trail, moving closer. It was quickly growing dark, which made it virtually impossible to make out any details of the silhouette. It grew larger as it approached until Kyle felt certain it was too big to be the sheriff.

He raised the shotgun and slipped his finger through the guard.

The figure stopped and raised its arm. "Come ... quickly."

Kyle sighed in relief, carefully easing off the trigger. It was the sheriff.

Kyle and Carrie emerged from the hiding spot and began sloughing their way back to the trail. It was tough going at first, and Kyle found himself struggling to keep up.

"What is it? What did you find?" Carrie asked, but the sheriff had already turned and was marching back up the trail.

Ahead, they crested a small rise. At the bottom of the hill were two black-clad figures, one leaning in the shelter of a rocky outcropping, the other kneeling next to him.

Kyle froze. He looked around anxiously, wary of a trap. But the sheriff marched on, apparently unconcerned. Carrie hesitated as well and looked at Kyle. Unsure what else to do, Kyle nodded for her to follow. They would have to trust the sheriff. Even so, Kyle kept a close watch on the surrounding forest as they made their way toward the two.

As they neared, Kyle was able to discern more about the two figures. They were both clad entirely in black, but they weren't just snowsuits. They looked like some sort of specially armored military or special-forces gear. One figure still wore what looked like a futuristic black helmet, while the other, the man kneeling next to him, had removed his. This second man had dark, curly hair mashed flat against his head and damp with sweat. Faint wisps of steam rose from his head. Even with the suit on, it was apparent that he was thin, almost frail. His glasses were canted at an odd angle, bent from wearing the helmet. He had a weary, strained look on his face.

"Oh, thank God," the man gushed as they approached.

"What's going on?" Carrie asked. The man in black stood as if she had been addressing him. Kyle pointed the shotgun his direction.

"No, no," he said hastily, holding his hands up. "You don't understand. This man is hurt. He needs medical attention."

Without pausing, the sheriff moved over to the man and knelt beside him. The man's head lolled back and forth, and he seemed to be speaking, but it was unintelligible beneath the helmet. The sheriff slipped the visor up. Beneath was the face of a young Hispanic man. His eyes were glassy and unfocused, and they were rolling around as he muttered something in Spanish.

"What happened?" the sheriff asked.

"We, uh ... were sent here on a rescue mission," the man stammered. "Some hikers got lost in the woods and ... and then he fell and hit his head." The man was a terrible liar.

"Give me a break," Carrie snapped. "You're not part of any rescue team. You were sent here to retrieve your monster, weren't you?"

The man stopped, his eyes widening in surprise. "I don't know what you're talking about."

"How dumb do you think we are?" Carrie said. "There aren't any hikers out here. And look at you—you're wearing what looks like high-tech military gear. Do you really think we're that stupid? We know what happened with the GenTech plane. Why else do you think we're here? This is Sheriff Greyhawk and Agent Andrews of the FBI. So why don't you tell us what really happened?"

The man just stood there and stared at them with a dumbfounded expression on his face before he looked to the sheriff as if requesting confirmation. Without speaking, the sheriff unzipped his snowsuit enough to reveal his uniform and badge beneath.

"I ... I can't," the man stammered. "If I tell you, they'll kill me."

"Who will?" Carrie asked. Kyle noticed she seemed to have taken the lead in the interrogation, but the sheriff didn't seem to mind. She seemed to be making progress.

"I don't know *who* exactly," he said with a glance toward the man on the ground. "I just know they will kill me."

"He doesn't appear to be much of a threat to anyone right now," Kyle noted.

"Not him. The people he works for."

"And who is that?" Carrie asked.

"I told you. I don't know. I just know they'll kill me if I tell you anything."

Kyle noticed that the sheriff, who had been watching the man, had subtly turned his attention to the forest around them. His eyes narrowed as he scanned the shadowy confines beneath the trees. The thought they might even now be in the crosshairs of a sharpshooter's scope made Kyle feel suddenly exposed.

"Are we being watched now?" Kyle whispered, lifting the shotgun slightly in readiness. "Can they hear what you're saying?"

"No, no," the man replied. "Except for him, the ones I was sent with are all dead, or at least I think they are."

"Dead?" Kyle asked. "What happened?"

The man looked down at the ground. "Mistakes were made … mostly by me, I'm afraid, and now we're the only two left."

"Then what do you have to worry about?" Carrie asked.

"You don't know what you're dealing with," the man sighed. "I don't even know who they are. But I can tell you that powerful people are involved, with tentacles that reach far and wide. They will know I told you. They *will* kill me—and you—to keep their secret quiet."

"I work for a newspaper," Carrie said. "Once we go public with this story, there will be too many people who know about it. They won't be able to cover it up by simply killing those who know about it."

"It's not that simple," the man said. "Even I don't know who is involved. If I tell you, can you promise to protect me? Put me in the witness protection program or something?"

Carrie looked to Kyle.

"I can't promise you anything," Kyle said, "But I'll talk to my superior. I'll do everything I can." Technically, Kyle hadn't lied to the man, but he knew he didn't have the authority to promise anything. In fact, as far as he knew, he might be arrested himself as soon as they returned to town. But he had come too far to be concerned about that right now.

The man seemed unconvinced. He remained silent for a moment, considering his choices. As he did so, he looked at the young man on the ground and then at something he held in his hand. It looked like a necklace made of dark beads. Then Kyle noticed the small silver cross dangling from it.

The man seemed to make his decision then. Looking up, he said, "This man has a serious concussion, probably a subdural hematoma. We have to get him to a hospital soon, or he's going to die. If you help me get him back, I promise I'll tell you everything."

Kyle looked to the sheriff. "What do you think?"

"If this was a setup, they would have already captured or killed us."

"Right," Kyle said, somewhat unnerved by that thought. "So now what?"

The sheriff pulled out the walkie-talkie.

"Uh, I'm afraid that won't work," the man said.

Everyone looked at him. "Part of the equipment we left back at Pentagon Cabin included a radio frequency jammer. That's why I couldn't call for help. I tried to turn it off, but I didn't have the passcode."

The sheriff keyed the radio. As expected, there was nothing but static. He turned up the volume, adjusted the squelch, and tried again, but he still received no answer.

The sheriff put the radio away. "Do you know the range of the jamming equipment?"

"About five miles, I think—"

The sheriff looked up at the near-black skies overhead. The concern was clearly etched on his face. "The storm will have reached the ranger station by now. It will be upon us soon. They will not be able to air-lift him out."

The sheriff seemed to make a decision. As he began to shrug out of his gear, he said, "Take off your packs. We must lighten our load. We are going to have to carry him out."

They all did as requested, and the sheriff began quickly sorting through the supplies, dumping everything that was not absolutely necessary and redistributing most of the remaining items between Carrie and the stranger.

"You're not leaving any of the weapons or ammo behind, are you?" the man asked, his voice wavering as shivers racked his body. Kyle found it odd that the suit he was wearing wasn't keeping him warm enough.

The sheriff looked at him suspiciously. "Why?"

"Because ... they might still be out there."

"Who might?" Kyle asked, concerned that the man might be in shock. "I thought you said everyone was dead?"

"They are—at least I think they are—but I can't be sure about the dragons."

"Dragons?" Kyle asked.

"The creatures, the chimera—that's what they're called: Mandarin Dragons. I don't know exactly how the name came about. The project was underway for years before I was brought on board. I think maybe it had something to do with Vietnam—"

"No, no, that's not what I meant," Kyle said even as the man continued to ramble on. "You said *dragons,* as in plural. You mean there's more than one?"

"Yes, that's how they managed to overrun the recovery team. We didn't know it at the time, but—"

"And they're still out there?" Kyle interrupted.

"Like I said, I can't be sure how many there were or if any of them survived, but it's possible. In fact, quite probable considering that none of the team returned. We really ought to hurry before it gets any darker."

"Why?" Kyle asked, even though he was afraid he already knew the answer.

"Because," the man said. "They're nocturnal. They hunt at night."

CHAPTER 93

With Kyle's help, Carrie shrugged into her pack. It was noticeably lighter. The only things left within were the first-aid kit, a small amount of food, the ammunition, and the digital camera she refused to leave behind. Even though they had an eyewitness, Carrie knew an actual photo of the creature, if they could manage to get one, would be infinitely more valuable in proving the authenticity of their story. The rest of the gear lay in a pile alongside the trail, including the sleeping bags and most of the water. It seemed like such a waste, but she understood why it had to be left behind.

At the sheriff's suggestion, Carrie and the biologist led the way. They were walking directly into the teeth of the storm now. Her face was becoming wind burned, and her eyes watered in spite of the goggles she wore. As a precaution, she walked with her right hand in her jacket pocket and held the grip of the Glock. Behind, Kyle and the sheriff struggled to keep the wounded man, Ramirez, upright and moving forward.

While the man had promised to tell them everything, Carrie wasn't willing to wait until they made it back to the ranger station. She was determined to get the answers she had come for while she had the chance. She began questioning him almost immediately.

"I don't really know where to start," he said. The visor on his helmet was up, or else she wouldn't have been able to hear him at all.

"Why don't you start with your name and who you work for," Carrie prompted.

"Yes … yes, of course," he said. "I'm Dr. Myles Bennett. I'm a biological engineer for GenTech."

Carrie perked up at the mention of the company's name. Excitedly, she glanced back at Kyle. She wanted to say, "See, I told you. I was right all along," but he was busy struggling with the Ramirez kid.

Turning back around, she said, "And you've seen the creatures?"

"Oh, yes," he said. "The dragons were genetically engineered in the black projects lab at GenTech. I was one of the scientists involved in the project."

Carrie could hardly believe her luck. Not only had they found a witness but someone who had firsthand knowledge of the project.

"But why?" Carrie asked, "I mean, what were they created for?"

"They were designed with a very specific purpose in mind," Bennett said. "The impetus for the initial experiments came during the Korean and Vietnam Wars. Our soldiers were fighting a very different war from any that had ever been fought before. Those wars were waged in inhospitable locations with unconventional tactics being employed by the enemy. They were in swamps and forests and rugged, mountainous regions, being attacked from virtually every direction with guerilla-style tactics. Typically, the army depends on our air superiority to soften up the opposing forces through extensive bombing prior to our ground forces moving in—a method that was employed with great success in the wars against Iraq. But this approach doesn't always work. In conflicts with less easily defined targets, such as Vietnam and Korea and more recently Afghanistan, this proved to be an ineffective method. The government was desperate to find an alternate means for dealing with these guerilla and terrorist forces, which typically move in small groups in remote and often harsh environments, and mostly at night. My understanding is there were numerous projects being worked on originally—everything from training small, elite, counterterror forces to small remote-controlled attack droids to chemical and biological weapons. But with the mapping of the human genome and the exponential advances in genetic research and recombinant DNA, the Mandarin Project, as ours was known, was seen to offer the most promising results for the near future."

"My God." Carrie could hardly believe what she was hearing. "So you're saying these things were intentionally created as some sort of weapon?"

"Created, yes, although 'designed' is perhaps a more accurate description. The dragons were developed with very specific parameters in mind. First, they were to be carnivorous and, if possible, to specifically seek out humans as prey. They wouldn't be a very effective weapon if they were herbivores. Second, they were to be warm-blooded, which would allow them to function in all environments. Of course, such characteristics require a lot of energy, which means they must eat a lot. They hunt almost continuously, although this isn't really a problem, since it fits in with the overall design criteria."

Carrie was shocked as she listened to Bennett's description of the creatures. It was as if he was detailing the specifications for a piece of hardware, not some genetically designed killing machine. He sounded like he was proud of their creation.

"Third," Dr. Bennett continued. "They were to be nocturnal so they would be active during the times of most guerilla and terrorist movement. The cover of darkness offers the added benefit of making the dragons more difficult to detect as well as playing upon man's innate fear of the dark. For the most part, the dragons were to be deployed in remote and often less technologically advanced areas, so the effect of rumor and superstition was seen as an added benefit. Fear is a great disrupter of cohesion and motivation among forces," Bennett noted.

"Fourth, they were to have the ability to fly, enabling them to travel in almost any region as well as allowing them to cover large amounts of territory in a short time. And fifth, there had to be a means for deactivating them once their work was done."

"In the end," Bennett said, "the creature's design wound up being a mixture of various animals, but its primary makeup came from the Nile crocodile, chimpanzees, and bats. Most people don't know it, but crocodiles are similar to birds in many aspects. The bats provided the nocturnal habits as well as sonar and echolocation and the ability of flight, although it was very difficult to increase the growth factor enough to match the size required by the dragons. It was all much more complicated than it sounds. It took years and years of work by dozens of scientists to develop a self-sustaining prototype."

"Wait a minute," Carrie said. "You said there was to be a way to deactivate them. What did you mean by that? Did you mean *kill* them?"

"Yes," Bennett replied. "Eventually, there were to have been tracking units implanted in each of the creatures. The plan was to install a chip into each dragon's head that would serve as a GPS locator as well as a radio frequency receiver. Once the dragons achieved the desired result, a signal would be initiated from a satellite and the implant would immediately sever the link between its spinal column and cerebral cortex, thereby deactivating it. There were also miniature radio transmitters developed to prevent unwanted attacks on ground personnel."

Hearing all of this was beginning to make Carrie feel sick to her stomach. To describe the program as a violation of human and animal rights was a gross understatement. But it still didn't answer what she wanted to know. "So why weren't these 'deactivated' after the crash!" she asked angrily.

"Unfortunately, they had not been fitted with the implants yet. The two prototypes were being transferred to a base in Alaska for further testing when the plane went down. A cleanup crew was deployed to the site immediately after the crash, but there was little time for them to get in and out before the NTSB investigators arrived. They didn't have time to search the area sufficiently, and therefore, they were unable to determine that one of the dragons had survived. Even so, it should never have become as big a problem as it did, were it not for several extenuating circumstances that even we didn't know about until it was too late. Apparently, the dragon that survived must have become pregnant at some point without our knowledge. After giving birth to what I now suspect are at least several litters, they began to put a strain on the local food supply—a problem that was exacerbated by the exceptionally harsh winter. The dragons were forced to range farther and farther afield in search of prey."

Prey? Something about the way he said it caused Carrie to snap. Without fully realizing what she was doing, she attacked the man. "Those goddamn things killed my grandparents!" she screamed as she began hitting him. In spite of his suit and helmet, Bennett cowered before her assault, holding his arm over his head in a halfhearted effort to defend himself. Arms flailing, she struck him again and again, screaming and crying until her throat was raw. "You bastard, you fucking bastard——"

Someone grabbed her from behind and pulled her off. She struggled to break free, but the arms around her waist held her tight.

She fought to turn around and hit whoever was holding her back, but as she thrashed about, she heard Kyle yelling in her ear. "Carrie, stop it! Stop! Settle down."

Hearing Kyle, the fight drained out of her. She stopped struggling, and as she did so, he loosened his grip enough for her to turn around. With hot tears rolling down her face, she fell against Kyle's chest.

She stayed that way for several moments before Kyle gently asked, "Are you all right?"

She nodded weakly and stepped back, wiping at the frozen tears on her face.

"I had no idea," Bennett said. "I'm sorry. I'm truly sorry."

After they gave Carrie a moment to gather herself, they started back down the trail again. They still had a long way to go, which included making their way through the bog of deep snow, and the light was rapidly fading. The sky was dark with angry, black clouds roiling overhead like a turbulent sea turned upside down. Tiny pellets of snow and ice fell like frozen spray.

Carrie remained silent as they trudged along, but Bennett started speaking again, as if now that he had started, he wanted to get it off his chest all at once. "I didn't start out to create monsters," he mumbled, as if talking to himself as much as Carrie.

"Shortly after my little brother, Douglas, was born, he was diagnosed with Dandy-Walker syndrome, a congenital malformation of the brain and, in his case, his heart. Douglas's head grew to be larger than normal, and he never fully developed mentally. He could never really hold his head up without it wobbling about, and his eyes never seemed able to focus on you.

"Throughout his infancy, we suffered as he was forced to endure numerous surgeries in an effort to correct the problems, but all they ever really did was prolong the agony. He cried all the time. It was horrible. Then, when I was in high school, I read *Flowers for Algernon*, and it changed my life. You are familiar with it, aren't you?" Bennett asked.

"Yes," Carrie replied.

"I was so affected by that story I decided to become a scientist in hopes of helping people like my brother, like they did in the book. Only I was determined to succeed where they had failed. I had just graduated from high school when my brother died. He was only six. My parents were devastated. I don't think they ever recovered." Bennett wiped at his eyes beneath the raised visor. He sounded sincere, but Carrie wasn't about to let her opinions of him be swayed that easily.

"I became more determined than ever to help make a difference," Bennett said after a moment. "Children shouldn't have to suffer like that. Unfortunately, genetic research is very expensive, and in the early days, there were no marketable products to help offset the costs. As a result, the company was forced to look for alternative means of funding. The Mandarin Project provided the solution. Although now I don't suppose it matters how it got started," he said. "The road to hell, right?"

Carrie didn't say anything, but as they continued to march into the teeth of the growing snowstorm, she was afraid that was exactly where they were headed.

CHAPTER 94

By the time they reached the stretch of trail passing through the bog, the storm had struck in full force. The wind howled through the trees, and what little daylight remained had been blotted out by the thick mass of churning clouds.

Javier's behavior had become more troubling as well. His head lolled from side to side, and he muttered continuously as he stumbled along. Even before they had started, it was obvious they were going to have a difficult time with him.

They paused while Kyle and the sheriff spoke among themselves, but it was impossible for Carrie to hear. The sheriff tried the radio again to no avail.

"Carrie," Kyle called out, and she leaned in closer. "Don't wait for us. You and the doctor go on ahead. When you get to the high point on the other side, try the radio again," he said, holding it out to her. If it still won't work, head for the snowmobiles as fast as you—"

"No," Carrie interrupted. "I won't leave you."

"You have to," Kyle shouted. "Take one of the snowmobiles and get to the ranger station as fast as you can. Tell Hank to bring one of the ski sleds back with him and meet up with us at the trailhead."

"But what about the dragons?"

"That's why you have to go now," Kyle shouted back. "We've got the shotguns. We can take care of ourselves."

"I won't leave you," she said again.

"Carrie, you have to. It's the only way. We'll be all right," Kyle assured her.

She started to ask, "And what if you're not?" but she couldn't bring herself to say it, as if saying it might somehow make it come true. She bit her bottom lip and nodded. As she took the radio from him, she looked up at him one last time, hoping he would change his mind. But he didn't. He just nodded at her in encouragement and offered one last, "It's all right. Now go."

Numbly, she turned around. Step by agonizing step, she began to slowly walk away. Behind her, Dr. Bennett paused to speak with Kyle and the sheriff, their voices too low for her to hear. After a brief conversation, he turned and began following her.

As they began trudging through the drift, Carrie felt as if she had been sucker punched in the gut. A gnawing emptiness bloomed inside of her just as it had after the death of her grandparents. She felt as if she stood on the brink of a yawning chasm, one foot out in space, as if she were about to take the fatal plunge.

God, how it had hurt—*physically hurt*—when he had told her to go.

It wasn't until now that she realized just how much she had come to depend on Kyle's presence to help her through her grief. And with that thought came the realization that she might have finally found someone capable of filling the void she had lived with for so many years.

All of which made the current situation even more devastating. The thought of losing Kyle was suddenly unbearable, especially when she was the one responsible for putting him in danger. She knew she wouldn't be strong enough to go on alone this time. The thought of her long, empty life stretching out before her like the dark forest corridor they were now passing through would be more than she could withstand.

She almost turned around then to go running back to him, but she knew Kyle would never leave Javier behind, not even at the risk of his own life. The best way for her to help him was to do as he had asked and get to the bluff and radio for help—and failing that, get to the ranger station as fast as possible.

With a renewed sense of resolve and energy born of desperation, Carrie lowered her head and plowed onward into the storm, heedless of Dr. Bennett. He could manage on his own. In a strange twist of fate, now that she had the story she had been so desperately chasing, she realized it was never what she had really been searching for. The story was no longer the most important thing to her, and she wouldn't hesitate to leave Bennett behind if he couldn't keep up.

CHAPTER 95

Atop the windswept bluff, Carrie frantically pressed the button on the radio again. "Hello?" she yelled. "Can you hear me? We need help. Please respond." She held the walkie-talkie against her ear, but again, there was nothing but static.

Carrie looked back down the trail. She wondered how Kyle and the sheriff were doing. She hoped to see them just behind her, climbing the rise out of the gap, but it was now too dark to see more than a few feet in front of them.

Beside her, Bennett had pulled down his visor and appeared to be surveying the mountain across the valley. Carrie looked at him, puzzled. He seemed like an odd duck, and his behavior now was only adding to it. She still didn't feel comfortable being alone with him. She slipped her hand into the pocket with the Glock.

Apparently, he sensed her watching him. He flipped the visor up. "It has a night-vision display," he explained.

"Oh," Carrie replied. "Did you see anything?"

"No, but that doesn't mean anything." He looked behind them. "The dragons will be stirring any time now. We should go." He slid the visor back down and began carefully making his way across the ice-glazed rock.

Carrie looked down the trail behind them once more, back into the black depths of the trees. The bad feeling in the pit of her stomach grew until it threatened to overwhelm her. Finally, she forced herself to turn away and scrambled after the doctor.

$*\ *\ *$

Neither Kyle nor George spoke of it, but as the storm blotted out the sky and twilight turned into night, it became obvious they weren't going to make it in time. They were still struggling to make their way through the defile, and their progress was slow at best. Nevertheless, they struggled onward. Between them, Javier slipped in and out of consciousness, his head lolling about like a rag doll's. He mumbled deliriously, uttering short passages of prayer to the Virgin Mary and calling out to his mother. Occasionally, he became more animated and cried out, "*El Chupacabara es aqui, aqui!*" before he lapsed back into silence. Kyle worried that Javier's ramblings would give them away, but there was nothing they could do to stop him. Fortunately, the spells didn't last long.

Despite the icy wind, sweat trickled down Kyle's back and under his arms. The muscles in his arms and back screamed in agony. Between holding Javier and the shotgun, they felt as if they were being slowly pulled from their sockets. He and George had switched sides several times, trying not to overwork one side or the other, but it didn't matter anymore. They were both past the point of exhaustion.

Kyle tried hard to focus on everything but the pain. He scanned the treetops, wary of any movement. At Dr. Bennett's suggestion, he had put on Javier's helmet, which provided a night-vision display inside of the visor. The otherwise pitch-black forest came to life in luminous shades of green. At first, it had been disconcerting to watch the display and walk at the same time—it was like trying to hike down a mountain while playing a virtual reality game—but after a few stumbles, he seemed to adjust. He had offered to switch off with the sheriff so that he could see as well, but the big Indian had refused, saying he could manage just as well without it.

In front of them to the right, something moved in the treetops. Branches swayed and snapped, and the sound was followed by a heavy thud.

Kyle jumped. Turning, he accidentally squeezed off a shot. The gun kicked hard against his hip and an explosive *boom* echoed through the gap. The treetop disintegrated in a cloud of powder and needles.

"Shit," Kyle cursed. It had just been a tuft of falling snow. "Sorry," he said, embarrassed by his jumpiness.

"Perhaps the noise will keep the monsters at bay," the sheriff offered, even though they both knew it was doubtful. The creatures had been intentionally designed to be aggressive killing machines. They hadn't been afraid to attack the recovery team. A little noise wasn't going to scare them away now. If anything, it was more likely to attract them, like blood in the water.

CHAPTER 96

The cold wind chafed Carrie's face and burned her lungs. Her hands and feet had gone numb long ago, and her legs felt leaden. She stumbled and nearly fell as weariness, darkness, and the rugged terrain continued to take their toll. Her body begged to stop, but she forced herself onward. They had to make it to the ranger station before it was too late. They had to.

Just audible above the wind, a low, rumbling sound that might have been the echo of distant thunder rolled down the valley.

Carrie stopped and looked back up the mountain.

She stood still and strained to hear over her own heavy breathing. *Was that gunfire? It could have been one of the shotguns.*

Dr. Bennett reached out and took her arm. "We must go," he panted. "There's nothing ... we can do. We must go. Now."

She nearly attacked him again. God knew she wanted to. She wanted to hit him and scream at him and wail on him for being a part of it all, for having the audacity to play God, for destroying her life. But even as she glared at the doctor, his face hidden behind the black helmet, she knew it was too late for that. All that mattered now was that they get to the ranger station as soon as possible. She refused to give up hope that Kyle would make it.

She jerked her arm free and took off again, moving as fast as her exhausted legs could carry her. She dared the doctor to try to keep up.

Another distant *boom* rolled down the mountain. This time, there was no mistaking it. It was gunfire. "No," she whispered, biting her bottom lip to keep from crying out. *No. God, no. Please, not again,* she begged as she strained to move faster.

* * *

After what seemed like an eternity, Kyle and the sheriff finally topped the bluff. The rocky shelf was about fifteen feet wide, the snow scoured away by the vicious winds. Only a few twisted, scraggly trees had managed to force their way up through cracks in the weatherworn limestone. The expanse was covered with loose scree and slick veins of dark ice.

They began to creep across. To their left, the stone face dropped away forty to fifty feet straight down, as if a large chuck of the mountain had broken away and fallen into the valley below.

They never saw the dragon.

It slammed into the back of them like a meteor smacking the earth. Bodies went flying. One of the shotguns, knocked from the sheriff's grasp, skittered across the stone and toppled over the edge.

Kyle was driven to the ground, face-first. The shotgun roared as he fell, chips of rock and ice exploding as the pellets shattered the stone. His vision bloomed in a shower of green and white sparks as his head slammed against the stone. The helmet saved him from cracking his skull, but the blow left him dazed. The night-vision display flickered, and then everything went black.

Screams rang out in the dark.

It took Kyle a moment to regain his senses. Ears ringing, he rolled over and sat up. The visor blinked a few times before it came back to life. A glowing silhouette rose before him. It was massive. It stood seven or eight feet tall on a pair of thick, powerful legs like those of a raptor. A pair of wings flared from its broad torso, fluttering and twitching as it knelt over something. There came the hideous *snap* of breaking bones and the *pop* of rending muscle as the thing raised its head, a man's arm in its mouth. The long, toothy maw clacked open and closed several times in rapid succession, swallowing the limb whole.

The screaming had stopped.

As it turned its head, the creature's eyes glared balefully at Kyle. With a rumbling growl, it pounded across the ledge toward him, its claws raking the icy stone.

Kyle kicked backward, driving himself back across the ledge. He raised the shotgun and pulled the trigger.

Click.

He had forgotten to pump it.

Desperately, he continued to scuttle away from the thing. The edge of the cliff drew nearer.

Then it pounced.

It landed on his legs with crushing force and pinned him to the ground. The claws ripped through his snowsuit and dug into his thighs. Warm, slippery blood welled forth. It crouched over him, its wings spread like a demon from hell. He could feel its hot, steaming breath; he could smell the fetid stink of it. Frantically, he tried to pump the shotgun, but it was too late.

He just prayed that Carrie had made it to the ranger station in time.

A piercing, ululant cry erupted from behind.

The creature whipped about. George Greyhawk charged across the ledge, slamming into the beast. Its breath exploded from it in a throaty cough, its wings flapping wildly as it struggled to maintain its balance. But the force of the blow was too much. The dragon stumbled backward, its claws scrabbling across the stone, failing to find purchase.

Then the ground was gone. It toppled backward over the edge with a screeching yowl. Its tail lashed out and wrapped around a scraggly tree at the edge, but the weight was too great. The brittle wood snapped.

"George!" Kyle cried out as the dragon and the sheriff disappeared.

Kyle crawled forward, peered over the edge and scanned the jagged rocks below. There were a few dark objects, too indistinct to make out in the green glow of the visor, but nothing moved.

"Sheriff Greyhawk!" Kyle yelled. The sound of his voice was ripped away by the wind.

"George!"

There was no answer.

After several long moments, he struggled to his feet, wincing in pain with every movement. He picked up the shotgun, racked a shell into the breech, and hobbled to the edge. He looked for a way to get down the cliff and into the valley below. It was hopeless.

Leary of another attack, he panned the sky to make sure another dragon wasn't bearing down on him. He didn't see anything, but just as he looked away, he caught the faint glimmer of something out of the corner of his eye. He spun around and braced himself for an attack, but like the flickering of a distant star on a cloudless night, it was gone.

Then he noticed the display at the top of the visor ticking off a series of numbers: 300, 320, 340. Something was out there. It was out of range of the visor's night-vision capabilities, but the helmet was tracking it, displaying the distance from his position in yards. It had to be another one of the dragons. Bennett had surmised that several of them might have survived the team's assault. Kyle was relieved to see it was moving away from him.

But then he realized it was headed up the valley.

Toward the ranger station.

And Carrie.

Heedless of the pain in his legs, Kyle rushed across the ledge and onto the trail leading down.

CHAPTER 97

In the distance, the glow of lights from the ranger station came into view just above the tree line. It looked to still be a mile or more away, but at least it was in sight. Here in the lower elevations, the road leveled into a more gradual descent, and Carrie took advantage of it. She twisted the throttle and felt Bennett's arms tighten around her in response. They flew down the last stretch of the road, slowing just enough to make the turn as they reached the final bend leading down to the river.

They shot across the bridge without slowing. Disregarding the road that curved away on the other side, Carrie took them straight across the ground in front of the ranger station and killed the engine as they slid to a stop just short of the front porch.

The night became deathly quiet.

Carrie jumped off the snowmobile and hurried up the steps, Bennett behind her. She grabbed the door, but it was locked.

"Hank! Help! Please ... someone help us!" she called out as she banged on it.

Behind them, the wooden floorboards creaked.

"Whoa, don't turn around," said a strange voice.

Carrie felt something hard shoved in the small of her back—the barrel of a gun. "Hand over your weapons, nice and easy," he said. Carrie complied, slowly reaching into her pocket and pulling out the Glock, which was quickly snatched from her grasp.

She was confused. *Where was Hank? Had he been relieved by another ranger, and if so, why were they doing this?* "You don't understand," she said.

"We need help. Where's Hank? Didn't he tell you what was going on?" She tried to get a look at the man out of the corner of her eye but was unable to make out anything.

"Okay, now you, buddy boy," the man said to Dr. Bennett.

"I ... I'm unarmed," Bennett stammered.

The gun was removed from Carrie's back, but she knew it was still trained on her as the man frisked the doctor. "All right," he said. "Step aside."

He moved to the door, unlocked it, and then motioned for them to step inside. It was too dark for Carrie to make out any details of his face, but she did notice his coat had the US Forest Service emblem on the breast. The door opened with a groan. The light caused her to squint as she was shoved inside.

The man closed the door and locked it behind them. As he walked past Carrie, she caught a whiff of something familiar—gum, cinnamon gum, the same sickly sweet smell of the man who had attacked her.

He wasn't a ranger.

Her breath caught in her throat as the man turned around. He held a silencer-equipped gun aimed at her midsection. He was muscular, with broad shoulders and burr-cut reddish hair. Smacking the gum, he grinned lasciviously as he looked her up and down.

Carrie shivered.

On the floor in the aisle between the counters, she noticed the body of a man wearing the dun-colored uniform of the US Forest Service. A pool of blood spread out from beneath him.

Hank.

"Oh, dear God," Bennett gasped as he spotted the body on the floor.

"Where are the others?" the man snapped. He casually backed to the counter and picked up a shotgun which he leveled at them before he tucked the pistol into the front of his pants.

Dr. Bennett began quivering. "They ... they—"

"They're dead," Carrie interrupted. It was the only thing she could think of that might give them a chance. "Are you happy? Those *things*, whatever they are, killed them. We're it, the only ones who made it back." To help sell it, she let tears well up in her eyes. After all she had been through, it was easy to do. Bennett looked at her, a mix of confusion and fear on his face. She hoped he knew enough to keep his mouth shut. She just prayed that nothing had happened to Kyle and the sheriff. Otherwise it wouldn't matter.

"Huh," the man snorted, seemingly unconvinced. "We'll see about that." He grabbed a sturdy oak chair behind the desk and shoved it across the floor in front of them. He tossed a pair of handcuffs to Carrie. "Cuff him to the chair," he said, nodding at Bennett. "With his hands behind his back."

Bennett started to protest, "But—"

"Do it," he shouted, which caused Carrie to jump.

"Okay, okay," she said. She pulled off her gloves and tossed them onto the counter.

Reluctantly, Bennett sat in the chair. Carrie's hands shook as she snapped the cuffs on his left wrist. She ran the other bracelet around one of the slats on the back of the chair. If something happened, Bennett might be able to break free.

"Unh, unh, unh," the man grunted, waving the gun back and forth like a schoolteacher shaking her finger at a student. "Run it around at least three of them," he said. "We wouldn't want the good doctor to accidentally break one of them during his interrogation." Bennett looked up at Carrie in desperation. The terror was clearly visible in his eyes. He would crumble at the first hint of violence.

"I've got to admit ... you surprised me," the man continued. "I didn't think you would make it back alive, much less bring back one of our own employees. To be honest, I'm not quite sure what to do with him. I guess I'll have to get clarification regarding his current employment status."

"I ... I don't understand," stammered Bennett. "What are you doing here? I haven't done anything wrong."

The man chuckled. "We'll see about that."

"But we work for the same company, you and I," said Bennett.

"Not exactly. Let's just say I do all my work outside of regular office hours," the man replied. "You might say I'm sort of like ... the cleaning crew," he said with a wicked smile.

"Cleaning crew?" Bennett asked, bewildered.

As Carrie's hopes collapsed, so did the restraint she had placed on her anger. "Don't you get it?" she snapped. "He's been sent to get rid of us. They're trying to cover up the link between GenTech and those creatures."

"But ... why?" the doctor asked.

"Because it's all falling apart on them," Carrie said. "First, the monsters started killing people. Then Charlie and I uncovered the truth. So they killed Charlie and sent him here to kill me. Then they sent you and the others to catch that *thing* you brewed up in your lab, but they all wound up getting butchered by it instead. So what do you think will happen if word of that gets out? Huh? Have you thought about that? The bigwigs at GenTech have decided to pull the plug. Your lab is probably going up in flames even as we speak. They intend to make sure there are no witnesses left to tell the story. Including *you*."

"Oh, God—" Bennett muttered.

"Now, now, doc," the man chuckled. "Things aren't quite as bleak as she would have you believe. If I'm convinced of your honesty and loyalty to the company, once I take care of her, we'll simply whisk you back to your lab. I'm sure General Colquitt would love to hear what happened to the rest of your team. Why, I bet you could be back to work as soon as tomorrow."

The man picked up a hunting knife from the counter and held it up, twisting it so the light reflected off its surface.

"Nooo," Bennett moaned, shaking and jerking the cuffs against the chair.

"Oh, don't worry, doc," the man said. "This isn't for you. It's for *her*," he said, looking at Carrie. His eyes seemed alight with an unnatural fire. She had seen that look before. She knew he intended to do more than just interrogate her.

Her mind screamed at her to run, but the cold emptiness in the pit of her stomach seemed to have frozen her entire body. Everything seemed to move in slow motion as he took another step. She had to do something while she still had a chance.

She bolted for the door, but he was too quick. Before she could reach it, he grabbed a fistful of hair. She yelped in pain as she was jerked backward and thrown to the floor.

She looked up to find him stepping toward her, a maniacal grin on his face. An image of her lying in the street as Bret walked toward her flashed through her mind. She waited as he took another step. Then she ducked her head and kicked out with her right foot, catching him squarely on his right kneecap.

"You fucking bitch!" he roared as he stumbled and hopped backward.

Then the plate-glass window behind them imploded.

Shards of glass blew into the room. A log skittered across the floor and banged against the counter.

The instant she saw it, Carrie knew what was coming.

CHAPTER 98

Kyle crashed through the undergrowth, limbs and branches cracking against his forearms. Time blurred as he stumbled through the luminous green netherworld. All that mattered was that he get down the mountain as fast as humanly possible in order to help Carrie. When he finally burst from the forest at the trailhead, he had no idea if it had taken him twenty minutes or twenty hours to reach the bottom.

He climbed onto the remaining snowmobile and started it up. Instinctively, he flicked on the headlights and was suddenly blinded by the blazing green-white light inside the visor.

Shit! he gasped, squeezing his eyes shut. He turned off the lights and took off for the ranger station in the dark. He drove slowly at first, waiting for his eyes to adjust again. But as soon as he could see, he twisted the throttle until he was flying down the roadway. He glanced over his shoulder repeatedly, each time expecting to see one of the dragons hurtling toward him.

As he continued down the trail without encountering the other snowmobile, his hopes began to rise. Maybe Carrie and the doctor had made it to the ranger station. But why wasn't Hank on his way back up?

When he came within sight of the ranger station, the first thing he noticed was the cabin door standing wide open.

Luminous green-white light spilled out into the night.

Carrie.

With a sick feeling in his gut, Kyle twisted the throttle more.

CHAPTER 99

It was as if Carrie had fallen through a hole in space where time hung suspended between one moment and the next. She knew what was coming, and there was nothing she could do about it.

A massive black shadow shot through the window, slamming into Bennett. He was knocked across the floor, crashing into the counter, a rippling black mass atop him.

Bennett screamed in terror as he flopped about, desperately straining against the cuffs. The dragon rose above him, towering over its creator. The beast's long snout opened wide, revealing row upon row of jagged teeth. It spread its wings and shook them as it released a piercing screech.

Bennett ducked his head into his shoulder, too terrified to look. The dragon struck, its mouth snapping shut on Bennett's shoulder with crushing force. Screams filled the air. The creature slashed at him with its long claws, gutting him. Blood geysered forth, spraying everything.

A loud *boom* shook the room as a shotgun went off.

The creature shrieked as the upper half of its left wing was blown off. With incredible quickness, it launched itself up into the open beam ceiling. Gripping one of the logs with its talons, it flipped itself about. Its tail flicked out from beneath it as it spun, the glint of steel flashing in the light. The shotgun roared as it fell to the floor along with the suddenly severed arm. The man looked at his missing limb in disbelief as the dragon dropped onto him from above. The two fell to the floor in a writhing, shrieking frenzy.

387

Carrie scurried across the floor. Glass dug into the palms of her hands. She grabbed the door latch, which became slick with blood. Her hand slipped off. She grabbed at it again and finally managed to jerk it open.

She fled outside, chased by the horrific screams. She stopped on the porch and looked for signs of other dragons bearing down on her.

The snowmobile was parked in front of her. *But where to go? And what if there were more dragons?*

Then it came to her.

The Hummer.

She took off around the building. She panned the dark skies as she ran, like a terrified rabbit running from a hawk.

The Hummer still sat out back, apparently undisturbed. All four of its giant tires still held air. Relief flooded through her.

She raced to it and yanked on the door handle. It was locked.

Damn it. The keys.

After Kyle had given them back to her, she had put them in the pocket of her jeans that morning. She unzipped the top of the snowsuit and then ripped it halfway off to get to her jeans. Relief flooded through her when she shoved her hand in her right pocket and felt the remote. She jerked it out and punched the unlock button.

Snap!

She jumped into the truck without pausing to pull her snowsuit back up. After she slammed the door behind her, she locked it. The keys slipped in her bloody fingers as she tried to shove them into the ignition. On the third try, she rammed it home. She cranked the ignition switch so hard she was surprised the key didn't snap off.

The truck roared to life.

She flipped on the lights, threw it into reverse, and tromped on the accelerator. Snow and gravel spewed from under the truck, pelting the back of the cabin. She hit the brakes and then shifted into drive. She was going to make it.

Something heavy crashed down on the hood, crumpling the metal.

Carrie screamed. The long, toothy snout and the narrow, golden eyes of a dragon appeared before her. *Were there two of them now?* But then she noticed the shattered wing dangling at its side. Broken glass covered the hood of the truck. The cabin's back window was now gone.

With an angry screech, the dragon bashed its forehead against the windshield, leaving a bloody smear across the glass. Carrie screamed. Snapped from her momentary trance, she stomped on the accelerator. The truck took off with a roar. The dragon sprawled across the hood, its head cracking against the windshield again.

She was heading straight for the cabin. She jerked the wheel to the left. The truck's floodlights swept the back of the building, sending huge shadows of the creature flying across the wall.

She wasn't going to clear the corner. She braced herself just as the truck's right front wheel slammed into the log that served as a parking stop. The front of the truck canted up crazily as it bounced over the log and slammed into the cabin. The airbag deployed with a concussive *bang*. Mortar and splintered timber flew as the truck rammed through the back wall.

The impact of the airbag stunned her and caused everything to flutter about crazily for a moment. The cabin of the truck was filled with a fine white powder.

Coughing as things slowly coalesced back into focus, all Carrie could see was the dark, pebbly skin of the dragon's underbelly through the window. It wasn't moving.

Crack! Carrie shrieked as the dragon's tail smacked against the windshield. She watched in horror as it rocked its body back and then sent its tail whipping toward the glass again. The steel blade struck the window with a *bang*, launching a spiderweb of cracks across it.

Without waiting for the next blow, Carrie threw the truck into reverse and floored it. The Hummer's massive engine roared as it strained to move, but it was wedged between the logs of the cabin's back wall and the parking stop. The front right tire spun against the log, smoking and stinking of burned rubber. The truck shimmied from side to side as the other tires spun, throwing up plumes of snow and gravel.

The tail slammed into the windshield again. The safety glass cracked and crumbled along a three-foot depression where the tail struck. The thin plastic laminate between the sheets of glass was the only thing that kept it from falling into Carrie's lap.

She let off the accelerator and then slipped between the bucket seats, over the center console, and into the backseat. The tail struck again. Safety glass exploded into the cab and pelted her with a spray of sticky pellets. Crackling and crumbling, the front windshield fell onto the dashboard and into the front seats.

The dragon's head snaked down into the opening. Streamers of blood and saliva dripped from its snout. Its amber eyes narrowed as they focused on her. It emitted a shrill, coughing bark and then slithered into the truck like a crocodile slipping into the water.

Panting and trembling, Carrie shoved herself up and over the backseat into the rear cargo area. The gap between the seats and the roof of the truck was confining to the dragon, which helped to slow it down. Its claws raked across the seats and ripped large gashes in the leather as it struggled to pull and push its thick bulk forward. One of its long forelimbs slipped off the center console, and it dropped down, momentarily disappearing from view.

Carrie groped for the rear door's latch, her bloody hand smearing the plastic as she searched for the handle. But there wasn't one.

She was trapped.

She looked about the cargo area, desperately searching for something to break the window with. She grabbed anything and everything, including the leather gun cases, and tossed them up front to get them out of her way and hopefully slow down the creature.

Then she saw it. Mounted in front of the tire well against the backseat was the metal jack. She reached over and began frantically working to unscrew the large wing nut holding the jack to its mount, but it kept slipping through her bloody fingers.

Up front, the dragon's head rose above the seat. Carrie became aware of a high-pitched, keening sound within the truck only to realize it was her own panicked whimpering.

The dragon pulled and clawed its way between the front seats.

The wing nut finally spun off, and Carrie jerked the jack free. She slammed it against the back glass, but it didn't break. She slammed it against the glass again, but the thing just bounced off, slipped from her hand, and fell to the floor.

She screamed as the dragon lunged forward, snapping and ripping out a chunk of the backseat. She could smell the rank stench of blood on its hot breath.

She grabbed the jack again and rammed it against the window. This time, it shattered, showering her in sticky pellets of glass and plastic film.

Carrie squeezed herself through the crumbling remains of the window, past the massive spare tire mounted to the rear bumper. She turned as she went and reached up and grabbed the back rail of the luggage rack to pull herself out.

The dragon lurched across the backseat, its jaws clacking together as Carrie started to pull her legs out. Searing pain flared along the inside of her left calf as its teeth ripped through her snowsuit. She cried out and kicked wildly at its head with her right foot, but its jaws had clamped down on the snowsuit, and it wasn't about to let go. She shoved against the back of the truck, struggling to free her leg as the dragon began to slowly pull her back inside. Jerking and kicking, she managed to work her left foot up through the leg about ten or twelve inches.

Then the dragon began to thrash and spin like a crocodile rolling its prey on the bottom of a river. The leg of the snowsuit twisted up and tightened around her boot. Carrie tried to pull it out, but her boot was caught in the ever-tightening noose of her suit. With her right leg braced against the tire well, she pushed with all she had and screamed with the effort. Her foot began to slowly slip out of the boot. There was the sound of ripping nylon, but the suit twisted tighter.

With one final surge, her foot came free. She fell backward to the ground with a heavy thud.

The wind knocked from her, Carrie struggled to her feet. Inside, the dragon had finished shredding the snowsuit, and when it realized there was no longer anything in it, it began pulling the rest of its bulk over the seat into the cargo area. Its head poked out the missing window beside the spare tire, but the space was too small for it to fit through easily. It shrieked in anger. Its burning eyes focused on Carrie.

She took off, hobbling across the frozen ground, one boot still on and one off. She wasn't sure where to go now, but it would only be a matter of moments before the thing managed to slither its way out again.

Running around the US Forest Service's Suburban, she thought about trying the doors, but she didn't have the keys. And after she had seen what the thing had done to the Hummer, she wasn't going to make that mistake again. She continued on around the cabin, desperately trying to think while keeping an eye on the skies above her. It was hard to see through the swirling snow. Another dragon could be diving toward her, and she would never see it. She ran on, wracked by shivers as the wind cut through her clothing like the dragon's teeth through her snowsuit.

Thirty yards ahead, the dark, steel framework of the lookout tower loomed before her.

CHAPTER 100

Carrie raced for the tower. She felt certain the thing couldn't fly with one of its wings blown off. She just hoped it couldn't climb a ladder.

The cold metal burned her skin as she climbed. Searing pain shot through her calf, but with each rung she passed, she began to gain confidence that she was going to make it, which only encouraged her to push herself higher.

Two-thirds of the way up, she heard the victorious screech of the dragon.

Seconds later, it came loping across the ground below, its powerful legs churning up chunks of snow. It flapped its wings as if trying to take off, but the shattered stump and tattered skin flopped about uselessly, keeping it grounded. Even so, it headed directly for the tower and Carrie as if she had been tagged with a tracking beacon.

At the base of the tower, it looked up and shrieked angrily. It moved closer, tentatively touching the steel framework a few times, as if unsure of what to do. Then it grabbed hold. Carrie watched in shock as the thing mounted the ladder. Slowly but surely, it began scaling the tower.

"Goddamn you!" Carrie screamed, cursing the creature and everyone responsible for creating it. The thing was unstoppable.

She started back up the ladder with renewed urgency.

When she reached the observation deck running around the outside of the perch, Carrie looked down again. The dragon was only a third of the way up, but it was still coming, slowly raking and clawing and pushing itself up. It used its tail as a safety line as it came, wrapping it tightly about the beams as it worked its way up.

Carrie pushed on the door leading into the observation perch and was relieved to find it unlocked. Inside, she looked about the octagon-shaped room. It was still filled with construction materials—stacks of sheetrock and ceiling tiles, spools of cable, sections of metal ductwork, crumpled plastic and tattered brown paper piled in one corner. To the left, opening from one of the back walls was a small toilet. Beyond that, sweeping around the front of the perch were six large windows, which were angled outward to maximize the viewing capabilities and gave the place the impression of an air traffic control tower.

She scanned the room for something to use as a weapon. Unfortunately, there weren't any shotguns left lying around or hanging on a rack against the wall just waiting for her to come along. She considered trying to use a section of the sheetrock to drop on the creature, but, it was too bulky and heavy for her to lift alone, and the ductwork and ceiling tiles were too insubstantial to be of any effect against the dragon's immense strength.

She looked at the built-in console/desk running around the room beneath the windows. It had been turned into a temporary plan table during construction, with rumpled blueprints and fast-food wrappers scattered across its surface. Beside the plans sat a metal toolbox. A wooden desk chair like the one in the cabin had been hauled up and shoved into the knee space.

Carrie grabbed the toolbox and picked it up to test its weight. Filled with tools, it felt heavy enough to do the trick. It took both hands for her to slide it off the counter and lug it out onto the catwalk.

The dragon had made it halfway up.

She hefted the toolbox up onto the railing and leaned it out over the edge. After she did her best to judge the distance, she waited until she thought the creature was within range before she let it go. It hurtled downward, twisting and tumbling. It crashed into the tower just above the creature's head and bounced off the steel structure. The lid flew open and sent screwdrivers, wrenches, and hammers raining down on the creature. The dragon screeched as the tools bounced off its thick, bony skull before the box sailed harmlessly to the ground and disappeared into the snow.

Carrie fled back inside and struggled to control her rising panic.

Giving up on the idea of knocking the dragon off the tower, she closed the door and locked it in an attempt to barricade herself in. She slid the chair over and did her best to wedge it firmly under the knob.

She looked around again, hoping for inspiration. She knew the door wouldn't hold forever, and while the tower's glass was thicker than ordinary windows, she wasn't sure they were impenetrable.

Then she saw the rungs leading to the hatch in the roof.

CHAPTER 101

Kyle roared up in front of the cabin and leapt off the snowmobile before it came to a full stop. He jerked off the helmet, grabbed the shotgun, raced up the steps and burst into the cabin.

It was like stepping into a charnel house.

He gaped at the slaughter before him. The maps on the walls were splattered with blood. Twisted and broken forms, severed limbs, and entrails were strewn about the room. Blood seeped into the cracks and crevices of the wood floor. The faint pall of smoke still hung in the air. And death. The stench was horrific.

Kyle gagged, nearly vomiting. He turned to run back out into the cold night air, but his knees buckled. He collapsed.

Overcome by it all, he no longer had the strength to pick himself up. He dragged himself across the floor, crawling on all fours like a baby. He struggled to reach the doorway.

He managed to pull himself out to the porch. He lay there, too numb to move. He had failed them all—the Joneses, Lewis, Sheriff Greyhawk, and now Carrie. They were all gone.

All because of him.

For so long he had tried to make a difference, to help people see that life was worth living no matter what might have happened to them. But now he wasn't sure. He wasn't sure if it was even worth living at all.

Then, from somewhere far away, he heard something. It sounded like someone screaming.

He lifted his head and strained to hear it again. It was barely audible over the howling wind, but it was there. He rose unsteadily and started in the direction of the sound and then stopped. He picked up the shotgun and pumped it once to make sure it was loaded. Another scream rang out and was quickly carried away by the wind but not before he heard it.

It *was* a scream. And it had come from the lookout tower.

* * *

Arctic wind blasted Carrie in the face as soon as she stuck her head through the hatch. Her eyes watered, and she had to blink away the tears to see clearly. The roof sloped downward in all directions in order to limit the accumulation of snow. A rectangular metal box that looked to be the heating and air-conditioning unit sat to one side, while the rest of the roof was forested with satellite dishes, radio antennas, wind and rain gauges, and other odd-looking monitoring equipment. A lightning protection cable ran around the edge, connected to metal rods located at each of the eight corners.

Braving the blinding snow and wind, Carrie pulled herself onto the roof and slammed the hatch shut. The latch was on the inside, so she lay across the door, hoping the dragon wouldn't be able to figure out where she had gone. She wrapped her arms around herself and shivered as she tried to shelter herself from the biting wind. Exposed as she was, she knew she wouldn't be able to survive long, but she didn't know what else to do. She had finally come to the end of her rope.

There had been a time not long ago when she had felt as though she didn't want to live anymore, when she would have jumped to her death with only the slightest provocation. But now it wasn't even an option. She was determined to fight until the bitter end.

She carefully scooted across the roof a few feet and grabbed onto one of the long metal antennas. Gritting her teeth, she pushed against it until it slowly bent. Then she pulled it back. She worked it back and forth until the metal finally gave and it snapped off. As she held her makeshift weapon, Carrie clung to the frigid metal roof, shivering and praying that the beast would give up and move on or succumb to its wounds—although, from what she had seen, it didn't appear to be slowing down.

Below, Carrie heard the first *bang* as the creature crashed against the door. She listened helplessly as the dragon broke into the room below her. It was silent for a moment and then, because it apparently sensed she had escaped, it screeched furiously. A barrage of pounding and smashing erupted below as the beast ransacked the room.

Kyle, where are you? she whispered between chattering teeth.

Below her, the room fell silent. She listened for a moment, trying to figure out what it was doing.

She screamed as the hatch bounced upward and nearly threw her off. She braced herself for the next attack, but she knew she couldn't last much longer.

When the attack came, she screamed again as she was dislodged from her position. She began slipping toward the edge. She tried to flatten her body against the roof, grasping for anything to stop her inexorable slide. Finally, the toes of her boot caught on the metal flashing and the lightning protection cable running around the edge.

She scooted to the side to keep from falling off. The hatch bounced up again, but this time, without her weight bearing down on top of it, it didn't fall shut. Slowly, the creature's head rose through the gap. It opened its mouth and hissed at her.

Carrie rammed the broken antenna into the dragon's face, spearing it right in the mouth. The thing thrashed about furiously and screeched as it fell back through the hole. The hatch slammed shut.

Overcome by a sudden surge of emotion, she yelled, "Yeah, come on!" at the top of her lungs. It was the kind of thing her grandmother would have done, and Carrie was proud of herself for doing it. She might not have much longer left to live, but she sure as hell wasn't going to go down without a fight.

Carefully, she began inching her way toward another antenna.

The hatch banged up again.

* * *

Kyle raced from the cabin to the base of the tower and looked for signs of someone inside as he ran. He desperately wanted to call out to Carrie and tell her he was coming, but he didn't know who—or what—was after her, and he was afraid to give away his presence.

He climbed the ladder as fast as he dared while clutching the shotgun. It wouldn't matter how fast he reached the top if he dropped the gun in the process.

When he reached the bottom of the platform, Kyle stopped. As he raised his head, he peered over the edge of the catwalk.

The tower's observation room looked as if it had been rocked by a bomb blast. The shattered door hung limply from the twisted remains of the top hinge. Tattered plastic and other construction debris fluttered about the room, swirling in the icy wind.

The most unbelievable sight of all was the dragon. It stood in front of the windows to the right of the console. It was perched on a series of metal rungs leading to a hatch in the ceiling. It jumped up and down, pounding its head against the bottom of the hatch in an apparent attempt to open it. As Kyle watched, it drove itself upward and knocked the hatch open with its head.

Carrie's scream rang out from above.

Kyle bounded up the last few steps and burst into the room. The dragon's head swiveled toward him. The amber eyes narrowed.

The shotgun roared, fire and powder flaring from the muzzle.

The blast caught the dragon in the side, spinning it around and knocking it from the ladder. Behind it, the window glazed, cracked by the stray pellets. The dragon landed on the console and roared in fury. It sprang to its feet, preparing to pounce.

Kyle was quicker.

As soon as he fired the first shot, he was already pumping the next shell into the breach. He fired again and struck the beast square in the chest, blowing it backward into the window. Glass exploded outward in a spray of glimmering crystals.

The dragon fell. It bounced off the railing around the catwalk and then tumbled over the edge.

Its whiplike tail shot out and wrapped around the rail, but Kyle had seen this trick before.

As he leapt onto the console, he pumped another round into the breech and fired at the tail. The blast severed it and sent the beast plummeting downward. Halfway down, it struck the steel beams with a wet, smacking sound before it bounced off and tumbled to the snowy ground below, where it lay motionless.

Kyle watched for several seconds to make sure it was dead. He then turned and began climbing the ladder, calling out Carrie's name as he went.

He pushed the hatch open and was nearly overcome with relief when Carrie's dirty, scratched face came into view. He helped her down the ladder into the observation room, where he pulled her into his arms.

"Is it dead?" she asked, shivering.

"Yeah, I think so," Kyle said, watching the doorway. He still held on to the shotgun.

Clinging to him, she said, "I was afraid I'd never see you again."

"I know," Kyle said.

"When you told me to leave, I—"

"I know. I'm sorry. I'll never do it again," Kyle interrupted.

"Never?" Carrie asked, looking up at him.

"Never," he replied, pulling her tighter against him.

CHAPTER 102

In spite of Carrie's protests, Kyle pulled off his snowsuit and had her put it on. It was too big for her, but she pulled her hands through and bunched up the sleeves while she let the legs cover her feet like the footies on a little kid's pajamas. Under other circumstances, it would have been cute.

Together, they carefully made their way back down, each watching the sky while the other climbed. Carrie went first while Kyle covered her with the shotgun, and once she was down safely, he descended.

Not knowing where else to go to seek cover, they scurried back to the visitor center. Although it was a pointless gesture with the window gone, Kyle pushed the door shut behind them. He then killed the lights in the front room both to avoid revealing their presence and to keep from seeing the carnage as they passed through. In back, they found an office with the busted radio equipment on the floor. The room had a window, so they moved on, turning out the lights as they went. Across the hall, they found a small storage room. In the corner against one wall was a cot. There were no windows.

"What do you think?" Kyle asked.

"I think it's as good as we're going to get," Carrie said.

"Yeah, me too," he agreed. "Stay here." He slipped down the hall to the back room.

What the hell?

The front end of the Hummer was sticking through the back wall. He couldn't imagine what Carrie must have gone through, but he was impressed by her toughness. He grabbed one of the chairs from the table and took it with him, killing the lights on the way out. The remaining headlight from the Hummer was still on, casting an eerie glow down the hall.

When he slipped back into the storage room, Carrie had already collapsed onto the cot. He pushed the door shut and wedged the chair up against the knob. He leaned against the door as the last of his strength seemed to slip away from him. Tiny tremors shook his entire body. He was cold and exhausted. At the moment, he would have given almost anything for a steaming cup of coffee.

"Do you think there are any more?" Carrie asked.

"No," he lied.

There was silence for a moment as the magnitude of what they had been through seemed to slowly sink in.

"You can sit down," Carrie said, scooting over on the cot.

She didn't have to ask twice. Kyle collapsed onto the cot beside her.

Without speaking, their arms slowly enfolded one another, and they huddled together, awaiting the dawn.

CHAPTER 103

The old trailer house creaked and groaned as if it might blow apart while the blizzard raged outside. The dream catcher hanging in the window jangled at the end of its string, tapping out a mysterious cadence as the trailer swayed and rocked. A low rumbling like the peal of thunder echoed in the distance, but it went unheard by the old lady on the bed. Eyes wide, she stared off into nothingness, her wispy white hair fanning out around her head.

Her breaths came quick and ragged, more panting than breathing. They grew more rapid and labored until there came a final, deep gasp followed by a long, slow exhalation.

A gossamer mist seemed to rise from her mouth as she expelled her final breath.

The dream catcher rattled against the glass and then fell still.

CHAPTER 104

Kyle woke with a start. He didn't realize he had fallen asleep or know how long he had been out, but something had awakened him.

And then he heard it—something scraping around up front.

He got up, grabbed the shotgun, and crept over to the door. As he pressed his ear against it, he listened for sounds on the other side. Nothing.

He slid the chair from under the knob and cringed as it scraped along the floor. He cracked the door and peered into the hallway. It was dark. The light from the Hummer had died sometime during the night, but a faint, lambent glow seemed to spill into the corridor from up front.

Kyle raised the shotgun and used the barrel to open the door wider. Leaning against the frame, he stuck his head out to get a better look.

He could see up the hall into the front room, where blowing snow swirled in through the open door. Something had made its way inside. His heart knocked against his chest in warning as he peered into the darkness, searching for signs of movement.

A dark, hulking form suddenly rose before him in the hall.

Kyle jumped, his finger tightening on the trigger, but something caused him to stop.

The form tilted awkwardly to one side and slumped against the far wall. It slid forward and then stumbled and fell.

As it fell, Kyle glimpsed the faint shimmer of long, black hair.

"George," Kyle gasped, rushing forward to help him. The big Indian lay slumped against the far wall. His breathing was shallow and rapid as if he were still in shock. In spite of the long exposure to the cold, his skin was dry and hot as if fevered. His right arm hung limply from a badly mangled shoulder.

Kyle whispered urgently for Carrie, who then joined him in the hallway. As gently as possible, they helped to lever the sheriff up off the floor. He never once groaned or cried out in pain as they helped him shuffle into the storage room, where they laid him on the cot.

When he turned on the lights, Kyle found two cases of bottled water wrapped in heavy plastic on the floor below the shelves. Carrie found a pack of paper hand towels for the bathroom, ripped them open, and pulled out a handful. Kyle dampened the stack of towels, which Carrie placed on the sheriff's brow.

Kyle trickled a little of the water into the sheriff's mouth, careful to make sure he didn't choke. The sheriff, still seemingly dazed, was slow to swallow at first, and a good portion of it just dribbled from his mouth and onto his chest. But then he seemed to come around a little. His eyes opened halfway. They seemed glazed and distant as he tried to speak.

"Grandmother ... came to me," his deep voice croaked. "Her spirit ... guided me," he managed before he fell silent again.

Carrie looked at Kyle, worry creasing her brow. "I think he's delirious. What do we do?"

"It's getting close to dawn," Kyle said. "As soon as it lightens a little, I'll try to find the keys to the Suburban out back, and we'll get him out of here as fast as we can."

A short while later, when the dark line beneath the door had begun to fade, Kyle picked up the shotgun. He wasn't looking forward to fishing through the pockets of the dead men up front, but it had to be done. They had to get the sheriff out of there.

He slipped into the corridor, still cautious in spite of the fact that dawn had arrived. The stench of death hung heavy in the cabin, and Kyle found himself wishing he had something—even if it was a menthol cigarette—to help mask the smell.

As he made his way up front, he heard the high-pitched whine of a hard-working engine approaching. He crept to the front door, which

Lance Horton

was still ajar, and watched as a black Expedition crusted with dirty snow and ice came lurching down the roadway.

The truck slid to a stop in the middle of the road, parallel to the cabin.

On the far side, the driver's door opened, and Mike Marasco got out. He stood there for a moment, watching the building as if looking for signs of movement. In the past, Kyle would have blithely marched out to greet him, but not anymore. Things had changed. Instead, he hung back in the shadows inside the doorway and waited. *Why has Marasco come alone?* he wondered. *Where are the other agents?*

Marasco began cautiously making his way across the snow toward the cabin. When he had made it about halfway across the open expanse, he reached behind his back and pulled a gun from under his thick coat.

Shit. Marasco must be the mole.

"That's far enough, Marasco," Kyle called out.

When he heard the voice, Marasco dived for cover behind one of the snowmobiles. Kyle tracked him with the shotgun, but he couldn't bring himself to shoot. At least not yet. He just hoped his hesitation didn't cost them all their lives.

"That you, Andrews?" Marasco called back.

"Yeah, it's me."

"I thought so. Man, are you all right?" He tried to sound relieved when he spoke, but Kyle didn't believe him. Something wasn't right.

"What are you doing here?" Kyle asked. His mind was racing as he tried to figure out what was going on. Could Marasco be the mole? When he had first met him, Kyle had pegged Marasco as someone who was loyal to the calling of law enforcement; someone with honesty and integrity in spite of his abrasive nature. But then Kyle remembered Marasco had been undercover in the mob. Even though he had been working for the government, it still showed he was adept at being deceitful. He could be doing the same thing now.

"I came looking for you," Marasco shouted. "You caused a real shit storm when you three disappeared yesterday. No one knew what had happened. Then I remembered hearing the sheriff talking with someone about a helicopter in the valley, so I figured you must have

406

come here. I was going to come after you yesterday. But then Deputy Johnson turned up dead, and all hell broke loose."

Clayton is dead too? Kyle felt a pang of grief over yet another death. The deputy had seemed like a kind, good-natured person.

"He was shot with the same caliber bullet that killed Lewis," Marasco continued. "But you already knew that, didn't you?"

"What are you talking about?" Kyle asked, suddenly confused. *Why would he think that?*

And then it came to him. Kyle remembered the confrontation with Marasco at the hospital, and it all made sense. Marasco wasn't the mole. He had come after them because he thought Kyle was the killer. Marasco intended to take matters into his own hands. It was the Jersey way. That was why he had left the other agents behind. In an odd sort of way, it was almost flattering that Marasco thought him capable of such actions.

As Kyle continued to sort things out, he realized that Clayton had been the mole. He had been killed in an effort to cover it up just like they had tried with Carrie. The fact that he had been killed with the same gun as Lewis proved it as far as Kyle was concerned. And Kyle knew Marasco wasn't the killer. The man who had attacked him at Carrie's motel had been much taller than Marasco. Thinking back, Kyle remembered that the deputy had seemed hesitant when the sheriff had asked him to get the phone records. And later, when Clayton had told them the phone company had turned him down, no one had checked to make sure he was telling the truth. It all fit.

"So I put two and two together," Marasco continued to talk. "You were there when Lewis was shot. Then you disappeared, and Clayton turned up dead. So I said to myself, 'What better way to get rid of the girl and the sheriff than to pretend to go along with them, then bring them out here and kill them?' I've got to admit ... you had me fooled all along with your sympathetic act. But you made one major mistake. You should have gotten rid of me first."

Kyle almost laughed at him. He sounded like someone from a bad cop movie.

"I didn't kill anyone, you idiot!" Kyle called out. "Carrie and the sheriff are inside. The sheriff's hurt—bad. He needs medical attention as fast as we can get him back."

Kyle leaned the shotgun against the wall and stepped out into the open, his hands held high for Marasco to see. He knew he was taking a big chance, but time was of the essence. And he *knew* he was right.

"Just come inside, and you'll see," Kyle said. "Carrie's with the sheriff in the storage room in back."

Marasco rose from behind the snowmobile, but he kept his gun leveled at Kyle. His eyes remained narrow, a look of hatred burning in them as he stepped closer. A sick feeling swept over Kyle as he looked down the barrel of the gun. Could he have been wrong?

But then Marasco looked past him, and a broad smile slowly spread across his face. He stood up and shoved the gun into the back of his pants. Relieved, Kyle turned around to find Carrie, the sheriff leaning against her in the doorway.

* * *

"Aay, no hard feelings, right?" Marasco asked as they helped the sheriff to the truck.

"No hard feelings," Kyle assured him.

"And you're not, uh … going to mention this in your report?" Marasco continued.

"I promise. You don't have anything to worry about," Kyle said. He suspected the only reports being written would be one by SAC Geddes detailing the numerous reasons for his dismissal.

Carrie got in the backseat with the sheriff, who leaned against her to avoid putting any weight on his right side. Kyle couldn't help but think about the similar situation with Lewis. It had been only thirty-six hours since they had raced him to the hospital. It had all been so surreal, like a bad nightmare.

As they pulled away, Kyle glanced out the window toward the lookout tower. The overnight accumulation of snow had obscured much of it, but the dark form at the base of the tower was still there.

CHAPTER 105

"Here you go, boss," Carrie said as she handed Allan the paper. It was a draft copy of the latest in a series of articles she had written about the events that had taken place in Montana.

Dilbeck picked up his reading glasses, leaned back in his burgundy-colored leather chair, and propped his boots up on the corner of his desk.

Over the last week and a half, Carrie's articles—along with the amazing photographs taken when the FBI returned to the site—had been picked up by all the major wire services, including *USA Today*. She had made headlines across the country. But that was just the beginning. It had been the top story on every national newscast and twenty-four-hour news outlet, including CNN, FOX, and MSNBC every day since. She had been on the morning shows of every local affiliate in Denver and had even been on the *Today Show* and *Good Morning America* to talk about her ordeal. Talk-radio stations across the country had lit up with callers as people endlessly argued the merits of GenTech's genetic engineering program and her exposé of it. Some praised Carrie's courage, calling her a hero, while others mercilessly blasted her as a traitor for blowing the whistle on one of the country's confidential defense secrets. In an effort to ensure her safety, the FBI had provided her with around-the-clock protection.

While debate on the subject had waged on, the military had quietly gone in—or so they claimed—to ensure that no creatures survived. Thanks to equipment left at the scene by the first recon team—which the military vehemently denied it had anything to do with—they had been able to locate the dragon's lair relatively easily. Three of the creatures had been found, one of which was fully grown and had been badly wounded. According to a statement released by the secretary of defense, all of the creatures had been accounted for and destroyed.

As of yet, they had not been able to determine who was responsible for sending in the first recon team. The members of that team had all apparently been highly skilled and highly paid mercenaries. None of the men identified were shown to have been actively employed by any of the national service branches. There were rumors of them having worked for something called the Terrorism Defense Agency, supposedly a covert branch of Homeland Security, but nothing had been found to validate the existence of any such agency. Unfortunately, the chances of identifying the specific entities and individuals responsible for the project had become even more unlikely as of this morning.

Anderson Colquitt, who had remained out on bail pending his arraignment, had been found dead in his home of an apparent suicide. Officials with the FBI, however, stated that there were suspicious circumstances surrounding the former general's death and that they would be investigating it as a possible homicide.

To Carrie, it meant that the cover-up was in full effect. They would never get all the answers now.

While Allan continued to read, she looked out the door of his office. Across the room, she could still see the one-eyed plastic Ogre perched on top of Charlie's monitor. No one had had the heart to take it down yet. It broke Carrie's heart every time she saw it. The guilt she felt for his death was something she would never get over, and it was part of the reason she had made the decision she had. Denver held too many bad memories for her now. She needed to move on and put the events of the past few weeks behind her. The same went for her personal life. That was why she had decided to sell the rights to her grandparents' place in Montana and why she had decided to accept the job offered to her by the *Washington Post*.

Allan lay down the paper and looked up at her. "The story's terrific, hon," he said as he pulled off his readers and tossed them on the blotter. "If you don't win the Pulitzer, they might as well stop giving the damn thing away."

Carrie smiled. "Not that you're biased or anything, but thanks," she said.

Allan's face took on a somber look then. "So I guess this is it, huh?" he asked.

"Yeah, I guess so," Carrie agreed. "I've already packed up my office. The movers should be here to pick it up in the morning."

"We're all going to miss you, darlin'. You sure you won't let us take you out for drinks one last time before you leave?"

"No, I'm not much of a drinker anymore, but thanks anyway," she said as she looked at her watch. "Besides, I've got to get going, or I'll miss my plane."

"Now where is it you're going?" Allan asked.

"I don't have to be in Washington until next Monday. I decided it would do me some good to get out of the country for a while, try to put all of this behind me. And I've had enough of the cold weather to last me the rest of my life. I figured I'd spend a few days soaking up the rays in Cabo."

"Won't the place be crawling with college kids?"

"Oh, I don't think they'll bother me where I'm going to be," she said with a grin.

"Well, good luck, hon," he said as he stood up. "You give those lying and cheating bastards in DC hell, you hear me? And you remember, if you ever need anything, all you've got to do is call me."

"I'll remember," she promised as he gave her a big bear hug.

Afterward, as she was leaving the office, she could hear Allan clearing his throat behind her.

CHAPTER 106

Kyle pulled into the driveway in the midst of a typical Texas thunderstorm. Heavy rain drummed on the roof of the car, and strong wind tugged at the door as he opened it, threatening to jerk it from his grasp. Thunder rumbled overhead as he dashed up the drive to the front porch, getting thoroughly soaked in the process. He reached for the knob, but the door opened by itself.

Valeria Sanchez stood in the doorway. "Mr. Kyle," she said and smiled as he stepped inside. "It is so good to see you." She reached around his waist with her short arms and hugged him.

"Careful, Miss Vera. I'm all wet."

She dismissed it with a wave of her hand. "It's okay. I don't mind."

"How have you been?" Kyle asked.

"I am good. Your mother is upstairs in bed."

Kyle looked at Miss Vera. It was the middle of the morning. Had Janet's condition worsened already?

Miss Vera apparently noticed his expression, for she quickly said, "No, no, she went out last night. She took her breakfast in bed this morning."

Kyle frowned and nodded. In other words, she was hungover.

He went down the hall to the downstairs bath to dry off before he went upstairs. The last thing he needed was to piss Janet off right from the start by dripping on the carpet.

After he dried off, he went upstairs and down the hall to the large master bedroom. When he stepped into the room, he noticed that

Janet had redecorated—again. She sat propped up in the bed amidst a swarm of decorative pillows. *The View* was currently on the flat screen television mounted above the fireplace.

She must have assumed he was Miss Vera, for at first, she didn't look over, but as he neared, she turned in his direction. The blank expression on her face turned to one of surprise.

"Kyle, darling, you're here. Finally," she said in an exasperated tone. He leaned over and put his cheek against hers while he reached around her in a halfhearted hug.

A wicker breakfast-in-bed tray sat on top of the extravagant comforter. The dishes from breakfast, if she had eaten anything at all, had been cleared away. All that remained was a half-full glass of what looked like orange juice but was actually, as Kyle knew from experience, a screwdriver. He could smell the alcohol on her breath.

"I'm so glad you're back," she said, slurring the words. Whether it was from alcohol or pills, Kyle couldn't be sure. "I can't begin to tell you how awful things have been around here." Apparently, she hadn't been watching the news lately. She acted like she had no clue of what he had gone through, or if she did, she just didn't care.

"I see you've redecorated," he said, sitting on the edge of the bed. The walls had been painted a sandy brown color. Floor length burgundy- and beige-colored drapes hung on each side of the French doors that led out onto the balcony overlooking the pool. Sheets of rain currently obscured the view.

"Yes, have you seen your room? You never got back to me, so I went ahead and had it redone, and while I was at it, I decided if I was going to be spending so much time in here over the next few months, I might as well enjoy it."

Kyle nodded. "Have you started the chemo yet?"

"No, I put them off for a week," she said with a dismissive gesture. She picked up the screwdriver and took a big drink.

"What do you mean you put it off?" Kyle asked.

"I wasn't ready. If I'm going to be out of commission for a while, I wanted to have a little fun first."

"You can't just schedule it at your leisure," Kyle said, the old frustrations with her arrogant attitude beginning to creep into his voice.

"I feel fine."

"Just because you don't want to admit it doesn't mean you're not sick," Kyle said.

"Besides, it will be easier for me with you here now."

There it was, the moment he had been dreading. There was no point in putting it off any longer.

"Janet," he said with a sigh. "That's what I've come to tell you. I'm not coming back."

"What?" she looked at him incredulously.

"I'm being transferred to Quantico to train as a special agent."

The offer had come as a surprise to Kyle. He had fully expected to be fired. Instead, in a typical political move, the FBI had decided to use all the publicity to their advantage. During one of the press briefings after the incident, the director of the FBI had stated, "Kyle Andrews is exactly the type of person we want helping to protect our country. That is why I am pleased to announce that Mr. Andrews will be transferring to Quantico to train as a special agent."

While it hadn't come about in the fashion he would have wished, Kyle knew this was his one shot. If he didn't play ball and go along with them on this, he would never get another chance. Besides, he owed it to Lewis. He had accepted the offer.

"Well, just tell them you quit," Janet said.

"I can't."

"Of course you can. It's not like it's the military."

"Okay, I *won't*. This is something I want. It's important to me."

"Oh, and I just guess that I'm not important, is that it?"

Kyle rolled his eyes. *Here we go again*, he thought. He wanted to tell her that she had never been there for him, that she had never cared about anyone but herself, but he knew that would only make things worse. Instead, he just said, "No, that's not it."

"After all I've done for you. And this is the thanks I get," she said, the bitterness coming through loud and clear.

Kyle didn't respond. Nothing he said would ever make her see things any differently.

"You ungrateful little bastard," she continued. Even the drugs couldn't rid the venomous tone from her voice. "I wish I had never had you!" she spat at him.

And there it was—the truth of the matter. She had never loved him and never would, no matter what he did for her. All she had ever cared about was herself.

Kyle got up and started for the door. He had felt bad about his decision before, but her behavior now actually made it easier for him. "Good-bye, Janet."

"Get out!" she screamed, throwing the glass at him. It shattered against the wall and sprayed the fresh paint with vodka and orange juice, which ran down into the expensive carpet.

Kyle walked out without looking back.

Miss Vera was waiting for him at the bottom of the stairs.

"Are you okay, Mr. Kyle?" she asked.

"Yeah, I'm fine," he said. "Trust me. I've been through a lot worse lately."

She nodded and then said, "I think you are doing a good thing. Miss Vera is proud of you."

Kyle smiled. "Thanks, Miss Vera." He put his arm around her shoulder. "Coming from you, that means a lot to me."

"So what you do now?" she asked.

"Well, I don't have to be in Virginia for another week. The bureau thought I deserved a little time off, and I've always wanted to learn how to sail, so I chartered a boat down in Cabo for a few days."

Now it was Miss Vera's turn to smile. "That's good," she said. "You have fun, and don't you worry about your mother. I take good care of her."

"I know you will. And thanks ... for everything," he said with one last hug.

Kyle stepped outside and headed for the car. As he did, he noticed it had stopped raining, the worst of the storm having already blown through.

And as the remaining clouds trailed away, he could see blue skies behind them.

ACKNOWLEDGMENTS

I would like to personally thank all of my friends and family members who read the early versions of my manuscript and who offered their comments, suggestions, and support. I would like to thank Sarah Valenzuela, my brother, Shane, my nieces, Courtney and Kiley, and I would especially like to thank my mom, Sandra, who read and reread it numerous times, always offering excellent comments and encouragement as I worked to improve it.

This novel would not be what it is if not for the excellent staff and students of SMU's Continuing Education Creative Writing Department. The courses gave me a great understanding of what makes up a novel while they also taught me how to become a better writer through practice and honest critique. A couple of members of the staff I would like to thank specifically include Joy Scallon, who read a much longer early draft and encouraged me to push on as I neared completion, and most importantly, Suzanne Frank. Suzanne, an author herself, is the director of the creative writing department at SMU and has created an excellent program for both published and aspiring authors. Suzanne always offered honest, insightful comments and wasn't afraid to tell me when something wasn't working or when she thought that I could do better. Thanks Suzanne!

I would also like to thank Pat LoBrutto for assisting with the editing of this book and for helping me to cut it down from its earlier version.

Finally, I would like to thank each and every one of you who bought this book and read it. I truly hope you enjoyed it, and I would love to hear what you thought about it. I can be reached through my website at LanceHorton.com and ShadowDragon.info.

CPSIA information can be obtained at www.ICGtesting.com
Printed in the USA
BVOW040059271212

309221BV00001B/8/P

9 781462 007660